Mentis and Ethos

BY R. HENRY PRICE

DORRANCE
PUBLISHING CO
EST. 1920
PITTSBURGH, PENNSYLVANIA 15238

Dorrance Publishing Co
585 Alpha Drive
Suite 103
Pittsburgh, PA 15238
Visit our website at *www.dorrancebookstore.com*

ISBN: 979-8-89027-032-0
eISBN: 979-8-89027-530-1

Mentis and Ethos

Disclaimer

This is a work of fiction. Names, characters, and events are the products of the author's imagination. Any resemblance to actual persons, living or dead, or events in the plot, are purely coincidental. The California Institute of Technology (Caltech) is a real place, and most of the physical description of it is true, as is the geography of the surrounding region. Some of the history of Caltech is reasonably accurate as are some elements of life at Caltech. But a great deal is modified or created in service of a more compelling story and more interesting characters.

TABLE OF CONTENTS

PROLOGUE
WEDNESDAY, NOVEMBER 21, 2018

Fang Lou worried that her heartbeat was too loud.

Her guard was named Wijers. She tried not to show any reaction as he rushed to the bathroom, leaving her unguarded in the large workroom. She had reason to hope for a major digestive problem. She had ground up a centipede and sprinkled it on Wijer's lunch. The internet said that centipedes are venomous. The venom was rarely fatal, but she could hope. At least he left her unguarded, maybe for enough time.

She was a prisoner – they called her a guest – in the large house. They told her that they were keeping her away from distractions so she could work. She did want to work, but not work for them, not for what they were after. She wanted to work for herself, on her innovative scheme to become a real-estate billionaire. She had the intelligence and the confidence to make it almost plausible if she had enough capital. Her captors had lured her with the promise of capital, but really wanted her to work on hacking into computer infrastructure. They were tolerating her scheme as long as they thought she was making progress on theirs. She thought she could fool them; she could fool most people.

Her hosts spoke to each other in a strange language, something like a mixture of English and Dutch. Fang spoke a little of many languages, so understood much of what they were saying. What she understood was that their patience was wearing thin.

She understood that it was time to get out.

The house was in the Culver City section of Los Angeles at the western edge of a residential sprawl; it was in the last row of houses. West of that row was a steep hill leading up to the Baldwin Hills Overlook, maybe 700 feet away. Beyond that, by another 700 level feet, was Jefferson Boulevard, Ballona Creek, and the densely populated part of Culver City. Safety and freedom.

The door to the room was on the western side of the house. Once she got past it, she could start running. A few hundred feet up the hill were trees. If she got to the trees, she could snake through them, a difficult target. But the door was locked.

There were two horizontal casement windows on the western side of the room, one on each side of the locked door. She was confident she could squeeze through a window, just as she was confident she could do almost anything.

Fang was a beautiful 19-year old born just outside Beijing. She had medium-length jet-black hair with a dyed purple streak that matched her purple contact lenses. She was barely five feet tall and had several years of gymnastics before coming to the US. The windows would not be a barrier, except that they were high.

That barrier only required that Fang slide a worktable under one of the windows as quietly as possible. She used arm strength to pull herself up to the window ledge. The width of the horizontally oriented window was six inches less than Fang's height, plenty of room. She led with her left leg, and got her left side through the window first. She rotated her torso through the window. The last step would be to push herself forward and down, head first. She was strong enough to hold onto the window frame and lower herself more-or-less gently.

She had moved quietly, but when she pushed off the table with her right leg the table fell over with a loud crash. Wijers bellowed from the bathroom. Fang hurried; she ignored the scraping of her skin against the window frame and dropped to the ground outside the house. She did not manage to land well, and limped her first few steps away from the house and up the hill.

She heard Wijers fiddling with his key to the exit door and yelling. She heard sounds of others rushing into the room. The outside door was flung open and Wijers fired his handgun. She saw puffs of dirt where the shots hit the hillside safely far from her. She was now moving fast, zigzagging left and right, getting further and further from the house. Wijers was heavyset, in his mid-fifties, and ill. Fang was sure that he could not run uphill to get closer to her. Then she heard a shot that sounded different from the handgun, and a bullet scraped her right thigh.

Others burst into the room. The leader, Sashi, carried a scope-equipped rifle. It was not adjusted for the uphill shots, and had hit Fang too low. He adjusted and fired again. Fang's life stopped. She fell over backwards. Blood flooded out of her head, some seeping into the ground, some forming a rivulet streaming down the steep hill. It was the end of Fang's brilliance and confidence.

Sashi, at the back door with Wijers, screamed at him, furious. He hit Wijers with the butt of his rifle knocking him to the floor. Though Wijers was a heavy man, Sashi's fury gave him the strength to drag Wijers by the collar through the room and past the kitchen. Wijers' terror was almost a match. Sashi opened the door to a room off the kitchen, a room with tools for working wood and metal. Wijers, though dazed and ill, fought to stand up and to escape from Sashi's grip. When he realized that Sashi was pulling him toward the large vice on the workbench, he went into a panic. He screamed and tried to grab onto anything he could, and to kick out at Sashi.

The others knew what was happening and ran out the back door to escape the screams.

CHAPTER 1
SOLLY, AN INTRODUCTION; 1993-1997

My name is Saul Sokolsky. (My parents either had no ear for the sound of that combination, or no stop sign on their senses of humor.) I am on the faculty at Caltech, one of those prestige educational institutions. Any Techie would frown at the wording "one of those..." To them it was *the* outstanding/scientific/educational institution in the world. They knew not to make that claim within the hearing of an MIT student or risk the violence of a game of Go. Seats at the Go table were also claimed by students from Stanford, Princeton, Tsinghua, Imperial and a few other sites in the academic prestigiverse.

Don't jump to the conclusion that I am one of the faculty geniuses. I was good enough, though, to be a grad student at Tech, and to leave with a PhD in physics and standard uncertainty about what comes next.

Around here, I am 'Solly.' It is a Caltech tradition to give nicknames, Tech tags, to members of the small community. Sometimes a name seems so right that it sticks. Mine stuck. I was known to be interested in too many things. Notable because breadth was not typical in the land of narrow focus. The other grad students tried calling me Jack, as in of all trades, but it didn't seem right, though the master of none was appropriate. My interests had great breadth and little depth.

I was a polymath, a generalist, a non-specialist. Full confession, I would have been a polymath if I were better at doing things, not just a dabbler, so shallow polymath, was dead on, but too long. It became just plain Solly, and still is. And should be. I am very much a just plain kind of guy. The name stuck so well that it is what I call myself, as in "Solly, you idiot, how could you do that?"

Long names often do well to shrink. That is not always the case with long stories. But they do have to start somewhere. This one can start in Omaha, Nebraska, 29 years ago, the fall of 1993, when – casting nervous eyes left and right – I entered high school. I was treading a path already trodden by my sister, Shoshana (parents, no ears). Shosh was born three and a half years before I was. I never caught up. She was always my older sister. When it served my purpose, I would cite research about the effects of birth order. What served best was the claim that an older sister made a boy less competitive. Though in middle school I meant this as a serious accusation, it evolved into a family joke by the time I reached the false maturity of high school.

Ironically, Shosh helped me be *more* competitive in the high school years. I was always good in math and science (if we leave out biology), but barely tolerated the subjects without equations: history, English, and social studies. Shosh was OK in science, and got by in math, but loved history and English. Those had stories, and that's what drew in Shosh. Our common feeling about social studies could have been a feeling about the way it was taught. Maybe it didn't have to be dull. I'm not sure that the experiment has been done.

I probably would have passed the no-equations courses without Shosh, but the mediocre grades would have hurt my college applications. Thanks to Shosh, my record was good enough to get me a nice merit-based scholarship to an Ivy. Important since the family was in the unfortunate middle ground: income too high for a needs-based full ride, and too low for the full burden of a prestige college.

My first year of high school was the first for Shosh in college. Her own college bill was not a family burden since Shosh had a full scholarship as an athlete and blossomed under college coaching. In high school my big sister was second in Nebraska in the 100 m backstroke. In college she ended up second in California, a much bigger state.

Perhaps I would have been an athlete even without an older sister. It surely wouldn't have been in swimming, which I liked as much as I did social studies. But I did need a sport, and for the usual reason: impressing girls. I wasn't bad looking. By my sophomore year I was already at my full 6'1" height. Experts in labels would have put me in the mesomorph bin. I had dark hair that looked best when in disarray, and eyes the color of Crayola indigo. My ears were slightly too large. This kept me from being annoyingly perfect. Overall, physically I was not a bad package. Not like Shosh who was annoyingly perfect, ears and all. She had been envied by every senior girl in high school. The hate rays from them would have been worse except that Shosh was so damn nice her perfection was generally forgiven.

In one of my rare philosophical moods in high school I thought about our looks, mine and Shosh's. Our parents were both physically attractive and their looks mixed together well. Lucky us. I understood how important it was for a high school girl to be attractive. I thought about the pain for the unlucky ones, and wondered whether they blamed their parents. I wondered whether an unattractive couple worried what would happen if they had a daughter. (You're now getting a glimmer of the way my mind works; it wanders. Solly, the peripatetic shallow polymath.)

Like Shosh, I was considered nice but that earned nothing with high school girls. They demanded cool. This meant a convertible, knowing how to dance, or athletics. The last was the most plausible. I needed to become an athlete.

Football was out; I didn't want to risk lifelong injury. Basketball was out; my aim was terrible. On the plus side, I had long legs and pretty good balance. On the minus side, no experience in organized sports. I needed to find a suitable disorganized sport, one that was performed individually. When I now remember Shoshana, what often comes to mind is my phone call to her. She had set the standards for effortless cool before leaving for college, but I knew she would understand my problem seeking cool. I was right.

She started by narrowing down what I was after.

"Sauly, you wouldn't consider fencing, right?"

"Interesting," I replied. "I have bad aim, but with a big opponent that wouldn't be an issue. What *would* be an issue is that fencing would not attract the right kind of girl."

"And just what would be the 'right kind of girl'?" she inquired suspecting the truth.

She had me on the ropes already. I didn't want to say 'easy,' and anyway it wasn't (completely) true. Even at that age I was a romantic.

"Well, fencing might attract nerdy chicks. I think that I want a kind of normal girl."

Shosh came up with the winner. "Triple jump," she said.

I stared blankly at the phone. She heard the stare, and paraphrased, "Hop, step, and jump."

This was a sport? Indeed it was, and an Olympic sport, although that was hardly relevant. I soon learned that it consisted of a hop off one leg, a landing on and pushing off from the other leg (the step) and a final jump.

And so it happened that in my sophomore year I became a triple jumper.

To make sure that the intended targets knew that I was a jock, I bought a team jacket. It was wonderfully nonspecific, announcing only 'Track & Field,' and I wouldn't tell girls that my sport was hop, step, and jump. I might tell them "I do field events in track and field." If I were trying to start a more truthful relationship, I would affect a modest expression and mumble that I was the best triple jumper in the school. (There *was* another triple jumper, Sean, a talented athlete limited in triple jump by his 5'9" height.)

The team jacket brought some attention. Brittany noticed. There was also an Ashley, a Danielle, and two Shelbys. The jacket was a success but it only started conversations. I was supposed to make something of the opportunities but was not as successful as the jacket. It was also too light for the Nebraska winter so I waited for spring. But in the spring I didn't return to wearing it. By then I had figured out the sociology of high school girls. They were interested in boys only as a form of competition with the others of their kind. I suspected that jewelry played very much the same role.

Sex was no doubt playing some part in the background and not always secretly. I regretted that I was not able to learn more about it during those years.

I had nerd friends in high school who were not using me to boost their status in the tribe. Ours was a totally different sociology and we laughed at the fatuous networking of the normals. But the grapes tasted sour, and we were missing the point that the hoi poloi were getting educated in social skills that would be more useful in their careers than AP Calculus.

Like a tunnel at the end of another tunnel, college loomed. We nerds knew we were going to walk that tunnel. Not so many of our Omahan brethren. All of us,

Nerds and Shelbys, were required to see the high school professional guidance counselor, who – like the Holy Roman Empire – failed to have the attributes of any word in their title. We were pretty sure that Mrs. Gompers had failed as a teacher and the school administration looked for something she

4

could do that would maintain her dignity. We and the school had very different views of dignity.

The nerdhood discussed our forthcoming visit. We knew the script. She would suggest community college or vocational school, ask what we wanted to do and tell us that we could be anything we wanted to be. In a way, keeping a straight face across from Mrs. Gompers was a lesson in dealing with the laughable incompetence that would be the default experience further along the tunnel. But for me there was an important lesson about myself.

My fellow nerd Paul wasn't going to take it straight faced. And keeping a straight face was Paul's talent. Poker could have made him rich. He said he was going to use that talent during his guidance session. And he did. When Mrs. Gompers asked him what he wanted to do he brightened, leaned in and excitedly said that he wanted to be a rodeo bull rider. Mrs. Gompers knew almost nothing about rodeo but the image of bull riding fell within the realm of almost nothing.

Her smile turned to seriousness. Perhaps she worried that Paul's imminent dusty death would be traced back to a guidance session.

"But Paulie, have you ever ridden a bull?"

"No, Mrs. Gompers, but I can learn.. you said we can be anything we .."

"Paulie, have you ever ridden a horse?"

"No, Mrs. Gompers. Are they like bulls?"

And so it went. Mrs. Gompers went to the Principal who bit the inside of his cheeks to keep from laughing. He was kind enough to limit the truth to "You've done all you can." Paulie ended up foreswearing rodeo for a scholarship at Berkeley and a career in biochemistry.

And me? I realized I couldn't do what Paulie did. I couldn't hurt someone even if they didn't know they were being hurt. The folly of Mrs. Gomper's position wasn't her fault. Maybe that was it. Not sure. But it was something important to know about myself.

I did not hop, step and jump in college, but the high school athletic involvement might have helped me look well rounded on my college applications. Something worked, since I was accepted at all four schools I applied to. I chose the most prestigious of the four, an Ivy. My parents immediately approved the choice since it was also the one with the best financial package.

With the unchanging three and a half year difference between us, this happened around the end of Shoshana's college career. During her time out of the pool she was outstanding in her literature major and was being encouraged by her major advisor to consider an academic career. She didn't.

Maybe Shosh had a lot of time to think while she was backstroking. She knew how difficult an academic career would be: grad school, postdoc positions, then – with luck– a junior faculty position and a slow ascent to tenure while her biological clock ticked frantically. Apparently, she did not find an answer to the 'for what?' question. To her very surprised brother, who had never asked that question, her decision came as a surprise. To our parents it was no surprise but more a fulfillment of hopes. Shosh chose marriage to Michael, who would soon be an optometrist; she chose family, kids, and braces, and nagging Michael to clean leaves from the roof gutters in the autumn. She chose the whole of Zorba The Greek's full catastrophe.

CHAPTER 2

SOLLY GOES TO SCHOOL; 1997-2001

In November 1997, my calendar said 'Apply to College' in bold marker, just to be sure I didn't forget. Forty years earlier only around eight percent of the population had finished college, the proof college was not a necessity for the species. I hadn't known that. I might have wondered what the other ninety-two percent did. Did they work? At what?

The undergraduate processing was useful for me. Four years of dabbling: a semester of this, another of that. Mostly a toe could be dipped in the water of knowledge. The toe dried quickly, and usually nothing much remained. No harm done. But there were exceptional puddles. I read Freud and Skinner in a survey of psychology, and was fascinated both by the ideas, and by how wrong those ideas seemed. It was educational in a skewed sense. I learned that there were a lot of bad ideas floating around and many of them got more credence than they deserved. I learned to be skeptical. I learned to be polite but not to give authority more respect than it earned.

There were history courses. From a distance history seemed to be a random unfolding. But when taught by the right professor it was a collection of stories all the more interesting for having been true. Possibly true. Partly true. The sources were always imperfect; the stories were always an interpretation. Their influence depended on the skill of the story teller, and the good ones could draw connections that didn't require full acceptance. They were still thought provoking. An example I never forgot was the Turner thesis: the connection of the American character and the existence of the frontier. It was exciting to think about it, and the way it brought together sociology, political science, and a good story. Historians wrote on both sides of this frontier-centric view of America and I loved rummaging through their arguments for the weak points. The exercise gave me an appreciation for the responsibilities of the skeptic. Thought and facts were needed; it was not enough to be a curmudgeon. (Damn.)

Ironically, and maybe it's typical, some of my best college experiences were during the summer breaks. I wanted to earn enough money for living costs, the sizeable costs of attending college away from home, costs not covered by a tuition scholarship. My parents could afford to pay those costs, so – I suppose – this was just my ego pouting. Or maybe I was just following in the backstrokes of my big sister.

Shosh worked as a lifeguard every summer. As a competitive swimmer she had the connections to get the jobs and the jobs gave her pool access so she could practice in off hours when the pool was all hers.

There was an amazing spectrum of specialized summer camps (flute, magic, basketball,..) available to the scions of the pretty well to do. I didn't bother looking for hop-step-jump opportunities and was, in any case, an ex-hop-step-jumper. In the usual manner, through who-you-knowism, I got a nice position as a counselor at camp AtenRos. (I was told this meant 'friendship' in Mohawk. I have been waiting for two decades to bump into a Mohawk speaker to have my skepticism confirmed.)

The living quarters for the campers were log cabins that bore names of the Iroquois confederacy: Cayuga, Cherokee, Huron, Mohawk, Oneida, Onondaga, Seneca, and Tuscarora. The names may have come from early American culture but the laser straight, smooth machine-processed uniform logs would not have been recognized as wood by members of the confederacy.

The campers slept in double-decker bunks, twelve to a cabin. Counselors were embedded with them like journalists with combat troops. I was the counselor for the Onondaga troops.

The AtenRos Big Chief (that's how the camp director referred to himself) liked to push inter-cabin rivalry, and to encourage each cabin to have a distinct character. I liked working with the kids. They trusted me. I liked it that they trusted me. It might have been a portent of things to come.

Interaction with other summer staff was a chance to meet different kinds of people. Hannah was a different kind. At a get to know other Iroquois social

I locked eyes with redheaded Hannah, a junior arts major from a nearby four-year college. Hannah was less shy than I and made the opening move.

She approached with, "Hi, I'm Hannah, the arts and crafts instructor. What's your specialty?"

I had no trouble answering, "Having twelve kids survive the summer. Hi, I'm Saul, chief of the Onondagas."

It was the perfect summer relationship, the romantic equivalent of an undergrad course. We explored the subject then at the end of the course it was over. No harm done. She was from a different college so there were no awkward accidental encounters. There were a few emails. They dwindled and stopped. We understood without expressing it: This was as it should be.

I must have done well enough the first summer since I was invited to repeat after my sophomore year. I even got to be chief of the Onondagas again. I had developed some loyalty and don't know if I could have tolerated being a Huron. (The shallow polymath in me found this kind of loyalty interesting. I made a mental note to look up some studies about this kind of behavior. That mental note is still lying around somewhere in a rarely visited lobe.)

I looked for an alternative summer job but my pool of connections failed me, so I took the AtenRos job, in spite of some hesitation. It did not pay well and I was a little nervous about Hannah returning. She did, but there was no need for nervousness. Within a few days we had restarted the studies dropped the previous August. Despite the romantic moonlight of our pine-scented trysts we became an old married couple. It was unthreatening. Even the following summer held no threat since Hannah would be graduating and entering the so-called real world, or at least the world of more expensive arts and crafts.

Sometime around 2010, I had a chance meeting with a woman who had also been a counselor during my AtenRos summers. She stayed in occasional touch with a few AtenRosers from that era, and told me Hannah was divorced. She might have been dropping a hint. If so, I let it lie. Some things are best as memories. What remains now is only an erotic frisson from the aroma of pine and a fading visual memory of Hannah at age 20. I wouldn't want reality to erase that.

I found it interesting but unexplained that, aside from Hannah, I had no other romantic life during my four undergraduate years. This was not a choice, was not welcome, and the reasons for it were not clear. Vestigial shyness? Lack of effort? Bad luck?

The following summer, the summer after my junior year, I qualified to do something relevant in the so-called real world. Deciding on a career would be relevant so I got a job as a research assistant working in a physics lab, doing experiments in condensed matter physics. It paid better than AtenRos and was more interesting. I was not distracted by the women in the lab, all several years older than I was. If they were distracted by me they kept it secret, and it was just as well.

The exception to academic dabbling was the choice of the next step: grad school, professional school, or marry rich. It was not an exception to the systemic dysfunctionality we laugh our lives through. With limited knowledge of ourselves choosing how to spend the next decades was like playing Russian roulette with only one empty chamber.

In the educational system we bred from the medieval guild system, we ask a barely fledged nestling to identify a lifelong career. That's an overstatement of course. On its own it is not an inescapable trap. It is turned into a trap by the human genius for inertia. There are investment bankers out there who still mourn the career as DJ they abandoned. And it's too late now. So much to learn. So much new music. Dub step. Could I learn how to DJ that? No. It's too late. I'm 53. Goddamn it. 53.

Later when I came to appreciate poetry (a little) I read with appreciation (a little) Thomas Gray's musing on careers not pursued. (OK. The comparison isn't perfect.)

> *Perhaps in this neglected spot is laid*
> *Some heart once pregnant with celestial fire;*
> *Hands, that the rod of empire might have sway'd,*
> *Or waked to ecstasy the living lyre:*

It motivated me to update the context and write *Elegy Written in a College Courtyard*. (OK. Only one verse of it.)

> *The sad physician checks old Goldstein's heart*
> *But stares unblinking to the great afar,*
> *Checks twenty boxes on the patient's chart,*
> *In his head only his youth's rock guitar.*

I might laugh at what I had to do but I still had to do it. Undergrad dabbling was perfect for me, the polymath-in-training; the choice of career not so perfect. Though I shared some of Shosh's love of stories and literature, I leaned at a very steep angle toward the sciences. Or maybe engineering. There were several reasons I chose physics. (I'm not counting the coin flips.)

First, there was that summer lab experience. I was told I was good at it. The work required bringing together lots of understanding and quick learning. Not to master, but to manage. I didn't always (OK, ever) understand deeply how some of it worked, but my own broad/shallow background and attitude seemed to be ideal for it. Experimental physics seemed like a polymath's playground. Maybe even a shallow polymath.

Then there was junior quantum mechanics. I was exposed to lots of things in college that gave me a snide smile and made me grunt a skeptical 'Hmpf.' But quantum mechanics made me frown and growl an insistent 'No way!' They were telling me the world worked in a way it could not possibly work. It was not a matter of belief. It could be shown in experiments. Everyone was either lying about the experiments or we were all wrong about what we were sure of. It wasn't a matter of figuring out something. We could figure all we wanted. It didn't change the fact: The physical world didn't give a damn about what we thought.

Physics seemed like an interesting way to make a living, so I looked around for a grad program that might have me.

CHAPTER 3
SOLLY GOES TO MORE SCHOOL; 2001-2006

I still tell the story of the envelope with the Caltech logo containing only a single sheet of paper. A single sheet. It's what I had expected. I didn't need to open it. I knew what it said: "You should be proud of your accomplishments, but unfortunately due to the large number of applicants this year blah blah." To avoid ego bruising I almost tossed it aside unopened.

I puzzled over my acceptance. It must have been the letters of recommendation for my summer research experience. Yet more evidence it isn't the coursework that's the important part of college. There was not yet evidence the acceptance had been a mistake so there I was, the dog who had chased the car and caught it. Now what?

Now: hard work. I discovered my new classmates were at the top of their graduating class at the best institutions. Some were hiding their lack of confidence behind veils of overconfidence. Some didn't have veils. And some, like me, were going to wait and see. They had no clue how they were going to eat the car.

It was a painful joy. There was pain in the catechism of the required courses. Most emblematic was the one book closest to being a physics grad program standard: *Classical Electrodynamics* by J. D. Jackson. To my fellow sufferers I used to call it 'Jacksonian electricity.' Like Jacksonian democracy it wasn't quite what the name implied. It wasn't physics as much as nineteenth century applied mathematics. Students had to use near impossible math to solve laughably impossible configurations, like the electric influence of a three ring pretzel, split into sections at different voltages; it was an applied math boot camp. From time to time we heard 'why, when I was a boy' rumors about the book that had preceded *Jackson*, the Smythe book, for which *Jackson* was only a warmup. We were sure these were myths, and we didn't want to know more.

The joy packaged with the pain was learning how the world works, and how clever nature was in the working. This was very different from what I had experienced earlier; undergrad math and physics were mostly training. Now, Jacksonian drudgery aside, I was asked to think. I was doing research. There would come a big day not too far off. On that day I would be the only one in the world who knew the answer to some question. Maybe not a crucially important question, but still, I would be the only one in the whole damn world who knew the answer. It's a big world. Lots of people. I would be the only one

The required courses were a bonding experience, but not so much as the soul baring sessions on our choice of research area. (Does the menu never end? High school choice of college major; college choice of postgrad path; now this.) That decision started with the theory or experiment fork in the road. The novitiates aiming for the theoretical path fantasized about having their breakthroughs added to the list of the major advances in human understanding. They would solve the problems haunting physics since the mid-1950s. Their names would be attached to principle, law, or theorem. This pursuit of glory came with a risk: Their job opportunities were restricted to academic research, teaching, or fast food. Those walking the experimental path had a less restricted future. They would acquire skills valued by the real world, especially the world of high tech companies.

The grad student bonding, with its where-will-we-be in 10 years bull sessions, was especially strong between me and Xi Luk, a peer from New York City via Columbia. He was short and slight, with a friendly round face well suited to a smile. His appearance wasn't going to frighten violent malefactors no matter how many Bruce Lee movies they had seen. He was, in fact, not interested in Asian martial arts. Ironically it was I who joined the Caltech karate club.

I had a clear vision of continuing to work in laboratory physics but in the commercial world. Xi had an even clearer vision: forensic science. I had no self-delusion about the Sokolsky equation and Luk didn't fantasize about Luk's principle. (We did joke, however, about Luk collaborating with fellow novitiate

Roberta Goode on the Goode-Luk principle in quantum gravity.) Luk wanted to master a broad a range of lab techniques and then work in criminal justice. While our theoretician-wannabe peers daydreamed of a big book-strewn office at an Ivy, Luk pictured himself in a lab at the FBI.

This was an unusual, maybe a uniquely strange choice, and hence a question crying out to be asked. And it was asked but was only one of many we were unable to answer during our graduate years. Early influence? From early on Luk was attracted to a career in law enforcement. Perhaps there had been a childhood experience with a role model police officer in the Chinese section of New York City. Perhaps not. Something about law enforcement had gotten under his skin and festered.

He was always happy to chatter about his vision of criminal justice via science so his career goal was well known to our crowd. With that, and the sound of his mumbled Mandarin name, Xi Luk, it was inevitable his Tech tag became Sherlock. Good tags stick. That stuck.

In any case, Luk became my closest friend during the grad school years. His research work involved silicon micromotors, more engineering than physics, but really interesting. We explained the latest steps in our work to each other. Often explaining ideas to peers helped us clarify our own understanding. (Ask any teacher about this.)

We also shared a love of low-brow detective novels, especially those with our hero, Archie Goodwin, Nero Wolfe's amanuensis (look it up) and factotum (look it up). When I later studied early American literature, I wondered about the relation of bachelor Archie to the freedom of the frontier, primarily the freedom from family life. The Turner thesis came back to haunt my thinking. It would return yet again later, with greater impact.

Luk and I not only shared thoughts about great, and not-so-great literature but also about the questions that have vexed great philosophers since the Big Bang.

"Luk, can people think without language?"

"They can certainly think that the pan is hot when they accidentally touch it. It is useful to scream Shit!, but unnecessary."

"Funny. You know what I mean. Like can one think about why ice cubes float, even though they're made of water?"

Luk made an astonished expression.

"Ice cubes float?"

"Cut the crap, Luk. Be serious. I read that neuroscientists are finding that language is not used in doing math."

Luk got serious.

"And I therefore conclude that science is not used in doing neuroscience. How the hell can they probe whether language is being used?"

"Positron emission spectroscopy, I think. The language centers do not light up when a subject does 2+2."

Luk saddled up and rode to the defense of language.

"Big deal. Two plus two equals 4, or even the sum of two 2 digit numbers, can be done with pictures in the head. Or maybe you're reading from a table in your memory. Why should you need language, huh?"

"But hold on. What about a multistep process like divide 72 by 4+5. You need to store an intermediate result, the 9 divisor. Murg and Throk invented writing on the cave wall because they couldn't remember everything. But the 9 divisor? Hell, we can remember *that*. And what are we remembering? What are we storing in our heads besides irate bats? We're storing a WORD! Nine, neuf, neuve, jiŭ.

Luk wasn't finished.

"And positron emission tomography, language centers. Hmmm. Could it be that these neuroscientists are *defining* what they mean by language!"

My rebuttal was, Uncle! (Oncle, tio, shū shū.)

Though Luk and I enjoyed each other's company, each of us would have chosen female company. But we weren't given choices. We waited for choices to come to us. They didn't, with one exception. During my third year, my research advisor said that her husband, an administrative law attorney, had a comely intern who had just arrived in SoCal, and might be grateful for a young man to show her around. I showed Deanna around. We were both grateful for a relationship that relieved some physical tensions but did not take time from our career pursuits. It lasted for a semester. I didn't tell Luk. I didn't have to. He understood that my luck wasn't my fault.

Aside from this, the wait-for-it choice produced only waiting. If we wanted more, we had to seek it. Such seeking was the design target of singles bars in LA so we chose one, almost at random, visited it, and spent a sedentary hour waiting for something to happen. Nothing happened. We left the bar feeling pretty glum and returned to the land we knew where we would be able to find solace in research.

Life had been a staircase, high school, undergrad, first year grad school and then the life-determining step: research. You out there in the real (vs academic) world, you Muggles, have no idea how the system works. Stay tuned.

Academic research depends on money. (You had no way of knowing.) The one with the money is a Principal Investigator. This is usually shortened to 'PI,' with little fear of confusion with Philip Marlowe. The PI's reputation for research brings in funds.

The PI has stopped doing research, rather, spends 90% of the time applying for grants. The grant funds support grad students and operations of the institution.

The remaining 10% goes for judging other grant applications, and squirming in chairs at panel and committee meetings, staring at the slow-moving clock. Oh yeah. There's teaching. It only seems like a scam. It works wonderfully well, and is good for the grad students, the institution, and scientific progress.

Is it good for the PI? Depends on the PI. I didn't have much self-knowledge but I knew that the coronation to PI required a type A+ personality. I was a kind of B-.

I hardly ever saw my PI. But my success implementing her ideas would attract future grants and future students to take her money and implement her ideas, fueling the student/grant cycle. It was like contributing to soil fertility after the dean's or manager's brief professional eulogy "..mumble mumble your decades of service."

It's worth mentioning that she also cared about me for the right reasons. Because I was a human being. But that attitude was not required. I was lucky. Also lucky in another way; the work acquainted me with much of the new lab and computer technology coming into the high-tech workplace, the place I would work.

Making the decision to get off the academic ladder allowed me to relax (a bit) and enjoy the grad student experience. There was actual pleasure staying up all night to get that one last data point that fit the predictions. There were the colloquia that gave a view of the ideas that would dominate the coming years. There were also things that played to the other side of the person. For me that was primarily the Caltech karate club where I learned how to be hit. I got my black belt (lowest level) at the same time I got my PhD (fortunately only one level).

I bought a used Honda Civic and explored some of the Southern California surroundings, and the culture, especially the culture. Venice Beach and its denizens made a particularly quaint impression. The place and the people seemed as if they were posing for a movie. It looked like fun, and I thought about spending some time there. But it would have been dabbling, and I was past dabbling.

A few times during those four years I emerged from my academic cave and visited the old homestead in Omaha. It took a day or so to readjust. My parents were loving, supportive, and well educated, but I could not convey to them the attractions of research. I could see in their expressions the question "You're in your late twenties and you're still in school?" I expected a deeper understanding from Shosh, who seemed always to understand, though she herself had taken another path. Eventually, I visited her. It was not as soon as I should have but my priorities were blighted.

This was my first visit, since Shosh and Michael had been too busy for a big wedding. They talked about having a big renewing vows ceremony sometime in the indefinite future. Such times never come but talking about them becomes a habit. They never did get to renew the vows, or to take a deferred honeymoon.

A few months after the non-wedding, I got a call from my mother, a call that edged out Shosh's call by an hour. I was going to be an uncle. This, and much more, led to my first visit to them in 1998, after my first undergraduate year. Was it worth the plane trip to the Bay Area? I met my one-year old niece Delia and my knees went weak. I think that means yes.

Soon after, in 1999, Shosh made me an uncle again, bringing Conrad into the world. My priorities were still flawed, and I missed Conrad's first year of life just as I had Delia's. By the time I met him, Conrad was already exploring the world with the curiosity of a physicist. Poor kid, I thought.

I liked Michael, although no one could be good enough for Shosh. Michael seemed like a great father. And as an optometrist he knew enough about physics that we enjoyed arguing. I think he was part of the reason that Shoshana was disgustingly happy. My misgivings about her choice were wrong. When I visited she had no time for me. A good sign.

CHAPTER 4

IN THE VALLEY OF THE START-UPS; 2007-2013

Those silly square commencement hats spent a few seconds in the warm Southern California air then rained down on the laughing students. It was commencement with blue sky over the green lawn in front of the squat silo of Beckman auditorium. Many of the celebratory products, like me, were hugging their parents and thinking about the future. The future would wait until the Sokolskys celebrated with a Lake Avenue lunch. The newly certified Dr. Sokolsky was wise enough in the ways of the Pasadena world to have reserved their table four months in advance.

The restaurant was only about a half mile away, and we walked west along California Boulevard basking in the weather. The walk gave us a chance to appreciate each other's company, and we did, but the love was mostly unspoken. There was the occasional joke so my father could remind me he was the source of my bad jokes, and my mother could remind me she was the source of my tolerance of bad jokes.

As we passed a store advertising pet food, my father mock seriously acted as if I were steering them in and said, "Sonny, I should have told you, we don't eat cat food any more. I got a raise." My mother rolled her eyes in mock exasperation, that made me nostalgic. What little was spoken was of the past, and only made awkwardly evident the separation growing in our views of the world.

For almost all the Beckman hat catchers, the future – or at least the next year of it – was determined. Some of us who had just commenced would go to graduate school, some would go to professional school (law, medical, business

school), some, like me, would descend immediately into the infernal circles of
the real world.

Around the end of the first decade of the new millennium, virality became
a meme and the meme entrepreneurship went viral. Joe DiMaggio and James
Dean were replaced by the superheroes of the new economy, billionaires who
had built e-whatevers in their garages. Educational institutions, themselves
entrepreneurial, were quick to develop and advertise programs to convey entrepreneurial skills, whatever they were. The everyone-a-millionaire delusion
of the roaring 20s became the everyone-a-billionaire entrepreneurship of the
new millennium. All it took was optimism, determination, and venture capital.
The emphasis was on attitude; the emphasis was off a good underlying product
or service. The separation of appearance and reality stayed in the closet.

For me this was an important part of the real world I skeptically entered.
I became Dr. Sokolsky at the start-up of the era of the start-up. Garages around
the country had become workshops with posters of Gates and Jobs for inspiration, if not worship.

I didn't so much have to search for a job as I did choose among the offers.
They came from big high-tech corporations, and from small start-ups, teams
of a half dozen buddies and optimists. The start-uppers were invariably young,
young enough to take chances on the hope of a big payoff. That fit me also so
with an attitude of let's see what happens, I opted for the start-up side of the
fork in my road.

I didn't completely shrug my shoulders over the choice. Many of the start-
ups were not paying salary but were giving stock in the company. This would
mean starvation now, yacht (or more starvation) later. I was in a position to
negotiate, and wouldn't know what to do with racehorses, so I insisted on a
livable salary along with some company stock.

Here's where you find out more about me. I already copped to shallow.
Now I hang my head and admit that in a world of pain and suffering I often
value what is trivial.

To me a livable salary included the cost of a car that would help me forget
whether start-ups were the right path. At 19 I took a test drive in a Lotus Elan,
a real Elan, not the M100, a Toyota/Isuzu automotive bouillabaisse foisted on
insensitive drivers after General Motors took over Lotus Cars in 1989. That
was the year I turned 19, but had no interest in the (sneer) front wheel drive

M100. It had the name Elan, it had modern engineering, but not the soul, not the ..well, elan of the real thing. I lusted for the perfume of the SAE 50, for the song of the dual overhead cams. But that reality had gone out of production in 1975. After the test drive my view shifted about money buying happiness.

In 2007 when money was a lower barrier than it had previously been, Elans had a museum aura. They could be admired, but not considered transportation. Along with the rest of my generation I faced the practical vs. spiritual in making a decision. I would have railed against the dark clouds of change except for one ray of sunshine. The Japanese company Mazda had seen the niche left by the passing of spiritual cars. They built a car, the Miata, with the explicit target of the Elan. And they hit the target dead center in 1989. It looked like an Elan; it walked like an Elan; it felt like an Elan.

But change moved the Miata a bit away from the spiritual, and a bit closer to practical. At the time I entered the Valley of the start-ups, the third generation (NC) version Miata had come out. The first generation Miata, the NA, could be mistaken for an Elan, if they had only made the NA in British Racing Green. The second generation NB was losing some of the wonderful simplicity, maybe a sign that the Miata was coming into its own, and no longer needed the green glow of the Elan. In 2007, the third generation NC had just come out. It looked OK, but it would never be mistaken for an Elan. What to do? Buy a used NA or a new, more practical, more reliable, more comfortable NC? These are the questions that try men's souls. My soul compromised on a gently (laughter here) used 2005 NB2. The selling point was the color: green.

The Miata was a toy that would fit whatever I negotiated with start-up suitors. Despite my insistence on salary in addition to stock, I had options among the suitors. I chose the one that looked most interesting, and even (with some mist of self-delusion) plausible. It was a company founded by two students, Bret and Arlene ("We use first names here"), who had dropped out of Stanford Engineering. The company, *ExecToy*, was going to build toys for the newly too rich, the tech principals (a segment they hoped to join soon). They wanted to answer the question: What do you give a filthy rich friend who is celebrating a birthday, wedding, divorce or IPO? The first product would be AbyssMiss (female version), or AbysSir (male) executive models. When placed on a desk, the toy would move in a straight line until it sensed an edge, at which it would stop in the nick of time, flail its little arms like a person trying not to fall into the abyss (business failure?). They had a crudely working model that occasionally crudely worked. And they had enough venture capital to pay me more than hopes.

The workplace was a large loft-like space and was student-apartment crude. Furniture was picked up at garage sales, and lab tables were made from exterior grade plywood on Home Depot table legs. The lighting could have been better. But the big corporation alternative would have been a warren of cubicles. I bought a lamp to improve the lighting, and did not complain about the setting.

They were in the Bay area, an important aid to my self-deception. I was within pestering distance of Shosh and Michael, so I could pop in and check on my niece and nephew. I took the position. I had trouble filling even the smallest U-Haul, small enough to be pulled by a Miata. I headed north.

It was fun for almost two years, and I got to know Shosh's family. Hyper-kinetic Shosh figured out how to fuss too much about her kids while letting them develop independence. She stayed in shape by continuing to swim and doing volunteer coaching of local youth. I got to attend Delia's tenth birthday party. The knee-weakness she inflicted at age one persisted and meant I had to grasp furniture to keep from falling. She reminded me so much of Shosh, and not only because – according to Shosh – she was already doing well in the backstroke. Conrad was almost eight. I asked Michael how Con was doing with optometry. Michael laughed. He understood my jokes. I liked him.

ExecToy did not make it out of the Valley of the Start-ups. Problems volleyed and thundered. There were problems with the costs; there were problems with the evolution of the tastes of the nouveau filthy riche; there were who's-in-charge arguments with the venture capitalists. I let it be known I was interested in new opportunities.

I was still a buyer in a buyer's market; I didn't yet need to put index cards on supermarket corkboards. My Caltech provenance would impress the human resources department, often the vice president of the start-up wearing one of many hats. The VP would see me as a cost-effective resource due to my breadth of skills. The shallowness was discovered only later.

The offers that were least unappealing were all in Southern California, so I slid 400 miles down the map with a U-Haul a bit more laden than its predecessor, and a promise to the Miata I would return for it. So Solly the shallow salmon swam downmap upstream back to SoCal. I found an acceptable apartment in Duarte, not too far from the start-up, but far enough to enjoy the Miata on the freeways. There wasn't much enjoyment at the destinations.

I cast my lot at the first of two rapidly failing start-ups. The first attempted to locate the origin of sniper fire by analyzing the pattern of echoes. My ambiguity about military work was assuaged by the start-up CEO/CTO/CIO/head of HR who pointed out the importance of the technology to domestic terror situations. I got into the company to replace an employee who jumped when he saw the writing on the wall. (Why was no start-up offering improved wall reading?) After eight months the start-up did not get the small business grant it had sought, and we shared a good-bye cake, a cheap cake.

My next stop in the Valley was a company that wanted to produce textiles with built-in strain sensors. The textile could be connected to send a signal indicating how and where it was being stretched. This could be used to improve athletic performance, support the development of prosthetics, and create animations. The company principals were quick to point out they weren't quick enough to think of all the possible applications. It had the potential to be a winner, but getting the signal out was a problem that needed much work and much work meant much money and much waiting. The short attention span of the venture capitalists balked at this cycle and sic transit talking textile.

The last was best in some ways, but not good enough in the money ways. The company, named Cyrano, was in the LA area (no U-Haul). It was a phone app that Bluetoothed to a nearly invisible earbud adapted from a hearing aid. In a conversation between a tongue-tied wearer and a speaker, the app would use early artificial intelligence to whisper suggested statements to the wearer. The app had options for professional and sales conversation, but its major market was expected to be in the romance-a-verse.

When Cyrano contacted me it was a surprise. I wasn't really a software guy, and aside from the conversion of the hearing aid, the project was almost entirely software. It turned out they noticed I had gone to an Ivy, and Solly the polymath had taken a literature course (Joyce and Yeats) at Caltech. They wanted me not only for the engineering, but also for guidance in finding suggested statements for the app. I left Cyrano a few months before Cyrano lost the duel with survival. Something worse than business failure upended my life.

Zorba had it wrong about catastrophes. The real catastrophe hit early in 2013. The good builds slowly. The bad happens fast, as fast as a telephone call from Michael. Out of nowhere, Shosh came down with amyotrophic lateral sclerosis, ALS. She was much too young for this (only three and a half years older than I). She went relatively quickly, two years of agony. The worst part, although all its parts were worst, was that she knew what was happening to her. Her husband knew, and her two kids, at the time they needed her most, also knew. So, on top of everything else Shosh had to act cheerful since creating pain in others was worse to her than her own dread of imminent departure.

I was there for the funeral in March 2015. Shosh had wanted to be cremated, but Michael disobeyed. He wanted a place he and the kids could visit and remember Shosh. So did I. But that was later. Consoling the kids was now and there.

Delia started college, at UC Berkeley. During a period of mourning, she stopped attending. Seventeen-year old Delia was being brave to help Conrad and Michael get by. I tried to be brave. From time to time I failed, and hid away until I could regain composure.

Distraction seemed like a good idea. Maybe I just needed to do something to think I was helping. My distraction was a rave-reviewed book store in the Richmond district of SF. We had dinner first. I hoped we would talk, but it was too soon. I timed the bookstore visit for a talk by the author of a new book. It worked for Delia, who was thinking about a career as a writer. Conrad was well behaved; I suspected he did this for his sister who was into the author's talk. Michael, Delia and Conrad, all of them focusing on helping each other. Families. Much is blamed on them but they are how the heart survives.

I visited every four months or so. Each time, I grew closer to Conrad and Delia. I watched them grow up; I watched them become adults. Delia was becoming a writer, and Conrad moved toward a science career. Michael never remarried. All of us became more like family. The love grew; the pain stayed.

CHAPTER 5

COURSE CORRECTION; FEBRUARY 2013 TO FALL 2014

Michael's call came on February 1, exactly one month before my thirty-third birthday. The Cyrano people were understanding about my need to leave (and understood they too would soon be leaving). For a couple of weeks I thought deep thoughts. Some of them about mortality. How could they not be, with Shosh's reminder and my birthday looming, but the real focus was: Why was I wasting my life?

From the perspective of my couch and unemployment, I was embarrassed by the last five years. I had strolled through technical jobs, occasionally distracted by engineering issues. There was no real joy in solving them. I envied the principals in the start-ups. Their goals were mostly selfish, but they had goals, they had visions, at least fantasies. I was just along for the ride, strolling through the Valley. I didn't have the right attitude because it wasn't the right path.

I had always read a lot (Shosh's influence), but in those few weeks after Shosh left, I spent most of my time reading. Novels, short stories, poems, essays by those presumptuous enough to tackle important questions. Much of it left me unimpressed, but some of it took hold. I began to wonder whether the best of it might be a guide to the right path. I couldn't get it out of my mind. In a seldom used corner of that mind, an errant synapse sent a signal and it metastasized: Books, stories, poems, essays. Human ideas. A career in literature. Really, Solly? Really?

I was not above lying to myself. But knowing that made me wary. I spent a week listening to the voices in my head make the obvious arguments against a new life direction. The counterargument was what? Returning to the Valley wouldn't be so easy. My employment history made me look like a curse to a start-up. Most start-ups failed without me, but small-tech founders were a superstitious lot. I could opt for the warrens of big tech but that option didn't light up a vision of right path.

The internal debate winner was to tread a new path and hope it was right. But the practical, skeptical side won a concession. I was seeking solace in literature, but had not completely lost contact with reality. I needed to think about a future job, and that meant an academic job. College literature programs had fallen into a rut of preparing graduates to apply for jobs in college literature programs. Jobs were few and applicants were many. Where there *were* jobs was to teach college students writing beyond the abbreviations of text messages. Poor communication among high tech engineers IMHO was becoming an expensive problem. I could combine literature and rhetoric (how to write good).

I had saved enough money from the start-ups that I could afford not to be employed for a couple of years, and I could pay some tuition. So, with a shrug of my shoulders and a steely focus on the middle distance, I set out to find a lit/rhetoric master's program. And I wanted it to be in Southern California; no more U-Hauls. You'd think this was easy, but you'd be wrong. Neither UCLA nor USC had a master's program that was terminal. That was a bad word to someone musing on mortality but I knew what it meant.

Finding the right program was a barrier but I had made the career-path decision, and I wasn't going back. (Interesting point this, one that marketing people must know: Once a customer has made a decision, returning to indecision is out of the question. I made a mental note.)

The forward direction turned out to be Cal State Los Angeles. This gave me the mixture I wanted, and I was happy with the location. I could continue living in the apartment in Duarte, far enough from the maddening crowd. Cheap and apartment could appear in the same sentence. Although Cal State was 17 miles from Duarte I avoided rush hour and the freeways made the drive 20 restorative minutes. The campus was on a hill, which seemed promising, and the views were interesting, even symbolic. (I'd be alert to symbols during the next two years.) Two miles to the west was the vague haze of LA's skyscrapers. A few miles to the north were the foothills of the San Gabriels. To the southeast, most symbolic, was the modern art cloverleaf interchange of the 10 and the 710.

I filled out the paperwork in March and won the argument for the Department to accept a late admission. (I was paying full tuition, an important part of my argument.) I would start with summer courses but knew I would have to deal with flaws in my attitude.

I had gone to an Ivy for undergrad, to Caltech for grad. Solid preparation to be an elitist. I could claim this was 'despite my best efforts,' but I had only made an effort to hide it. Then there was my science elitism. Was literature really as hard as science? As valuable? I was like a Peace Corps newbie who smiled indulgently at quaint cultural practices, hiding – even from himself – a mild disdain. I really didn't like these stains in my otherwise perfect nature but at least I admitted it to myself. That's something, right?

Fortunately, this elitism vanished quickly and almost completely.

Elitism aside it was exciting to start on a new path at Cal State. That start was the climb up the steep hill from the parking lot to King (as in Martin Luther) Hall, the site of the English Department. Before entering the building, I turned, looked east over the parking lot to the 710 and, as if to say goodbye to the previous Solly, hitched up my shoulders and entered the world of new corridors and bulletin boards, but a familiar schoolness.

My goal was the office of my master's degree advisor Dimitra Murphy. I already knew what I wanted to do for my master's thesis, so I had looked through the faculty blurbs for who would support, or at least tolerate my thesis idea. Prof. Murphy was the in-house scholar of American literature. Though her focus wasn't precisely what I wanted mine to be, she would have to do. I soon learned she would do quite nicely.

What I wanted to do had a seed way back in my junior undergrad year. Remember that history course that led me to the frontier thesis of nineteenth century historian Frederick Turner. Turner explained how Americans broke from European roots, why they came to revere individuality and practicality. Turner told us they became the rough-and-ready individuals who were the foundation of American exceptionalism by the need to conquer the frontier. Something about the idea seemed right to me and I said as much in a post-midnight dorm room pizza and beer meaning-of-life session. Horace, chair of our know it all club, said I should read Leslie Fiedler's book. I did.

It turned out to be literary criticism. (Solly was really going out on a poly-mathematical limb) and it was fascinating, Freudian analysis, homoeroticism, God knows what. I ignored much of this. Like a puppy with a baseball glove, I ignored its intent and put it to my own purpose. The American character, Fiedler announced, was rooted in the male drive to escape from the airless oppressiveness of family obligations and move on to new places.

Fiedler made much of the buddyism in early American lit. The example I liked best was Fennimore Cooper's Hawkeye and his companion, the Mohican Chingachgook. (I didn't wonder at the moment whether my Camp AtenRos experience was part of my interest in Fiedler's claims.) Yes! I said to myself. The Lone Ranger and Tonto adds fuel, and the movie High Noon proves it. (I did not yet have a rigorous standard for proofs.) I later added to my list the Cisco Kid, Red Ryder and whoever, Hopalong Cassidy and someone. The cowboy, the paradigmatic American individual, had a buddy, not a wife. But homoeroticism? Really? Maybe.

The tie-in to the frontier hypothesis got me excited because I had my own application of these thoughts. In the middle of the twentieth century, California had become the frontier. Students would get their degrees in the east and seek their future in the west. California became America. The Beach Boys. The Berkeley Free Speech movement. It was where all that was new was being invented.

It was so damn obvious!

I thought back to that inspiration as I approached the office of my new advisor and knocked.

She barked, "Enter!" A sign of a forthright person. She also won a point for the piles of books on her desk. I wondered whether she had to be careful with her gestures to avoid toppling the precarious piles. In fact she showed no such constraint during our talk and one of the piles did topple. That was good for my ego which was going to suffer as we discussed American literature.

She rummaged around on her desk for her appointment book. She saw it on top of one of the piles, consulted it, turned to me and said, "You would be Dr. Sokolsky."

"Please call me Solly."

"Very well. Call me Professor Murphy."

Some people give descriptions like "in her middle late thirties," as if they had counted tree rings. How do they do that? I only had confidence she was between birth and death. Tiptoeing out on a limb I could guess she was between late thirties and a well-preserved sixty. She had olive skin, long dark hair, and a broad face with a friendly scowl. She had a body that was cylindrical: solid, no frills. Her attitude was not unfriendly, definitely a double negative. I grew to appreciate her a great deal.

I laid out my thesis idea being cagey to hide some of my ignorance. She listened and seemed interested. Then it was her turn to batter my cage.

"What about Don Quixote and Sancho Panza? A pair of buddies but no frontier. Maybe buddies is a broad theme and not confined to your frontier idea."

She paused. I took a moment to think. A moment wasn't nearly enough. She continued: "What about *The Scarlet Letter*, a widely acknowledged masterpiece of American lit. No frontier. No buddies."

Years later I would be able to give a rebuttal, but at the time I could only silently squirm.

"What about Poe? Was *The Cask of Amontillado* a metaphor for entrapment by a family?"

I was on the ropes. I had read the short story, and had a few remarks in mind. When you're on the ropes anything in mind can be comforting. She took another whack at the dying horse: "What about *Moby Dick*?"

It was time to fight back. I was going to step away from the ropes and out onto thin ice. I hadn't read the book, but I had seen the movie. I ventured an insight.

"What about it? Ishmael has Queequeg, a parallel to Hawkeye and Chingachgook."

(Had I read the book I would have been able to push the argument for Fiedlerian homoeroticism; I was glad I hadn't read it.) Imagining that I had scored a point, I continued.

"And the whole idea of a sea voyage, escape from the family, escape from women."

"Good, Solly! You're going to be fun to work with. You need to read more American Lit, and you need to read more literary criticism, more than just that one Fiedler book. We'll have many meetings to discuss literary ideas. But for now, tell me if you have a punch line. Does your thesis end with the argument California is the new frontier?"

"No, not at all. It ends with the question: What next? With no more frontier what is going to happen to the American psyche?"

"Interesting, but it's not a literary question. It falls somewhere in the fuzzy realm of sociology and political science. I suggest you concentrate on how the disappearance of the California frontier is affecting the modern American novel."

"Suggestion accepted. And there's another unrelated matter."

"And that would be...?"

"What do I do about the rhetoric part of my master's?"

"Mmmm. Yes. I can tell from your admissions paperwork you already write acceptably, but that's not at all the same as knowing how to teach writing. I see you took one of the courses during the summer. You'll benefit more from the other one. Buck up. It won't be bad. And don't whine; you've got to do it.

"Solly, I hope you understand I will be giving you a hard time, as I did today, as a way of educating you."

"Professor Murphy, I not only understand it, but I appreciate and look forward to it."

I left the meeting happy and an elitist no more.

CHAPTER 6

SWEET CAROLINE; FALL 2013-SUMMER 2015

After meeting Murphy, I was as high as I had been low a few months earlier. Part of it was my relief that I might actually have made the right choice of path. I proceeded on that path at a very fast jog. I attended, and almost enjoyed, the two Cal State courses I was required to take. Aside from that, I stayed in the apartment I had turned into the Duarte Tome Depot, reading, reading. One day I missed a meal and realized I was overdoing it. I headed for the street.

There were good things about my Duarte digs besides its rent. It was close enough to, and far enough from, where I wanted to be and not to be. And it had a wonderful symbolism for my thesis: It was only about 200 feet from historic Route 66. For those who were on the way to a new life Route 66 had been the path.

I walked the one block south to Historic Route 66. (Others may call it Huntington Drive but they would be asking for a fight.) I turned inappropriately east and walked to a nearby tavern I had visited in my previous life. From the outside it was camouflaged as an IHOP clone. Inside was very different. The management called it a dive and tried to live down to the description. The lighting was kept very low as if to hide the dirt that wasn't there. The chef's masterpiece was a vertical tower of three meat patties, bacon, and a fried egg held together with cheese adhesive. It sat on the bottom half of a burger bun that had lost visual contact with the top half of the bun far above it. I wouldn't have eaten one on a dare but I liked the attitude it showed.

I sat down at the bar, ordered a local brew, and waited for a nibble. A few minutes later a nibble arrived named Jesika. When I saw the spelling on her big 'Hi I'm Jesika' button I knew it wouldn't go well. I kept saying "Solly, get over yourself and just enjoy someone different." Anyway, I wasn't going to be rude.

Jesika could have been quite physically attractive scraped clean of tattoos and piercings. I sensed her disappointment that I was unaccessorized. She broke the ice with, "You ever considered a tattoo?"

I (politely) probed her sense of humor, "Yes, I had my parakeet tattooed."

She understood it was a joke, but she was not a joker.

"You're funny," she said, in an accusatory tone, and moved on. I guess she was not looking for funny…

I returned every few days when I felt a need to get away from the books. Jesika and I chatted when she was there. She was always there; she worked there and we had met on her break. I kept my sense of humor tucked in. Eventually I got to tell her what I was up to, and learned she did a lot of reading of mystery novels.

A chat about them made the visits relaxing, but wasn't a cure for the isolation.

Then came Sweet Caroline, not at a dive, but at the USC library where, as a Cal State grad student, I had library privileges. I drove there one afternoon after my class to look for a book of literary criticism many other books attacked. I wanted to see it for myself, thinking I might want to defend it.

Caroline came through the library entrance carrying a stack of eight, maybe ten, books. I thought of the tower-burger at the tavern and when the top book slipped off concluded that there was no cheese *inter libros*. Everyone saw the problem. She couldn't bend over without all the books falling. They looked at the book on the floor, looked at her, looked at the book on the floor.

These situations are awkward. There were several students who stared, thinking about helping, but scanned the crowd to see whether anyone else was about to help. She was pretty, so the males worried that helping her could be misinterpreted, or correctly interpreted. I was one of the worriers, but at age 33 had shed some of my shyness baby fat and was not terrified of doing the wrong thing. I moved quickly to the fallen book, picked it up and said, "I was wondering whether this might be yours?"

She smiled a beautiful smile and said, "It might be. What's the title?"

Thank you Lord. She has a sense of humor. I told her in a voice loud enough for those nearby to hear, "How to Murder Your Professor."

"Yeah, that's mine."

We both started laughing, then dealt with her burden. I made a motion to lift the top half of the stack. We both realized this would run the risk of my hand brushing against a breast. So, with a conversation via eyes and eyebrows, I lifted the top three books, left her breast untouched, and escorted her to the desk to drop off the books.

Caroline turned to me and said, "Beasts of burden are usually watered. Might you accept being coffeed?"

I signaled acceptance with a smile and a nod, and asked whether she would be bringing many books. She indulgently smiled and led me to the nearest campus site for beast caffeination.

"Do you have a name?" she asked.

More about me: For you to understand me you need to understand the challenge I now faced. I wanted to answer with a simple "No," or with "Call me Ishmael," but I sensed – with regret – it was a time to throttle back on silly. I might have stumbled into an interesting development. Wouldn't want to kill it too soon.

"My name is Solly to my friends, Saul Sokolsky to my enemies."

"Then I'll call you Solly. I'm Caroline Berkey to everyone. What do you do Solly?"

"I'm a professional hop-step-jumper." Damn. So much for throttling back. But Caroline could play in this league.

"That's good. I'm getting so tired of meeting javelin throwers."

We laughed, and she gave me a mock stern stare and said, "No, really."

So I told her really. And she gave me her really.

"I'm going to finish my bachelor's in sociology then off to the Peace Corps for two years."

That stopped me for a moment, before I asked a stupid question (the first of a series): "The Peace Corps is still in business?"

"Oh yeah! It's only about a tenth the size it was sixty years ago, but it's alive."

Mixed with my flirting was honest curiosity.

"This is a sign of the changes in attitude of young people?"

"Yup. But more the change in our government; it's not being run by JFKs anymore. Funds have been slashed. The Corps actually have as many volunteers as they can handle."

Caroline had to run off to a class and was not one to miss a class just for an ex-hop-step-jumper. We didn't want it to end there. I simply said, "I'd like to hear more about the Peace Corps, and about you. I'd like to see you again."

We negotiated for a meeting place more convenient than USC, which has three students for every parking place and two cars for every student.

We met in Pasadena for dinner and hit it way off right away, agreeing on classic noir movies, flavors of ice cream, dogs vs. cats, the important things. She was a decade younger than I and that meant that there was different pop culture in vogue during our formative years. It wouldn't have been much of a problem anyway, but it turned out we were both fans of culture that went back further than we ourselves did, back to the peak of American culture: Rocky and Bullwinkle, Fibber McGee and Molly, Sid Caesar, Pogo. People in the restaurant turned to stare at us as we recited remembered bits and rolled out of our chairs laughing.

There was something else good that I associated with an earlier era, and I turned to it.

"Peace Corps?"

"Ah yes. The Peace Corps. They had 7,000 volunteers participating last year, so I'm not the only one."

"Do you know where you'll be going? What you'll be doing?"

"Yes, and sort of. I'll be going to Sierra Leone, and I'll be helping with education.

Time for the second stupid question.

"Do you speak Spanish?"

She looked at me with mock pity and said, "Fairly well, but I won't be using it. Sierra Leone is in western Africa. It's right next to Liberia. You can't miss it."

She paused before sweetly adding, "Did you graduate from college?"

I did a mime version of Japanese self-disembowelment, then wondered whether it was culturally insensitive. I looked around and saw no offended diners drawing Samurai swords. Relieved, I turned to salvage my ego.

"Hey, c'mon, 'Sierra Leone.' I took a semester of Spanish, and *that* is Spanish. It means 'lion saw.'"

"Completely understandable, the fifteenth century Portuguese explorers are to blame, not you."

"Indeed! I'm going to write a stern letter to the Federation do Exploradoros Portugeses."

"Nice try. C+."

Despite the silliness, it dawned on me that she was headed for a dangerous place. I didn't know about Sierra Leone, but I knew about Liberia and Senegal. These were in the western bulge of Africa, and were places the State Department warned against. I tried to raise the question of motivation without adding to the list of stupid questions.

"Is Sierra Leone dangerous? I've heard scary stories about Senegal."

"Dangerous? Yes. So is Chicago. I am not going to do anything stupider than it has to be. The Peace Corps is aware of the danger, and has in-country training to deal with security, language, customs, the whole pig roast. They do the training well."

"And yeah. I'd be a fool – maybe I am – to deny that violent crime is a problem. But the crime is mostly in Freetown. It's the capital. But you knew that."

"Of course. And you won't be in Freetown?"

"No, I'm going to be in the north, near Kabala, a town of 20,000. It's about 30 miles south of the border with Guinea."

I thought to myself "Guinea is in Africa?" but didn't want to interrupt. Caroline had warmed to her subject and was ladling it out.

"The plan is for me to set up a school in a village called Koinadugu. That's also the name of the region, so don't get confused."

It was far too late. She continued.

"Koinadugu is small, maybe 100 huts. There's no school, and there's no school close enough. Their way of life is being threatened by heavy logging in the area. They'll be facing change; they need school."

"And the language? Not Spanish, but…"

"Yeah. Not Spanish. And full disclosure, I am a repressed linguist. I pick up languages pretty easily, but this is going to be a new experience. The official language of Sierra Leone is English, but in Koinadugu the dominant language is Temne. Only about 30,000 people in the world speak it. I'll make it 30,001. It's not going to be easy."

I was heartened by this confession. She dug into her pocketbook, handed me a pamphlet, and explained, "Here's the 1987 Peace Corps manual of Temne."

It reminded me of educational materials produced by underfunded elementary schools. Not wanting to be rude I faked an interest which soon lost the fake. It was probably just bad luck that the first vocabulary word I saw was nɛnɛ, 'cockroach.' I then learned that the most difficult consonant was 'Gb' which is the sound of a 'g' and 'b' pronounced simultaneously. I was testing whether that was possible, with gbɛngbɛ (pepper), but Caroline became disturbed at the choking sounds.

It was time to move away from the Peace Corps. I asked about her early years and learned some things more interesting than the alveolar consonants of Temne.

Caroline made a big mistake. She told me that in high school she had become 'Sweet Caroline,' inspired both by the Neil Diamond song and by Caroline's personality. Like a good Tech tag it stuck and she would be Sweet Caroline to me ever after. She didn't mind. In fact, she didn't very much mind very much of anything. She shrugged off the little stuff; she put things in perspective. It was wonderfully comfortable being with her.

God, I wish I could do that, but I didn't even make a mental note. Why bother?

Chapter 7
THE FUTURE LOOMS; FALL 2013-AUGUST 2015

In addition to some rudimentary Temne, I learned from Sweet Caroline that her parents had been missionaries. I pictured Stanley and Livingston. It was the wrong picture, but it crushed a fantasy that was pre-crushed by a pin Sweet Caroline wore; it showed a stylized flame next to a crucifix. Just as it was obvious that Spanish would be spoken in Sierra Leone, it was obvious Sweet Caroline would be a religious 'good' girl. Sic transit fantasy.

Sweet Caroline was not a classic beauty, but classic beauty is overrated. You get tired of looking at it. Sweet Caroline had the kind of looks you can keep looking at.

Her face was broad. Her hair was a radial mop, all hairs the same length, like hair glued onto a doll. But her smile made everything else go unnoticed. Her mouth was wide and set off by unusual dimples, not in the cheeks, but right at the edge of her lips, like parentheses setting off her mouth. Her smile was slightly skewed as if she were always smirking in the kindest, sweetest way. Her figure was medium, but so what.

With not-so-good girl dreams fading I hid my disappointment, but was silent. Sweet Caroline asked where and how I was living. The answer wasn't interesting, so I made the Duarte story brief, then turned the question to her.

"What's life like in the dorms?"

Sweet Caroline suggested, right there and then in the Pasadena restaurant, that she move in with me. She wasn't in the dorms; she was sleeping on a couch in the apartment of another student she knew from way back.

The big question mark lit over my head and in a break with tradition I came up with just the right way of asking the big question.

"There's a problem. I don't have a couch."

My heart and other parts of my body reacted at her response.

"But you do have a bed."

The new path was turning out to be pretty good. I was enjoying the master's program and could see myself happy teaching writing. Caroline not only added sweetness to my life, but had me considering a more flexible attitude towards the world. Her parents were not B-movie missionaries. Her father was a minister in the United Methodist Church. I learned that the UMC was coming apart. It spanned too wide a range of progressive and conservative leanings. Sweet Caroline's dad was *way* over on the progressive side. That provided part of the missionary answer.

There was a more important part. Her parents had served in China on a mission organized not by the Methodists, but by the OMF, the Overseas Missionary Fellowship. Yeah, it was evangelical Christian, but they were awfully open minded, and had the Peace Corps approach: Become part of the local culture. Gnaw your way into their lives. Become an infestation. Yeah, there was some overlap with what Sweet Caroline was doing. Some.

We had great talks, make that arguments, about what Caroline was doing and why. She was excited by what an adventure it would be, loved the challenge of saying pepper in Temne, but mostly – she claimed – she wanted to make a difference. I admired, though I didn't really understand, the attitude. I was very careful to make the admiration clear and hide the lack of understanding. We were so alike and so different.

Was I in love? I still hadn't read enough books to know what that meant, but I was happy; I knew what that meant. Was it perfect. No. I also knew what that meant.

Back at the Pasadena restaurant, when we were setting up the surprising living arrangements, there was a horizon: In a year and a half we would both finish degrees and start new lives. There was distant haze over that horizon. But just as kittens become cats, the future becomes the damn present. It had been many months. Our haze was dispelling. I would get my master's and job-hunting license in two months. Sweet Caroline would get her bachelor's degree, do the US segment of training, and sail off. The horizon became the terrible cliff marked decision.' We avoided looking over the edge but the day came.

We took a break from work to play tennis at a nearby public court. We were silent, unusual for us, as we walked back to the apartment. I couldn't help but notice, with my newfound sensitivity and vocabulary, we were at a denouement. We both sensed that it was time.

Caroline's serve was, "Solly, have you thought about what you're doing?"

I returned serve: "I've thought a great deal about what I'm doing."

We both contributed to a protracted silence.

Caroline's second serve was unexpected.

"Solly, do you realize that you are being selfish?"

This was a surprise, so my return lob really was a question.

"How am I being selfish by preparing myself to teach?"

Her return of my lob was an emotional overhead smash.

"Teach? Are you intending to go to an inner-city school? If not you'll just be helping already overprivileged kids move undeservingly forward in a system that already favors them too much. And you're doing it because you see it as a comfortable life for yourself."

Damn. She was right, at least partially right. I was doing this for myself. I was a bit sad that this did not make me sad more than just a bit, but that was the way it was. I guess I *was* selfish. But was I really that different from Caroline? I re-entered the game.

"You're right, Caroline. My motivations aren't selfless. Are yours? You want to make a difference. Why? Isn't that your ego speaking? You want to be important, at least to the people in those huts."

This upset her, maybe because it rang true. She was as angry as I had ever seen her. Her complexion became redder but shouting was just not in her skill set.

Louder was as she came back with, "So Solly, the view from your pulpit is that no one can ever do anything that is purely good?"

It wasn't really a question so I didn't answer. If I had, the answer would have been, "Yeah. And that's not so bad."

Caroline moved out. It only took her a few hours to pack; she wasn't much of a hoarder. She drove away. We hadn't said a single word since she started packing.

She returned a few hours later. We had both cooled down and were careful to be polite. It was over, why incur pointless pain? She told me where she would be staying, and said that she would return sometime in the next few days to pick up her remaining things. There was the awkwardness of whether she could hold onto the key until then. Each of us tried to emphasize how much well we wished the other, but it came out in short bursts of mutual interruptions. And that was that.

It's interesting the way you miss someone. You get used to the minutiae of daily activities and when things change you miss even the annoyances. Caroline would park her ancient Corolla more in the middle than to the side of our two-car space, often leaving less space than I needed for my tiny Miata. Now every time I parked I was reminded of the space in my life. She had commented sweetly on the way I left mail unopened. With her gone, I found myself dealing with mail as soon as it arrived. These minutiae were the bricks that built our lives. My life had crumbled.

But there was another feeling. It was a lighthearted feeling of freedom. I thought about it a great deal. Freedom from what? Sweet Caroline and I would soon have to make a tough decision. People hate making decisions. Change is hard. Being responsible for it is harder. Now the decision was made and, at the cost of some emptiness, the future was simplified. It was the best explanation I could come up with.

The future didn't lie too far ahead. It was May, a bit late to get a teaching job for the coming academic year, but the late date could work to my advantage. There would be colleges, even major universities, that needed someone. Since it was very late to hire, they might overlook a minor shortcoming in my application: no teaching experience. I would be Walmart's one remaining bouquet of flaccid daisies late on Valentine's Day.

Reality exceeded my hopes: Caltech was looking for someone to teach writing and literature. It wasn't a permanent position, but nothing is permanent and this was a great door to stick my foot in. I sent in a mostly true application which led to an appointment for an interview. I bought a tie and crossed my fingers.

Hope springs eternal (Pope, the one who's a poet). I was pretty good at not fooling myself, so that eternal springiness of hope had some justification. Caltech should be very happy to have someone with a strong science background, along with a degree in teaching writing. If they were thinking it through, they would also see that my experience with the, umm, unusual nature of Caltech undergraduate fauna would be more valuable than experience teaching writing at Random State University. It turned out that I was 75% correct.

CHAPTER 8
SOLLY RETURNS; AUGUST 2015- AUGUST 2018

The 25% error was Prof. Maurice L'Hommedieu, Chair of the Caltech Department of English. He was the longest serving, and oldest member of the Caltech faculty. From my student days I remembered the suggestions that he was one of the first life forms to crawl out of the sea. He was not popular with the students, but he had tenure so it didn't matter very much. What mattered very much to L'Hommedieu was his English Department, his bastion of literacy surrounded by the illiterate hordes, Philistines who write equations and programs, not novels and poems. He was badly outnumbered and saw any prospective hire as either an addition to his tiny army or yet another Philistine. There were no doubts about where I pitched my tent.

He was the first at bat in the interview. Peering over his heptafocals, he stared at what must have been a fuzzy image of me and asked: "Who is your favorite poet?"

This was yet another opportunity for my sense of humor to make trouble.

I thought about looking literate and saying, "The guy who wrote 'There was a young lass from South Bangor...' "

I bit the insides of my metaphorical cheeks. I knew that L'Hommedieu's specialty was Blake. I liked Blake as much as I liked any poet, but it would have been an error to move the jousting to L'Hommedieu's terrain, so I played it safe and named a golden oldy, Tennyson. I wrote a paper on him in my master's program and rather liked his straightforward poetry.

L'Hommedieu sneered and scoffed "That clichéd filler of templates? How unoriginal!" L'Hommedieu and I exchanged a few unpleasantries in which I more or less held my own.

L'Hommedieu very slowly took a fountain pen out of his pocket. He was agonizingly slow. I wondered whether this was to give himself time to think of his next insult, or he just wanted to be annoying. When the pen finally cleared his pocket I was surprised to see that it was not a simple black Montblanc.

I expected a Montblanc the way you just know that someone drives a Mercedes. (Just to be sure you don't miss it they often toss their key fob on the table). But when I saw the white star on the top of the pen's cap I realized that it was indeed a Montblanc, just not an off-the-rack black one. It would be the right instrument to jot down a half-witty scathing remark, which is what he presumably did, dragging it out manipulatively.

Fortunately the other three members of the hiring committee had the same affection for L'Hommedieu the undergraduates did, so his obvious distaste at the thought of hiring me dispelled hesitation about my lack of experience.

That was that. I was hired in a two-year position, renewable if performance was deemed successful. It was and was again for a third year. After three years, near the end of the summer, the administration demonstrated creativity in the exploitation of auxiliary faculty and made up a position, Senior Lecturer, that had no benefit in substance over my previous position (indentured instructor) but it had implications of permanence. Also it sounded nice.

My initial teaching load (that's what they called it, a load): one literature course and one writing course. Like many new faculty members, I started out not knowing what I was doing, but muddled through adequately. Students are kind. As I learned how to teach, it became more and more enjoyable for me and for them. The students understood that technical writing would be valuable in their careers, and they viewed it as a form of engineering: The goal was to optimize clarity with the constraint of keeping it as brief as possible. They ate up little tricks like moving adjectives adjacent to nouns and repeating words like "to" in order to search, to find, and to destroy any antecedent-ambiguity.

But literature? Why did they need literature? To ignite their interest, I tried an old trick: having them relate the lit to their own lives. They were not impressed. They had done that starting in fourth grade. I came up with a new trick: criticizing literary criticism. After making sure that they respected good literary criticism, I sharpened their appreciation of what was good by showing them what was bad. I told them – and these smart kids could have figured it out for themselves – much of lit crit was professionals trying to impress other professionals, and to insult yet others. Ironically, the rhetoric of this shlock lit crit was terrible. I instituted a contest to come up with the most biting mock literary criticism. In my second year, a biochem major won with:

> *"Unless, during the storms of the last dark, anyone-can-write dec-ades, one has confined reading to the last chapters of the lesser of the sold-by-the-pound mystery novels on the supermarket shelves, one cannot have avoided, despite understandably desperate at-tempts, the transparent bathos appropriate to what is revealed in Schlafting-LePew's disgraceful praise of Czymzky's "Harry the Hamster."*

PhD at age 27; five years in Start-up Valley; two years to get a master's in English; four years (so far) teaching writing at Tech. There I was, at 38; I had a permanent temporary position. Despite the downsides, there were many rea-sons that I was happy (not just the escape from the Valley). I wondered whether that was about to change. The Caltech administration failed to overlook the fact that, despite my dotage, I got along very well with the undergraduates. This led to an invitation for me to chat with Louis Horvath, the head (the Master) of Caltech Student Housing.

I had a suspicion about the invitation. I would be asked to be a Resident Associate, an RA, at one of the Caltech Houses. I had 10 days to think about it. Oh bother. Another change, another decision. Of course, I put off that deci-sion until lunch, right before the chat appointment.

The lunch was at Caltech's Athenaeum (the Ath), a sort of faculty club. (Because Caltech is small and unusual, many things are only sort of; students, for instance, are allowed to be members of the Ath.) It exhibits its nature in its architecture, sort of Mediterranean. It has survived earthquakes, but it is not the place I would run to after an earthquake warning. It also exhibits its nature by the mixture of the formality of its interior, rich dark wood everywhere, and the California attitude toward dress. (You need to be dressed.)

I was sure that the Resident Associate offer would be proffered. And I wanted the lunch to be a time for mulling. But as any Scottish mouse can tell you, intentions gang aft agley. I had steered clear of the English Department's traditional table for my traditional reasons, but was caught from my blind side by Prof. Ian Sturdley, who asked to join me and sat down, assuming that the answer was yes.

Ian is a geophysicist. His stocky body and small feet give the impression of a brown bear on its hind legs. This is reinforced by his beard, a face covering that suggests fur. He is used to the ursine comparison and is good-natured about it. He smiled when I asked him, as I always did, whether he had come to the Ath to beg for food.

I enjoyed Athenauem conversations with Ian. I learned about the frustrations of predicting earthquakes while I looked nervously at the cracks in the Athenaeum walls. Ian was interested in literature, and believed himself, in that sense, to be literate. That belief was held by everyone at Caltech, but in Ian's case there was justification; he was knowledgeable about literature, and – more important – he was truly interested. So, I listened to his original ideas in geophysics, and he listened to my unoriginal thoughts about the role of the American frontier in early American literature. In this way, 1 pm, the Resident Associate chat hour, snuck up and I hurried out like Cinderella at midnight, to protect my reputation for reliability (an actual Solly virtue). Also, I still wanted to process the idea a bit, and the walk from the Ath to the Housing office was one last chance to introspect.

Caltech is small. The main part of campus runs about a half mile east to west, and about the same distance north to south. Olive Walk, the spine of the main campus, runs east and west, with the Athenaeum at the east end, smack up against the eastern border, South Hill Avenue. I imagined old campus maps with 'Here there be dragons' in the terra incognita east of South Hill Avenue. But I was walking west, away from South Hill, toward the Pacific Ocean which lay sixty miles off. I would stop sixty miles short of that. The Housing Office was only about fifty yards ahead, but they were an important 50 yards, and maybe an important part of my next few years.

I still hoped for some insights as I ambled. On my left, south of Olive Walk, were the four original undergraduate dorms, built in the same faux Mediteranean lack of style as the Ath. On my right, north of the Walk, were the three unoriginal houses, built in lowest bidder, sturdy but sub-plain mode. A strange hybrid, Avery House, held a few homeless undergrads after a housing shortage around 2004 created the need. But Avery House was in the northern hinterlands, not on Olive Walk, and not part of what, for want of a more pejorative term, could be called the Caltech House culture. I told myself I would reserve judgment; I knew that I was lying and it was about to get worse. As if the Housing Office had pressed CNTRL-D, a new, shall we call it out house, would be opening in September, Bechtel House. I thought about culture change; I thought about Rocky and Bullwinkle. It was too sad to think about. I ambled on.

The Houses could maintain culture because the characteristics of each House perpetuated themselves through a ritual near the start of each academic year. The frosh would rotate through the Houses getting to know and be known to the inmates. There followed a choosing. Each House in turn claimed a frosh who was still in the dwindling pool of increasingly glum frosh, until all the frosh were linked to a House. It was necessary for the pool to be drained since all first-year undergrads had to live on campus. In that way it was unlike the cruelty of fraternity rushing. The ritual was more like choosing sides for a game of playground baseball. The kid who trips over untied laces while walking across the field knows his limitations, but knows that a place is guaranteed.

Each House selected students who were the best fit to its beliefs about its own character. And these characteristics were preserved and enhanced in every generation. It's a process engineers call positive feedback, and social anthropologists call cultural evolution (about which my knowledge is typically shallow). The cultures that evolved are fascinating, but can be found elsewhere, and should be sought elsewhere if we are to amble forward.

The Housing Office sat between two of the new Houses on Olive Walk. If I were prone to drama, I would have considered it a fateful walk since it might end in a change in my life. In view of this I looked around, rather than casting my eyes downward in the thoughtful rabbinical posture of the typical Techie. I stopped walking for a moment. I had never noticed the cornerstone of the new Houses, marking the 1960 start of construction. I had not noticed, right above the date, the question кто Иван Галт? I chuckled to myself. (Laughing out loud was so uncool; chuckling was tolerated.) So arcane. Fortunately my shallow polymathism had prepared me for just this kind of Techishness. From my one semester of Russian, I knew that this was "Who is John Galt?", and from my time wasted reading *Atlas Shrugged*, I knew that this was a meme (though memes were born long after the shrug) for a very self-reliant stern conservative view of the world. I admired not only the interesting mixture of ideas and irony but that the lettering, added by Techies to the cornerstone, very accurately duplicated the carving of the date by serious construction artisans. It was so damn Techish, ironic ideas presented with top flight technical craftmanship.

I started walking again and was passed by two eastbound undergrads arguing about the meaning of Gnosticism. I made a note to myself to look it up after the interview, just in case.

CHAPTER 9

SOLLY GETS A FAMILY; AUGUST 2018

The door was open. The location and open door gave Master of Houses Louis Horvath an opportunity to watch some of the comings, goings, and goings-on of the students. But he eschewed (English Department word) that opportunity. A martinet would have been a hilarious failure as the Master of Houses. The students would use him as the target of practical jokes that would become legends. Louis, an antidisciplinarian, would not be legendary. His rule was there was no point in pointless rules. The students had very much the same view so appreciated that House Master Louis delivered a sermon, or meted some punishment, only when a student action was seen by all (except perhaps the perpetrator) to be improper, unfair, or dangerous.

Louis was a very fit, broad shouldered 50-something. He had facial hair in the middle ground between goatee and honest beard. It was grey-white on the chin, darker around the mouth, and then grey as it ascended to blend with the grey top hair. He had rimless glasses and I knew that behind the desk his pants were tucked into his western boots. I didn't find it flattering but wasn't there to give fashion advice.

The interview started by Louis standing and breaking the ice: "I am told they call you Solly."

I responded "Yes. I'll take the position."

We both laughed. I knew why I was there; he knew I knew; I knew he knew I knew. Why not get on with it? We got on with it.

Getting on with it did not preclude petting Mentis and Ethos, who shared Louis' office. Louis thought a dog or two would be good company for the many hours Louis spent in his office between sparse emergencies. Since the dog or two represented Caltech they needed to be representative. The question of dog intelligence seemed to attract many dog owners of limited intelligence but poodles and border collies were near the top of everyone's list. So Louis bought a mix, a bordoodle, from a breeder who had foreseen the market. The bordoodle was Mentis.

Louis wanted the students to understand there was more to life than brains; there was soul, or heart. Something like that. He rummaged the internet for guidance, but 'dog with soul' didn't get hits. The proxy would have to be loyalty. He read about Hachikō, a Japanese Akita who continued to go to the train station to meet his master for ten years after his master had died. It is told that Louis remarked "that dog must have been incredibly loyal or stupid." Whichever Louis believed, he did go out and buy an Akita, Ethos, to fill out his canine brace. Mentis and Ethos, mind and soul.

A footnote to the campus lore was a freshman who visited the Housing Office and told Louis his pets were grammatically incorrect. Since 'Mentis' was Latin genitive, the dog's name should be 'Mens.' Louis explained, "Dogs are terrible with Latin declensions." The lore goes on to relate the student didn't know what to make of this; he wasn't sure Louis was joking. But lore tends to favor amusing rather than actual, so who knows.

All three of us were reluctant to see my petting end but we needed to get down to business.

I would live and dine free of cost, and would receive $1,500 per month. That, of course, was in addition to my Senior Lecturer pittance. Never mind the $1,500. The elimination of living and dining meant I would be relatively well off, almost as if I had stayed in the Valley, but much more interesting. The commute to the classrooms was also an attraction, being provided by shoes.

Louis went through a brief discussion of rules. It was extremely brief. The rules were in a short pamphlet and Louis had been told I could read. More delicate was the discussion of the extent to which the rules would be enforced. Though delicate, this was also brief, since Louis was told I could think.

He now switched to a formal tone. I sharpened my attention.

"I'm sure I don't need to mention this," he said, letting me know he needed to mention something, "but it would be a bad idea for you to get romantically involved with one of the students."

I was surprised. Indeed, it didn't need to be said, nor did my response.

"But I'm twice their age. I can't imagine one of them being attracted to me."

In a more or less kindly way he said, "Then you don't have much imagination for someone who reads so many books. You may become a father figure to some of them."

The more or less kindly part was his smile as he said it, but the smile was slight; it was not a smiling business. He wanted me to take it seriously. I did and I wanted him to know it.

"Point taken, very taken, but this is the last thing you should worry about. What worry is higher on the list?"

"The danger of getting involved with a student cannot be overstated," he overstated.

Don't you hate it when a conversation is like a scratched 78 rpm record, and repeats? I closed my eyes so I could roll them without Louis seeing. I responded with my sarcasm veiled in the sheerest civility.

"Nor can my resistance to such involvement be overstated. What other worries are on the list?"

"Highest on the list is mental health."

An important part of my position was to serve as a first line of psychological counseling and to be on guard for worrisome signs. I would receive student profiles, including mental health profiles, but these were only professional guesses. I would make my own amateur guesses.

Louis looked off in the distance, or where the distance would be except for a wall, and opined: "It's probably going to be a great deal of fun 70% of the time, very rewarding most of the time, and perhaps very sad 5% of the time."

We both knew what he was talking about: the recent, and not-so-recent suicides. Students at Tech were used to being at the top. In school, pre-Tech, they suffered only from boredom and jealousy-generated ostracism. But when thrown together with others like them, they experienced fragility of confidence. With no practice in such things this could get the better of them, and that had happened in Blacker House the previous year. Louis made the relevance clear.

"As you know, a student, Jim Boyd, died in Blacker House last year. He made two unsuccessful attempts to poison himself, though perhaps successful is the right description, since he survived. It is generally believed his attempts were meant to get him attention.

"Both times he drove to Blacker immediately after taking the poison, and his friends rushed him to Huntington Memorial Hospital. His stomach was pumped and all was temporarily calm, though hardly well. He tried again, a third time, but when he drove to Blacker, all his friends were away. He wasted some time looking for help, and then it was too late.

"Last year there were two RAs in Blacker, a married couple, Lana and Phil Jones, both postdocs in biochemistry. I like having an RA couple. It exposes the students to a good adult relationship; they may not have come from a home with one."

Neither of us mentioned that this strategy might have been questioned after the divorce of another Blacker RA couple, a decade earlier. Maybe that was also meant to prepare students for real life experiences.

"Lana and Phil's RA-dom was going fine, except most of the males were developing a crush on Lana, but it never led to any real problem."

"The danger cannot be overstated," I interjected.

Louis stared at me for a few seconds before continuing.

"Obviously the suicide was a real problem for Blacker, but it was also a real problem for the Joneses. The wife thought they needed to intervene forcefully after Boyd's second attempt. The husband thought it would be best to deal with the student's need for attention directly, by seeing to it that Boyd got the needed attention. Jones – the husband – took it upon himself to give Boyd that attention. The death of the student almost broke up the marriage. They ended up getting counseling (as Boyd should have) but obviously had to leave Blacker. A retired Chemistry professor, Gerald Tarsdale, took over on an emergency basis for the remaining months of the academic year, and did an excellent job of arranging grief counseling.

"So, this may be the sort of thing that will be mixed in with the fun, rewarding experiences, palatial lodging and gourmet food."

I hadn't known some of these details of the suicide, and I was somber, but not discouraged. I took a deep breath and asked the obvious question, "I assume I will be assigned to Blacker House."

He took a deep breath and gave the obvious answer, "Yes."

It wasn't quite over. He added, "One more thing, a new thing, that might signify nothing."

"Sound and fury," I interjected playing the role of the English instructor. He was kind enough not even to pause.

"Some Caltech undergrads are very skilled at hacking into computer systems."

"Yes, I know."

Where was he going with this?

"Well… there is a vague rumor, and it might be nothing more, that some miscreants are hanging around trying to enlist students to help with ransomware attacks. They can be good at trapping students. Many of our students are not street smart and might be caught in a very awkward, even dangerous position."

I understood that "…might signify nothing" was a throwaway line. The hacking business needed to be watched. But rather than taking this as a scare I saw it as a challenge I would be better prepared for than an RA who had not dealt with the miscreants and traps of the Valley. Yes, a challenge. I told myself I liked challenges. I was almost convinced.

There seemed to be nothing more to be said, so I affected a Bogart lisp, and baring of the teeth, in a pitiful impersonation of the last line in *Casablanca*, "Louie, I think this is the beginning of a beautiful friendship."

His lack of expression showed his disappointment that I should think this funny. But he affected an 'oh yeah' tone of a *Colombo* episode for an addendum.

"I almost forgot, and this may be important. One of the students in Blacker, Fang Lou, quit a month before the end of spring semester. She filed the right paperwork, but did not show up for an exit interview. There is a slight suspicion there is something going on we should know about. The members of Blacker may know more than we do, so if you learn anything, please let me know what you can."

I didn't miss the implications of the passive phrasing "There is a slight suspicion…" Who was suspicious? I figured I would learn before too long.

"Got it. I'll keep my ear to the rail."

He was old enough to understand the metaphor.

Chapter 10
OPENING NIGHT; AUGUST-SEPTEMBER 2018

So that was the beginning of that. It was the third week of August and the calendar was ticking; the main horde of students would be arriving on September 23rd, a little more than a month off. Students anxious to get on with it, or to get away from another it, were tolerated a few days earlier. I had much to do, and as long as I told myself September 23rd was a long way off, it wouldn't get done.

There was the apartment in Duarte. I had five months to go on my lease, so I would have to seek a sublet (in violation of the standard lease contract that no one took seriously). There was moving/selling/donating most of my furniture, that sort of thing. As that sort of thing always does, it turned out to be a time consuming pothole in the road. RA *pro tem* Gerald Tarsdale had departed on September 13th, leaving a message to me in the RA suite that said only 'Good Luck.' That could mean anything. I never understood chemists.

I had visited Blacker many times during my grad student days. The four original Houses, Blacker, Dabney, Fleming and Ricketts, were squares that together made up a large rectangle south of Olive Walk. The Houses had very similar layouts, with appropriate mirror inversions so the House corners, meeting at the center, were the four dining rooms, all served by a central kitchen.

The Houses had long-established relations. Ricketts and Blacker, the eastern two Houses, had a weak bond with each other, but they were Houses of individuals and paid little attention to each other. The western Houses, Dabney and Fleming, on the other hand, had a very strong relationship, rivalry and exaggerated mock enmity.

Within Blacker itself there were yet further social subdivisions: the alleys. The corridors were only four feet wide, encouraging bonding or claustrophobia, and the many corners of the architecture meant many alleys, segments of corridors.

Each alley had a fanciful name, Swamp, Cannes, Pub, and a half dozen more. From time to time, they would engage in alley challenges, competitions in which silly trumped athletic.

The House, the alleys, the Blacker lounge, the Blacker courtyard. These were the setting of student lives, the creative silliness, the formations of friendships they would experience during a perhaps wonderful, perhaps difficult transition in their lives. There would be no perhaps about memorable. Decades later they would remember the people, the scenes, many of the events.

The RA suite was on the first level, south side, facing California Boulevard. It was convenient to an exit but inconveniently far from most of the rooms. In due time this would be a source of a quite a bit of exercise. The suite itself was nice. That's the perfect description. Nice. Or maybe nice enough. Besides a private bathroom with a great shower stall, the suite consisted of a small bedroom and a large living room/office. There was a full bed, a desk, and four chairs: the desk chair, two guest chairs, and a very nice easy chair I knew to avoid if I wanted to stay awake.

The RA suite was where I would meet with students and feel guilty. The suite had been converted from five single dorm rooms when the dawn of two genders among the students seemed to require two genders among the RAs. But now it was just a single Solly who couldn't forget he was taking up the space of two RAs or five undergrads.

In those first days, and occasionally weeks later, in my always troubled mind, there would be a review: Duarte apartment vs RA suite. The RA suite was smaller than the apartment, but was more than big enough and nice enough for my needs. And I was relieved of poverty, travel, food preparation, and worries about apartment problems. (Caltech was a good landlord.)

But there was something else. One thing I would miss about Duarte: Solitude. Getting away. I would no longer have two worlds. I could no longer leave the world of work (OK, teaching) and escape into the awayness of home.

In any case, it came to pass that on September 23rd, when the bulk of the students arrived, I was ready. And they were ready. They had heard about me through the digital networks, and my reputation among the students was good enough they smiled as we passed each other in the halls.

I would say, "Hi, I'm Solly. Your RA. Welcome." (I didn't say 'your *new* RA.' It would link too easily to last year's events.) They responded in a wide variety of ways, some shy grunts, some self-confident pleased to meet you's. Most important there were no scowls suggesting a lingering squad of diehard Lana/Phil loyalists.

The dining room was filled with history and nine round tables, each with 6 to 8 chairs. Waiters (work/study students) would bring food. Students would nourish themselves and be alert for violations of the many rules. The seriousness of these rules can be judged from the rule governing butter pats stuck to the ceiling.

I was optimistic when we all entered the dining room. I looked around at the faces of 68 students and thought about the vast set of possibilities of what may come. A voice in my head put it,

"So here I am; at 38, I have a permanent temporary position. And now I have a family."

First impressions are important. I wanted to come across as friendly and funny, but not too cute, not needy, not an older form of a Caltech prankster. I allowed myself just a bit of a light touch by putting a paper plate in front of every place setting, and announcing,

"Hi, I'm Solly. I see many smiling faces. I think the other faces belong to former students of English 136 or Writing 118. And, no; now that I'm your RA we can't get the grade changed.

"The RA/student ratio is 68 to 1. I assume you did not have trouble memorizing my name, but I may have trouble memorizing all yours. You know how us elderly people can be. For this reason, I have left paper plates in front of you. Please write your name on it, or Tech tag, or however you want to be known. And write in letters large enough for an elderly person to read. To repeat: I am Solly; please call me Solly. If I hear someone yelling Dr. Sokolsky I will try to be helpful by also yelling Dr. Sokolsky."

An introduction to Blacker naming: Assigning individual nicknames ('Tech tags') was widespread at Caltech, but it was a religion at Blacker. Residents were known by the generic name Moles, since moles lived in dark tunnels, dark as in black, as in Blacker. Moles used the adjective Molecular to describe

House characteristics, To describe a group of Blacker residents, they used the appropriate collective noun 'labor,' as in a labor of Moles. When three of them solved a problem, they appropriated a term from chemistry and called it a three Molar solution. And so on. And on and on.

Two years earlier, a new Mole, Artless, or Less (born Arthur) proposed that Molestation be used to mean adapting something to Blacker. The nasty side of that word gave it a bad aroma and it was rejected. Several older/wiser Moles explained this to Less with some difficulty.

My paper plate shtick went over well. It showed I had a sense of humor, but I wasn't trying too hard. It broke not only the RA-student ice, but the slight frostiness between the veteran Moles and the newly arrived frosh trying to fit in. The fledglings hadn't realized that Blacker was very much a universal fit. I read as many paper plate names as I could, and tried memory tricks for getting the names associated with the faces. I had already read the files on all the Blacker vets, so had a head start on the ones I should worry about. I had not forgotten about the hacker issue, but it was a first dinner. I told myself, "Slow Solly; take it slow." As for hacker stalking, the Fang enigma and the father figure fantasy, I would relegate those to 'be aware.'

CHAPTER 11

STUDENTS AND ROOMS; OCTOBER 2, 2018

Dust was settling slowly as the semester began, and Louis called me about a dust-up in Page House. A new student, née Barbara (not yet renamed) had been assigned a double room, but was not getting on well with her assigned roommate. This wouldn't do, and there was an as yet unshared double in Blacker.

Louis gave me detailed instructions: "Go to Page. Fix it." I went and took with me the Blacker House President Nidan and his consigliera, Jillrabbit (JR).

We walked the short distance to Page, waving to Mentis, Ethos, and Louis, as we passed the Housing Office. Along with its peers, Ruddock and Lloyd, Page sat on the north side of Olive Walk, facing the old Houses more or less the way the troops faced each other in World War I trenches. The old Houses had character; the newer northern concrete slab Houses weren't quite examples of brutalist architecture. That would have been a commitment to style; the new Houses were stylishly uncommitted. In any case, what was interesting was not the character of the buildings but the characters within, some of whom I already knew from my classes.

Lloyd House has been renamed, but it was still Lloyd in 2018. The change, for whatever reason, saddened me. I didn't like change. The *new* new houses, Avery and Bechtel, didn't depress me, since I didn't acknowledge that they were Caltech Houses. They weren't on Olive Walk. I suppose they had electricity and indoor toilets, but they were elsewhere. For a very different reason, I had no negative emotions about Page, Ruddock and Lloyd. They were born in 1960, before I was.

Why did I feel this way about change? It seemed completely wrong, since I was (OK, *had been*) a scientist and a technology worker bee. I had toiled to advance change, and had no misgivings about my efforts. Was change a reminder of mortality? Was it the clock we would prefer to see stalled? Psychologists should look into this. They probably have.

At the entrance to Page, we were greeted by Gerald Tarsdale, the retired Chemistry professor who had gone above and beyond by taking over as RA of Blacker when the Joneses had their troubles. He explained that the new Page RA would not be arriving for another few days. She was coming to Caltech as a postdoc in civil engineering and had been interviewed by Louis during a visit she had made in June. Louis had been impressed by her. I wondered about the impression Louis had of me.

Once we were inside Tarsdale asked a passing student to please find the Page House President. The student went off anxious to be helpful. Nidan and JR had encountered some Page friends and were nearby in an involved discussion involving laughter. This left me alone with Tarsdale and I was never one to remain silent when I could be gathering information, or at least talking.

Tarsdale was in his mid-seventies, almost four decades ahead of me. He was walking a section of life's road I would eventually tread, barring intervention by an SUV driver or an errant cell. I wanted information about what the road ahead was like?

"Prof. Tarsdale, I hope it's not too awkward a question, but why did you retire?"

He hesitated as if he had never dealt with the question but smiled as if he had thought about it a great deal.

"I think maybe my work was seeming less interesting to me. It had been a while since I had really started something new. But there's more to it. I had reached the stage where I was being asked to be on this panel, that review board, this committee, that whatever. I felt I owed it to my science community to agree to many of these, but it was not interesting. It was drudgery."

"But can't you do these things now that you're retired? In fact, maybe you'd seem a more likely target of a request."

"Ah Dr. Sokolsky, what you say makes sense but I have learned that now I can simply say 'I'm retired.' They accept it and it's over. Interesting, eh? Maybe it's the simplicity. If I said, 'I'd be happy to, but I have a grant proposal due,' they could say 'it will only take three days,' but there is no way of arguing with 'I'm retired.'"

The Page House President had not yet arrived so I pushed on.

"If you are not accepting requests for volunteer tasks why are you the go-to substitute RA?"

"Because that is not boring and it's pretty damn easy. But most of all it continues my connection with the Institute. And the students are usually fun."

His professional career was different enough from mine that his thoughts were not directly relevant but still I wondered how I would feel in a few more decades. I didn't have time for much wondering. The Page House President Polar had just arrived.

We got down to business. Barbara and her roommate were not happy together. Tarsdale was too smart and experienced to volunteer an analysis, but I pushed against the House leaders. It would be important to know whether Barbara would have problems with any new roommate, in particular her new Blacker roommate, if we went that way. The pushing was controversial but the Page House President and the Blacker leaders thought it very wrong not to discuss the point. Polar said she had interacted only briefly with Barbara.

To Polar, Barbara seemed pleasant and Caltech-normal. Useful. A bit off topic, Polar mentioned two guys who had shared a room in Page the previous year and had not spoken a word to each other; it was the way they got along. But Polar's time with Barbara was far too short for a judgment to be meaningful. JR could do better. She had talked at some length with Barbara during the House rotations. Her guess was Barbara would be average in the getting along department, and thought she would work out OK in Blacker.

The decision would be up to the students. I knew they wanted my blessing but what they got was a shrug of my shoulders. We all stood for a moment in silence finally broken by the wisdom of age. Middle age.

I asked, "Polar, could you fetch Barbara? I suggest that you four students then go over and look at the double room Barbara would be sharing in Blacker."

They were grateful for being given a direction, and went off. Tarsdale and I knew it would be a while before they returned, so we began to meander around Page, and meandered into a too small room used for social interaction. (When more space was needed the dining room was used. Its movable chairs and tables allowed this, but made for an institutional ambience very different from the old-wood feeling in the Blacker dining room.)

We stood silently, looking through the photos on the wall. There was one of Richard Feynman, the Nobel laureate and star of the campus in the 70's and 80's. He had visited Page sometime in the past; from the clothes I guessed it to be the early 80's. In the photo he was surrounded by Pageboys with adoring expressions.

There were pictures of politicians from California and from the wide world outside it. I recognized most of them. One photo stood out as very different. It was a man in blue jeans and a leather jacket leaning against a Harley-Davidson motorcycle. If the Harley was of typical size, not a miniature reproduction, he was a very large man. A large, heavy man. The kind of man who evokes the word threatening.

His full beard hid most of his face, but the smile wrinkles at the corners of his eyes contradicted threatening. I asked the nearest Pageboy, Spider, a very lanky long-haired youth, "Who is this?!" He seemed to think "That's Clarence," was an explanation.

If I were going to guess the first name of the threatening/smiling behemoth, Clarence would not have been among my first few guesses. Spider perceived the inadequacy of his answer and glossed on it: "Clarence Hunsucker," as if that explained it. (Spider has a future in teaching I thought to myself.)

I clarified my question, "What is his connection to Page House?"

"He kinda got friendly with one of us, Tobee, and was invited to dinner. Then he became a kinda auxiliary member, showing up kinda irregularly, like maybe once a month or so, just to chat and joke."

This was too kinda interesting to let slide by. I had to meet Toobee. Spider directed me to Toobee's room. I knocked to no avail. I would return.

But for the moment we were still doing Housing business. The students had returned from the Blacker visit. Barbara was smiling. It turned out she had met her Blacker roommate-to-be during rotation, and they bonded. In Barbara's words they found they had many distastes in common. Indeed, the relationship worked out well. There were spats during the year but only the average number.

CHAPTER 12

SOLLY PRESENTS; EARLY OCTOBER 2018

"The doctor is in," I thought, when classes began Monday, October 1. I knew the best technique was to have them come to me. And they did, slowly at first.

Dome (pronounced doam-ee, birth name Domokos), a junior of Hungarian background, bumped into me by prearranged accident. Dome was less shy than the average Mole, but he was being shy about something that was bothering him. Dome was a computer science major, an expert in codes, networks, and such things. The conclusion I jumped to was hacking. But no. I was confusing Dome's worries with my own.

When Dome graduated as a computer science major at the end of the year, he could sit back and let the offers roll in. He could let the trucks full of money dump at his doorstep. But he was thinking about the quality of life, not just the quality money could buy, but the feeling of making a difference not just making a buck (or a truckload). Some students tell themselves they will take a high paying job and, after saving a great deal of money, take a high road and turn to something more spiritually rewarding. (This fantasy always strained my ability to keep my mouth shut. I never saw it work out but there was much I had never seen. Maybe for some it did work out. Researchers should study this kind of thing. Maybe they have.)

Dome first came to see me on Wednesday, the third day of classes, and very little came out that first visit. I think he was just trying to see how comfortable he was talking to me. He must have seen lots of comfortable since he returned twice more and really opened up on the last visit. His worry was that he would seem to be boasting about his idealism. Visions of Sweet Caroline threatened to distract me but I focused.

I felt good about helping him, but I don't want to boast about my own idealism. My own feelings had a lot to do with my ego, my feeling that I was doing a good job.

I did what should be done in my role. From time to time I would ask a question, especially if he wandered too far from the issue. Mostly I listened, and made it clear I heard what he was saying. I'm pretty sure he also heard what he was saying. I made a mental note to watch what he did in the early spring when his career decisions needed to be finalized. The note remained even after all that happened before we got to spring.

An interesting early encounter was with a sophomore, Joy (née Aanandita), a young lady born in the Tamil region of India, well known to the Caltech math nerds as the birth region of the Indian genius Ramanujan. Her problem was not special to Caltech, or to bright STEM kids. Her boyfriend was pressuring her to relax the rules of her upbringing. He wanted her to sleep with him. (She couldn't bring herself to be explicit with wording, but it was obvious.) This was one of the few times (full confession: maybe the only time) I showed some out-of-the-box cleverness. She was a math major; I used math.

"Joy, estimate the probability you will be with this boy in two years. Would you say 60%? Maybe 70%?"

This moved the issue from the emotional to the rational side of her brain and her expression changed. She thanked me and ran off to her class. I didn't know which way her decision would go and I was worried, but I felt I might have made a difference. I would find out later I had.

Something she said, an off the cuff remark, got my focused attention. She said, "...like Fang and Darryl... ." I thought if I tried to press this point I would lose her trust, so I kept my mouth shut. Something I did frequently but always with difficulty.

It was a tradition in the Houses for one of the members to make a presentation after dinner. Not at every dinner, but frequently. This could be standup comedy or a new theorem. A student could report on something the Caltech administration was doing wrong and how *he* would do it. There was a nice example on Tuesday, the second day of classes. A senior Mole, Sparks, dual majoring in electrical and mechanical engineering, updated us on solar car competitions. Her presentation had an interesting twist.

Caltech and MIT were rival-colleagues, like siblings. Solar car competitions had become a big thing but the origin was a 1968 electric car cross-country challenge between Caltech (the winner!) and MIT. Caltech had stopped competing, and directed its cheering to its sister tech monster. Sparks told us about new ideas MIT was implementing, and emphasized the need to keep these secret. We all knew she was joking.

These after-dinners were the ideal place to start a discussion of hacking. After the solar car talk, it was not too early so I looked at the list. When I saw no one else was signed up to give the next presentation, I wrote down 'Solly, Hacking.'

After complaints about dessert died down, I stood and raised a piece of chalk.

Since there was no blackboard this caught their attention. (Sometime I'm so clever you have to cut me slack for boasting.)

I started with a reminder that 'miscreants' (I had settled on this word for the time being) were out there to exploit Caltech 'creants.' (There were more groans than laughs.) Among the very little I had learned in the Valley was a marketing trick. A snappy phrase would help my Moles remember the danger, so I told them the bad guys were potential 'hacker trappers,' but it never caught on. So much for a Valley education.

I knew a sermon would do nothing but lower the opinion of me, so I opted for a variation on role playing. I suggested the Moles might not be able to see through the techniques the trappers use. I turned the question to the Moles. How would *they* recruit a student to do something unethical, illegal, and possibly dangerous.

A senior chemical engineering major, whose Caltech name was Tetra (as in tetraethyl lead, real name Ethel), raised her hand to tell us how she would do it. She was a tall young lady, handsome, rather than pretty, who exploited cosmetics more than her peers. She started with a loud wood on wood screeching as she pushed her chair back to stand up. I suspected it was done on purpose and admired the technique. (Later a Mole told me Tetra practiced this.)

In the now quiet room she continued with a theatrical pause. She showed confidence by leaving 15 seconds of dead air. When polite coughing indicated the end of patience she spoke the single word, "sex!" She followed with another theatrical pause, then quietly sat. Brava, Tetra, great timing, nice way to get them involved.

She didn't expand her thesis. She didn't need to. The room broke out into local arguments, mostly on whether this could happen to Techies. I listened for about a minute and got the feeling the vote was pretty much 50/50, not completely along gender lines.

After another minute the conversations in the dining room died down and it was time to end the dinner. But a few Moles nearest me pointed to a raised hand. Others, soon all others, stopped whispering and silently stared at the young man whose hand was raised. The hand belonged to Darryl. I was looking forward to meeting him, especially after Joy's comment about Darryl and Fang.

I had already identified him from the picture in his folder and had been glancing in his direction as part of glancing in all directions to get to know my Moles. I had noticed something different about Darryl. He was not part of the discussions going on around him among the other seven Moles at his table. Ordinarily an excluded student will try to barge into the conversation, or at least look anxious about exclusion. But not Darryl. He was perfectly relaxed about it, as were the seven Moles excluding him. Darryl was asocial not antisocial. He was choosing not to be one of the Moles, which seemed OK with all concerned.

When Darryl's hand went up, so did many eyebrows. Asocial Darryl was going to make a contribution. This was interesting to the gathered flock. Darryl stood up at his place. I noticed the absence of screeching as his chair moved back. His way of getting attention (hardly ever speak) was an interesting contrast to Tetra's.

When Darryl stood he had a neutral posture, neither aggressive nor timid. On a checklist of appearance attributes, Darryl fit the middle of the scale on most everything. He was medium height, maybe five-eight, maybe five-nine, and slight, but not skinny. He looked young. Of course, he *was* young, but he looked as if he didn't yet shave. His fair skin made up a nice ensemble with his fair hair. I imagined him instructing his barber 'medium.'

Chapter 13

DARRYL EMERGES; EARLY OCTOBER 2018

Darryl was efficient. It took him less than a minute to deliver his message.

"I would get the student target to do something wrong, but minor, a misdemeanor. I would say it's really not more than a prank. Caltech, prank; it would sell. Maybe a couple of weeks later I would tell the target that the prank stirred up more trouble than expected. Sorry. Something was needed to cover it up. This cover up would be a big step further into the forbidden, but the trapper would say still only a prank. Key idea here. People hear what they want to hear. They would go for it; they would do it. There might be another cycle of cover-up/deeper trap. The trappers would be upselling."

I was impressed. I knew the term 'upsell,' from my purgatory period in the Valley, but how did Darryl know? Did Darryl have a side hustle? (Anyone who knew Darryl would laugh and stare at me disapprovingly.)

It was twenty minutes past the end of dinner and a few Moles were already standing to signal it was time to get on to other things, so a clueless frosh made no friends when she raised a hand and raised an objection.

"I can see how the cycle has feedback with bad going to worse. Yeah, once it is *started*. But how does a hacker trapper get it started; how can you fool a smart hacker into being involved?"

Darryl had the answer ready as if the questioner was a shill.

"The hacker trapper just has to trap *any* student. Not the wily hacker target. No, *any* student. Once the trapper has one Techie there is an example to help push the message that it's not a big deal. 'Hey look, others are doing it.'"

(In my always intrusive mind, I heard the voice of my mother: "Sauly, if your friends jumped off a cliff, would you?" and my rebuttal, "I would if I were a lemming, Mom.")

Darryl gave the impression of confidence but there was something about Darryl even more interesting: He wasn't trying to impress anyone. I'd seen this in a few adults, but very few, and never in adult precursors. In her brief performance Tetra clearly was aiming to make an impression. Darryl wasn't trying to impress anyone.

I thanked Darryl for the useful commentary. Attention in the room had waned. Both veteran and frosh Moles quickly disappeared lest another hand be raised.

I watched as Darryl left the dining room. Most others were leaving in chatting groups. Darryl left by himself. He didn't look downcast; he didn't look cheerful. He had a Mona Lisa smile. This in fact was his default expression.

When the evening settled down I went back to the RA suite and took out Darryl's folder, the folder with the name Larry Lagerstrom. My linguistically oriented, no off-switch, English Department mind pondered whether Lagerstrom might mean beer storm (I never did get around to looking it up, not even making a mental note). It wouldn't be hard later to find why Larry had become Darryl, so I pushed forward through the file.

Darryl (né Larry) had a stamp on his psych evaluation: Suicide Watch. I had already been paying attention but I increased my payments. I read hurriedly. Darryl's older brother committed suicide at age 19, six months before Darryl entered Caltech. The psych eval stated Darryl was handling his brother's suicide well. In fact, too well. The evaluator would have expected to see more emotional involvement.

Darryl accepted it too well? Was this really worrisome? I reminded myself I was an amateur.

There was also the suicide last spring. Not all the Moles had psych sessions after the Jim Boyd suicide, but the suicide watch made it required for Darryl. The notes on the session commented that Darryl was not 'unduly upset' by the Blacker suicide. Again I wondered about the expectations of the psychologists. Duly upset?

Who's to judge?

Then there were the results of his psychological inventories. One was the Myers-Briggs, which assigned people to one of 16 possible personality types. It was based on the Jungian theory of archetypes, so was as scientific as reading goat entrails, but was taken seriously by some psychologists. Darryl had taken it 5 times, and had wildly different results each time. The psychologists caught on that he was gaming the test. He admitted that his goal was to take the test 16 times and come out with all 16 different personality possibilities. I caught on that Darryl could be a smartass.

The Minnesota Multiphasic Personality Inventory was a greater challenge. The test had a built-in evaluation of consistency, to probe whether someone was trying to do what Darryl would try. He got away with outwitting the consistency check once but set off the alarm the second time. The evaluators gave up after that but did ask Darryl why he was playing games with the evaluations. According to the notes he told the evaluators he was giving them the answers they deserved. I more or less agreed with the judgment but not his way of presenting it.

The family background in the folder gave me no answers, only lots of room for speculation. Darryl grew up in Indiana, near Purdue university, where his mother had a permanent temporary position (staff scientist) similar to mine. His father taught history, government, and English at a local high school, and had some administrative duties. This seemed to be an academic, intellectual environment, but what was their emotional relationship like? What was Darryl's relationship with his brother? And what was his relationship with Jim Boyd, the Blacker suicide?

People stories can be absorbing but it wasn't just curiosity for me. I wanted to know how much worry and attention should be directed to Darryl? And, what made me think I was well suited to this job? Almost nothing was clear except I really needed to talk to Darryl. A few days later I took some clumsy action to that end.

I looked up Darryl's schedule and assumed he was attending class according to the schedule. There was a three-hour break in the middle of his day, so it was a good guess he would be coming back to Blacker during that time. I had a teaching break during those three hours, so this was my chance.

Darryl had room #68, a single (of course) almost at the northwest corner of the second floor. This was about as far as a room could be from my RA suite at the south side of the first floor. But, for the moment, room #68 had an advantage: It was easy to predict what path Darryl would take when returning from class. From Olive Walk, he would turn south along the eastern edge of Ricketts house, in the shaded exterior corridor, then would turn east at the inner corner, where the corridor makes a small jog as it enters Blacker air space. There was a chair in that corner. I was in that chair.

Darryl appeared, walking in his not-downcast way. When he saw me he came straight up and said, "You wanted to see me?" I was getting used to being surprised by student behavior so I was speechless for only a few seconds.

"How did you know?"

"I thought about what you would be thinking and watched what you were doing."

When we got to know each other better, or at least more, Darryl explained his predictive prowess. Most people, didn't use much of their attention to observe or think about the actions of others. Most people, according to Darryl, were concerned with themselves, with the impression they were making on others. If you forget about the impression you can focus on the important things about those others.

When he said this I remembered how I noticed Darryl, unlike Tetra, didn't seem to be trying to make an impression. This salved some of the damage to my ego for not being a Darrylic observer. I didn't think that Darryl was full of BS nor did I think that his behavioral theorem had law status. Someone should study this.

I've wondered in the years to follow whether Darryl's insights about not making an impression were a form of showing off, of making an impression. If you want to figure out people I suggest you switch to an easier challenge: quantum gravity or the holy trinity.

In a later conversation Darryl came a little cleaner on his magical insight that day at the corner of Ricketts and Blacker. He told me he caught me looking at him during dinner and trying to hide it. He didn't miss the context. I was a new RA who would want to learn what he could about the Moles of interest. He knew he was of interest.

So there we were. And I was nervous. I was starting to think of Darryl as a mind reader, and to worry he could see through me. It would be futile to try to be opaque with Darryl. We began to stroll aimlessly on Olive Walk. I eschewed (that English Dept word again) the obvious gambits, "Why do you think I wanted to talk to you?" or "Is there anything you would like to talk about?" or maybe even "Anything on your mind?" Obvious was a bad strategy with Darryl. I decided to leave a real conversation for a later time; better to say nothing than to be obvious.

I hoped to be a scoche unpredictable and said only, "See you at lunch."

He responded, "Yes, see you at lunch." I turned off towards the RA suite.

CHAPTER 14
TOOBEE; SATURDAY, OCTOBER 6, 2018

The semester chugged along with minimal drama. Perhaps I needed some, so I persisted in my quest to interview the elusive Toobee about Clarence Hunsucker. After walking the short distance from Blacker several times, I finally found Toobee in his room.

His door was a preview of what was to come; it was covered with pictures of motorcycles. It wasn't surprising. I had picked up a bit about Toobee from undergrad chatter. The name 'Toobee' was from the motorcycle-themed song *Born to be Wild*. More interesting was the common assessment: Toobee was a bit strange, but a nice kid. Everyone here was a bit strange, but there were many flavors of strange; I was curious about Toobee's flavor.

Most student doors had pictures, patches and stickers. Toobee's was atypical, a neat arrangement of pictures cut in precise rectangles with clean straight edges. One of the pictures was familiar from the Page House social mini-room: huge Clarence dwarfing his Harley. Another on the door showed a normal sized young man next to a similar motorcycle. I assumed it was a Harley, an error I was to regret.

I knocked. A normal sized young man opened the door. To exhibit my alertness I said "Ah, the young man next to the Harley."

"You're either mistaking the man or the bike. If I'm the man then the bike is an Indian."

As if to provide evidence he nodded to his left where a Harley-like motorcycle left space in the room only for a bed and a desk. Toobee did not invite me in.

The motorcycle was a mixture of serious colors. The saddle was of a tan leather suggesting misplaced luxury. The rims, wire wheels, and tires were black. If the phrase 'dark black' needed examples, here they were. There were massive fenders covering more than half of the front and the back wheels. They were a color more scarlet than red, and all this metal was polished to a solemn shine. The tear-shaped fuel tank was the same color with the same shine. On the tank's side the tear shape was duplicated on a smaller scale by a plaque, in silver and white, that mocked me in all caps with the word '*INDIAN*.'

I noticed the four sparkplugs, more evidence that the bike was something special. Toobee noticed my focus on the engine and helped out with a bit of technical detail and much too much history.

"Yes, it's a *four-cylinder* motorcycle. The 1940 Indian Four. Indian was the original American two-wheel cruiser. They were first built in 1901, two years before Harley-Davidson started production."

Thus started a lecture on Indian motorcycles, one in which I heard many facts but remembered only the fact of a monologue, not its content. My mind drifted off, remembering a similar experience with monologues in Shakespeare about the British royal succession. Was it King John? Something about the problems caused by Eleanor of Aquitaine? Maybe. Something about whether an illegitimate child could inherit the throne? Or was that another monologue?

I sensed we were approaching the final scene when Toobee said, "… and now Indian is back in production and is a threat to Harley-Davidson. It's a much better bike, so just watch."

The words suggested pride, but they had a subtle undertone that made me wonder whether Toobee would prefer to remain a member of a very small club. The possibility was supported by his next statement.

"This is almost identical to the 1940 Indian Four Steve McQueen had."

I already had a sense of Toobee, how definitive he seemed about everything. He wasn't an 'almost' sort of guy. I had to ask.

"Almost, just almost?"

I had ruffled a feather, but he stated bravely, "It's the Crocker steering damper. It was missing when I bought the bike, and I couldn't find a 1940 model."

Pointing to the center of the handlebars he added: "This is the 1945 model Crocker."

Though the Crocker steering damper was certainly the best I had ever seen, there was something on the bike much more important to me. Toobee's license plate read 'HACKR.' I gently raised the subject.

"Toobee, are you into hacking? Can you tell me something about it?"

Toobee laughed.

"Weird. The Blacker RA asking me about hacking. Blacker has the king and queen of hacking."

When he saw the blank look on my face, he filled in the blank.

"Darryl and Fang, the king and queen!"

Only the fact that it was attached kept my jaw from hitting the floor. This was information I would have to, as they too often say, process. To hide what was going through my mind I turned back to Toobee's beloved bike.

"It's really beautiful. How much did it cost?"

"I picked it up pretty cheap, just $55,000. It needed a lot of work, but I wanted to do it myself to be sure it was done right."

With some pride he added, "I paid for it myself, with money I made over the summer working for a tech firm. I'm good with writing assembly code. It needs precision, no errors, and I seem to have a knack for it."

Toobee had a medium build leaning toward scrawny, and a medium height leaning toward tall. His sprinkling of freckles was consistent with his ginger farm boy hair. The ginger colored moustache seemed just a bit off. He could tell I was trying not to stare at it.

"A lot of actors have harelips."

I anxiously agreed.

"Yeah, the guy who played a crime boss in the new movie about John Gotti."

"You mean Stacy Keach. Yeah, he's one, but there are lots more. Lots."

I was seeking information about Clarence but found Toobee of interest on his own. I made a clumsy effort to say something relevant.

"You seem very concerned about details, Toobee."

"Damn right. I have Obsessive Compulsive Disorder, and I'm proud of it."

There was a pause as Toobee was overcome with honesty.

"Actually, not completely true."

He managed to climb over the bike and remove a thick volume from the row of books on his desk arranged in order of size. Using the book as a prop he said, "This is the *DSM IV*, the fourth version of the Diagnostic and Statistical Manual of Mental Disorders."

"Yes," I said, "I'm somewhat familiar with it."

Assuming (correctly) that my familiarity was slight, he continued.

"OK, really I don't have OCD. What I almost have is OCPD, 'Obsessive Compulsive *Personality* Disorder.'"

Again, I had to ask: "Just almost?"

"Yeah, I only have a few of the symptoms. I'm hardly any better than someone who would just be called a perfectionist."

"So Toobee, are you going to try harder?"

He got it, but he didn't laugh. Instead, he made his own joke.

"So, Dr. Sokolsky, forgive me for being rude. It's one of the characteristics of us OCPDs. But you didn't come here to chat about motorcycles or the *DSM*."

"Right. I was curious about Clarence. I was told 'See Toobee.' So I'm here, seeing Toobee."

"What do you want from Clarence?"

"Just to satisfy curiosity. He doesn't seem like someone whose picture would be in an undergrad house here, so I'm guessing there's an interesting story. Maybe he'll be in the novel I'll never get around to writing."

"That seems believable. OK. I'll set up a meeting."

"Set up a meeting? Can't I just call him? Or email him?"

"No, Clarence is kind of off the grid. I would need to go to the place he hangs out."

"Can't you just tell me where the hangout is?"

"No. It wouldn't be safe for you."

Wow. My guess was right. It is going to be interesting.

"Why is it safe for you, Toobee?"

"Look, here's the deal. Clarence is in a motorcycle club. You probably don't know much about motorcycle clubs."

Though it was a statement there was a slight interrogative lilt at the end of it. He saw my expression and took it as "No, I don't." He was getting used to my ignorance, so helpfully added, "You should read Hunter S. Thompson's book about the *Hell's Angels*; it's journalism as literature.

"You probably think of the old Marlon Brando movie, *The Wild One*. The movie was a vision of an Outlaw Club, filtered through the 1950s idiot censors.

The real Outlaw Clubs, the One Percenters, like the *Hell's Angels* or *Bandidos*, are a whole lot worse than Marlon Brando's movie *Rebels*. It's an interesting subculture, the logos, the "rocker patches." It really *is* a culture."

When he said this, in the back of my mind a small voice asked "Like the Caltech Houses?" But Toobee was still expounding.

"Clarence's club is not an outlaw club, but neither is it a 99-Percenter, a member of the American Motorcycle Club. Some of Clarence's buddies have police records and have stepped on some toes. Clarence's club is as a mama bear; it's in the middle. Maybe they are a rounding error when you add the One- and the 99-percenters. They are not one of the good guy clubs that are springing up, like the *Soul Survivors*. Most of those are guys kicking habits or finding religion. So, imagine you've got a bunch of guys who like bikes, but aren't into the AA kind of thing. That's what we're talking about here. These guys are different. They're pretty smart. Lots of times they are really funny. They crack me up."

"What are these motorcycle comedians called?"

"They're the *Reprobates MC*. The in joke is *Reprobate*'s a word the outlaw bikers wouldn't know. In fact, the *Reprobates* are scared one of them will look it up and be offended. Outlaw bikers offend easily."

"And how is it that Toobee Grant, assembly code expert and electrical engineering sophomore, is safe riding into the lair of the *Reprobates*?"

"They know I'm Clarence's friend."

"This only shifts the question: How does it happen that Toobee Grant, blah blah is Clarence's friend?"

"I was exercising my almost Steve McQueen bike one afternoon last spring when Clarence pulled up on his Harley and started talking bikes. He knew all about the four-cylinder Indian I was riding, so we went in for coffee and chatted about the leaf springs on the front suspension, the desmodromic valves on a Ducati. That kind of thing. We seemed to have a lot of strong opinions. We agreed on most of them, but it was more interesting when we didn't."

"So...?"

"So, he brought me to his hangout. The motorcycle repair shop the *Reprobates* call home base. And told everyone I was his friend, and should be treated appropriately.

"I got some funny looks. I thought because of my motorcycle. But Clarence is gay, and his buddies were jumping to a wrong conclusion. In fact, Clarence is monogamous, and has a partner with no interest in bikes. Funny, isn't it. Just like the problems of heterosexual couples."

"So, Toobee, there's never been any …"

Toobee could have taken offense but instead he joked.

"No, Clarence doesn't go for kids with harelips."

I laughed. How could I not? Toobee was so adroit in handling the tense moment. It was time to wrap it up before I created another tense moment.

"Toobee, how did Clarence get to be a sort of auxiliary member of Page House?"

"I invited him to dinner; he loved it and the Pagefolk thought he was really something."

"I'm sure I will also. Please *do* set up that meeting."

"No problem Dr. Sokolsky. I won't delay the novel you'll never get around to."

CHAPTER 15
CLARENCE I; SUNDAY, OCTOBER 7, 2018

Toobee assumed I would be free on Sunday, and set up a 3 pm meeting with Clarence at a coffee shop, Kallie's, that Clarence favored. It was gay friendly, so Clarence might run into some buddies. They wouldn't be from the motorcycle crowd though, since there was no nearby street parking and bikers like to keep eyes on their mounts. I had been to Kallie's a couple of times during my years in Pasadena. Though it was only two miles from Caltech, a straight shot up Lake Avenue, we probably wouldn't run into anyone from Tech there. Not that it would matter if we did.

I used Sunday morning to prepare Monday's classes. For my course in American Literature and Culture, prep only involved a light refresher of my previous trips through the material. I went over the order in which I presented ideas. More important was sensitizing the students to bad literary criticism. I had continued the competition for the funniest mock lit crit. No award was needed. These kids loved calling out academic nonsense. More and more, I realized those who were competent tolerated those who weren't, but hated those who faked it. The kids often were on a par with the lit crit experts who were competent. They lacked the broad background of those experts, but that lack could be an advantage. It sometimes spiced their insights. I always looked forward to the surprises in store as I walked into the classroom for AmLitCult.

More work was required for Professional Writing II, the more advanced of two writing courses offered to students early in their undergraduate years. They had to take one of the two, with the choice imposed after an exploratory writing exam. I used to attend writing conferences. I remembering hearing one instructor bitching that correcting writing was drudgery, that it threatened instructor mental health. One instructor from a state institution fantasized about an inner circle of hell for those who confused 'infer' and 'imply.' I didn't think that such distinctions – while important – were what good writing was all about.

The students got it. They quickly caught on that writing was a chance to express opinions, and they had many. They (eventually) caught on that their ideas would be taken more seriously, or at least more frequently, if they were expressed clearly and even (dare one hope?) eloquently.

Correcting writing was also a distraction, and distraction could be therapeutic.

Sunday morning passed with a continuation of grading and a few counseling sessions with Moles who needed someone to listen, not to give instructions on what to do. That was a perfect fit to my ability and nature.

Soon after, on the clear afternoon, with a clear conscience about grading, I pointed the Miata north on Lake Avenue and arrived at Kallie's right at 3 pm. It was one of those establishments started as a small dining spot known only to the locals. It grew to be a small chain but kept much of what was attractive in its origin.

The Pasadena location was one of the first expansion sites. It sat on the northwest corner of the intersection of Lake Avenue and Las Cruces, a sizeable cross street. Tables lined both the Lake and Las Cruces sides of Kallie's. The tables on the Lake side were the coveted ones, inspiring early arrival; they gave a view of the foothills and the mountains of the Angeles National Forest to the northeast. They were also baked less by the sun than the tables on the south side, the Las Cruces side. The solar bother, on both the Lake and Las Cruces sides of Kallie's, was mitigated by big umbrellas and awnings.

To further the comfort of al fresco dining, the curbs on both sides were painted no-parking red, so it was not a surprise I didn't see a Harley as I drove by. I turned west on Las Cruces in search of my own parking. As I passed, I saw Clarence, the man, parked there, occupying a chair and a large section of sidewalk, and casting a huge shadow against the wall of Kallie's.

I left the car at a space about two blocks away, and spent the walk back east to Kallie's trying to think of a good opening line. My criterion was ultimately 'don't be a smart ass,' so when I got to Clarence I sat down, reached out my hand and said, "I've been looking forward to meeting you." He responded in kind. So far, we were acting like normal people. Had that continued it would have been a disappointment.

I recognized Clarence from the Page picture and already knew he was huge. He was impressive even seated. I put him around 6' 8" and maybe 320 lbs. He didn't have the body type of a bodybuilder, but of the strongest worker in the steel mill. His features and coloring were more farm-boy than even Toobee's. His expression was not particularly farmerlike; he was curious and nonthreatening. So was I.

We ordered our choice of coffee drinks (both boring unadorned dark roast) from a waitress who was trying out a goth look. I got down to the obvious, telling Clarence I was curious about him and hoped my curiosity was not offensive.

"I might have been a little offended if you had not been curious. I certainly would have been more than a little disappointed. This is going to be an interesting conversation because we have a lot in common – more than you suspect - and obviously a lot that isn't. Could you go first? Could you start by telling me how a Caltech physicist ended up in the English Department?"

The question was always asked, and I was bored of my own story. I sometimes yielded to the Sirens of Silly and said I lost a bet. But I wanted to know about Clarence, so I played it straight. Of course, like a good lecturer, I made some changes to fit the audience. For Clarence there was a bit less about Shosh, that was too personal, and much more about Sweet Caroline, since that had more of a universal theme. (And I asked myself: Dwelling on Caroline, was I trying to make the point I wasn't gay? I don't understand myself enough to be sure.)

He was either less insightful, or more polite than most people and did not probe the question whether I was avoiding maturity by coming back to Caltech. Perhaps he felt his Harley made him vulnerable on the maturity score. In any case, he was a very good listener. So few people are.

It was my turn to be a good listener. I didn't even need to ask the obvious question for him to start. What followed had a strong flavor of rehearsed lines, but that didn't make it any less interesting.

"My size has shaped my life. Some people are smart, some are musical, some are artistic. I am large. For a while –in middle school– I was a target of boys who were unsure of their masculinity and wanted to prove it by giving me a hard time. This got worse when they found out I was gay. I took the verbal abuse for a long time. An opportunity arose with lots of witnesses and an unfortunate young moron got into an argument with me. I worked it so he would look foolish if he didn't carry through with some physical action against me. When he did I hurt him without doing lasting damage. (He's probably recovered by now.) After that, the reverse bullying was kept to sideways glances and whispering behind hands.

"I struggled against the arguments of the football and basketball coach (same guy, different arguments). I could have been useful to them. I'm actually pretty coordinated and athletic when I want to be, but I didn't want to be, and I didn't see it as my obligation. My interest was literature and writing. Ah hah. I see the predictable widening of your eyes.

"My greatest love was theater. Yeah. Gay. Drama. I know, I know. There was a theater club in high school, and I joined. We did some of the usual high school productions, but I always looked out of place towering above the rest of the cast. So, after two bad experiences I was no longer cast. I understood, and they were nice about it.

"Later, when I moved to LA, I joined the Glendale Community Theater Group to be around theater people. I was lucky. They were doing a dramatization of Steinbeck's *Of Mice and Men*. Do you know it? Oh yeah. You're an English prof. Of course, you know it. And you know a major character is big dumb Lennie. I was cast as Lennie (surprise!) and got pretty damn good reviews. That's saying something for a town near Hollywood.

"Another way I was lucky: There were real actors, or at least professional actor wannabes in the Glendale Group. It was a way of getting some free acting experience to go with the very non-free acting classes they were taking. One of them was a good-looking guy named Steve. Dark curly hair, eyes the color of robin's eggs. I thought: 'Here's a guy who can make it on looks alone.'

"After one of the Mice-Men performances he came up to me and told me I was really effective in projecting the idea of large. It was love at first wisecrack. Steve and I have been together since then. It's getting on to two years. He's doing OK with his career but needs a big break. Sometimes I feel I'm living my acting ambitions through Steve. I cringe when he isn't chosen after an audition. He's really pretty damn good, but there are a lot of pretty good pretty boys out there in this town."

I smiled hearing Clarence's devotion. Most likely his statements were polished by repetition but they were sincere. I remembered Toobee's comment about Clarence's partner not being a biker, an interesting thread.

"Toobee told me your partner isn't into bikes."

"Yeah, life's like that. We are close but we're not identical. He's not into motorcycles. I tried to get him onto a Harley but it just didn't turn him on. And he was worried about an accident that would ruin his looks. I was worried about his looks too. I have some pride in ownership.

"Anyway, he's got interests I don't. He loves baking! Baking, biking, sounds like a bad joke. I tried to get interested in baking, but I don't get it. The joy of creation? Creating a cake? An eighth of a teaspoon of zest. Do you know what zest is? Never mind. You get it. I've become accustomed to people who are too damn thick."

Clarence was thick, but only in body. That thick body leaned back, making me think about the thin wall tubing of his chair and the manufacturer's design goals. I leaned back in my own chair. We were pensive about the damn thickness of people. We both had a lot more to say, but not at that moment. Clarence was the one to take action.

"Hey Solly, this has been interesting. How 'bout again next Sunday?"

I was relieved to hear that and responded, "I thought you'd never ask. Next Sunday at 3 pm."

We smiled; I left a ten for the waitress and I exited stage west.

CHAPTER 16
ZONKERPEDIA; OCTOBER 12, 2018

A very informative Darryl chat took place a few days later, but not with Darryl. I found myself talking to Zonker (birth name Zachary), a chatty, friendly student. Zonker came from Iowa but identified as a surfer despite his Midwest upbringing and the fact he had never surfed. "It's an attitude not an activity," he said too often.

He wore tropical short sleeve shirts and no footwear except for flip flops. In the dead of Southern California winter, when high temperatures could drop below the seventies, he wore socks with the flip flops. I wondered whether he chose Caltech because he hadn't bothered looking at a map and thought all of California is a beach.

He was unusual also in his academic direction. He decided that he was not majoring in science or engineering, but hadn't yet decided what he was majoring in. He had been in one of my courses and I knew he was as smart as he was odd, smart enough for whatever path he chose. I also knew smart enough was not enough.

Blacker names were assigned by the Blacker House Naming Commission (MolNomCom), headed by Zonker, the Grand Gopher of 2018, and of the previous year. He was particularly proud of the name Darryl. The root of it was a television show from the 80's about a couple who ran an inn in Vermont. Reruns were still accessible in the mystical streaming waves bathing us and our devices. Zonker had all the devices, and had accessed every episode at least twice.

In the TV show there was a bit repeated as often as Zonker's surfing philosophy, and always got loud guffaws from the laugh track. Three hyper-rural characters appeared in the inn and the one who was capable of speech said in a monotone, "I'm Larry, this is my brother Darryl, and this is my other brother Darryl." The two Darryls never said a word but had the appearance of being very slow, even stationary. It seemed like a kind of arcane touchpoint but perhaps not on the beaches of Iowa. I didn't want to be rude but I did want to understand.

I put on a weak smile and said "I don't get it. Why does that make Darryl a good name for Darryl?"

Zonker tried to explain.

"The MolNomCom always tries to make the name fit the Mole, and 'fit' could be whatever we think is fitting. In Darryl's case we wanted a name to fit his academic smarts. So using the Brothers Darryl was *irony*."

He looked at me judging whether I understood the word irony.

"I get irony Zonker, but academic intelligence? Everyone on this beach (nice verbal flourish, Solly) is smart. So what's the deal here?"

"Oh man, Dr. Sokolsky, Darryl stood out among those who were already standing out. Do you know about the Putnam exam?"

I did know about the Putnam exam. This was a math competition for undergraduates, an exam so difficult it was compared to the Inquisition. It was said to be a test of whether a student had enough pain tolerance to become a mathematician. Several thousand students took the exam every year, competing both for themselves and for their institutions. These were typically the top math majors at the top universities and still only about a quarter of them got more than a single problem right. The top five every year had it made in the penthouse of the academic ivory tower; they were the Putnam Fellows. It was like a Nobel for a faculty member. A Nobel laureates brought so much prestige they could get pretty much whatever they wanted for agreeing to join an institution. Chauffeured limo with shower stall? Sure. Just pleeeaase let us use your name in our ads.

I remember looking at the exam when I was a sophomore. I thought I could do one of the problems. But only one, and I wasn't sure. So I opted for not risking my ego and never checked out my idea of how to solve that one.

The Putnam has some interesting sociology entangled with it. There are special summer camps specializing in training for math competitions, and why not?

As I learned in my search for summer jobs, there are summer camps in most everything, sports, music. (Would you believe harp? Believe it.) All these were threads in the rich-get-richer tapestry of American life. Serious Putnam aspirants would not miss a math camp, or go to an institution that did not coach to the Putnam. These institutions tended to do very well, but they were also the departments that attracted the best math students (who probably went to math camps in high school).

The Putnam did have some correlation with success in math and physics research, but the linkage was not perfect. Many of the best research mathematicians hadn't done well, or hadn't taken the exam. Some who did well on the exam did not rise to the top of their fields. Probably the strongest competitor at the turn of the millennium was a top-five Fellow each of the four times he took the Putnam. He also walked away with many of the top awards from the American Mathematics Association.

When word spread he had been home schooled many math genius wannabes started nagging their parents for home schooling. Worse, many parents started nagging their budding mathematical offspring. The Harvard math department had its own worries. The four-time Putnam hero at age 35 had not completed his PhD; he was too busy making important contributions to computer science. Harvard hoped this would not cast a cloud over finishing PhDs.

The natural conclusion inviting a jump is the difference between competence and creativity. But don't jump too fast. The Putnam emphasizes out of the box thinking. The problems do not involve any math beyond what is covered in a standard undergrad curriculum but often require innovative application of the math. The needed smarts are outside the box, otherwise known as creativity.

There is a story, with some evidence behind it, about Richard Feynman, the Caltech legendary physicist (a fictional character who actually existed). Feynman took the exam in 1939, the second year it was given. He was then an undergrad at MIT (talk about irony!). The grades of the Putnam Fellows were supposed to be secret, so no one could know how the top five compared. Secrets were hard to keep back then and word got around the graders were astonished by Feynman's exam paper. It was so far above the other papers of the Fellows.

Zonker told me Darryl had been talked into taking the exam in December 2017, his freshman year. Darryl made the top five.

The story started spreading that Darryl had done a Feynman, that he had been far above the other Putnam Fellows. But secrecy was much better in 2018 than in 1939, so no one really knew. It didn't matter all that much. Starting in the spring of 2018, Darryl was viewed as a special hominid. This was compatible with his growing reputation of being a loner, and maybe a quarter molar annoying. He had no close friends, Zonker told me, except *maybe* Fang.

Zonker went on to tell me that, to the great disappointment of the Caltech math department, Darryl said he wouldn't be in this year's competition. When the Department asked why not, Darryl didn't answer. He seemed to feel he didn't owe an answer. To its great credit, the Department didn't nag him.

"Zonker," I asked. "What about Fang? How did she do on the test?"

Zonker looked surprised at the question.

"No. No. That's not where Fang was at. She's a whole different kind of smart. Maybe that's why they got along so well. Hmmm. Maybe 'so well' is not the right phrase. Maybe that's why they got along."

"Zonker," I said, "You've been helpful beyond my ability to describe, and I am good with words. Thank you."

CHAPTER 17
MIA ENTERS; OCTOBER 12, 2018

It was now mid-October, almost two weeks since instruction began. Housing assignments were tentatively determined. The dust had settled and most everyone had made the transition to the long haul. Louis proclaimed a get-together, before the dust unsettled again, so the RAs could meet, share insights, and outrages. We met in a private room at the Ath for cheese and wine, especially for wine.

Representing the seven Houses were three postdocs, a single grad student, two RA couples, and one Senior Lecturer/former physicist. One couple was two grad students in geophysics, both hoping to finish their degrees by the end of the year. It is good to have hopes.

A young assistant professor and his wife were the other couple. They had been married only a few weeks earlier and this would be their first year together. The professor, a new hire from Cornell, was a 29-year old hotshot. His wife had a librarian job as part of the hiring deal. Their plan was to save money for a SoCal house. I wasn't sure this was a good idea. I wasn't sure it wasn't. They were going to be in Ricketts, right next door to Blacker. I figured I would be called on from time to time and might have to pretend I knew how to handle some student situation.

At 38, I was the oldest.

All the Houses had been coed for decades. The early plan to have only RA couples had proven unworkable and unnecessary. Of the uncoupled RAs, three were male. Then there was that single female, a postdoc in civil engineering, the new Page House RA. Most male eyes were furtively aimed at her, Mia (née

Ewa) Kulpa. Her last name was a not uncommon Polish surname and was, indeed, the Polish version of 'Culpa.' The replacement of Ewa by Mia, had already been made by friends who self-identified as witty; this eased the task for the Page House Naming Committee. How could they do better than Mia Kulpa?

She was a typical Polish beauty, tall, blonde, perfect features, perfect body. If there were a calendar featuring beautiful civil engineers, Mia would be a month in spring. She was not my type. Her looks scared off most men. I wasn't so much scared as biased. Beautiful women were usually not interesting. Besides, she was too young. And I had no interest in civil engineering. And she probably had no interest in early American literature. And why was I telling myself these things? Why was I making up these excuses? Would an interest in her come close to Louis' warning to beware of entanglements. But she wasn't one of my students, and anyway I wasn't interested in her. Right?

I did wonder whether her looks would interfere with her RA role. Could the Pageboys share their problems with her and seek advice without being distracted? Could the Pagegirls carry out those interactions without being jealous?

Louis played host. Everyone gave a bio sketch during introductions. Most of the other RAs had served a year or more, and already knew each other; one of the couples was new. Mia was brand new and shiny and quite the focus of interest. She gave us a short version of her life, a life a bit longer than I had guessed. Before grad school, she took time off to work as a model (who would have guessed), so she was an old maid of 29, the same age as our new, married assistant professor.

I was new as an RA, but had loitered around campus for three years. Presenting a bio sketch is an opportunity to present personality. In my case it was 'I don't take myself seriously' stand-up comedy.

With introductions over, wine was downed, and small talk was exchanged to no particular purpose. People talking, people not listening. A lot of shaking of heads as we all agreed on the strange things that go on at the Houses. I was on my third glass of wine, staring at the bar and telling myself out loud it was time to stop, when Mia appeared alongside me.

"You're funny," she said.

"You're observant," I replied.

She giggled. It seemed strange for such an elegant, cosmopolitan woman to giggle. She should have had a low throaty laugh followed by a drag from an

Audrey Hepburn signature cigarette holder. But no, she giggled. I had a weakness for giggling. My weakness overcame my bias.

"Louis, our boss, has already announced my name is Solly. If I said 'Hi, my name is Solly,' I would be suggesting you don't pay attention."

"Very inconsiderate of Louis, to give you no opening line. But I'm anxious to see what you can do to overcome that."

I liked this. She was anything but predictable. So, the battle was joined.

"Mia, did you know I am the best hop, step, jumper at Caltech?"

She tried not to smile, failed, and said, "That is a great achievement. I'm impressed, Professor Sokolsky."

"Oh please Mia, don't call me Professor Sokolsky. This is an informal little soirée. Just call me Dr. Sokolsky. Do I sense an undertone of sarcasm in your remark. Perhaps I'm not being clear. How does one say sarcasm in Polish?"

"There is no word. Everyone in Poland is polite and straightforward."

"We could change you, with a week in New York if necessary. But for now let me reward you with a glass of wine. I think there is some Chateau Trader Joe that has been well reviewed."

There was more to my bias than a reaction to her beauty. I (Sokolsky) was sort of Polish, but more sort of Jewish; Mia was sort of only Polish. My mom remembered the atrocities of the Holocaust. She had not experienced them herself but had relatives who came back with stories of horrors in Poland. It hovered in the background. Maybe. I wasn't sure.

We were well into a slight buzz. An extra glass of wine erased the slight along with the self-protective veneer on my ego. I held the wine glass up, looked at it as if making a judgment and, with a sneer and a faux French accent, pronounced it to be surprisingly drinkable for American swill, lacking the usual aftertaste of saddle blanket. I was rewarded with a giggle.

People were beginning to drift away from the get-together, and Mia must have sensed we needed to maintain appearances. She smiled and winked. (Winking *and* giggling; I was in love.). She thanked Louis and took off.

I was the last to leave. I thanked Louis and turned to go. I thought I saw a twinkle in his eye when he said, "I see you get along well with Mia."

I turned back and tried my Bogart lisp and grin a second time.

"Louie, I think this is the beginning of a beautiful friendship."

The twinkle in his eye disappeared.

CHAPTER 18

CLARENCE II; SUNDAY, OCTOBER 14, 2018

It was Sunday and Clarence was waiting for me at 3 pm, casting a shadow on the wall of Kallie's. I was looking forward to getting back together with him. I had heard elementary school teachers were so desperate for adult conversation that the single (and maybe not so single) women among them were easy targets for male predators. Was I that desperate for off campus conversation? Probably not. It was just that Clarence was so damn interesting. So easy to talk to, and easier to listen to.

After greeting each other, we sat silently for a time. It was one of those moments. You've probably had them. We thought we had really hit it off a week ago. Were we now going to find out we couldn't repeat it? It been a fluke. We sat there quietly, both understanding the risk.

Our tentatively goth waitress quickly noticed us. She may have remembered the ten-dollar tip and of course Clarence is hard to forget. She sauntered over showing no awareness of the awkward silence.

"Gentlemen," she stated with no hint of goth, "How about coffee? And like could I interest you in our pastry specials?"

We both nodded yes to the coffee and no to the pastry. Clarence had a good aside to me that helped the awkward moment: "Maybe I should have tried the pastry as research for Steve."

We both laughed. It wasn't funny, but it softened the tension.

Time to get into it. I was anxious to hear more about Clarence.

"Last I heard you were getting rave reviews – at least from Steve – about your portrayal of Lennie. What then? What happened after Glendale community theater?"

His answer explained what he meant by we have a lot in common.

"This is going to sound familiar. I decided to get a master's in English and have a life as a teacher."

"Wow," I said, "we're like clones. Next you're going to tell me you focused on early American lit. Yeah. It fits perfectly. Heroic loners and Harley riders. The frontier and freedom from domesticity!"

"No Solly, No. No. No. But I can see where you're coming from. I know about those theories, the American character and the frontier, the Turner thesis. I've read *Love and Death in the American Novel*. Your bible, right? I can see the claims of homoeroticism in the really early stuff, but most of that theorizing is more fun than probable. No. Not early American lit. My real interest was the comparison of western and oriental themes in writing. Pretty much the opposite."

As he said this, he leaned forward provoking a complaint from the chair. I leaned forward also, interested in the topic but clueless about 'opposite' and a bit sensitive about my shallow preparation to teach literature. It was a learning moment for me.

"What do you mean opposite?"

"Glad you asked. Western lit is all about the individual. What's he thinking? What's she feeling? Eastern is soft on the individual and feelings. It's more about structure, obligations. That kind of thing. Early American heroes were looking for individual freedom; the Eastern protagonists didn't believe such a thing existed; they were locked into the inevitability of fate. A little voice in my head keeps asking whether the difference was the western frontier and the restrictions of a society on an island. Hmm. Island. Yeah. With the island business I guess I'm focusing on Japanese lit, but that's what I focused on in grad school. Have you read Mishima?"

I wasn't going to fake it. I confessed to my shameful ignorance of Mishima, while reminding myself Clarence probably didn't know the spacetime transformations in special relativity. Unaware of his ignorance of the true nature of space and time he continued to chide.

"You should read his stuff. Mishima was one of the finalists for the 1963 Nobel in literature."

In my head I thanked the Nobel committee for not choosing him. Still, I made a mental note to look up Mishima. I actually did a few days later, and umm wow.

We sat for a few moments in silence except for the creaking of Clarence's chair. I was anxious to get away from my ignorance. I also wanted to hear more about Clarence, so I posed an interrogatory "And…?"

"After grad school I thought I should go into high school teaching in some tough inner-city high schools where my size would get the students' attention. I could make a difference. And that brings up the sensibilities of Sweet Caroline."

"Uh oh," I thought.

"While I don't readily approve of heterosexual relationships," he joked, "you were a schmuck to let her get away. Do you know the word 'schmuck'?"

"Hell yes. It's my middle name. But Clarence, I didn't exactly let her get away. She decided I wasn't worth her time and she got herself away."

"You might have considered making yourself worth her time."

"But then I would have been making myself someone I'm not."

"Ah," said Clarence, "It's good we're not agreeing about everything. This is so much more interesting. More like hearing Toobee rant against Harleys."

"At the risk of boring persistence: my curiosity is waiting. What happened to your teaching career?"

"I was a middling success for three years. Couldn't take it longer. I got involved in those kids' lives and it hurt too much to know what they were going through outside the classroom. The abuse within the families, the gangs,.. Caroline would have left *me* too. I was selfish. In the clash between what I should have done and what I could bring myself to do, I failed the Caroline test.

"I asked for a transfer to a middle-class high school, and taught there for a year. Some of the kids were interested in lit, but I wasn't very interested in them. They just weren't very interesting. It started to seem like a waste of my life.

"You're going to want to know what comes next and it's going to sound ridiculous after the wasting-my-life line. Let me start by being as misleading as possible: I made it pretty big in theater."

I was confused.

"Um. What about everything you said before …"

"Ah, I found the right *kind* of theater: professional wrestling. It's not real wrestling; it's a kind of a theatrical morality play. If you squint real hard it's something like Japanese Noh dance-drama. You know about Noh?"

At last! *Something* I knew *something* about. I rushed to show off my knowledge.

"A bit. It's a highly stylized ancient dramatic form. Masks. Strict conventions. I went to a Noh performance when I was an undergrad."

"Great. But it's not quite Noh I really have in mind."

Shit.

"The seriousness of the Noh drama is broken up with short comedy intervals, something called Kyogen. Drama, highly stylized, with the devils and heroes of Noh, but comedy relief."

That was a cue to inject my own comedy relief.

"Here's an idea: Maybe pro wrestling could be used between acts in Shakespeare. It could broaden the appeal of both."

Clarence gave a strained smile. I still think this addition to Shakespeare is something they should look into. Maybe they have.

Clarence continued.

"Pro wrestling required some athletic ability and I had enough. The acting was more important than the flying body slams, and I loved the acting. There are heroes and villains in wrestling; I was a hero. When I got into it my agent did some research and came up with my 'stage name.' I was the Decatur Destroyer. It was brilliant marketing. Brilliant! For one thing, there are at least four Decaturs in four different states, all small with populations less than 70,000, some way less. The fans could choose to believe I came from the one they knew. These are poor towns, with incomes way below the national level. (OK. Decatur, Georgia is an exception, but it's really a part of Atlanta, with all Atlanta's bad influence including income.)

"The pro-wrestling fans want drama, want to experience the good old days of rural America. They want to remember an America that never really existed, but they need the image. They need the clarity of good and evil. They need to believe in heroes."

He paused as if acting thoughtful, and it was good acting, then said (as if thoughtfully), "You want to know something funny? I don't get hassled by the cops. They recognize the Decatur Destroyer. Many of them are pro-wrestling fans. One in particular seems to like talking to me about nothing much. I think he's gay and hasn't come out. They're a complicated bunch, the cops. They do a lot of stuff they shouldn't, but I think they want to believe in some clarity between good and evil. We don't always live up to how we want to see ourselves. I sometimes wonder whether I would be hassled if I were a pro-wrestling villain.

"End of story, Solly. That's it. I'm the Decatur Destroyer and a used-to-wannabe English teacher."

"But what about the Harley?"

"What about it, Solly? You listen to the wisdom of Springsteen? I love to put my engines across a suicide machine looking for the glory of the American dream. I'm making a mockery of some great writing. Poetry, really. But it gives a hint of what it's about and damn it Solly, you must understand a little or you wouldn't drive the little bumper car you do."

My time had come for an admission.

"You're right. For a few months, I had a motorcycle back when I was a grad student – a Triumph 500. Another biker student got hit by a cow Buick driven by a senior citizen who probably couldn't see anything as small as a bike. The student died after lingering for two days. I knew him. I visited him in the hospital; he didn't know I was there. It shook me up. After that I sold my bike and went one click up on the sensible ratchet. I lusted for a two-seater sports car. I bought a Miata when I rented my soul to the start-ups."

"Yeah, Solly, sensible. And yeah, the Miata's a great piece of engineering and marketing. But not for me. Think about me in a Miata. The top would have to be down or my head would bust through the canvas. I would look like a circus clown riding a kiddie car. A thousand-pound Harley goes well with my looks."

He was right. It was time to satisfy another curiosity.

"Clarence, what's the deal with you and Page? You seem like an auxiliary member."

"Those kids are smart. They are special. I'm philosophically into 'special.' Can you tolerate a small side trip?"

He asked it like a lawyer requesting permission from a judge to introduce new evidence. I knew this would be interesting.

"Please trip where you want."

"OK. You know about statistics, right? It's the heart of most science now. Big databases. Using computers to search for patterns not obvious to us inferior bio-beings. But Solly, statistics misses what's more important than averages and standard deviations. It misses the outliers. The special cases.

"Drivers. They're hurtling along in two tons of lethal metal. Most of us don't stray far, maybe 10 mph, from the posted speed limit. Maybe partly to avoid a speeding ticket. But only partly. Then there are the assholes. Going way faster than the other traffic, cutting in and out of lanes, missing other cars by the thickness of their paint, then hovering four inches behind some minivan in the left lane to frighten some soccer mom into pulling over so the jerk can move up to terrify the next vehicle in the left lane.

"It's these jerks behind most highway traffic deaths. Not averages. Not standard deviations. It's the tiny fraction of drivers who are total assholes. The special cases."

"Really Clarence. Is that true?"

"I may have read it, or I may have made it up. If I made it up, it's true."

I knew the direction Clarence was going, but I let him have the pleasure of laying it out.

"And so, Clarence, highway safety is why you hang out at Page?"

"Cut the crap Solly. You know what I'm getting at. Those kids are special. The world needs good scientists, sure. There's a role for Southwest North Dakota Polytech. But we can't do without those weirdo outliers like Newton, Turing, Feynman, Picasso, Mozart. To keep the discussion civil, I won't add William Harley and Arthur Davidson. I'll just leave it at 'statistics vs special cases.' Both are important. The special cases are much more interesting."

I had to smile to myself at the way Clarence could smooth out a mini-diatribe with a light touch at the end. He drained the last bit of coffee and added an epilogue.

"The kids like me. The bike is not an important part of it, except with Toobee. The kids like hearing about pro wrestling, and I like telling them about it. They can't learn too early, or too much, about the bullshit – the wrong kind of theater – in American life. This may not get me by the Caroline filter, but it's a contribution."

It rang true. Clarence was a great story teller, and I could picture him keeping the Pagefolk entranced, while slipping in some important lessons. I had guessed he would be interesting. It was a good guess. I should have been writing notes for that novel. I'd have to rely on mental notes.

The previous Sunday hadn't been a fluke. I left a twenty as a tip, and wandered off in the wrong direction to find my Miata. I had a lot on my mind.

CHAPTER 19
TRUTH IN VENICE; OCTOBER 17, 2018

It was a day past the ides of October. The veteran students knew it was not too early to beware. Exams were coming up and the smell of fear would fill the halls of Blacker.

It would be noticeable but under control.

For many of the frosh pre-Tech school had been a breeze and they now found themselves in a tornado. The administration woke to the problem years ago and ruled there would be no grades for frosh, only pass/fail. The tension was reduced but not eliminated. For those beyond the first year stress hadn't changed but most of them had adjusted. Jim Boyd may not have. We don't really know.

In the late morning I was walking to the RA suite when I saw Darryl walking toward me. Always alert, Darryl saw me before I (not so alert) saw him. It wasn't clear whether I was his goal, or he was simply not avoiding me. It was a muggy October day and muggy was always a downer. I decided to try for some communication. Had there been a wind I would have thrown caution to it

"Darryl, you wanted to see me?"

I thought I saw a slight smile as he responded.

"No and yes."

I was half encouraged.

"I wouldn't mind at all a chance to talk to you, Darryl."

"Dr. Sokolsky, I am pleased you wouldn't mind at all."

He was being snide. I'm not anti-snide as long as it's funny. Darry wasn't funny, but we shall see what lies ahead. For now keep options open and lighten the tone a bit.

"Darryl, please call me Solly."

"It would make me uncomfortable, Dr. Sokolsky, although I can't explain why."

"I want you to be comfortable. You can call me what you like. Would it make you uncomfortable for us to discuss your family?"

Darryl stood silently for a moment, and not for effect (effects weren't his style) before saying, "Let's try it for a bit."

Fully encouraged, I went for broke.

"Darryl, would you mind going off campus for lunch? Or do you have to study?"

Again, he was silent for a moment.

"I can get by without more studying. I'm probably already overprepared."

"Fine," I said. "Let's get in my car and see if we can find somewhere with a breeze. I have a particular somewhere in mind. This will take a little while. Is that OK?"

He nodded noncommittal assent, keeping his emotional cards to his chest. We walked in silence through the sticky air to my Miata parked in the Ath lot (a perk of being an RA). Darryl got in and said, "This car doesn't seem like you, Dr. Sokolsky."

"Who does it seem like?"

He didn't pull the punch.

"It seems like someone who is trying to make an impression and is willing to sacrifice safety."

"Guilty as charged," I said in what I hoped was a good-natured way. His analysis was (I hope) wrong, but I didn't want to take our discussion there.

The trip was something of a tour of the history and character of LA. The wind noise in the small open car discouraged conversation as we drove west on East California Boulevard to the 110 Freeway. Like Caltech students, it had several names. It was the Arroyo Seco Parkway and, even more historically, the Pasadena Freeway. Dating back to the early 1940s, it was the first freeway in the country. I would have commented on this to Darryl, but I didn't want to break the comfortable silence. Besides, Darryl probably knew the history. He seemed to know lots of things like this.

Going south on the 110 we passed Dodger Stadium on our right and Chinatown, a distance off to our left, then went through the famous four level interchange that proved Los Angeles was built by and for cars. A few miles later, with the convention center on our left, we entered the whirlpool of one of those California cloverleafs, and came out of it going west on the 10. We got off on Centenela, took it to Venice Boulevard and, after being buffeted for almost an hour, pulled into the Venice Beach public parking lot.

I said to Darryl, "I know a place. Follow me," as we staggered our first few steps, getting our land legs. We had grown used to not talking, so we walked in acceptable silence in the clear air and the blissful ocean breeze.

I did, indeed, know a place. The food was pretty good, but more important, it was quiet. We could talk, and that's why we were there. The absence of background noise was important to me. I was ahead of schedule with a touch of age-related hearing loss, and my best hearing years were behind me. Darryl had a too-soft voice. If I asked him to speak louder it might make him uncomfortable. Why chance it when we could solve the problem by going to a quiet place?

I was using the trip away from campus to change Darryl's mind set, and maybe get him to open up. He was too insightful not to realize this but I hoped it would work anyway. Darryl asked about ordering. I suggested the rockfish tacos; he dittoed. We sat in a continuation of our silence for around ten minutes waiting for the food. The silence didn't seem to make Darryl uncomfortable, but I was still a newbie to comfortable silence.

I allowed time after the food arrived so that eating would not provide a pause in answering questions, then started with, "A few weeks ago, your last statement to me was that you thought about what I would be thinking."

"Not to be picky, Dr. Sokolsky, but I think my last words to you were "Yes, see you at lunch.'"

Oh crap. On top of everything else he has a scary memory. Dealing with his insight and memory gave me a tiny whiff of self-pity. I lied to myself that I too was clever, and I continued.

"I admit the mistake and hope you admit it's not important. Can we talk about your family, about communication in your family?"

He was courteous enough to go beyond a minimal answer. And, as he spoke, he seemed to peer out of his shell. Just a wee bit.

"Yes. Communication was good. We were aware of each other's moods and didn't need to whine or give verbal pats on the head. We didn't waste time on small talk; we all considered it a waste of time. We would almost always have dinner together, but we would read not chatter while eating. We each had a book stand in front of us. When there was a substantive issue to resolve, the books would close. We would discuss the issue and resolve it."

His tone implied that families that chattered and argued were a bit lower on some scale. My mind, lacking an off switch, flashed the name 'Spock' and wondered whether Darryl came from a Vulcan family. This thought was mostly silly but a good organizing principle for pushing on. I pushed on.

"Darryl, did you ever feel a need for more warmth, for hugs as an example?"

"We did hug. We understood mammals had a need for contact and we were proud of being mammals."

This was such a surprising statement I turned to look at Darryl. He was smiling. I think.

"Darryl, do you want to talk about your brother? I guess I mean, are you willing to talk about your brother?"

"Want, no; willing, maybe; later, maybe. Shouldn't we be getting back?"

Chapter 20
DARRYL OPENS UP; OCTOBER 17, 2018

We walked back to the car in silence, another comfortable silence. I was getting used to it. The breeze was a blessing as we drove back. I wondered whether Darryl was thinking about the history of the Pasadena Freeway, about the Dodgers moving to LA, about the proof of some theorem, or about his brother Michael. He was thinking about something. As soon as we parked I found out what. Without either of us being explicit it was clear we needed to continue the discussion. We started walking west along Olive walk. We passed Blacker and continued.

"My brother Michael was different from Mom, Dad, and me in many ways. He didn't live in the world of ideas. He was social, very social. He liked getting to know people, especially people he couldn't figure out. In a way I guess, his interest in solving people was a bit like an interest in science, literature… He was musically gifted and it was expected music would be his career, but he could just as well have ended up in clinical psychology. He would have been good. He was very empathetic and very sensitive."

"Do you have any idea why he committed suicide? You don't have to answer if it makes you uncomfortable."

"Dr. Sokolsky, it doesn't make me as uncomfortable as it makes you. I don't *want* to answer but I might if I knew the answer. It might be connected to what was special about Michael: he was so sensitive. Mom, Dad, and I didn't have that sensitivity. When we heard about tragedies we felt bad, but we knew these things happened; it was just a question of to whom. Michael couldn't do it. It's possible people around him, his friends, were having troubles and Michael was affected by their pain. Maybe too many things were happening at once, too many friends in pain and too much pain for Michael to handle. Drugs might have been involved. Please don't consider me naïve for saying I'm pretty sure they weren't. Summary: I don't know why Michael did it.

"But it left me with a belief. No, more like a suspicion. Sensitivity probably is an important part of creativity. I'm just guessing, but sensitivity has a disastrous down side."

In our strolling we had turned and were walking east. We walked past Blacker a second time, now in silence. We hadn't yet finished; we both knew that. I sensed (due to my sensitivity?) Darryl was turning something over in his mind and I was very willing to wait and hope it would tumble out. It did.

"Sensitivity. It's something I've been thinking about. Maybe a micro-obsession. I *know* I'm special. In some ways at least. Like, I'm really good on tests, have no trouble learning things that are supposed to be really hard to learn, but I've never *created* anything. Look at my parents. They're both very bright, but they have never really made a contribution, no theorem, no novel, no concerto. Their intelligence just amounts to extreme competence. What does that mean about me? About my future? I'm impressive here as a sophomore, and everyone expects me to go on to do amazing things. If there were a course 'How to Do Amazing Things 101' I'd probably get A plus, but it doesn't work that way."

We walked a bit more, again in silence.

Wow. That opened so many questions. I had to tread carefully now that we were buddies. The ice could be fragile, but I *had* to glide a bit forward; this was no time to stop. The theme was sensitivity and Darryl had turned it (intentionally?) away. I had to turn it back. I was keeping a very open mind. Was Darryl really downloading his thoughts? Was he trying to sell me something, or sell himself something?

"Darryl, do you intentionally avoid being sensitive? Do you intentionally avoid making friends? Are you afraid you'll feel that pain?"

Darryl gave his Asperger's smile.

"Dr. Sokolsky, you probably worry the question is too obvious and I'll poke fun at it. But I won't. I often ask it to myself, and I don't ask obvious questions."

Was he joking again? I looked at him, and doubted it. His small range of expressions was tilting toward serious.

"Did you have friends in high school? Do you have friends here?"

"High school was a problem. Even in my special program in high school, some of the students were having trouble and wanted me to help them with homework and projects. I'm sure Michael would have helped them, but I thought it would be better for them to work things out for themselves. They would learn more that way.

"I want to be honest. It's kind of true about learning more, but that was secondary and was an excuse. Really, I didn't want to be bothered. If I helped one, others would want help. There were also some awkward interactions with girls."

Bells went off in my head, and they clanged 'Fang!' But it was too early. I didn't want to interrupt and I didn't want to test thin ice. This was the right (failure to) move. An important insight was about to be added.

"There was something else. My father was a teacher at the high school. He was a great teacher but he was not popular. His focus was on teaching, not entertaining. They were used to history teachers who were also the football coach, or directed the school musical. The kids didn't appreciate my father, and that really put me in a 'they don't deserve him' mood through most of high school. So, I didn't go out of my way to make friends. There were a few, nerds like me, two in fact, who I slightly bonded with, but it wasn't 'I understand how you're feeling.' It wasn't Michael's way. And I lost contact with those two after we went off to different colleges."

He had answered only the first half of my question, the part about high school, so I repeated.

"Darryl, how about here? Do you have friends? You're surrounded by nerds."

"But Dr. Sokolsky..."

"Please, call me Solly."

"That makes me uncomfortable."

"Right. Sorry."

"OK. About nerds. It's not only what interests them that matters but what doesn't interest them."

"Are you saying you don't seek friendship with students who are well rounded?"

"That's an interesting way of putting it. Not completely off target."

"Getting back to the target, Darryl: There are plenty of unrounded nerds wandering around here. This is sort of a game preserve for unrounded nerds. But no friends?"

"Well, there are a couple of kids I sometimes chat with about far out ideas, but no 'best friend forever' kind of thing."

I took a hidden deep breath and faked being casual in asking,

"How about women? Were any of those kids female kids?"

Darryl hesitated for a moment before Darryl-smiling, and saying, "Next question please."

I debated whether there should be a next question, or whether our session had already opened enough doors and wounds. It might be better to call it quits and resume later, but I might not be able to recapture what had become a good interchange. I rolled the dice.

"Darryl, last spring, a Blacker House member, committed suicide, perhaps by accident. His name was Jim Boyd; I'm told he was known as Float. How well did you know him?"

"Not especially well. He wasn't a very academic type but he seemed like a nice guy, one who tried not to hurt people. What I knew of him made me suspect he was kind of sensitive. Interesting, hmm?"

"Were you in Blacker when he came looking for help?"

"I was. I would have helped, maybe by calling for an ambulance, but I didn't find out what was going on till too late."

"How did you feel about his suicide? Sorry, stupid question. I mean... Look, the psychologists thought you didn't seem very upset by it."

"I *was* upset. But people are dying every day. The psychologists think I should be more upset about Jim than about some random 20-year-old in Tajikistan. I don't get it."

"Did you feel worse about the death of your brother Michael than about the passing of the random Tajikistani?"

"Well... yes, because Michael was a special person, with special gifts and abilities."

"Whoa. Huh? I don't get it. What if the Tajikistani was talented?"

Darryl hesitated for a while and gave me a strange look before responding.

"Sigh. Five points for Dr. Sokolsky. You caught me. Yes, I admit it. I was shading the truth. I felt bad about losing Michael because ...well... because I lost him. I wouldn't benefit from knowing him anymore. I think I didn't feel bad for him. I felt bad for me."

As an adherent of the Lucy Van Pelt nickel school of psychiatry I was often surprised by people. And fooled. I think that Darryl was really opening up, and what came out wasn't pain – what I had expected – as much as confusion. Or was it a skillful act.

There was a pause and he added "I've got to get ready for class." I fished around for something light to say to brighten the mood of a conversation grown dark, some nice conversational epilogue.

"Your father taught English. Did you enjoy reading fiction and discussing it with him."

"Absolutely. We were both fans of J. D. Salinger."

I responded, "Wow. I am also. What work do you like best? Catcher in the Rye?"

"No. That's my least favorite. I like the stories about the Glass family, especially about Seymour."

"Interesting Darryl. Again, me too. And it's ironic: Seymour's strongest characteristic was his sensitivity."

"Yeah, ironic. Well, enough irony. Time for math. Bye."

I watched him walk off and pondered the fact Seymour Glass had committed suicide.

CHAPTER 21

THE DUCKLING PRANK; WEDNESDAY, OCTOBER 31, 2018

It was early autumn. A few leaves were falling. Not many. Pasadena leaves weren't the falling kind. The tension of first exams had faded and student attention turned to relieving tension, and hence to pranks. One of the pranks involved Page and Blacker and an email from Mia.

It had been almost two weeks since we flirted at the RA wine and cheese and I wondered how to take the next step. Now I wondered whether or not Mia was taking that step, but it really *was* about a prank. Of course that didn't mean it wasn't also an opportunity.

We met for coffee at a little place on Lake Avenue, a short walk from campus. I arrived a few minutes early. Mia was right on time; I liked that. People around us were ordering coffee concoctions with a list of instructions to rival Normandy invasion plans. Like me, Mia ordered just plain coffee; I liked that. She was polite in her interaction with the waiter; I liked that very much. We quickly got down to business; I didn't like that so much – I was hoping for some foreplay.

"Solly, there has been a theft from Page house. It's a ducknapping."

"A ducknapping?" I echoed, with an interrogative lilt to my voice and tilt to my head.

"Well, more precisely a duckling napping. One of our Pageboys was nurturing four duckling orphans in his room. This is against regulations, but we know how much that doesn't mean. There is a ransom note written in blood-red ink."

"My heart goes out to your bereft student."

I shook my head showing my sadness about the cruelty in the world.

"There's more. Endora, a Pagegirl, was pretty sure she saw ducklings in the Blacker courtyard."

"But Mia, those could have been other ducklings, any ducklings."

"Always possible, but it looks very suspicious and ducknapping is a felony in California. The penalties are particularly harsh when the ducks are underage. I hope you can look into this."

"I do not take this lightly, and you have my word; if the ducklings are in Blacker they will be returned forthwith, and will be returned unharmed."

"It is always good to talk to you, Dr. Sokolsky. I look forward to our further dealings. Perhaps a dinner sometime to discuss mutual concerns."

We were both biting the insides of our cheeks to keep from laughing, but now we were past the comedy into interesting but slippery prospects.

Late that afternoon, after teaching, I returned to Blacker, approached the first student I encountered, and spoke only the single word "ducklings." The single word response was "Xena," the name of a senior chemistry major Mole. It was the only word needed.

Just before midnight someone reported to the Pagefolk that four ducklings had been spotted in the reflecting pool of the Millikan library. They were physically unharmed but seemed slightly confused, though it's hard to tell with ducklings.

Dinner plans with Mia fell somewhat short of the fantasy when, on the following day, I received the invitation to dinner at Page House that same evening. For many reasons, I accepted.

In the Page dining room Mia introduced me to her flock.

"We have a faculty guest this evening, Dr. Saul Sokolsky, RA of Blacker, a professor (not really, Mia) in our English Department and a holder of a PhD from Caltech's own Physics Department. He will hang around for a while after dinner in case you want to ask about the strange paths through his several careers."

My face smiled but my mind said, "You're a civil engineer who was a model, and you call my career paths strange?"

Mia, clever girl, decided it would be better for us to be separated by several seats. We couldn't whisper anything to each other and generate suspicion and gossip among the nosy kids.

The Pagefolk were friendly, and minimized the good-natured hissing expected when Blacker was mentioned. Perhaps they wanted to be gentle with a senior citizen or perhaps would take an English course from me. In fact many of them already had taken one of my courses and had done well. Others had not done well. But there were rarely hard feelings. The students perceived that I was fair, and besides, in the view of these future scientists and engineers it was only English.

I left the dining room and wandered into the small room used for social interaction. The room where I had seen the picture of Clarence that ignited my curiosity. I was followed by a cluster of eight Pageboys. They shared an interest in only one question, and it was not literature or physics: "Isn't she hot!" There was no need to specify who she was.

They seemed to realize their own nonprofessional relationship with Mia was confined to daydreams and were interested in my own plans, hoping to enjoy them vicariously. I tried to sell the idea this was ridiculous. They didn't buy it perhaps because I didn't either.

With some difficulty I turned the discussion away from Mia, and looked through the photos on the wall. I pointed to the one of Clarence and said, "That's Clarence, right? Tell me about him."

The boys were happy to switch their focus. It was clear they liked him. One of them took the lead.

"He's a really interesting guy who comes over at random times. He's cool to listen to because he's had some weird experiences, and he gives us his view of things and advice. Hey, some of it turns out to be really useful advice. The guy who brought him here first time is Toobee, our motorcycle enthusiast. If you want to know more about Clarence talk to Toobee. Oh. And some advice: Toobee has his motorcycle in his room. Don't call it a Harley. It's an Indian."

I thanked him for the warning then returned to Blacker.

Early November is a time of mixed feelings. It had now been nine weeks since the beginning of the semester, so exhaustion – too strong a term really - was setting in.

We were past midterms. The obsession with coursework and grades had not disappeared but it was showing gaps. There was still a month to go before final exams, too far away for worry to be driving the students. We were in the doldrums of the semester. The dominant mood was glum.

I could sense this in my students and had learned the strategy of having the most exciting and controversial discussions during this part of the semester. Sometimes it worked.

It was the prime time for students to get entangled in minor trouble. Joy, the Tamil student who consulted me about a boyfriend problem, was walking around as an example of the doldrums glum. I jumped to a conclusion about her relationship decision. It made me sad, but not guilt-ridden; I had done what I could. Dome, the idealistic computer science student, was not looking glum, and I inferred he had made a decision about his career path. I made a mental note (better than nothing) to chat with him at the end of the academic year. There was already a note there, but two are better. Other student issues arose during the two months since the start of the semester, and I did my best to help. This usually meant just listening, but sometimes I could make suggestions of how to deal with logistical details.

One nonissue was the ransomware hacker threat. There was no news, and very little mention. It began to drop off the bottom of my list of worries.

Darryl was never far from my set of concerns. I had not spoken to him since our mid-October chat at Venice Beach. That was about two weeks earlier; a lot can happen in two weeks. Darryl's mood remained hard to read, so I sidled up to him one day and asked if he would like to chat. His answer surprised me a little: a snide-free, even polite, "Not right now, thank you."

It wasn't a pure no. Something was up but I had to wait.

Since it was the semester doldrums, I thought it might be a good time to suggest to Mia I cheer her up by taking her to dinner. She would recognize this as a pretty poor excuse. For one thing, as a postdoc Mia was past courses and exams. Problems with research might depress her but not the season of exams. The doldrums affected her only through airborne transmission within Page.

Mia was not coy in immediately accepting my invitation to dinner the following Wednesday, without the Page or Blacker hordes. Our tryst would have to be handled with care. I doubted that Louis Horvath would object. He wasn't one to impose pointless rules, but would this be pointless? Would our House residents change their images of us and become less likely to bring us their issues? Or might they be more likely? Better not to do the experiment. What was pretty certain was that we would be the focus of undergrad sniggering.

We both preferred to be out of focus, so plans were kept secret. We communicated by email, a bit nervous at the hacking skills of our students. Ditto our worry about phone calls or messaging. We could have passed notes via a spy craft dead drop, but that would have been a bit much. I even chuckled at the secrecy of our email messages and I pictured Mia giggling.

Chapter 22
CLARENCE III; SUNDAY, NOVEMBER 4, 2018

It was Sunday, and the Decatur Destroyer was again casting a shadow on the wall of Kallie's, waiting for me at 3 pm. Through Toobee we had confirmed that our coffee date was on.

It was three weeks since we last tested the furniture at Kallie's; Clarence was away, doing wrestling gigs around Pennsylvania and Ohio. I would have been looking forward to seeing him anyway but now there was a new element. I'd be sneaking away for dinner with Mia the following day and couldn't stop thinking about what-may-be's. I was disappointed in my lack of ability to stop thinking about her, but it was what it was. I would be embarrassed to tell Clarence "I talked to a beautiful woman for 20 minutes, we subsequently discussed a theft of ducklings, and now I'm besotted."

Fear of foolish appearance would defer that. But it would be interesting to turn the conversation to relationships.

After greeting each other we sat silently for a time. It didn't worry me like the start of our second get-together. Maybe we were just waiting for our goth waitress, so we wouldn't be interrupted later. She came, no longer goth, but something unidentifiable. It had to do with cosplay; later some Moles explained cosplay to me.

I don't know what was going on in Clarence's mind. In my mind the question was how to turn to relationships. I was lazy, or anxious, or something, so I just blurted out, "Clarence, did you and Steve ever think about having kids?"

It didn't knock him off balance.

"We thought about kids, but Steve didn't want to get pregnant. It would ruin his looks. You know I'm joking. Yeah, of course you do."

He repeated his line from a week ago, "Sorry, but a lot of people are so damn thick."

"Clarence, seriously, what about kids? You ever think about adopting?"

Clarence had tried to brush off the issue with a joke but his expression changed. The question might be a contentious one in their relationship, so I was hesitant about pushing after he said, "Thought about it. Still thinking." He shifted his weight. The chair had my sympathy.

This was just too interesting to drop. I came in at an angle.

"Do you think you would be good parents?"

I worried he would be annoyed. If he was he didn't show it and answered pretty quickly. He must have thought about it.

"Good parents? Can't be answered. Just guessed. My guess is I wouldn't be a good parent. Steve would be."

Clarence's chair creaked. I also sensed the creaking of thin ice so I tiptoed back. But it seemed Clarence did want to be serious.

"OK, Solly. It's like this. We're just so damn at ease with each other. I don't get comfortable easily. I'm no good at arguing with someone I'm close to. I'm always kind of suspicious that the person is mad at me and it gnaws at me. There's none of that with Steve. He doesn't hide his feelings; he doesn't carry grudges; there's no passive aggressive grouchiness.

"You know the scene: 'Is something bothering you?' 'Bothering me?' Then, after a just-right pause, in a soft voice. 'Bothering me? No' (an obvious lie a half octave up). So you go around knowing a fight is coming; you aren't quite sure why, and you can't do anything about it. It's hard to concentrate on anything else. You waste time waiting for the fight. Life is just too damn short for that shit. And there's none of that with Steve!"

Clarence leaned across the table. A this is important, pay attention look came over his face.

"Solly, if you are thinking about getting your life entangled with some woman, make sure she passes the Steve test: No wasted time trying to figure out why she's pissed at what you did wrong."

Great advice, but how often do we listen to great advice?

Clarence returned to the kid question.

"Steve and Clarence. We don't agree about everything, sure. But Harleys and cakes don't threaten our relationship. A kid is something very else, eh?

So, yeah, what it comes down to is I'm a coward. You know what the deal is with kids?"

No response required; it was rhetorical. But what *was* the deal with kids?

"Here's what it is: In *Fiddler on the Roof*, Tevye struggles whether to give his daughter's hand to Motel, the poor tailor the daughter loves. Tevye is basically a soft-hearted guy and he gives in. He gives his blessing. But then the fear hits him, and he cries out something like 'Oy. How am I going to tell Golde!' Golde is his wife. He's afraid of her. That's it. Kids bring strains that can sour a relationship. Sour was as bad as it could get in a Russian shtetl at the start of the twentieth century; they were stuck with each other. But here and now it could mean breakup. That's what it is. I'm not taking any chances."

There was a long pause as we stared at our empty coffee cups, not so much pensive as embarrassed by honesty. The goth/cosplay transitioning waitress must have heard our stares since she appeared. She demonstrated her consistent unawareness of awkward moments.

"Gentlemen," she stated with no hint of irony, "Like, how about refills? And like could I interest you in our pastry specials?"

Both Clarence and I replied yes to the coffee. I said, "No pastry, thanks." Clarence answered with an echo of the joke he had used at our last meeting.

"No thanks, I have a pastry chef at home."

Maybe it was the moment of Kyogen, the relieving of tension. We both smiled. The waitress, blissfully clueless, went off.

We sat, with the unspoken excuse we were waiting for the coffee refills, but Clarence's expression didn't fit that excuse. Usually Clarence was 'on stage.' He was playing to the crowd, even if the crowd was me. But now there was no stage smile. He was considering whether or not to go into particularly fragile thoughts about relationships. He considered, and decided to go for it.

"Solly, I'm going to open up to you. Don't know why. Maybe I'm fool enough to trust you. And this really isn't a big deal, except… Shit, let me stop talking about what I'm going to say, and just say it. I think I want to say it, and it could be useful for you to hear. Maybe even useful for me to say. Damn you Clarence, say it already!

"When we exchanged our nutshell bios, I said Steve was a good actor; I said I was living my acting ambitions through him. That's what I said a month ago when we first met. You remember?"

"Yeah. Clearly. Of course."

He paused before the big revelation.

"I lied. Steve sucks as an actor. I've watched him and I'm in pain. It's like watching your kid on stage. I'm gritting my teeth and inside I'm saying 'No! Steve. Leave a pause there. Steve! React to the other actor's line!' Act surprised! Act upset! Act something! I've stopped watching him act. It's too painful. It's like the spelling bee when you hear your kid spelling chaos starting with a k.

"But that's not the worst part. Not nearly. No. The worst part is I lie to him about his acting. He'll never make it big as an actor, so it bothers the hell out of me that I'm misleading him. Hell, it bothers me when I lie about anything. But this is different; it's worse. I'm feeding false hopes. Maybe he would drop the acting thing if I told him the truth."

I asked the obvious question. He gave the obvious answer.

"I don't tell him the truth because I'm afraid it would hurt him. Worse, I'm afraid he would have a meltdown and move out. So, Solly, keep this in mind: Relationships can make you a coward and a liar."

"Now you, Solly, are you being honest with yourself?"

Clarence shifted in his creaking chair and slouched into a new position and a new expression. I tried to act as if I didn't understand what he was really asking but I wasn't as good an actor as Clarence.

"Huh? What do you mean?"

"You know damn well what I mean, Solly! I mean Mia. I've got my sources. What happens on Olive Walk doesn't stay on Olive Walk. So what about Mia?"

What was I going to say? "You want an honest answer?"

"Always," he said, looking at me very seriously.

I gave an honest answer.

"Honestly, I don't know."

I left a ten as a tip, almost a fifty by mistake; I was dazed. I left walking in the wrong direction as I tried to remember where I had parked the Miata.

CHAPTER 23

THE POLISH DINNER; WEDNESDAY, NOVEMBER 7, 2018

We would be going on a – yes, on a date – so we would have to keep it secret from the students, and that was going to be a hassle.

I had the bright idea it would be interesting to go to a Polish restaurant. On the microscopic chance there'd be nothing else to talk about, Mia could educate me on her native cuisine. (I could claim some Polish background but my knowledge of non-Jewish Polish food was limited to Polish sausage.) Mia was enthusiastic about a Polish restaurant in Glassell Park, a hilly area of LA. It wasn't a particularly Polish neighborhood. In fact, the Polish population of LA was well dispersed; there were no concentrations. Surprising. Immigrants to a new land usually coagulated, the first arrivals acting to nucleate ethnic neighborhoods. Why not with the Polish immigrants? I made a mental note to look it up, but knew I wouldn't.

The location of Glassell Park was made to order, a 20-minute drive from Caltech, and far from any place you would expect to find Techies. Our dinner was on Wednesday evening, an unusual time for restaurant dining. And before meeting we could both show up for dinner at our Houses. No one would notice we weren't eating. Had we both been missing at dinner rumors were likely to start. (Working with these smart kids was wonderful, but not when you're trying to fool them.)

Mia would take a taxi to an address in San Marino, a ritzy neighborhood that was safe in the evening. I would pick her up and we'd head southwest. It was a pleasant evening, but I had the top up on the Miata. The best route started with us going back through the Caltech area. With the top up we were invisible.

More than half the trip was on the Ventura Freeway, the 134. When we were a few miles past Pasadena we entered one of those only-in-California one square mile interchanges. After being turned around several times we found ourselves going south on the Glendale Freeway.

With the top up, speech was possible, and nervous about silence, we engaged in the possible. From her questions, I discovered Mia knew nothing about cars. In 2018, possessions were no longer highly gendered (boys-cars, girls-shoes) so this was a surprise, particularly because Mia chose to be a civil engineer, a builder of sewer systems. But then, Mia must be used to being driven around by adoring men. Why shouldn't she take advantage of it?

She thought my tiny car was cute, and I gave her the very brief story of how the Miata had the engagement of the classic British two-seater without the range anxiety of repair. She didn't understand what 'engagement' meant. I tried to explain it as a feeling of control and involvement, a bonding, but it's something that has to be experienced, and even then often not understood.

There were no obvious name labels in the interior, so she asked what the name of the car was. I told her 'Margaret,' for no particular reason.

"No, really, what is the name of this kind of car?"

"It's a Miata," I answered. It's Japanese.

"M I Y A T A?" she spelled out a reasonable guess.

No, it's "M I A T A," I corrected.

She smiled and said, "It starts with my name. In fact, it means 'this Mia' or it would if they turned it around to Ta Mia. Is that where the name comes from? Polish?"

I didn't really know so I shrugged and guessed it might be a Japanese family name. Later I learned it had, of all things, a German origin. Some day on a TV quiz show I might win a refrigerator for knowing this.

The destination restaurant had a very Los Angelic location, in a mini-mall at the intersection of two four-lane streets. The other three corners of the intersection had gas stations. This seemed so symbolic it was hard to believe it happened without a Hollywood set designer.

The mini-mall corner consisted of a square parking lot bordered by a row of four storefronts on one side, a row perpendicular to that, also with four storefronts, and a ninth storefront in the apex joining the two rows. I chuckled at the shop with the sign DON T that had been a donut shop. Clearly, this was not an upscale location. That was fine with me.

Polska was the name of the restaurant. It means Poland, though it can also mean Polish. It was at the end of one of the rows and abutted the street. That could threaten street noise, but there were no windows facing the street, and the walls were concrete blocks. Then too, it was a Wednesday evening, although a Los Angeles Wednesday evening.

The interior, a big step above the exterior, was an example of cost-effective low-level elegance. There were linen tablecloths, covered with glass; they would be changed infrequently. The napkins, which had to be changed frequently, were paper. There were curtains with a pattern echoed in decorations on the tables, and that complemented the interior colors. The curtains would help those inside forget the outside.

We sat at one of the booths in the nearly empty restaurant. A waiter hurried to us with the heft and motion of a rhino, but the face of a favorite uncle with a big smile surrounded by a big moustache. He called out "Ewa!" (Evh - ah) followed by a string of words I assumed were Polish.

He and Mia/Ewa exchanged words and laughs. The waiter turned to me and introduced himself, "Good evening, I am Wojceich." It was not a just the way it sounds name. The sound was Voy check. He owned the restaurant. He and Mia were buddies.

Mia explained to him this was to be my discovery voyage into Polish cuisine. Would I like for him to make suggestions? I preferred for this to be part of an intimate goût-à-goût, with Mia so I thanked him and asked him to give us a few minutes.

The menu had English versions of the Polish names but this wasn't enough. I was fascinated, for instance, by the 'Ryba Wigilijna, given in English as 'Christmas fish.' I looked at Mia and managed to keep a straight face as I offered a mock opinion.

"Say! The rye bah wigg ill eej nah looks good."

She stared at me blankly since the sounds I made were meaningless to her. To be helpful I read her the English, 'Christmas fish.' She burst out giggling, and shook her head.

"No, too oily, too fishy."

We moved down to the pierogis, the dumplings, and I realized I was, after all, familiar with a Polish delicacy beyond sausage. Mia took over and ordered a sampler plate. We were allowed to make our own choices of pierogi and Mia chose to go cross cultural with pierogi z serem i jalapeno. (Serem is spinach; jalapeno is what you think it is.) Mia spouted some more Polish at Wojceich. His look of approval signaled she had ordered well.

It took a while for the food to arrive. I guessed Wojceich, was doing his best for a favorite customer. It gave us a head start on talking and laughing (or giggling). When the food arrived, we were so deep in flirting we didn't pay the attention Wojceich's labor warranted.

I don't know what Mia was thinking. I know what I was thinking: What would it be like doing the Times crossword puzzle in bed with her on a sunny Sunday morning? We'd be great on physics, sewers, American literature and Polish food.

We were at that unique moment in a relationship, the moment at the cusp of curiosity and intimacy, a moment glowing with the possibilities ahead, but also a fragile moment when the possibilities can be crushed by the wrong question, the wrong statement, the wrong tone. I stumbled through trying to say this to Mia.

"It's strange poets have not written about this."

"Maybe you are reading the wrong poets. What do you know about Polish poetry?"

I answered truthfully, "Not as much as I would like to." Sure, I would like to know more about Polish poetry, early papermaking, algebraic topology, and the Salem witch trials, but there's only so much time. In my master's program I studied poetry, grudgingly, only to the extent it was required.

"You probably do not know the poems of Wisława Szymborska, but surely you know she won the Nobel prize for literature."

"Of course!" I lied. But I lied wide-eyed as if I were offended by the possibility I wouldn't know about a Nobel for lit, so Mia knew it was a lie, which meant it wasn't really a lie.

"Wisława Szymborska would agree with you about fragile uncertain moments. At least about unique moments, moments that cannot be repeated. Would you like to hear what she says about our moment? I can recite the lines in English."

"Yes. English. I would prefer English."

"In *Nothing Twice*, she wrote:

Nothing can ever happen twice.

and then,

...you can't repeat the class in summer: this course is only offered once."

"Yeah. She's got it! I like the simplicity, like Rock and Roll, no thous and wherefores."

"Yes, you should look her up. I'll write her name for you."

Mia wrote down Wisława Szymborska.

"Mia, you crossed your L. How is that pronounced?"

"Very much like your English w, like this." She pursed her lips in kiss/w position and stared at me wide-eyed with false innocence. If there were prizes for teasing, no one could challenge her.

"Surely you have much more sophisticated examples of your philosophy. I am just a civil engineer to be, not a Senior Lecturer in writing and literature. Please, dear sir, give me your sophisticated professional poetic version."

I decided to move the borders of poetry. Popular music, after all, is the poetry of our times. I was ready.

"OK, from the Eagles' *Take it Easy*. The singer, searching for a love that can save him, crawls into the truck of a girl who drives by. He makes his case with the words, *We may lose, and we may win, but we'll never be here again*. That's the heart of it, the special moment that will never be relived."

"Oh Senior Lecturer Sokolsky, your students must love you."

"Yes, they are easily fooled."

It had gone well. We had impressed each other with literature, and impressing is what the magic moment called for. It was time to move to biography.

Mia wanted to know how my path went from physics, to start-ups, to literature and writing. I didn't really understand it myself, but barriers between us were falling and I opened up the right amount, the amount the special moment called for. I told her about my feeling of being lost after Shoshana died. I told her about Sweet Caroline. Maybe most important, I told her I was still lost, but happy with my life, and I wasn't very much concerned that I didn't understand it.

"Solly, you're back where you were a student. Did you even consider you are not facing growing up and moving on?"

It wasn't said in an accusing way. She was curious. So was I.

"I've thought about it, but I don't know. I did take six years to work with grownups and I didn't like it. Maybe I would have liked other grownups. But your question is a great one. I wish I had a great answer. Now it's my turn to interrogate you. So Evh-ah, how did a beautiful model end up having dinner with a failed scientist?"

Now, a normal woman would have said something boring like, "Oh *no*, you're a success as a ...," but Mia, looking totally serious, said "I've always been attracted to failure."

She went on to the real story. She had done very well as a student, especially in science. Marie Skłodowska Curie aside, women scientists were not strongly encouraged in Poland. Many people told Mia she should be a model. She figured they couldn't all be wrong. After thinking about it for almost a year, she gave it a try and discovered they all *were* wrong. At first it was all new and shiny, but within three years it got old and smudged. She looked pensive in telling this. The experience had left memories.

"Don't stop there!" I said.

"I went back to Poland to see old friends, to heal, and to think about what comes next. I wandered around Warsaw looking at the buildings and thinking about the way buildings affect people, the way they mix engineering, art, sociology and psychology. Their shapes and colors alter moods; their interiors can make people encounter each other, perhaps to start a conversation, or a collaboration or a friendship. So I decided to become an architect."

"I went into a church to talk to myself about it. Churches have some purpose, Solly. Remember how Caroline told you something about yourself beyond what you could see by yourself? The church did that for me. It told me I was kidding myself. I had the ability in engineering, but I never showed any particular ability in art, or in psychology. I would have been a failure, like you."

She didn't have to worry about me understanding that the last part was a joke.

"I thought about what I could do that would help people, but was heavy on the engineering, and light on everything else. I happened to read an article about the way asphalt roads can be designed to prevent the buildup of water during rainstorms, and reduce accidents. To grab the reader the article started with a description of a family killed when their car hydroplaned. I was hooked.

I started reading more about the importance of civil engineering to health and safety and – as they say in New Jersey – bada bing."

I was in awe of her grasp of the American idiom.

It was a little after 10 pm. We had arrived at 8:30 pm, and were at the point of taking shallow breaths and pouring coffee down our throats onto a week's worth of carbohydrates, when the evening took a sharp turn to the worse. Two men and a woman entered the restaurant, all dressed in outfits that cost as much as my car. I took a dislike to them, although that opinion was justified only later.

The one who acted as if he was the leader noticed Mia, smiled and walked over to our table. He looked older than I by a few years, but still able to walk on his own. He had classic good looks, which seemed inconsiderate. I stood up to be polite and to defend myself if necessary. He held out his hand and said "Gilles de Patou." I realized he was telling me his name. (I heard "Zheell luh.") My mind swam back to the interview with Maurice L'Hommedieu, but I was successful in suppressing all the witty things I could have said. I grudgingly took the straightforward route and said, "Saul Sokolsky."

"Ah," he said, "then you are Polish?"

"Not really. – And you?"

"No, I am a friend of Mia, and if she is at all representative of Polish women, I am very sorry I am not Polish."

"Surely you could convert."

Sarcastic and not really funny. Shame on you Solly. Meanwhile I was using Solly's intimidation technique 3B: Eye contact. Don't blink. Don't smile. It wasn't working. Gilles made a huffing sound that might have been his version of a laugh. He then tipped an imaginary hat and departed with, "Forgive me for interrupting your dinner. I must rejoin my associates."

He sashayed back to his group and tut tutted Wojceich, who insisted it was too late for new diners.

Mia's demeanor, even her complexion had changed. By way of explaining, she murmured, "Fashionistas from my previous life. I introduced Gilles to this restaurant."

I suspected there was more to it. For a change, I was right.

CHAPTER 24

MIA AND SOLLY GO TO A BAR; WEDNESDAY, NOVEMBER 7, 2018

We went outside and got into Ta Mia which was dwarfed by the 700 series BMW limousine parked next to it. We started the trip back in silence.

As we got back on the Pasadena Freeway, I figured maybe a mention of Clarence would lighten the mood.

"Mia, I noticed the picture of Clarence Hunsucker in Page. There must be an interesting story there."

A smile struggled to appear.

"There *are* interesting stories; talk to Toobee."

She said it in a mood that was hard to read, and became a bit harder when she asked, "Do you know a good bar we could go to? Do you know *any* bar we could go to?"

I dropped the idea of chatting about Clarence and responded to her question.

"Yes, I know a bar that allows in English teachers and civil engineers."

"Well, please apply the spurs to Ta Mia."

I had white lied. I didn't really know the bar scene in Pasadena, but for a lady in distress I could fake it. It wasn't really lying.

We would soon come to the end of the Pasadena Freeway. It didn't so much end as fade as it became Pasadena. The six lanes continued, but the speed limit dropped to 35 mph and the name changed to the Arroyo Seco Parkway. There were commercial buildings on both sides and there was on-street parking. The direction (due north) and shape (due straight) of the Parkway were a contrast with the romantic history of nearby Route 66.

In a half mile we could have turned east on California Boulevard and taken it to Caltech. But our plans had changed, and we drove on. Less than a half-mile further was the intersection with Colorado Boulevard. A right turn would have us continue on the historic Route 66 on our way to Chicago. A left seemed more appropriate; it would bring us to Pasadena's Old Town, which had its own claim to history, though only local history. Old Town had urban decayed, but was rejuvenated in the 80s and was now a yuppie haven, a center of craft beer, vegan calves' brains, and – of current interest – bars.

But there was too great a chance of bumping into the wrong person in Old Town, so I came to my senses and aimed Ta Mia to the terra less cognita of East Pasadena. Mia was lost in her own thoughts while I scanned both sides of the street. We needed a place where we could talk; I had no idea about what. That meant no live music, no juke box, no karaoke.

I thought I was focusing on those requirements, but we passed a foreign car repair shop. I had been looking for one so I made a mental note to check it out later. Funny, the way the mind works, at least mine. A likely bar appeared on our right, about one mile east of Hill Avenue, the eastern border of Caltech. Not a large distance but it was in the right neighborhood for avoiding awkward encounters.

There was a parking place right in front. Safe over sorry I went another short block and found a parking place in a mini-mall not very different from the one we had left in Glassell Park.

As we walked west, back to the bar, we saw, around ten feet away, a cat torturing a sparrow. Mia stood staring. She was transfixed, but only stared and spoke. "It's nature. It would be wrong to interfere."

I thought of Darryl not helping high school peers. His excuse was that he would be interfering with learning. But Darryl admitted that was a lie; his real reasons were selfish. Was Mia covering up some real reason? Huh?

She turned away. The light was failing and it was hard to read her expression. I wondered what Shosh would have done. I think she would have thought nature was wrong, and would have chased the cat away. I'm not sure what would have been right. This is what generates faculty positions in philosophy departments.

A more disturbing thought bounced between my ears. Was Mia really broken up about the display of nature's cruelty? Why was I even asking myself that question? What the hell was wrong with me. It had to be something. The image of the sunny Sunday morning crosswording with Mia made responsible thoughts wait in line. Yet here I am questioning whether she is coming clean about a cat's actions.

We walked back and went in to see whether the place would serve. It was dark and quiet. The walls looked faux Chinese and might have been annoying had there been any light. There was a stage that foreshadowed music, but not on a Wednesday night. It would serve. We slid into a booth and waited for a waitress. I saw the name Bobby embroidered on her shirt. After an evening of Wojceichs and Gilles's, I decided Bobby deserved a big tip just for her name.

I would be driving, so I ordered a light beer figuring the Polish food it would soon meet would render it innocuous. Mia asked what wines they had, and Bobby answered "red and white." Mia smiled (which was very nice to see) and said, "red."

I didn't know how to play it, so I just waited. It wasn't long.

"Gilles and I were lovers."

That hurt, but why? I didn't want to admit that it could be simple jealousy. Maybe a reaction to Mia having gone for such a jerk, if he was a jerk. Anyway, I couldn't think of anything to say that might not be exactly the wrong thing so, again, I waited.

"It started when I first got involved with modeling. I guess I had the looks, but it was a weird world of narcissism, insincerity, jealousy, anorexia... all treated with self-medication. I had no one to talk to. Gilles was a major figure in fashion. Not as major as he thought, but he was an editor and a designer and did seem to know everyone and everything about fashion. He became a father figure and one thing led to another."

It was interesting how the sparse last sentence was blurted out quickly. It was so get it over with, so different from the way she had spoken in Glassell Park. Maybe this was just her embarrassment at having fallen for the father figure routine. I didn't know what to say, so said nothing. It was enough. Mia continued.

"You could probably fill in most of what followed. He became less gentle and more critical. It was gradual, and it's always hard to know when to take a big step when changes are gradual. Also, his advice always seemed good, always seemed right. He did continue to help me, at least until... something happened."

There was a long pause, meaning I had to decide whether to say something. I said something.

"How did it end?"

"What do you think?"

"Another woman?"

"I found him wrestling with one of the new, young exotic, dark-haired, dark-eyed models – that was the look that was in fashion for that year. He wasn't even embarrassed; I certainly was. She laughed at my embarrassment, and my looks, saying to Gilles 'Is this the Barbie doll you've been servicing?' I had too many commitments simply to walk away from modeling but I left as soon as I could. It took four months."

This was bad, but Mia's mood, the strength of her reaction, the near-tears, the stumbles in her speech, made me suspect, again, there was more to the story.

I was right yet again. But I didn't think right was becoming a habit.

We sat in silence for a while. She didn't rescue me from not knowing what to say, so I crossed my fingers and tried.

"Mia, I can't help feeling there's more to the story. Something you're not telling me."

There was silence and she looked as if she was trying to decide how much to say. Or maybe how to appear that she was trying to decide.

"Yes, there's more. But I'm not ready to talk about it. You will lose respect for me. I will have to tell you sooner or later. It's got to be later."

"Mia, did you take part in a crime?"

She had a strange smile.

"No. Nothing like that. Maybe not as bad. Maybe worse. Sooner or later I will tell you, and you can judge me."

Her hand started shaking. Just a little. She tried another sip from what was now an empty wine glass. Bobby was on the ball. When Mia looked in her direction Bobby was already walking towards us with another glass of red. Bobby saw the shininess in Mia's eyes that meant tears would be involved. Bobby scurried away.

On the way out, I thought - again - I might improve the mood by letting her know about my developing friendship with Clarence. I was hoping for a giggle.

"Mia, you still haven't said anything about Clarence."

The mood did not improve. She said only, "Talk to Toobee."

CHAPTER 25

WEEK OF WAITING AND CLARENCE IV;
NOVEMBER 7-NOVEMBER 11, 2018

It was after midnight, but we still wanted to be careful about the return to campus. I dropped Mia off on South Wilson, just north of Del Mar. After a half-mile walk she would approach Page from the direction of the labs and academic buildings. If she were seen it would look as if she was returning late from working at research. From the same abundance of caution, I wanted to avoid returning to campus too soon after she did, so I decided to drive for a while, to kill some time. I knew where I wanted to do the killing.

I hesitated for a few moments and watched Mia walking in the right direction. (Nondrivers sometimes don't develop a sense of direction.) I then turned right on Del Mar, away from Caltech; I was getting too close. I turned right on the next street, Catalina, went three blocks, turned right again, and was back on Colorado Boulevard, Historic Route 66.

It *was* historic, and it was connected to the ideas I had shared with Dimitra Murphy five years earlier. It was the psychological importance of the frontier. Route 66, America's main street, the highway that carried the Okies from the Dust Bowl, the highway that was Steinbeck's mother road. It linked the middle of the country to the West, the frontier, and shaped the American character. Frederick Jackson Turner would have understood.

In 1890 the Superintendent of the Census said the US was fully settled. There was no more frontier. It was true in some ways. The great migrations and gold rushes of the nineteenth century were over. The transcontinental railroad had replaced Conestoga wagons. California, Texas, Alaska had all become part of the United States. Horace Greeley, or someone, said Go West young man, and in the nineteenth century many of the young heeded. Along with hope for new opportunities there was the spirit of Manifest Destiny, the sacred American obligation to settle the West. But the American character was shifting away from obligation, to one of liberty, freedom, and individuality.

The automobile was an important part of it. Between 1910 and 1920, the number of motor vehicles in the US increased by a factor of 20. There was another factor of 3 increase by 1930. The growth had to slow. By then 20% of the population already owned a motor vehicle. The car dictated the new American world view. At around the same time, California made the American vision into a dream. The land of movie fantasies inspired real-life ambitions of a brighter future at the left edge of the continent.

During the westward expansion some routes became important and symbolic. The Oregon trail, in particular, came to symbolize the hardiness and perseverance of those who crossed from the Midwest to Northwest, around the middle of the nineteenth century. But for imagery and romance, Route 66 was the star.

That star had its roots in some old trails; it connected them to some new roads; it included some surfaced trails. The name Route 66 was new, a 1926 compromise of several political concerns. What is important about it, and what led to its legend, was the plan to have it go through many rural communities, communities not served by other highways. It linked small town America to the California dream. Route 66 was part of the development of the car culture, drive-in burger joints with car-hops on roller skates, roadside attractions, cheap motels.

The romance of the Route was enhanced by popular culture. In 1946, Bobby Troup wrote 'Get Your Kicks on Route 66,' with lyrics that traced the route from St. Louis to San Bernadino, and invited the audience to come along with,

> *If you ever plan to motor west,*
> *Travel my way, take the highway that is best.*
> *Get your kicks on route sixty-six.*

An even stronger boost was the TV series *Route 66*, that ran from 1960 to 1964, and tried to cover the idea of adventurous youth looking for answers in the changing country. It tried to cover just about the entire Zeitgeist. The characters, Tod and Buz, were two good looking all-American boys, one blond, one dark-haired, in an all-American car (the 1961, 62 and 64 Corvette). Tod came from money; Buz came from those on the way up. The episodes took place in different cities, showing different slices of the American landscape. They were both pure of heart, eager to try different kinds of American work, and to help with different kinds of American problems.

The early 60s. It was a different time, but so was 2018. I was focused on what we would do without the frontier, without the TV optimism and the vestige of Manifest Destiny. I still didn't have a conclusion, and it was time to head back.

I hadn't gotten much sleep by Tuesday morning. The nice thing about teaching is it doesn't care about your sleep; you've just got to do it. I filled my bladder with coffee and set out to teach the craft of rewriting to future writers of important journal articles. The nice thing about coffee is it's a drug that's legal.

The week dragged by. I thought more about Mia than about Route 66. I called her once; she called me once. The calls were awkward. We were both unsure, and we weren't even sure of what we were unsure about. I felt like a teenager all gaga over some teenager-ess. One of many crushes. But those were candles that burned brightly and died quickly. Maybe this too would dim, but I didn't think so. You know what it's like when you can't get a song out of your head.

The song echoed for me at Friday dinner. The Pagefolk struck. They had a growing affection for their beauty queen RA and were tickled by the just-a-smidgeon against the rules Montague/Capulet romance fermenting with the Blacker RA.

They felt that it was their obligation to acknowledge the relationship Techishly.

And so, during dinner on Friday, cupid entered the Blacker dining room. Cupid had the nom de stork Brandon, and the Tech tag Iron. On this evening he was wearing a diaperlike wrap, sporting large flaccid wings and threatening with a small recurve bow. (Where do they get this stuff?) He had been chosen by the Page House instigators because he was the furthest thing in Page from cherubic. Iron had 200 wobbly pounds carried on a 5' 9" frame. He was bare except for his diaper, though his thick pelt of body hair was keeping him warm. The cherubic aura was enhanced by the stub of a cigar clenched in his teeth.

He approached me, and from a distance of around two feet, shot his rubber-tipped arrow. His aim was true, but the arrow bounced off. Undeterred, Iron closed the distance between us, picked up the arrow, slathered some mashed potatoes in the cup of the rubber tip and pressed it against my heart. It stuck. Innovative engineering. The noise of approval from the Moles delayed Iron's closing. He handed me a large red heart-shaped piece of construction paper and said, "You've been served."

Cheers accompanied him to the exit, and the Moles turned to plot their response.

Maybe Sunday coffee with Clarence would help. I confirmed the meeting with Toobee, who told me Clarence would be out of town the weekend after, wrestling in Tennessee or Kentucky, or something like that (Toobee's dismissal of these states, not mine).

As I approached Kallie's I wondered what our goth/cosplay waitress was trying this Sunday.

Two Mole cosplayers had explained cosplay to me. I described to them the costume the waitress wore. They were initially stumped but not defeated. They came back to the RA suite a half hour later, and proudly said "Rachael, from Blade Runner. We're pretty sure." This week was less of a challenge. The waitress was all blue.

Clarence stress tested his usual chair and cast his usual shadow, or would have if the sun were out. The calendar was creeping towards the icy horror of the Southern California winter. Our blue waitress came over. We didn't need to say anything; two head nods from us and she was off to fetch.

I wasn't quite ready to talk about Mia, so I made a strategic opening gambit.

"Anything interesting in your world this past week, Clarence? Something good? Bad?"

"Not really a good vs bad thing, mostly funny. Steve got a gig doing a commercial for a Chinese restaurant specializing in Peking duck. You know how much one of those ducks sets you back?"

"No idea, Clarence. I only deal with ducklings."

"It's $125, and you've got to order an hour and a half in advance."

He repeated the last part, sure I wouldn't believe it, and continued.

"Hell, I don't know what I'm hungry for even 15 minutes before. But anyway, this restaurant is in Alhambra – not far from Caltech if you ever inherit a wad and feel a Peking duck hunger coming on very slowly."

"At the cost of one of these birds this restaurant can afford to advertise, so they commission a commercial for TV and streaming. Steve, *my* Steve, gets the part. He is supposed to flash his seductive smile and say 'Come in and taste the best Peking duck this side of the Pacific.' Steve gave me his version of what happened, but I got a better version from a friend on the production team.

"Steve is jazzed. He thinks maybe this is his big break. And who am I to rain on his fantasy. But just listen.

"Solly, I'm sure (OK, not really sure) you know professionals like Steve are supposed to be experts in where they aim their eyes. If an actor is talking to another, the eyes go there, not offstage. In the case of this commercial, Steve is supposed to be talking to the viewer, which means to the camera. At the last moment he's supposed to turn to his left where the camera shows a covered metal platter. It looks like silver. I think it *is* silver. The restaurant figures it emphasizes the elegance of the overpriced experience. Right? Customers might say '$125 for a duck, but, hey, it's served on a *silver* platter.'"

"Clarence, did anyone ever accuse you of dragging things out, or am I the first?"

"OK, so there's a problem. Steve knows it's Peking duck, for the capital of China, not peeking, like a duck at your bedroom window. But every time he says 'Peking duck' he looks over at the platter as if he's worrying there's a duck under it peeking out. He can't help it. It's kind of obvious what's happening because of the way he delivers the line and his eyes go to the platter exactly as he says 'Peking.' The crew cracks up the first time. The second time, it's already getting old. By the third, the producer, who's probably getting paid like a paper boy, is pissed. They're on a tight schedule. But what can he do? The producer has an idea. Go with Steve's look at the platter, and in post-production, edit in a slight tilt of the cover and a big question mark.

"No one tells Steve, so his nervous glance at the platter is very natural and the commercial is a small hit. The restaurant starts out furious because they take Peking duck seriously and the commercial doesn't. But that changes when they realize they're getting a lot more orders for Peking duck; they have to hire an additional duck chef. Steve actually gets some feelers for more commercials because low-budget producers think he's got great comic timing. So how's your week been?"

"Dull. Nothing much happening."

"Bullshit. Something's bothering you. I'll bet it's a civil engineer, former model."

I grunted, stayed silent for a moment, and then asked, "Clarence, you hang around Page. What do you think of Mia?"

"I think she must be a real loser to hang out with anyone who would ask a friend a question like that. When you're ready to talk about it, I'm ready to listen.

"Solly, I've really got to go."

And he left. He didn't seem mad, but he was not smiling. What the hell?

CHAPTER 26
MIA CALLS; WEEKEND, NOVEMBER 17-18, 2018

Midterms were over on November 6, and students were settling in for the second part of the semester. Finals were still five weeks off. Too far away, not real threats. It was the season for more pranks.

Two Mole physics majors were arrested at LAX, the airport, for dressing up in brown robes and soliciting funds for Isomorphism, a church that had broken with Unitarianism. They handed out a sheet advertising their cause. They answered questions keeping straight faces. It took great control, since unitary and isomorphism were terms from mathematical physics.

The LA police were not as familiar with Caltech students as the Pasadena police were, so calls were made. The Moles had collected $4.75, and swore they had donated all of it to LARFPA, the Los Angeles Fire & Police Association. The fact the Moles knew of LARFPA seemed to carry some weight, and the cops backed off, but without appreciating the humor. Imagine that. Going into police work without a sense of humor.

Two weeks earlier another prank came to light, a production by a team in Ruddock. They put together a fake midterm for Math1a, the introductory calculus course at Caltech. It was a single sheet of paper, very official looking, with three problems on the front side and three on the back. The front problems turned out to be unproven theorems and conjectures. (One was the Riemann hypothesis, in case you're interested.) The back problems were just silly. (What is appropriate punishment for an improper fraction?) No one could be fooled, except a goody-two-shoes senior from another house. He had found a copy of the faux exam before the stated exam date, and reported it to the Board of Control, the guardians of the honor system. The Board had their first post-midterm meeting on November 12, so the campus was still chuckling about it.

But these were pranking side dishes. We all sensed a main dish was being prepared.

Every spring MIT has a 'Campus Preview Weekend,' at which prefrosh and parents are given MIT high-tech dog and pony shows. At the 2005 weekend Caltech pulled off a major multi-pronged prank. To me, the best part was the distribution of 400 T shirts with MIT logos on the front, and on the back *Because not everyone can go to Caltech*. This required a major response from MIT. It came in spring 2006, and it was epic. On Olive Walk, in front of Fleming house, is a 1.3 ton nineteenth century artillery piece, a souvenir of the Franco-Prussian war. (Flems claimed to have taken part.) Blanks are fired from it several times a year for special occasions (any occasion deemed special by the Flems). Its main function is to be the prop in pranks. And it served heroically in 2006. Thirty MIT students, with nothing better to do – in the Techie telling – managed to steal the cannon and have it appear on the MIT campus wearing a giant MIT alumnus ring. The Caltech crowd was very impressed with the skill and chutzpah it took to pull this off. And they were jealous.

During the dozen years since there had been a few minor MIT/Caltech pranks, but at Caltech a heavy sense of incompleteness lingered. MIT deserved a world-class prank. It had to be something big, very big. And it had to be something original, very original.

The world was waiting for that response. Now there were stirrings one was being formulated. The stirrings began in Fleming since they were the aggrieved party. But representatives from all the Olive Walk Houses, and even some of the newcomer outhouses, were attending the third planning session on Friday evening. It was Blacker's turn to host.

True to Caltech tradition, they mixed the serious (sort of) with the humorous (very). The Pranker in Charge, a Flem, wore a khaki tunic with medals (actually, old election buttons and painted barrettes). She had a riding crop she slapped against her palm to emphasize her statements. Behind her was an easel with a map of MIT.

As RA of Blacker, there were several reasons I shouldn't know anything about the prank, but I couldn't think of any of them at the moment, so I listened and got a bit of it. I heard them say that they were going to hit MIT at a strong point. What would that be? Better to be surprised. I went back to the RA suite.

There was another prank and another surprise earlier on Friday. Mia was laughing when she called to tell me about it. Like guests at a successful dinner party, my Moles had carried through their obligation to reciprocate for cupid's visit the week before. It was Friday, the traditional day for fulfilling such obligations.

Some preparation is called for. Like many beautiful women, Mia had big feet. This goes against the common unwisdom of petite equals attractive. In the famous *Pulp Fiction* dance contest the camera focused on Uma Thurman's size 11s. She isn't alone. The size 11 club also has Meg Ryan, Gwyneth Paltrow, Nicole Kidman and a whole red carpet of others. Elle Macpherson is size 12. Elle Macpherson! Mia was a model. She knew about the gorgeous bigfoots, and was not sensitive about her own size 9s. Yet there are some who think that the Chinese had something in that foot binding abomination. For them I have only two words: Audrey Hepburn (10.5).

The cupid payback started with the sounds of horses outside the Page dining room. No horses. Just sounds. Two Moles entered dressed in what they supposed was 1850s business casual. (Where do they get this stuff?) One was carrying a clipboard, the other a glass, maybe acrylic, slipper, size 5, maybe 4.

They both looked around squinty-eyed before one unrolled a faux-parchment faux-proclamation and declaimed:

"The Leader and CTO of Techistan is searching for the nubile visitrix to last evening's rave. She rushed off, but in mounting her motor scooter lost this dainty slipper." (He held up the prop.) "The Leader has developed an obsession for this winsome vixen. In service to his addiction he has commissioned us to search his entire employee base so that he may woo the maiden whose foot matches this slipper. If the shoe fits, she'll have to split."

It was a shame that the last words were lost under the sound of laughter.

The two commissioned searchers looked around and spotted Mia. One squatted down to look under the tables. He stood up looking disappointed, turned to his associate, and shook his head. The sound of horses accompanied their exit. In reporting the laughter in the Page dining room, Mia swore she saw food coming out a Pagegirl's nose.

I went back to my RA suite. The subplots of my life seemed to be on pause, but mid-morning on Saturday two unrelated messages arrived, almost at the same time.

The first one was from Mia, who put aside our caution and used email. She hoped we could meet on Monday evening. The daring use of email suggested something was up. That was supported by a brief second paragraph describing a minor breakthrough in her work on gravel dynamics, interesting but then so many things are. It was obvious that this was an attempt to dilute the message so the meeting need would seem less needy. It was not an impressive attempt.

Since we were being reckless I used email to suggest we meet at Bobby's place (that's what we were calling it) Monday at 8 pm. She immediately responded.

"Good. Don't drive! I'll explain later. Till then. M"

Don't drive? What was that about? I was pretty sure it wasn't related to gravel dynamics.

Then there was the second message. Toobee, acting as go-between, wanted to remind me that Clarence and I were on for coffee at Kallie's the next day.

"Got it. He's here now, gone in a week."

"Good. I wasn't sure. Have you guys had a disagreement?"

I thought "What!" but went with "Why do you ask?"

"I dunno. Something in his tone, but hey, I'm no good at reading people. Assembly code, sí; people nyet."

Despite Toobee's struggle to back away from his indiscreet question, I was curious and cautious as Ta Mia reached the cross street by Kallie's. I remembered a week earlier Clarence had let me know friends didn't ask each other for evaluations of romantic partners. I was driving on distracted when I turned west, parked and walked back to Kallie's. Clarence smiled as I sat down, but hell, he's an actor, so that didn't mean anything.

Our ever-changing waitress was wearing a perky outfit and a pout. We didn't need to ask beyond raising our eyebrows. She explained without using verbs.

"New company policy from the national bullies. The usual, gentlemen?"

The gentlemen began.

"Clarence, are you upset with me? Was I just too stupid last Sunday? I mean when I asked you what you thought of Mia."

He was slow to answer.

"It's complicated. First, yeah, let's talk about last Sunday. I wasn't mad, but slightly surprised. Very slightly. Think about it, Solly. You were smitten. You wanted me to say, 'Yeah. Mia. Great gal. Hell of a lady. Lucky you. Go for it, man.' If I hardly knew her, and said something like 'I dunno; she seems nice,' you would have sulked while trying hard not to show your annoyance. The odds are strongly in favor of bad outcomes. So friends just don't ask what you asked."

Our perkily attired waitress returned, giving me a few seconds to dwell on what Clarence said. Often a conversation is a battle of who can show off more with clever questions. Clarence and I were beyond that. More important, I had real questions.

"But hold on Clarence. Suppose you really had something to say that would be useful to me. Suppose you, unsmitten, rational, objective, could perceive something. Or you encountered some useful information. Wouldn't you want to share it?"

Clarence kept silent for a very long time. He didn't speak, but the length of the silence said something. Too much dead air. It was time for me to pump life back into the air.

"Forget it, Clarence. I get it. You've already answered the question and I'm being stupid. More stupid than usual. It's just that I'm irrational, unreasonable, illogical…"

"Enough! OK. Yes, you're all of those things. Let me share with you my feelings about your feelings. Nothing specific to civil engineers. More like another chapter in *Deep Thoughts and Questions*, by the Decatur Destroyer as told to Clarence Hunsucker.

"It fascinates me, this business of infatuation. This mental aberration when you can't think of anyone else but that special someone. It's forgivable in a teenager, when it's called having a crush, but it's exactly the same damn thing when you're 38. It's not as if you make up your mind to be hopelessly in love with someone. There are two reasons. First, you don't make up your mind; it has nothing to do with your mind; it's not a damn choice; it's an affliction. Second, it's not love; love builds slowly when lives are entangled. Third…"

"But Clarence…"

"Shut up and listen. Third, how can people possibly believe that there is a unique soul mate for them, and by incredible luck, in a world of eight billion people… that's billion, Solly, with a b…, by incredible luck they just happen to have encountered that one person in a bar, a party, a classroom, or a wine and cheese get-together?

"Maybe you can help. I've got some questions. Sort of scientific, and you're sort of a scientist. First, you believe in Darwinian evolution, right? OK. How the hell, did this sickness evolve? It has no value. It's a short-term thing that disappears when the smitten victim gets to know the crush object. It's such goddamn nonsense that it almost points to a God messing with us for her own amusement.

"Then, closely related, is chemistry. Attraction is linked to dopamine and norepinephrine squirting around in our bodies. Yeah, Solly I am internet educated. Anyway, these juices have nothing to do with love. That's a completely different hormone; that's oxytocin. So, Solly, why the hell do we need the attraction chemicals?

"Think about it. Are they bait to get couples hooked? But that's a disaster most of the time. In the US 30% of marriages end up in divorce, and my own informal conclusion is that 80% of the others are unhappy couples who stay together for the kids.

"Think about doves. They bond for life – at least some species do. They've got the oxytocin thing working well for them, but are there dove crushes? Solly, why aren't you scientists working on this? It's important."

It is indeed. With that off his massive chest, Clarence's mood seemed to have lightened. He knew he had given a good performance. I knew he had given me things to think about. But we both knew I wouldn't.

We said good-bye. I got up to leave and thought about whether to leave a ten or a twenty. Then thought, 'She's got to learn that in life you can't always get what you want.' I left a five.

Chapter 27

MIA SPILLS IT; MONDAY NIGHT, NOVEMBER 19, 2018

I was antsy all day. In class, my students saw it and asked where I was, because I sure wasn't there. They were good natured about it; they understood distraction. But they wouldn't have understood my reason: the worry about the meeting with Mia, and the curiosity. What was so urgent? And what about the car? Why shouldn't I take my car? There had to be a good reason so I followed orders.

At 8 pm I got an Uber and gave an address a few blocks short of Bobby's. The address turned out to be a nail salon which at 8 pm might have seemed curious to a curious Uber driver, but like many people he spoke a lot and listened a little. Unlike most of them, he was interesting.

My driver, Stavros, came to the US from Greece three years earlier. Several of his relatives preceded him and found the work and the lives they were looking for. The American dream still existed for those with reasonable dreams and expectations.

His were reasonable. They had been fulfilled for his relatives. He was following their life template, and using their connections. He was set up to work at a legendary restaurant on Lake Avenue, a restaurant that for 45 years, had been a waypoint for immigrants from peripheral Europe. Like his relatives and many others, he expected to learn the language, make connections and live out his reasonable dream.

But Stavros was stymied by American food safety laws. The business plan of the restaurant was not compatible with Pasadena Health Department regulations and the restaurant was forced to close. Just as Stavros appeared in Pasadena, his job disappeared. With a few hundred words of English, a cell phone navigator, a car borrowed from relatives, and not many choices, he became an Uber driver. Hearing his story gave me mixed feelings I didn't understand. There were the dreams of the huddled masses yearning to be free, and the golden shores of California, but they clashed with digital navigation and the changes happening to the land of dreams.

Stavros was resilient but resentful. He came from the country that gave us the word politics, so it was not surprising he went on at some length on the nonsense of pointless arbitrary health laws no one wanted, laws that were denying Pasadena such a fine restaurant. Had anyone ever died from eating there? No! He turned to me in the back seat, a practice much more dangerous than foodborne pathogens, to develop his argument further. Stavros's face had the same mustache as Wojceich, but not the warmth. It showed intelligence, and energy. Another variation on the immigrant theme. Perhaps he would mature into a Wojceich.

He got to the point that had driven him to turn in his seat.

"Lots of students from Caltech ate there. Even professors. You know about Caltech?"

I told him I heard it was a local engineering school. He wasn't really listening. Instead, he went further into a rant about the proper function of government. I wasn't really listening. I did pick up that his central theme was 'If it was up to me…'

We survived his driving and he dropped me off at the nail salon. I stood still for a moment watching him drive off and, in my head, wished him well. A few minutes later I entered Bobby's and saw Mia sitting at a booth, finishing a red wine. When I slid in next to her a few men at the bar turned back to their drinks.

Bobby was on duty (perhaps always was) and came over exhibiting an impressive professional memory.

"Light beer 'cause you're driving Champ?"

"No," I responded, "I can drive better when I'm drunk. Do you have Wild Turkey?"

"As a client or in a bottle?"

"In a glass, for now – a double. And a refill for the lady."

"You got it, Champ."

Mia and the Champ sat in uncomfortable silence for a while. I could see that Mia was flushed. From the wine? I was no better with this than with pickup lines. I was still testing out good silence-breakers in my head when Mia began. She wasn't looking at me, but was staring hard at nothing. She began slowly and softly.

"It's about Gilles."

Pause. Continue.

"It wasn't only the affair. Before I met Gilles I knew there were some questions. About whether he could be trusted. You know about Alexander McQueen, right?"

I thought about lying, but I would make a mess of it, so I tried to look embarrassed and admitted I didn't.

"He was the British designer of the year *four* times, and international designer of the year once."

I figured it was like the Nobel prize for fashion, but the insincerity of my embarrassment showed through. Suppressing a sigh and maybe a smile, Mia continued, though with a slight slur.

"He was really, well, different. Kind of refreshing like one of those really hot chili peppers. More news event than great fashion designer. He got attention by shocking people, by being outrageous. Some people confuse being creative and propres.. what's word?"

"Preposterous?" I offered.

"Right, preposterous. Anyway, point is McQueen and Gilles were having hush-hush meetings back around eight, nine years ago. Gilles was already established, but wasn't a star. His style was classical, traditional, pretty much opposite of McQueen, so was interesting they were meeting."

"So… what came of it?"

"Maybe nothing, maybe tragedy. No one knows. Maybe just no one is saying. But it's interesting, no?, that McQueen committed suicide soon after, and Gilles' work became a little less conservative. Maybe coincidence, but there were whispers. Could mean nothing. In fashion world whispers are how people communicate."

"Mia this was before you got involved with Gilles. In fact, before you got involved with fashion, so… ."

"Right. Right. 'S background. I heard gossip and insinuations. Great word, eh? Insinuations. Sounds like a snake. I told myself 'Ewa, there are always insinuations in fashion.' I didn't want to believe any of it, so I told myself pay no attention. I shouldn't have listened to myself.

"And there's more."

She stopped with a bitter smile, took a big sip of wine, and continued.

"At the beginning… ah, the beginning… we spent almost all our time together. There was not only the romance. Also was fashion. Both of us. (I was interested in fashion only to please him. Didn't see it then. Seem so ridiculous now. Trivial now.) Around that time, he worked with a young designer, Tommaso Russo, American barely in twenties, who introduced new look: shaped vertical stripes that fool the eye and make woman's figure look slimmer, or make her bulge where she wants to bulge. You remember that. Right?"

I tried to fill in the blank expression on my face, but it didn't fool her. She smiled to acknowledge the distance between my world and fashion. She went on.

"Was big hit for a year and Gilles was very much into it. Worked well with his conservative style. I was also interested. Really. Not just faking it to please Gilles. I loved way Tommaso studied the workings of vision. It is like something artists called *trompe l'oeil*, fool the eye. I figured it had been important in fashion, maybe always, but by trial and error. Intuition. This young guy was doing it kind of scientifically. And I guess I have that science module always sputtering in my brain."

Another big sip, another continuation.

"And Gilles stole it. Tommaso had not locked up ownership of the idea or of designs. The basic idea maybe couldn't be copyrighted. I don't know. Tommaso also had a father-figure attraction to Gilles, in a different way from me. Or maybe some of the same way – who knows. Anyway, he trusted Gilles with designs. He didn't trust anyone else. But I, I was always around, so I knew the designs were not Gilles' idea. Gilles built his new fall line around the idea."

Mia stared at me for a few seconds before the big reveal: "He never mentioned Tommaso."

"There was a lawsuit. Tommaso's lawyer came to see me. He avoided Gilles who was watching for someone to approach me. This lawyer said Gilles had the reputation, the connections, and the legal team. Tommaso didn't have chance unless I testify about what I saw and heard. Tommaso tried to call me himself, but I didn't answer."

Yet another long pause. This time it didn't seem Mia was going to continue but she had to. There was an important thread hanging loose.

"Mia, what did you do?"

"Nothing. I did nothing. Please. Please, understand. I was very different then. I knew something very unfair, maybe not legal, was going on, but I thought about what I could do, and I told myself no good outcome. Another example, hmm?, of how I shouldn't listen to myself.

"So Tommaso's lawyer laid it out for Tommaso. They would lose and it would look like Tommaso was trying to extort Gilles. That's the word lawyer use, *extort*. He told Tommaso they should try to get something in out-of-court settlement. Gilles agreed to pay legal fees and give Tommaso $10,000 in exchange for a binding agreement Tommaso was barred from revealing anything about the settlement. Tommaso went to Milan to get distance from the New York-Paris gang. Gilles gave him $10,000 'to encourage a bright young talent in his new setting.' Everyone thought Gilles was a great guy."

I didn't know how to react. My go-to philosophy was evil can exist because too many people remain silent. I thought about Shoshana, who would never remain silent when she saw something wrong. And here I was, sitting across from someone I was smitten with who remained silent when she was a witness to evil. Okay, it wasn't the rise of the Third Reich, but it was evil, and someone was hurt. And she believed she was the only witness who could help. I thought about the cat and the sparrow.

Mia looked at my face and could read my mind.

"You are disappointed in me," she said in a colorless tone.

I fell back on a cliché, "I need to process this."

"I understand. Maybe our friendship will be different. Just professional."

She tried another sip from what was now an empty wine glass. Bobby was on the ball, and when Mia looked in her direction Bobby was walking towards us with another glass of red. She put it down quickly, and hurried away.

"Mia, there's still a question."

She tried to relieve what had become a very dark mood with a forced smile.

"You mean about Clarence? See Toobee."

I couldn't even smile.

"No. I met with Clarence. Long story. The question is why you warned me not to take my car."

Her smile faded when she said, "Gilles last Wednesday at Polska. Not coincidence. I think your car is bugged. We are being watched."

CHAPTER 28

MIA CASITA; MONDAY NIGHT, NOVEMBER 19, 2018

"Jesus!" I stated without thinking and then apologized.

"Sorry, I forgot you're Catholic."

"Jesus!" she said, "You think that really matters?"

What mattered was that she was very upset, though her reaction was probably an overreaction to Gilles' showing up at Polska, with a wine enhanced expression of her feelings. I played the role of the calm rational consoler, a role that always pissed me off when it was turned on me.

"Hold on Mia. Is there any chance Gilles was at Polska by accident?"

"None. Zero. Zaden. Gilles hates Polish food. Hates anything not elegant and expensive. Went to Polska just once, when we were starting together, and wanted to please me. Or seem to."

I continued acting the role of the calm rationalist.

"But why would he bug my car and 'accidentally' run into you? Do you think he wants to rekindle the affair?"

"Ha! Impossible. I am too old and too fat."

It wasn't a moment for laughter. By US standards Mia needed to eat a bushel of pierogis. She may not have been translucent, like Gilles' underage models, but she was underweight by my standards or sensible standards (always the same as mine).

"OK," I said. "Let's assume he wasn't there for kielbasa. And it was important enough he that he might put a bug on my car and break laws."

Allow me a relevant aside here: I hadn't actually known whether it was illegal to plant a bug, but the subject had just become very interesting and I looked into it the next day. It depends on state law, and in the Golden State, according to California Penal Code section 637.7, it *was* illegal without my permission. Gilles may not have been familiar with the California Penal Code (one could hope about his future needs) but that wasn't the issue. He would have someone else plant the bug for him. The Gilles that Mia described wouldn't touch anything except fabric and female skin. I continued my failing attempt at rational calming.

"He must have a strong reason, and you must have some idea."

"I must?" Mia asked, with a touch of irritation. "But I don't! I hear rumors Gilles get into financial trouble and maybe borrowed money from some mob. But what does that have to do with *me*? Could Tommaso try legal action again? If yes, then I become important to Gilles. A wild guess, but best I can do."

Her shiny eyes threatened.

Women have ways to protect themselves in a dangerous world. There are small handguns- purse guns. The Glock 42, just one example, weighs less than 14 ounces. Knives are relatively rare for womanly self-defense, though interesting for the personal connection they involve. The list goes on to include snakes and lawyers. But the most common and reliable method women use is tears. I say this not as a misogynist, but as an admirer of those who make expert use of the tools they have.

I felt tongue-tied and helpless. I reached out across the table and experimentally put a trite hand over hers. She grabbed my hand, squeezing too hard. She was surprisingly strong.

This didn't make sense. Mia didn't seem fragile, but she was frightened. Patting her hand, and feeling awkward, I probed.

"Mia, help me understand. Gilles may be stalking you. But c'mon, he's not that scary. Is there something else?"

There was a long pause; it became a longer pause. I used a teaching technique: Wait. Let the pressure of silence weigh heavy on the student, or in this case the postdoc. It paid off. Mia finally spoke.

"Yes. Something happened. It was Friday afternoon. There was this guy. I noticed him hanging around, in cafeteria, in bookstore, and just walking around. I would say didn't look like Techie, but that wouldn't mean anything. What does Techie look like? Still, I don't know."

She paused added, "There was something," then paused again.

"Late in afternoon I was walking back to Page from my lab and he stopped me.

Didn't feel threatened. We were out in the open and I can scream very loud, but was nervous. Then he looked me in eyes and said something like 'You should know. Do what asked. Pay attention. Gilles in much danger. Remember. Do what asked.' He takes off, makes quick turn around a building and I couldn't see where he was headed. I thought about following him, but thought too long, then too late.

"He had mistakes in English and an accent. Maybe German, but not quite. Dutch? Maybe. I'm not sure. Not Polish. This is Tech. Maybe it was prank?"

That wasn't likely. The undergrads loved pranks, but they had a good feeling for limits. And Mia was well liked. They wouldn't do this to her. I wanted to comfort her, but not lie to her.

"What did this guy look like? What age? Tall? Short? Beard? Limp? Missing limbs? Parrot on his shoulder?"

She paused, as she often did, and she had the attentive expression she often had. She appeared to be listening to herself as if it were news to her.

"Yes. His clothes. Cheap European fabric, poorly cut, with patterns not well matched at seams. From distance he looked like undergrad. Slender, quick moving. 'Lithe,' is that right word? Made him seem young. But when I got close, I see there are lines on face. Much older close up. Not undergrad, not even grad student. Solly, up close I could see a scar down one cheek, far back almost to his ear. Medium height. His skin color was slightly olive. Or maybe not; maybe it was lighting. Dark brown hair. Not much noticeable. Kind of funny I *had* noticed him before Friday, at distance, and didn't pay much attention."

The focus on details calmed her, and we sat there in silence for a long time. It was 9:30 pm. I didn't know what to say, and hoped Mia would take the lead. Things suddenly got very complicated.

"Solly, I don't want to be alone tonight."

I didn't hide the expression on my face, but I'm not sure what the expression was. It had to be something seeping out of the debate going on between those voices in my head. As they argued, Mia continued.

"I know this is very forward of me. Don't have to sleep with me. You know what I mean. You don't have to make love to me. Just have to keep me from being alone."

The head voices loved this. They agreed this was a hell of a deal, but weren't sure I should take it. I hadn't decided what to do, but I found myself looking at my phone for motels, and realized I really had decided.

Yes, it was a hell of a deal, but it wasn't the Sunday morning bed strewn with the Times and flooded with sunlight. It wasn't my fantasy, but yeah, a hell of a deal.

The go-to motel was the Nomad on Colorado, so it was my unthinking first impulse. Then I came to whatever was left of my senses. The Nomad was over a mile to the west of us. Too far to walk. I envisioned Stavros heeding an Uber call and collecting award-winning gossip. Also, the Nomad was Tech territory and being noticed there would have Grand Canyon class downsides. I switched to a search for motels near us and found there were six motels within just a few blocks east of us. Six motels. A cluster. Huh. Why? Was this karma testing me with temptation? If so, I failed. Or succeeded. I didn't know what karma had in mind.

All the motels were two-star so I chose the closest one, and tried to act manly and decisive when I paid the bar bill (cash, no record), and took Mia's hand helping her out of our booth and out the door. I hadn't said anything (part of being decisive and manly) and didn't know what Mia was thinking. When we turned east on Colorado Boulevard, any doubts she had probably vanished.

We walked east for a block, crossed San Gabriel Boulevard, went another block and crossed a secondary street. One of the voices in my head mentioned we were walking along historic Route 66. The route to adventure. But we were headed east, the wrong direction. Did this mean something? A metaphor? I wished the voices would shut up.

We came to two motels adjacent to each other and we entered the first, *Mia Casita*. Mia noticed the name and gave a smile. I wondered again about karma. It was nice to see the smile. Neither of us had said a word since leaving Bobby's.

The motel differed only in minor details from standard two-star SoCal lodging. A detail was the large A-frame portico that would have shaded the entrance if it hadn't been nighttime, and hadn't been November. The pool, just beyond the portico, wouldn't be any more useful. The small reception area was neat and clean, but I hardly noticed as I dealt with embarrassment. I was 38 damn years old and I felt shame about entering a motel with a woman.

I tried to act as if I had nothing to hide. The clerk, Rusty, if he was wearing his own vest, didn't care. It was his job not to, and I was grateful for his job performance. My pangs of shame had minor aftershocks as I filled out the register with a false name. I thought about using "Alexander McQueen," but hesitated. A paranoid voice told me this could provide a lead to anyone clever trying to track us. I fell back on a venerable Caltech pseudonym and filled in Mr. and Mrs. Albert Luvial, from Boalsburg, PA. (There is such a town. Our pursuers could waste time looking for us there.)

Rusty didn't bother asking whether we wanted two queen sized beds or one king, and didn't bother telling us how to use the TV or connect to the motel Wi-Fi. I was relieved to see I had enough cash and would not have to leave the spoor of a credit card. I considered slipping Rusty a tip, but that would only be a reason to remember us.

We ascended the stairs to our second-floor room, and I sensed one of the voices in my head clearing its throat in preparation. The room was about what I expected, indestructible carpet, neutral color walls. We stood for a moment, still silent, and took the obvious next step, a step that is always awkward the first time.

As we lay in bed and felt each other's warmth, the storm in my mind would not abate. A voice told me there was nothing wrong with what I was doing. That voice lied to me too often. I wasn't buying it.

A more thoughtful voice was raising questions about why Mia was doing this. I didn't want to think about that, and it didn't stop the inevitable. Afterwards, while we remained entangled, I fantasized about Sunday mornings.

CHAPTER 29

SMITTY AND THE BUGS; TUESDAY, NOVEMBER 20, 2018

Tuesday should have been mostly the day after Monday, the day for calming down and mulling over what had happened.

It started with us getting back to campus separately. Mia called an Uber. A half hour later I took a taxi, not an Uber, to be sure I wouldn't run into Stavros. Both of us were dropped off several blocks from campus and first went to our offices so we wouldn't lie when we said we were at our offices.

A loose thread that had to be snipped: the bug on my car. I would use it as a learning opportunity.

As a grad student I was above average with digital electronics, but a bug on a car was a transmitter and my expertise had not been in radio and microwave signaling. Anyway, things were different now. There had been big advances in the technology during the preceding decade. But no worries; I only needed to go around two corners and talk to Smitty. (This was her Tech tag from transmit. I could have found her birth name in her file, of course, but it wasn't important. And I was bleary-eyed. And lazy.)

Smitty was a large friendly young lady with short brown hair, broad shoulders and suggestions of impressive musculature under her loose clothing. She was the star of the water polo team and was the major reason they were having a very good year.

She was also a star on the volleyball team. The year before I shared a couple of beers with the volleyball coach who whined about having to lose Smitty. He went on about how aggressive she was, how her spike had her opponents cowed. Her reputation gave the Caltech team a psychological edge. When I met her during my first few days as RA in Blacker, I was surprised by how gentle and friendly she was. Some highly competitive athletes are like that. The term I hear is compartmentalize.

Confronted with the idea of a college-age woman who is star athlete in a pool, I had trouble keeping Shoshana off my mind. But today I had to get down to business.

Though Smitty did OK in coursework it was clear to her and everyone else her future lay in electronic design and in helping some callow entrepreneurs to retire as young billionaires. She loved electronic design even more than water polo.

She answered my knock and looked surprised but smiled.

"Solly! I would say 'It's always nice to see you,' but I think this is the first time I've had the pleasure of a visit.'"

"I need a favor."

"Men! They always want something," she said in mock exasperation.

Her chunk of Blacker was more a lab than a dorm room. There were two plastic parts cabinets with lots of small drawers, each drawer neatly labeled. There was also a bevy of unlabeled parts on her desk. A few brought back memories. On a shelf were expensive-looking electronic instruments, a high-end oscilloscope, a lock-in amplifier, and three power supplies.

"What's up?"

"There's a radio bug on my car; I want to know as much about it as possible."

"My pleasure," she said in a tone that let me know for her this really would be pleasure. "Lead on," she added, getting down to business and grabbing a small instrument from a shelf.

As we approached my car, she looked at the readout on the meter in her hand and mumbled "Looks like 9 Gig." When we got to the car she reached under it, felt around for a few seconds and we were soon looking at a small device duct taped to a 9-volt battery and a ceramic magnet.

"Yup," she said. "Off the shelf Huawei hardware. Reliable range of one mile, maybe two miles or so, considerably more if they have line of sight. Who is playing a prank on you? It wouldn't be, ahem, someone from Page House? Maybe the Resident Associate?"

It would be better to have her suspicions linked to campus gossip than to alert the undergrad network of undefined danger. So I played along and acted embarrassed and evasive (well within my acting range).

"Not sure, Smitty. Who knows. Anyway, I want to be able to check by myself for bugs. You use a wide band detector of radio signals?"

"Right, Solly. I keep forgetting you are an excommunicated physicist."

She smiled. It was a good-natured jab. I smiled.

"The simplest thing: Buy one of the commercial units made just for detecting bugs. A few words of advice: Some bugs only transmit every minute or so, to save battery power and avoid detection. So, if you're sweeping for a bug, do it for more than a minute. Also, some bugs get power from a car's electrics. These are set up only to broadcast after the electrical system is activated, when the car is turned on. You probably shouldn't worry about that. Wiring the bug into the car's electrics isn't something that can be done by some sneaky Page House dweller ducking down by a wheel well for a few seconds while pretending to tie her shoelaces. Just get a cheap commercial unit and scan for at least a minute."

"Smitty, though I am in the English Department, an expert with words, adequate words of thanks fail me. My failure will be even more painful if you write down suggestions for the particular scanners you recommend."

"Sure thing," she said as she wrote down three suggestions including approximate prices.

"Gigathanks Smitty. Oh, and ummm, it would be great if you didn't mention this to anyone."

"Got it. What happens in Blacker stays in Blacker. Even if it involves Page."

She smiled knowingly, though she didn't know.

I had a surprise waiting for me at the RA suite, an old friend standing by the door.

"Sherlock! Long time!" I said with real pleasure. Then thought for a moment and asked, "How did you get in?"

"Horvath bows to the wishes of the FBI."

"Jeez, I forgot you're with the Feds now. Congrats. I want to hear more."

"Oh, you'll hear more than you want. Don't worry. Or maybe worry."

Luk always figured his contribution to law enforcement would be in forensics. His Caltech background would make him valuable in state and national labs. His very attainable fantasy was to work in scientific analysis for the FBI. He was living his fantasy.

We went into my RA suite, and the conversation started predictably with some catching up.

"Solly, my Sherlock tag is in the past. Now I'm senior agent Xi of the FBI. I'm in forensics. Surprise! I made it!"

He was proud but he wasn't there to boast about his career.

"Yeah, so I'm in forensics, but I've been moved temporarily to act as a field agent because of my connections to Caltech. The FBI has become very interested in Caltech."

"Do tell."

"I intend to, but first tell me what the hell happened to you. I know you're teaching English. Didn't see that coming. But I know about it. In fact, I probably know everything about you; we're the FBI and it's what we do. We know things. But I'd like to hear it from you, if I'm not exploiting a longstanding friendship."

I told him most of the story, including the chapter about Shosh, but not so much about Sweet Caroline. He probably knew anyway.

"OK, Luk. Your turn. Let's skip the saga of your ascent and your imminent coronation as FBI director. Let's get to the Caltech connection."

CHAPTER 30

LUK AND A STRANGE TALE; TUESDAY, NOVEMBER 20, 2018

Luk got to it.

"Our interest is Fang Lou. We're hoping you can help us."

"Keep hoping. You know more than I do. She withdrew from school a few months ago and it's a mystery. If I knew more I might tell you, but there'd be questions of ethics and privacy."

"Would you consider it a breach of ethics to tell me about Fang and Darryl?"

I don't know why this gave me a bit of a chill. Of course the FBI would know if there was something there. Why did this bother me? Maybe because I myself didn't know if there was something there.

"Right, Luk. I don't know anything, so no ethics worries. Let's make a deal. Tell me everything you can about Fang and I promise, if I learn anything I'll tell you whatever is ethical and complies with privacy laws. If it's information that can help protect Darryl or Fang, my ethics will get very practical."

"Deal. We can skip the pinky swear. Most of what I'm going to tell you is in publicly accessible material. Not all. Here's something not accessible, but maybe a smart guy like you guessed it: The FBI is putting lots of resources on Fang at the request of the goddamn State Department."

Huh? I wasn't that smart a guy. Where was this going? Luk continued talking. I continued listening. My jaw continued descending.

"Last March was the first session of the 13th National People's Congress of the People's Republic of China. Xi Jinping (no relation) was unanimously elected

President and Chairman of the Chinese Military Command. No surprise. Another no surprise: Xi Jinping is moving toward being an autocrat. He has rolled back some of the changes Deng Xiaoping made, and has a new vision. Xi calls it Chinese capitalism. It's not a wild success, so he's worried about his political future. He's not a risk-taker so he's focused on bolstering popular support.

"His main tool: increasing the stature of China in world politics. The Chinese people are very proud of their culture and history. Xi is exploiting this, a standard page from the autocrat playbook. Anyway, Fang Lou is the daughter of a Chinese big-shot billionaire, and some of the time –when it's to his advantage – he's a political opponent of Xi. It could be bad for the outside view of China, and hence for US-China relations, and hence for Xi, if the US is not seen doing everything possible to find her. If this doesn't make sense, it's because Chinese politics doesn't make sense."

It didn't make sense.

"Wow. But I don't get it. Sorry, Luk. There's got to be more. Why is the goddamn State Department involved on the side of Lou, not Xi Jinping? Or *are* they on the side of Xi? Or what?"

Luk took a deep breath and pondered how much to say. I think he decided to say a lot, but maybe not. I don't know what he was keeping to himself.

"OK. I'm going to tell you some goddamn State Department stuff. You don't really need to know it. It's going to sound top secret. It sort of is, but sort of isn't. You can find speculations about this in political science journals. But that's speculation. I wouldn't want any of it to have confirmation. So I'm trusting you. You used to be trustworthy."

"Still am, Sherlock."

"Here's the deal. Short and sketchy. There are people in the Chinese government and people in our government who get it that there are problems that affect the world, not just individual countries: atmospheric pollution, ocean pollution, pandemics, international arms sales, yada yada. Near the top of the list, of course: Climate change.

"But it's not at the top of the list. Climate is a slow death for the planet. But it might be irrelevant because we are facing a fast death. Remember MAD."

"Yeah. Mutually Assured Destruction. Use a nuclear weapon on us, and we use one on you. It's unthinkable so we don't think about it, and we don't have to worry about nuclear Armageddon."

"Right. And you're a smart guy, so you see the flaw?"

"The assumption that the players are rational?"

"Bingo, smart guy. We were fed this scheme by academics, by game theorists, by professors! Solly, you're a professor. Would you trust the fate of the world to professors?"

"Plead the fifth. Refuse to answer on the grounds. And anyway I'm not a professor; I'm a senior lecturer."

"Potayto, potahto. Yeah, you get it. We've already got nut cases with nuclear weapons; North Korea will be joined before long by Iran, no matter how we connive with the Israelis. Think about the tension between India and Pakistan, long border, nuclear weapons on both sides. And technical progress moves on making it all even worse. Drum roll please.

"There's going to be a big expansion of nuclear power plants as we turn off the fossil fuel spigot. Even the Greens are catching on that it will take too long to harness solar, wind, and – let us pray – fusion. With those nuclear power plants around every corner, fissionable uranium, and plutonium will be the new meth. Nuclear weapons will be as common as guns in high schools. With so many weapons and so many potentially unstable leaders, through stupidity, or a willingness to go down with the ship, one of them is going to light the nuclear fuse. You want to have terminal insomnia? Think about some new Idi Amin with nuclear weapons. Yeah, they won't have missiles for delivery but they'll have suitcases and smugglers.

"Striking multiparty deals doesn't work. You want a rigorous proof, you've got it: history! So what to do? Here's what: There are joint Chinese-American secret working groups discussing bipartite world oversight. They believe it's the only way. Xi Jinping is very much a player. We want to keep him in power.

"That's the reality. On the surface there is conflict but it's mostly a scam."

It made me think about Clarence and the scam of professional wrestling. People knew it was a show but they wanted to believe it. That's what was going on here?

"Luk! This is in journals? Why isn't it on the front page of everything?"

"It's speculations and there are lots of speculations. Political experts, academics, they think about possibilities and threats, and this China-US partnership becomes almost obvious. Of course, other possibilities are also almost obvious. The experts have cried wolf too many times. The batting average of political predictions isn't great, so speculations don't get headlines."

"Let me see if I get it. Bernard Lou may not be an ally of Xi, but he can hurt Xi if his daughter is lost or hurt. He can claim that under Xi, China gets no respect from the US. Is Lou in on this secret US-China bipartite thing?"

"Who knows. Maybe. Probably not."

"OK. I'm beginning to get it. Maybe. But not the urgency of finding Fang. College age students take off on larks all the time and can be hard to find. What's the big deal?"

"Yeah. There's that. But then there's this: We're pretty sure Fang has fallen in with some very bad people. Make that 'very very bad.' Strange creeps. I'm going to tell you about them; some of it will be certain; some will be guesses. I hope we have an understanding you will keep secret what I tell you unless it's a matter of life and death."

It turned out that life and death were very much the matter.

CHAPTER 31
SASHI AND THE HUNS ; TUESDAY, NOVEMBER 20, 2018

"I can tell you it's a small band. A half dozen we think. They were state-sponsored criminals, paramilitary secret police, bodyguards, small private militias, that sort of thing. They were doing well in the Balkans, in the old Soviet hegemony, and in some places that crawl under the radar. But things changed; new people came into the old world; even worse, new attitudes came in. Brutality and torture were the classical modus. They didn't end, just went behind closed doors. The old creeps couldn't adjust. They weren't closed door types. They became an embarrassment to the new overlords. Embarrassments are soon removed. They figured it was better to remove themselves. They needed to look for a new world, and quickly.

"They met at various times and communicated using EncroChat, an encrypted network frequented by European criminals. Solly, I'm not making this up. There's lots of stuff going on that you have no hint of. Joint efforts of Dutch, French and British law enforcement to hack EncroChat are underway. I can't say more; I think you'll hear about that before long. Anyway, these creeps first tried the Netherlands.

"Surprised? Yeah, the Netherlands. Seems like a funny choice, right? But only at first. It was an opportunity because of the surge in illegal drugs, and the loose Dutch attitude toward drugs. So off to the land of tulips but a little late. Our displaced criminal friends missed the front of the wave. By the time they arrived the police were cracking down in Rotterdam and Amsterdam, so the creeps set up shop in Harlingen. It's a minor port and they used it for bringing in drugs. We have information one of them grew up in that region,

Friesland, so they had a head start in connecting to networks. Also, the dominant language, West Frisian – exotic, eh? – was not Dutch, but something close to English, and they all spoke some English.

"It came apart after they were there for around two years. Maybe Encro-Chat was hacked. Probably not or we would have been told. Dutch cops found torture chambers built into shipping containers. There were dentist chairs, saws, pruning shears, and lots of blood stains. The Dutch gendarmes figured these were used both as part of ransom schemes and to deal with rival gangs. It caused such an uproar that the poor devils had to move quickly again. They looked west.

"Like Americans in the 60s, when they looked west they saw California. They knew very little about this new world, but they were sure there would be opportunities in the golden land, a land of dreams for enterprising young businessmen like them.

"They were not the smartest rats in the sewer. In fact, one of several reasons they were banished from their old jobs is the new autocrats worried they would do stupid things. One of the rats was a step up the ladder, a mastermind compared to the others. He attended university in the UK, and considered himself an intellectual. He was intellectual enough to manipulate six mindless cretins with stories of sunshine and bikinis.

"The leader had a vision he sold to the half-witted half dozen he collected. They were ronin, a band of samurai warriors who no longer had to bow to the authority of a leader. It escaped their notice that they had a leader and they were bowing to him, but lots of stuff escaped their notice.

"The head guy took the name Sashi, for Miyamoto Musashi, Japan's most famous ronin and swordsman. The others found appropriate noms de criminalité. The second in command, the largest of them, though far from the smartest, was the Harlingen native. He took the name Wejirs Jelckama, a sixteenth century Frisian warlord. Another of the gang chose the tag Roman Shukhevych, a white supremacist Ukrainian neo-Nazi. Other names came from a rebel native-American warrior, a Chechan turncoat, and two bad guys from American Westerns. The Huns. The ronin. Like a bunch of satanic kids playing robbers and robbers.

"We could have written them off as low comedy but Sashi is not a joke. We don't know much about him but we know something.

"But first, a *very* serious aside. You're going to suspect from what I tell you we've got someone on the inside, so I'll try to make this absolutely clear: If you ever mention your suspicion to someone, I'll cut out your liver and feed it to my cat. I can do it. It's standard FBI training. So, to continue…

"Sashi was smart enough back in the old country to see the end coming long before it came. He started stealing from his generalissimo who paid no attention to financial details. He had an even better source of kopeks: As head of the terror squad he arrested rich VIPs and demanded huge ransoms to set them free. He was smart enough to store his acorns in tax havens with bank secrecy, Switzerland, Monaco, Lebanon.

"From the info we have, our psyche evaluators say he is a classic psychopath. No tears need to be shed for him. His criminal behavior has nothing to do with mistreatment, abuse, a tough childhood; it's due to a neurophysiological defect. Bad wiring, not bad coding."

"Criminal psychopaths. Bad amygdala. Right?"

"Jeez, Solly. Just like the old days. You may have changed from physics to whatever, but you haven't really changed. Good old Solly, the shallow polymath. So to continue…"

"Sashi has the smarts to study history, and the mental leanings to become obsessed with things he finds (example: Miyamoto Musashi). He became obsessed with the bullies of 1500 years ago, the Huns. He loved their mastery of terror, and according to the source you will mention only at the risk of hepatectomy, Sashi goes on and on about the Huns. Solly, perhaps I should mention hepatectomy is removal of the liver."

"Yeah, yeah. I get it."

"Anyway, he started to use the name Attila, but it was too recognizable, and he sensed it might seem silly. He was very sensitive about looking silly and he expressed his sensitivity in violent ways. You make him look silly, he makes you look dismembered. The name Sashi carried little baggage.

"Let me give you some flavor of what this guy is like. The historical Huns were into cranial deformation, squashing the head to give it a conical shape. The Huns would do this to their *own* boy children to make them look scarier. Sashi had no boy children at hand, but couldn't get over the idea of cranial deformation. We have some evidence he used it for torture and murder. It's an example of his tendency to have obsessions, about which stay tuned.

"Sashi may have been a fan of the Huns partly for a professional purpose. He believes the Huns, clever little barbarians that they were, used terror as a business plan. If your enemies are wetting themselves they don't put up a good fight. They just surrender. He thought the Huns used that early on. He believed the stories that the Great Wall of China was built because the Chinese were terrified of the Huns. Sashi was fascinated. Look where scaring people can get you. He had no respect for the attitudes of the new autocrats. What was the point in terror if no one knew about it? His role models, along with the Huns, were the Haitian Tonton Macoute. Our source tells us the name choice was touch and go between Huns and Tontons."

I thought of Smitty terrifying her water polo opponents with the threat of her overhead smash. Same principle, different context. Luk continued.

"Sashi decided that his gang of miscreants would be the Huns. We sometimes call them that. We've got to call them something, and creeps is not specific enough. His horde of a half dozen may not have liked the name, or the obsession, but arguing with Sashi ran a risk of head renovation.

"Our source of information (liver, Solly, liver) tells us that in his new life Sashi has developed another obsession. Pay attention now. He made a fortune by holding people for ransom, so he went nonlinear when he heard about hacking and ransomware. It's the ultimate weapon for your typical power-hungry psychopath. He can have power over corporations, or local governments. And the threat to close everything down is powerful enough to allow him to dictate the rules of engagement, and to remain out of the grasp of the police, FBI, whoever.

"Our psyche guys, and they're pretty good, guess Sashi can't get over the idea of the power ransomware would bring him. Not getting over something is what psychopaths are known for. His dream was to hold hostage a municipality by taking control of their electric grid, water supply, and so forth.

"Ransomware was just beginning to be a big thing, so Sashi was not far from the front of the wave, a megalomaniacal criminal visionary. He was still smarting from being slow getting to the Netherlands. Being a sort of pioneer with ransomware appealed to his sensitive ego."

"Luk, are these guys expert hackers? Can they pull off a ransomware attack?"

"Hah. In fact, hah hah. Not even close. They know almost nothing about the tech side of it. But remember they have a powerful weapon, terror. Our guess: they're going to use it to get themselves the experts they need. Sashi has not given up the old ways."

"But how the…"

"Be patient, Solly; I'm getting to it. Sashi had arrived in southern California with a big bankroll but weak connection to the LA mob."

"There's an LA mob?"

"Yeah. There's lots of reasons it doesn't get much publicity. It's nothing like the classical Sicilian families. In fact, a past LA Police Chief called it the Mickey Mouse Mafia. But it's there, in Newport Beach, Westwood, Burbank, the Valley, all over, really. It sort of grew out of the Sicilian Mafia, but it's more like it replaced them. The old boys were entangled with lots of local corruption, but they got frustrated by the dispersed nature of SoCal municipal governments. The mob bosses complained there were too damn many people to pay off. It cut into their 90% profit margin. They moved out. See Solly, even the Mafia has business problems. Life is hard.

"Crime abhors a vacuum, so others moved in. The LA mob is not organized crime. It's more like disorganized crime. Lots of ethnicities have joined the party, Mexicans, Armenians, Asians, lots of small groups dominating their own ethnic areas. The Russian group may be the biggest.

"Sashi didn't know the territory. He hired four low level locals, but they weren't much help. So he reached out to what there was of the LA mob, probably the Russians, or the Belarussians. He offered to cut them into his dream of billions from ransomware hacking. They wanted nothing to do with this strange outsider. They were conservative; they did loan sharking, auto parts, prostitution, the traditional time-dishonored activities. Business was not slowing down, so why look for trouble? But Sashi's wad made them hesitate to cut off connections. Ransomware wasn't competition, so – as a favor – they gave him some advice. Sniff around Caltech."

Then Luk laid out what I should have realized myself.

"Caltech is the obvious place to look for hackers. Consider: It's in SoCal; how convenient. Many Caltech students are off-scale competent with computer systems. Caltech has a history of pranks, and breaking into a municipal power grid could be presented as a really cool prank. Caltech students have a tradition of picking locks; isn't that just a version of hacking?"

My jaw had been rising to its normal position, but now it dropped again. It *was* kind of obvious! And that was chilling. Darryl and Fang. And a brutal, obsessed psychopath.

"Luk, might this have something to do with Darryl or Fang?"

"Is the Dalai Lama Bhuddhist? It has *everything* to do with Darryl and Fang! Or at least with Fang. Our don't-risk-your-liver source of information witnessed discussions with a hostage that must have been Fang.

"We know some of the Huns' locations, and we think we know where they are keeping her. Anyway, if we go in, guns blazing there's, a good chance Fang would end up dead and our heads would be deformed by the Director."

Luk's buddy attitude evaporated during his narration. He was now a professional. He sat there in my guest chair as if waiting for me to say something. I couldn't say anything. He walked the few feet to the door. He let himself out with a noncontroversial exit line.

"Hell of a thing, isn't it?"

I was in a state of mild shock and strong confusion. Hell of a thing indeed. I looked down in my hands. It took me a moment to realize what I was looking at: the bug that Smitty removed from my car. Less than an hour ago I was chuckling to myself about it. I was going to put it on one of the campus patrol cars as a prank. I stared at it.

We had gone far past pranks, but where had we gone?

CHAPTER 32

CHINESE HISTORY; LUNCH, TUESDAY, NOVEMBER 20, 2018

It was 10:45 am when Luk left, and he had left me in a state of needing to know more. Mobsters, hacking, Chinese politics. I had an idea, crossed my fingers and called the Baxter Hall office of Prof. Emeritus Lee "Woody" Woodley. I was in luck.

"Woody, you've been looking a bit underfed recently, so I would like to buy you lunch at the Ath. Please say yes."

"Yes. But I know this is going to cost me something. Hmmm. Lemme see. You want me to support your candidacy to be President of Caltech?"

"Great guess, Woody, but I'm deferring my campaign till next year. My rice bowl is kind of full right now. Lunch will cost you a discussion of Chinese history and politics."

"So this will be a two-week lunch?"

"How about a condensed version for the attention-span deficient?"

"You got it. I'm going to prepare by checking what the most expensive meal is at the Ath."

It was always a pleasure to joke around with Woody, but I knew that once we got down to it he would be clear and efficient in sharing his expertise.

Woody's PhD was in Chinese history. It was his second love and was closely related to his first love, his wife Hua (Wanda to us). He had met her during his second stay in China, and had been taken in by her idealism and intelligence, though they disagreed on almost everything. She felt that the government was losing the spirit of Mao Zedong. She raised some hackles and found herself exiled to rural confinement where she had limited ability to make trouble. She pointed out that Xi Jinping had also been exiled, so she treated her clash with the government as an honor. She came back to the US with Woody and became a naturalized US citizen a decade later.

The Chinese took a hands-off attitude toward Woody. For one thing he was a US citizen (unnaturalized, Woody would like to say). For another, Woody was careful not to take sides or step on toes. Most of all, the Chinese respected Woody's knowledge of all things Chinese, and of his ability to speak their language. At home he and Hua spoke Mandarin and in mid-life he was beyond fluent; he was eloquent. After 70, however, he began to lose his hearing and the sibilant-heavy sounds of Mandarin faded out for him. That loss of hearing was one of the reasons that Woody regretfully gave up teaching at age 81 and ascended to Professor Emeritus.

I got to the Ath early to secure a good, quiet table in a remote corner. Woody arrived early also but had trouble making it through the tables of long-time colleagues. He was unbent at 84, but the aging process would not be denied. Woody had been taller than I when I was a grad student, though not by much. Now it was easy to see that he was shorter. I put off the depression about yet another horror of the aging process. At the moment I was too busy for aging.

Along with his upright posture, and regal white hair, was Woody's unaged baritone. He could still youthfully transmit, though receive only with great difficulty.

Woody greeted me and sat down. The waiter hurried over since he was a student born in China. For the Chinese at Tech Woody was a rock star. Woody made a few remarks in Mandarin to which the waiter responded with nods and smiles; he was aware of Woody's hearing.

"Solly, I'm going to keep to myself how great it is to get together with you, so that we can get down to something that must be serious. Spill it."

I spoke as clearly as I could, facing him so that he could supplement his hearing aids with some lip reading.

"First I'll have to be ever so slightly rude and ask that what is said in the Ath stays in the Ath."

"Oh my. This really must be serious. My lips are zipped. I hope that you will repay me by telling me about this what you can, when you can."

"It's a deal. This is all related to Fang Lou. She was in Blacker, and still has some ties to the House. I know that you've acted as an advisor to the administration on her admission. I've been alerted to the involvement of the US State Department with her disappearance. Could you give me some background on her father, Bertrand Lou, and anything else that might be useful background to her disappearance."

"Here we go: The roots of it reached back to US-Chinese relations early in the 20th century, when China saw the US as a potential protector, but things changed, and changed again and changed yet again. And so forth. The really relevant part started around the death of Mao Zedong, and the rise of Deng Xiaoping. In the early 80's, Deng gradually rose to control China. He moved China away from government and Maoist economy based on revolutionary ideals, to a pragmatism with increasing elements of a market economy.

"With the relaxation of the Mao era constraints, and with the Chinese work ethic, the economy flourished in an economic miracle. But there were problems. For one thing, miracles have a limited duration. Opponents of the Deng modernization waited for the miracles to fade. They complained China was abandoning revolutionary idealism. There was also the business of corruption, a Chinese art form.

"The loss of revolutionary spirit and the escalation of corruption gave rise to new threads in the Chinese leadership and led, eventually, to the ascent of Xi Jinping, and yet another change in directions. The changes required that Xi have greater control than Deng, or his successors Jiang and Hu. Xi's philosophy seemed to include the belief China needed an autocrat, not a lively exchange of ideas and programs. To that end, Xi started taking steps toward broad and complete control.

"Xi knew his approach would work only if he had strong popular support. In addition to the usual manipulation of state run propaganda, Xi pushed two principles. One was the traditional tool of populists, playing on national, cultural and ethnic pride. This was an easy goal in China. Still imbued in the national spirit was the contrast between the achievements of early Chinese culture, the science, art and philosophy, and the later status of China in the world.

"Particularly stinging was the century of humiliation, starting in the middle of the nineteenth century. It was the basis of what historians call the never again view of the world. Xi's promise to have China return to previous glory was easy to sell but a challenge to deliver.

"Xi also had to solve the previously unsolvable problem of corruption. Deng accepted it as a cost of doing business. But like most everything else, corruption changed with Deng's modernization, the loosening of regulation and oversight led to an explosion in corruption, with more sophisticated cadre corruption, or cronyism, than the time-honored bribes and embezzlement of Chinese business.

"The new corruption involved much higher stakes than traditional practices, and a Chinese don with sufficient ambition, sufficient connections, and insufficient morality, could become obscenely wealthy, though in constant mortal danger from those who saw stealing from a don as easier than stealing from the government.

"Bertrand Lou was one of the earliest and wealthiest of the new dons. He constructed a home that was a fortress protected by an army. It was not paranoia. In addition to would-be thieves of his wealth, there were complex political threads woven into his life. In particular, he had well-known connections to a political faction opposed to Xi's anti-corruption campaign. Lou's gang, in fact, generally opposed an autocrat who could afford not to woo the new Chinese ultrarich.

"Lou was careful to cultivate political allies also on the pro-Xi side. This meant big payments and gifts to some of the strongest opponents of corruption. But such hypocritical both-sides connections are an old story in China. And, of course, not unknown in our own country.

"These complicated and entangled facts made it clear why the US State Department was interested in Bertrand Lou and, by a natural extension, in Fang Lou.

"Despite his fortress, his army, and his connections, Lou knew there was no such thing as absolute safety, and he was fixated on the safety of his daughter Fang. He gave her a name that meant (more or less) pleasant, in the hope of letting his rivals know she would not be a threat to any of their criminal plans. Indeed, he did not *want* her to be involved in the same kind of life he had, since he could be proud of her conquering other worlds. She was academically brilliant, and he wanted to bask in her reflected glory. She had been at the top in most subjects in school, learned languages easily, came in high in math competitions, and was one of the top Go players in the country. All this was known to the world since it was known to the internet."

As I heard about Fang and Bertrand Lou I thought, as I often did, about the many forms of love between a parent and a child. Was Bertrand Lou's love of Fang an extension of narcissism? Was any parental love a form of narcissism, although not always in the form of indirect showing off?

"Bertrand Luo did the obvious; he had her apply to MIT, Harvard, Stanford and Caltech. She had enjoyed a family trip to Santa Monica three years earlier, and had visions of the southern California lifestyle. She wanted Caltech. Being less than 100% certain of the honesty of the American system, Bertrand Lou thought it wouldn't hurt to slip some money across the Pacific, and for the past few months the days have been disturbed by the concentration-shattering construction sounds of the *Genji and Bertrand Luo Center for Geophysics*. I am sometimes grateful for my bad hearing.

"The donation for the building was delicate so I was brought in as an advisor to the negotiations. I found Bertrand Lou to be impressive. Unemotional, to the point, reasonable, and on top of all details."

"Woody, can you tell me what Lou's attitude was.. what his feelings were for his daughter?"

"No. Bertrand Lou kept his cards close to his chest. Sorry for the cliché. Like any good businessman he wanted others to know as little as possible about what he was thinking."

"Fang's disappearance, of course, was of great concern to Bertrand Lou, who worried what one of his enemies might have done. Was it primarily fatherly love, or primarily politics/business? I can't say. But either way it was a great worry to the Caltech administration, which would have been very concerned even without the Lou building.

"Your turn Solly. Can you answer a question I've had in the back of my mind for more than a year: How did Fang choose Blacker in House rotation?"

"Great question Woody. I discussed this with my flock and think I have the story more or less straight. Fang was not an obvious fit to Blacker, a house with a diffuse character. It was a live and let-live House in which different personalities interacted well, or comfortably ignored each other, despite differences. Not everyone was easy going; there were a few aggressive characters, but there was no one like Fang. Somehow, she appreciated this. Perhaps it was enjoyable not to be competing every moment, especially on her home turf. She showed this appreciation by trimming her behavior to fit Blacker; the old Procrustean approach. Anyway – though it would have been hard to predict – she was well liked in the House, an interesting new individual. Different, as are all Moles.

"A new Blacker name for her had to be created. But after her first few days, Zonker and his MolNomCom group became familiar with Fang's aggressive, though intriguing, personality. Zonker started the discussion with 'Our work has been done by her parents. She will be known as Fang.' It was approved unanimously, and Fang, known only as Fang, settled in as a Mole, until the spring of 2018."

It would have been interesting and educational to sit there with Woody for the rest of the day, but teaching called, and I had already learned a great deal.

It was clear to me why the goddamn State Department was also concerned. Although the precise connection was open to several interpretations, one dominated: If harm were to befall Fang, Bertrand Lou might use his influence with the Xi administration to argue for a more untrusting relationship with the US.

Chapter 33

DARRYL DESCRIBES FANG; TUESDAY, NOVEMBER 20, 2018

Back in the RA suite I saw the electronic bug on my bed, and put it away in my closet. You can never tell when you'll need one, right? I made a mental note to ask Smitty for a tutorial on how to pick up its signal.

As I waited for what would come next, it turned out to be a call from Mia. We hadn't communicated since the awkward good-bye at the motel. The call was more awkwardness. We exchanged questions about any aftermath of our Monday night. We both thought there wasn't any, then didn't know what to say. I wanted to say how much I wanted to be with her this very moment. I wanted to ask about us sneaking away to be together late in the evening. I wanted to ask her about sneaking off to Boalsburg, PA. But all I said was an awkward good-bye for the second time that day. The awkwardness was reciprocated. I wish there were something like a sigh but stronger.

I wondered if she felt as strange and confused as I did about Monday night. When I tried to think about it, thoughts of the FBI kept getting in the way. My head just couldn't parallel process. When I managed to focus on Mia I got a sort of out of focus picture of two confused not-so-young-sters in a dating phase, with secrecy and possible danger adding to the ro-mantic flavor. If we went past this, should I apply the Caroline test? The Steve test?

I wondered why I was so fascinated with her, and wouldn't allow myself to think it was her beauty. I just wasn't that superficial. Really. I wasn't.

I toyed with the idea of talking to Clarence about it. Strange how quickly I had come to trust him. But the Mia thing would have to wait. The FBI thing wouldn't wait.

On Tuesday afternoon, I had tutorials with students doing writing projects as part of their degree requirement. It was one of the many times I was grateful for the distraction of teaching. Performing in front of a class pushed everything off my mental stage. Maybe it's the ego stepping onto that stage to direct the action? Do actors forget whatever slings and arrows lie waiting off stage? I wondered what Clarence, the (sort of) actor, would say about this. And then wondered again why Clarence had become my therapist, my rabbi.

The tutorial wouldn't have the distractive power of strutting and fretting in a lecture, but 'tis enough, 'twill serve, I said to impress myself. I could try to compartmentalize, like Smitty and her athletic aggression. I would put Mia in a compartment, and Fang and the FBI in another. The compartments were adjoining. I didn't know where to put Gilles. Maybe in a wood chipper? For now I just put him out of the picture.

My labor of Moles was cut by about a third. Thursday, and Friday would be the Thanksgiving break. This made Wednesday a sort of lame duck teaching day. Lots of students didn't see a reason to stay around for it.

Some instructors would give last prefinal exams during the weeks after the break, but were almost never cruel enough to schedule them during the first few days back. Worries about student mental health, or simple kindness, dictated the Thanksgiving break should be a break.

I thought getting off campus might help, so hiked over to Lake Avenue. My mind didn't accompany me. I walked an aimless block or so, then aimed back at Blacker. I forgot that I had already eaten lunch and yielded to the seduction of a vending machine. I was reminded to unwrap its droppings by the taste of cellophane.

I had about an hour or so after the tutorials and before dinner. I needed to prepare for my strutting and fretting on lame-duck Wednesday, but the flesh was weak. I was grateful for the looming low-key day, with no looming high-key crises. (A Mia decision was slouching toward the horizon, but not yet looming.) I thought I might look into some more Chinese politics and history to get a better feeling for Fang's father and what it means for Fang. But another thought came knocking; the knock was neither gentle nor aggressive. "Darryl?" I said to myself then to the door.

It was indeed, and he was showing an emotion very much unlike Darryl. That is, he was showing emotion.

"Dr. Sokolsky, I think I need to talk to someone."

This wasn't going to be good.

"Of course, Darryl. Let me know how I can help."

"I'm not sure you can. In fact, I'm not even sure I should be taking this problem to you."

He needed a little push. I pushed.

"Be sure, Darryl. You did the right thing coming to me. So let's hear how bad it is."

Note: I carefully avoided something inane like "It can't be that bad." For one thing, I was worried it was that bad. Also, Darryl would not suffer inanity gladly. I wanted Darryl to know that he was right to come to me.

"OK. It's not going to make sense unless I tell you the whole story. Maybe even if I do. It started last year. You know Fang Lou quit school during spring semester. There are some weird things that led to it.

"Fang and I were friends. Not the right word, but there's no right word. We were both top students. I know I'm not supposed to boast, but modesty can be an obstacle to telling the story. So, OK. We were the smartest. Almost always at the top of whatever class. Freshman year there are no grades, but everyone knew we were at the top. In fact, for this year, Fang and I were going to avoid taking the same courses. We wouldn't be doing this behind each other's back. It was one of the ways we got along well. She was really smart, but she and I weren't clones. I was strong with abstraction, details, and computer codes. She had incredibly broad knowledge of things, and she was more insightful and creative than I. She would come up with incredible new ideas synthesizing what she knew. And her ideas were ...*adventurous*. She was adventurous with ideas. I think that's what got her in trouble.

"I said friends wasn't the right word. But maybe now you get what it was like."

I didn't. And I needed to.

"Would you say you were like partners? You worked together effectively but didn't share affection?"

"No. There was some affection, but it can be hard to distinguish affection from a sort of respect, from appreciation of how the other is special. That's the best I can do: appreciation, also maybe respect."

I was beginning to get it. Maybe. But we needed to get down to the important thing, the reason Darryl was here. Trying to describe his relationship with Fang seemed to calm him. I asked the crucial question.

"Might she have confided in you anything she wouldn't confide in anyone else?"

He knew what I was really asking and took over control of the narrative again.

"Yes, but you're interrupting … sorry, that was rude … I guess. We'll get to that, but it's probably best if you let me tell this in the order that makes the most sense to me."

"Yes, certainly. Sorry. Please continue."

"OK. Dr. Sokolsky, I understand you are interested in why Fang disappeared last spring. Everyone is. The story is bizarre and you would really have to know Fang for it … for the story to be credible.

"I don't want to dwell on a psych analysis of Fang, but I think she had a powerful urge to impress her father. It's more complex than that. Very complex. She was desperate to impress him, but she also wanted to outdo him. It was like a mixture of love and competition. An example: her hair. She dyed it. It was purple. Kind of disappointing because it was a short-term fashion among Chinese students and Fang usually ignored fashion. She may have followed it this time because she thought it might irritate her father. She was right. He saw it as a rebellion against her Chinese background. That was nonsense; she was very proud of her background. Her father didn't know that. In fact, she felt he didn't know much about her at all. They didn't have good communication, like my parents and me."

Darryl, the little snit, was chiding me for my Venice Beach interrogation.

"The hair was no biggie. It annoyed her father but didn't impress him. She wanted a biggie. She wanted to do something spectacular. This is where her creativity and adventurousness came in. What didn't come in was any sense of caution. For her it never came in."

He was editorializing, but I didn't want to interrupt and didn't have to. Besides, this editorializing was telling me a lot about Darryl. He seemed to be explaining all this to himself, as much as to me. He got back on the main path with no nudging.

"Pretty much all last year she was thinking about the future and how she could use her abilities to become rich and powerful. She was a believer – this is sort of a theme in Chinese philosophy – in taking advantage of being in the right place at the right time. She thought she was, and it was her chance to show her father.

"Here's how she would do it. She saw Los Angeles was becoming unlivable. It was a city built for cars, not people. It had been the future but that future was now the past. It's now dystopian and people aren't facing it. People are spending almost as much time in their cars as at their work. It keeps getting worse and worse. Neighborhoods are far apart; buses are too slow. Rail on dedicated lines maybe. The answer had always been cars, but it was becoming more and more obvious they couldn't be the answer. She saw this, and she thought she was in the right place at the right time.

"She said real lessons could be learned from the map. Take a look at the map of the Los Angeles County light rail and subways. There's a handful of stations. But it's not only the small number of stations. It's the distance covered!"

To my surprise Darryl seemed invested in some idea, Fang's idea. He might even have been passionate about it. I tried to be patient. Darryl continued the lecture, or maybe the sermon.

"The distance is roughly 35 miles from the SoCal Rail station in North Hollywood to the Long Beach station. A huge distance with very few stations along the way. Think about it: The equivalent distances in the DC system is around 12 miles, and in the Boston area around 15 miles. With many more stops, remember. And this is not surprising. The population density of Los Angeles County is around 2,000 per square mile. I forget the exact number."

I think it was a clumsy attempt at modesty. I was told he had an astonishing memory, especially for numbers. He was about to give a few numbers whose exact values hadn't escaped him.

"By comparison the population of the greater Boston area is around 14,000 per square mile, and for DC is around 12,000 per square mile. Do you see what these numbers point to?"

I had become a student questioned by the teacher, and hoped I didn't disappoint.

"Yes, rapid transit can't work in LA."

He went back to lecture/sermon mode.

177

"It doesn't because distances are large, so trains have to be fast. But if there were many stops, they couldn't be fast. And if there are few stops, most people would live too far from a station, and rail transport would become a problem that generated another problem. How to get to and from stations. Did they drive 10 miles? Did they then have to find parking? What did they do at the destination end? This is what Fang called the local transportation roadblock, the LTR, which seems to be the end of the rail transportation dream."

"Got it. Los Angeles needs rapid transit but it is fatally unsuited to it. And Los Angeles was not going away. I paused, left the student persona and added, "How does Fang figure into this?"

"Fang thought she had a vision of the way things were out of equilibrium, off kilter. From her knowledge of the sciences, she deeply believed, things would always move back to equilibrium. The pendulum would always seek the middle. Her visions were always interesting, usually unique, and sometimes valid."

That was a general comment that added no insights. I knew it was just a prologue, and a long explanation was coming up. I had a feeling that Darryl himself was fascinated by Fang's ideas, that he was, in some sense, *proud* of her. Their relationship really was hard to describe.

He was a good explainer, but I wished I had another cup of coffee and maybe some way to put my feet up as the explanation began.

CHAPTER 34
FANG'S PLAN; TUESDAY, NOVEMBER 20, 2018

"Fang's vision was based on two principles. The less important one was the American obsession with home ownership. She saw this was a complicated mixture of economics and psychology. People believed it was the way to build family wealth. There's some misleading truth there. Americans overbuy the idea and overbuy houses. They go into debt as deeply as they can. The mortgage leaves the average family with none to waste on nonessential things and activities. The monthly mortgage payment is a forced savings plan, pushed by the threat of losing the home.

"It's also pushed by the government's tax structure. The government gives tax deductions for mortgage payments since everyone knows that home owners are better citizens. Makes sense, right? The homeowner's financial welfare is based on the welfare of the community. No politician would dare question the stability that comes from the 68% rate of home ownership in the US. No one would dare point to the 50% rate in Germany and trending downward, or the 43% rate in Switzerland. These seem to be pretty stable countries, but who knows.

"The second principle is – sorry Dr. Sokolsky– the romance of the car. This country, especially the west, has never overcome the cowboy image, the lone rider. A driver alone in a car has a self-image with a bit of Marlboro man thrown in. (These are Fang's words. She was better at making this case than I could ever be, and with great images like the Marlboro man.) There was also some therapy in the love of a car: During the travel from home, the driver escaped the family; car time was when the driver could be alone, could have the solitude that was a human need. (Fang's words, of course.)

"For some people the car even becomes a kind of love object. They buy small red impractical two-seaters. You probably know some people like that."

He was trying to make light of what he saw as one of my flaws. At least he was trying.

"But things shifted. Really obvious in California. The car became an expensive, frustrating, lengthy experience of sitting in traffic. Driving during rush hour became as nerve-wracking as family life. (Yeah, Fang's words.) People were beginning to get it. Most would happily convert their garages to museums if they could. But they couldn't. It all changed too fast; they still needed the car.

"Fang had a solution. It sounds crazy; *please bear with me*. Her vision was a hierarchical private transportation system integrated with real estate hubs. The hubs would be communities of maybe 25 homes, mostly single-family stand-alone homes. This is regrettable, but in the near term, it would be impossible to break the homeowner addiction. (There could be some multifamily units. Fang was excited at using these to wean families away from stand-alone singles.) The hubs would be served by a private minibus, funded by the hub real estate developers. These inexpensive short-range vehicles would carry a handful of passengers to an aggregation point where minibus passengers would transfer to a larger bus running on a dedicated lane. This would be an express to the nearest rail station. At the destination end there wouldn't be a local transportation problem since the destinations would typically be in areas where stations could be dense.

"There would be several transfers, minibus, big bus, train. Doesn't sound appealing or efficient, right? But everything would be governed by computer scheduling and internet communications. The transfers would be quick and reliable. The first level of this hierarchy has been floating around for a few years as an idea for improving the use of the Long Island Railroad. There's a report you could look up if you're interested.

"Fang thought the Long Island Railroad scheme failed – and anything like it would fail – unless it was really big. It had to involve the whole infrastructure. The real estate, the local minibuses, and the transportation to railroad stations. It couldn't be done one piece at a time. It had to be built as a package. 'No toe in the water,' she would say. 'Gotta be a big dive off the high board.' And that would take huge amounts of capital.

"She ran some computer simulations. (I thought that was ridiculous but I kept my mouth shut. I'm not sure if this makes me her friend. Maybe it shows I wasn't.) From the simulations she figured she would need at least 30 hubs. If each hub had 25 family residences, then, at typical Southern California real estate prices we're in the neighborhood of three quarters of a billion dollars. And that's just for the real estate, without neighborhood infrastructure, the local transportation system and payoffs to politicians. She made a wild guess a billion would be needed. But anyone investing early on could rake in enormous gains, especially as the innovative urban hub system expanded."

Fang's scheme didn't sound real. It sounded like a fantasy, something a handful of college frosh would come up with during an all-night session of being young, imaginative, sharing a pizza, and maybe filling the room with funny smelling smoke. It wouldn't affect their lives except for a short-term lack of sleep, so I said what I thought.

"Darryl, this sounds unrealistic."

"Yeah. I know what you mean. It's why I started by saying you would have to know Fang to believe she followed through on this."

"And following through is why she disappeared last spring?"

"Yes, but please let me keep telling it the way I want, the way it will make the most sense."

I apologized again. He was right. I was too impatient. He did seem to be getting to the point. And what was the point?

"Fang really wanted to go through with this. She knew nothing about real estate, but had confidence she could learn what she needed. Damn it, she was probably right about that. If that was the hurdle, and if I had any money, I would invest in her idea. It's good I don't have money. She hoped she could convince a bank to loan her a starter fund, $10 million or so to support the development of research, hiring a few experts, and developing a professional presentation.

"She went to see appropriate loan officers and vice presidents of a few banks. She could be very persuasive, but not persuasive enough. And she was a teenager, a foreign national, with a purple streak in her hair. She thought about asking her father for a loan, but hated the idea.

"OK, here's where the problems really start. One of the bank officials she spoke to had some connection to a mob. I don't know much about this mob, but I know they're shady, and not offshoots of the classic East Cost/Las Vegas Cosa Nostra. They seemed to be something new, at least partially new and different. I only know what Fang told me, and even she didn't know much. She told me they were very international. Some eastern Europeans, maybe. More likely a mixture. They called themselves the Huns."

Alarms were going off in my head. Those alarms must have had an effect on my face, and Darryl must have seen it. Oh, hell. The brain alarms were so loud he might have heard them.

"Dr. Sokolsky, you look as if you know something about this."

I didn't want to lie to Darryl. And it would be pointless. He could see through me and it would be the end of his trust.

"Yes, Darryl. I might. But I can't say anything about it. Not now. I hope you'll trust me to tell you what I know when I think it is the right time."

He looked at me. He was thinking through what I might know, and – since it was Darryl – he might come to the right general conclusion. That changed the background for our conversation. I think he appreciated my choice not to try to lie. I'm not sure. In any case, he continued.

"The bank official must have reported Fang's case to this mob. A top guy, maybe the leader, arranged to meet Fang at a café off campus. This was early in spring semester, so Fang hadn't yet dropped out. This guy said she could call him Sashi. She was sure it wasn't his real name. He spoke perfect English, with a slight British accent. Fang was fluent in several languages and tried speaking to him in Russian and, of course, Mandarin to get a clue about his background. But he wouldn't take the bait."

Where was this going? Did the Huns fund Fang's fantasy. My left leg was doing the restless leg thing in frustration. It was hard being patient as Darryl continued.

"Sashi told Fang they were interested in Fang's real estate idea, but needed to know more details. Would she be willing to meet with several members of his investment group? He told her it was crucial to keep competitors from getting any hint of this, so the meeting location would have to be secret. In fact, they would have to blindfold Fang during the drive to the meeting location."

I wanted to scream "Didn't she know she should get out of that immediately and tell the cops?" but I waited. I don't think I took a breath for several minutes.

"She went to the meeting. You're getting impatient Dr. Sokolsky, so I'll skip over some details, and get to a kind of bottom line. The place they took her to was a rented house in Culver City. They had blindfolded her but she could just look out a window, or – better – look at her screen. She saw she was in zip code 90043. She saw a steep hill out the back window.

"At the first meeting she thought the plan was definitely a go and she dropped out of school. At the next meeting though, she developed some suspicions. She caught on that the mob was more interested in ransomware hacking than in real estate. She wasn't deterred. The money to be made in her scheme would bring them around. They'd forget about hacking. Meanwhile she'd hold them off by faking some hacking."

I couldn't stay silent.

"Did she? Did she have the skills for the hacking? Even for the faking?"

"For the hacking, no, not at all. She was good at faking anything, so who knows."

The bell rang for dinner and Darryl looked anxious.

"Dr. Sokolsky, I didn't get to what I wanted to say, the reason I came to see you."

I realized it was mostly my fault; I hadn't really given him the chance. But another part of it was his own eagerness to tell Fang's story. His attitude towards her was unusual. He wasn't a teenage boy fascinated by a beautiful young woman. For a brief moment, I thought about my attitude towards Mia, and wondered what someone would think if I tried to talk about her. Someone other than Clarence.

"Darryl, I apologize. This is my fault. What did I keep you from saying?"

"I can explain more later, but I really want to say something about it now.

"It finally hit Fang that she was playing a dangerous game, and she wanted some kind of protection. I was the protection. She sent me an email every day. The bad guys were too tech-illiterate to monitor what she was doing.

"She told me if the emails stopped I should immediately go to the police, and tell them everything I know. This way she could threaten them with exposure if things got out of hand. She swore she would not reveal my name to them."

A strange look came over Darryl, the look of wrestling with emotions, the look people get when they might break down. Because it was Darryl, I didn't expect this. But people are always surprising. He stopped speaking as he tried to get control. I waited while, then asked, "So, Darryl, what changed? Why did you come to see me?"

"The messages stopped yesterday."

We both sat silently as Darryl completed getting under control. He then stood and left the RA suite. I followed, and we went to dinner.

CHAPTER 35

LOVE IN THE FOG; TUESDAY, NOVEMBER 20, 2018

Ordinarily Darryl wouldn't have been distracted from his own thoughts at dinner, since he didn't engage in discussions. Tonight was an exception. Darryl was distracted, and in a bad way.

The buzz at dinner was about an FBI agent coming to the RA suite. A Mole had seen a charmless car, with a federal license plate, parked in the lot near Blacker. Finding the FBI association with the license number was easy. The Blacker grapevine then spread the word, and Luk was noticed in the corridors. A little light duty Molar hacking revealed that Xi Luk was an FBI scientist who had been a Caltech grad student at the same time I was.

A leading theory was that the FBI scientist was an old buddy of their RA, and the buddy was just dropping by to shoot the breeze. But there were theories trailing not too far behind it, theories involving hacking and Darryl. Fang played a co-star role in the theories, with her disappearance providing many possibilities. It's not surprising that none of my Moles bothered to ask me why Luk was visiting. That wasn't the way the game was played.

Though Darryl was not contributing to the discussions, he was attentive and even visibly upset. His table buddies were too sensitive to try to draw him into the discussions.

Darryl rarely missed a trick, so I was sure that he remembered my expression when he started talking about the Huns. And I was sure he combined that with what he heard about Luk's visit, and came to a conclusion within a spitting distance of dead bang on.

It was a relief to get to the end of dinner, but our patience was stretched by an after-dinner presentation of a student petition. The speaker wanted signatures in a campaign to stop the noise of campus construction work; it was making concentration impossible.

Finally, we could leave. When Darryl got up I headed him off and told him we needed to talk more; we needed to talk about hacking. Soon. In the morning. I took his silence as assent. He headed for the stairs and corners and I headed for the phone.

"Luk, it's me. Oh, of course you can see that on your phone. Listen, Darryl knows where Fang is being held. It's in a rented house at the bottom of a steep hill in Culver City. I've got the zip code."

"Thanks Solly. We know about it, zip 90043, at the east edge of a steep hill, right? We've got the address."

I was deflated at not knowing something helpful. It was like spreading gossip only to find out everyone already knows it.

Luk wanted to be sure that I continued to spread gossip, always to report any information, even if I think the FBI already had it. I went on to give him a nutshell version of everything that Darryl had told me, especially about the email safety valve. That was interesting news to him. He thanked me and hung up to relay that tidbit to his team.

I turned to the bed, but my phone objected. The screen said Mia, and I said nothing. I wanted to speak to her as much as I didn't want to speak to her. Both wants were intense. I was an exemplar of decidophobia. I didn't make up the neologism, a Princeton philosopher did. I was pretty sure that it would never have made the big time had the philosopher been at Springfield Community College. It's how this stuff works. Anyway, decidophobia isn't yet in the *DSM*, but give it time; I think the *Zeitgeist* and internet are ripe for it to catch on. That's how this other stuff works.

My finger oscillated over the red and green choices and went for the green.

"Solly, I couldn't stop thinking about you."

"There is mental help available through Student Wellness Services."

"Can we be serious?"

"Sorry. I'm acting like a middle schooler at a junior prom."

"I want to see you. I'll keep my words at middle school level and try not to frighten you."

"I'm not frightened, but when?"

"Right now."

"It's almost midnight…" It was 9:50 pm, but it had been a long day.

"Yes, how romantic. Let me pretend to be rational and see whether I can persuade you. First, it's a dark night. It's foggy, almost as if a cloud has descended on us. We'll be invisible if we choose the right meeting place."

"You've already chosen haven't you?"

"The southwest corner of the athletic field. By the batting cage. That way we'll have a very specific meeting point instead of bumbling around in the dark mist."

"Clever girl."

"Engineer. See you in 10 minutes… Oh, Solly. We might be crossing California Boulevard at the same time. So you cross at Hill; I'll cross at Wilson."

"Clever girl."

"Engineer."

The RA suite was convenient for sneaking out, and I snuck out, tiptoeing to the walkway en route to… Damn. Was I supposed to cross at Hill or Wilson? I shrugged and crossed in the middle. It was almost midnight and traffic was light. I didn't see Mia at Hill. In the heavy mist I couldn't make out the corner at Wilson.

I appreciated the cleverness of my civil engineer heart throb when I realized that it would be impossible to find another person on the athletic field, but it wasn't a challenge to find the batting cage. It was at a corner of the field so I walked west along the south edge of the field until I saw what must be the batting cage, near the western edge. Mia was waiting.

I approached close enough for us to see each other, and we had an echo of our awkwardness. We stood looking at each other, not sure what to do, for maybe five seconds before embracing. Sic transit awkwardness.

It really was romantic, maybe because it put us in the final scene of *Casablanca*. Humphrey Bogart watches the love of his life, Ingrid Bergman, fly off forever in the darkness of misty black and white. OK, the comparison wasn't perfect.

Mia had come prepared, a quilt, a bottle of wine, and two wine glasses. (There would be wine in them, so they were wine glasses.) She proudly announced, "These are for our picnic. And you know what's most important about our picnic?"

"No ants?"

"No, my hopeless romantic. It's that we're together."

"That too."

She spread out the quilt on home plate, gave me a glass, and produced a chunk of Swiss cheese. The wine/cheese symbolism wasn't lost on me.

"So, you're the new RA in Page."

She giggled. I kissed her. We spilled some wine, then turned to pretend to look at the stars, appreciating each other's sense of the absurd.

"Mia, Mia, Mia. What are we going to do with our … Hmm. In fact what are we going to call our…."

"Relationship?"

"Yuk. Terrible word, something you'd hear from a counselor whose therapy consisted of 'I hear what you're saying.'"

"OK. How about a word from physics. We have an interaction."

"What would a civil engineer call our whatever?"

"It's a configuration."

"It'll do for now. OK, Mia. What are we going to do about our configuration?"

"Why do we have to do anything?"

"We can't keep this secret. Hell, the kids know we're configured. That's OK as far as it goes, but we can't keep meeting. It violates… something."

"OK. Alternatives: A) We stop meeting. All in favor? I don't see any hands. Of course I can't see anything.

"B) We convince Louis that we should be an RA Couple. Grandma Solly, your eyes are so wide!

"C) We run off, abandon engineering and senior lecturing, and open a tea shop."

"Can we make it a bike repair shop?"

"Oh, Solly, we're bickering already. It's just not going to work out."

"Serious, Mia. Remember serious. We were going to be serious. Please forgive me. I'm going to be depressingly serious. Would it work? Would we be good together? We love amusing each other. Our senses of humor resonate. I love driving you to giggles. Maybe that's the ideal match for dating. Maybe it isn't the ideal match for lives together."

"What is ideal Solly? What really matters if not the way we make life fun for each other?"

"Maybe what's important is being comfortable together."

Yes. That's right. I was thinking of the Steve test.

"I think that we *would* be comfortable together. Maybe we need to test being together. Maybe next summer."

"Yes, maybe. Interesting. For now, let's do the serious thing and procrastinate. There's lots of stuff going on now, dangerous stuff, FBI stuff…"

"You mean about Fang Lou."

"I can't talk about it, even to you, even if everyone knows about it. But now is an impossible time to weigh tea sales vs bike repair. The current craziness will end soon. For now, let's just enjoy what we have. OK?"

"OK Solly. I hope you enjoy this." Mia wrapped the quilt around us and wriggled out of enough of her clothes for us to enjoy what we had.

CHAPTER 36

FANG AND THE HUNS; WEDNESDAY, NOVEMBER 20, 2018

I hoped to catch Darryl at breakfast on Wednesday. When that hope was dashed, I went up the stairs and around corners to knock on his door, and bade him continue yesterday's lesson.

"Darryl, I don't see any reason to keep this confidential. You suspect that the FBI visit involved Fang and the mobsters. You're right. Now it's your turn to tell me more. How was Fang fooling them? What do you know about it going bad?"

"Yeah, I know some of it. Of course, damn it, she should have run away as soon as she got a sense of them, but no. Fang always thought she was smart enough to get away with anything, and she kept faking it. She went along with their ransomware project and – incredibly – kept believing she might get the mob to fund her real-estate start-up.

"She spent a day learning html and css, the markup language used for websites. She took the Caltech login page and copied it (the innards are publicly accessible). What she changed was the login information. In her version it got emailed to her private email account. She rented a domain and the website name www.caltek.net. She showed it to Sashi. He was impressed, but no fool. This was beyond him, and he knew it. He was skeptical, but kept up his side of the two-way scam; he continued to tell Fang they were arranging investments for her real estate start-up."

"Sorry to interrupt again. Darryl, this was in the house she had been taken to in that early meeting, the one they took her to blindfolded? The Culver

City house? You said she had some doubts by the second meeting. When did it really go bad?"

"About a month ago. Maybe six weeks. The mobsters were making a big show of conferring with her about plans for the real estate idea. They did their best. They brought in fake experts to discuss housing construction, water lines, and so forth. They actually had her uncertain. Not easy to do.

"For her part, she was making a good show of bitching about how difficult it was to find the right section of the Monrovia public utilities file structure. She would point to a screen full of meaningless code and tables and mention that she was almost stumped and thinking of trying another municipality."

"And...?"

"It went along that way for quite a while. I said it started going bad about a month ago, but maybe it was gradual, so it's hard to pin down just when it started. Anyway, not too long ago it started to wear thin. She could tell that they were getting suspicious, and she decided to sneak away when there was an opportunity. That's the last email I got from her. It was yesterday. When there was no message from her by this afternoon, I got very worried."

"And I am also. Do I have your permission to share what you told me with the FBI?"

"Yes. Absolutely. Thank you."

"Maybe I can understand this better if you explain something to me. Toobee says you and Fang are the king and queen of hacking. Why can't the queen do the hacking that the mob wants. I don't get it?"

Darryl started to explain. I thought this might be like his description of Fang's urban transportation fantasy and I was glad I had the foresight to grab a cup of coffee, just in case.

"Fang could use computers. Of course. Techies all have to use computer programming for courses, and Fang could write programs in Python. She was competent. Of course. But there are different attitudes about computers.

"For some Techies, I guess I should say some people, computers are tools. Great for communication. Also, for quick math using high level easy software like *Maple, Matlab, Mathematica. Python* is the next step up the hill. It involves actual programming, but the learning curve is almost level. Then there are steeper hills, no-holds barred programming like C++. But even then, the computer is just a tool. For Fang, the computer was a tool.

"So, Darryl, Fang used computers, but was not, let me say, facile with hacking?"

"Again, no. God, no. Not the way you mean it. She was like the average Techie with that stuff. I think she could have been a great hacker, because she was so damn smart, but she wasn't interested."

"So how was she the queen of hacking? I'm still confused."

"Yeah. I can see how it's confusing. Can we step back to the question: How do you break into a system?"

"Darryl, step back. Step back as far as you want. I've always wondered about that. How *do* you break in?"

"OK. The answer will surprise you. Breaking into a computer system usually takes no skill. People are sloppy with their passwords. They use birthdays or ABC123, or they have the password on a slip of paper taped to the bottom of their desk. The careful ones are proud they have long passwords with special characters, and they never share their password. But these same people use home Wi-Fi with the default WEP security!"

"WEP?"

"Oh. Sorry. That's the weakest encryption for Wi-Fi. Ironically, it stands for wired equivalent protection, or wired equivalent something, which is ridiculous! How can a broadcast signal be as safe as a signal on a wire? Anyway, WEP is easy to hack. You don't need to be an expert. You can get the software, free I'm pretty sure, to intercept and decipher a WEP-protected signal.

"There's much better encryption, WPA2, that's been available for a long time. More than a decade, I think. And WPA3 is coming soon. Anyone who can operate a cell phone can switch home Wi-Fi to WPA2. Most don't bother."

There was exasperation and disdain in his voice. I was going to tell him I had used the default WEP in my Duarte apartment, but I didn't want to interrupt. He continued.

"Let me tell you about Kevin Mitnick. He's a legend, the most famous hacker ever. He claims two principles of hacking. The first is a kind of hacking Hippocratic oath: Do no damage. The second principle is what explains queen Fang: It's easier to hack people than to hack computers. Mitnick claims to have broken into carefully protected systems without using any of his skills with software or electronics. You would like him."

"Why would I like the world's foremost hacker?"

"Dr. Sokolsky, you have a sense of humor. Many of Mitnik's escapades were really funny, especially early on when he was a teenager using phone phreaking and interfering with the mike/speaker ordering at drive-ins."

I decided to leave phone phreaking unchallenged so we could get to Fang's role.

"How did Mitnick's people-hacking work? Can you give me an example?"

"Mitnick has written a book, a funny book, with lots of examples he claims are real. Maybe they are. But he has a loose relationship with the truth, so maybe you shouldn't believe every detail. Let me make up something to show what people hacking means.

"You want to get some information about, say, a checking account for J. Random Victim, so you can take out all his money. You know where J.R. works, so you call human resources at the company, call it Spamatics, and tell them you are doing a background check on him for whatever, maybe a mortgage application. You chat with the HR drone and charm the drone. You find out lots of info about J.R. You find out lots of info about the HR drone. Next you call J.R.'s bank. You *don't* ask for any very sensitive info; it's too early; that would set off alarms. You identify yourself as the HR drone at Spamatics, and say you want to confirm J.R.'s been paying his bills. You come away with his bank account number, and maybe his balance. You call his mobile phone provider and tell them you are J.R.; you just got a new mobile phone, and want to change the number on file. And so on and on. Eventually, you'll connect to someone gullible. Eventually you'll have some information that you shouldn't have. The next day you call the bank, using a different voice, just in case. You tell them you need to change your card pin; you're afraid your teenager has learned it. And so on and on. It's kind of a game of hop, step and jump, but over people.

"The whole game has to be played by ear. It takes someone with, let me call it agile intelligence, to change the game plan quickly. It takes someone with charm. It takes Fang."

"Thank you Darryl. I understand. Sort of."

CHAPTER 37

KING HACKING; WEDNESDAY, NOVEMBER 21, 2018

Wednesday, the lame-duck day, started way before I was ready for it. Mia called at 6:30 am. (Is there a Polish word for sleep?) She said that we should have breakfast together. She clarified: off campus. I had to meet Darryl in the morning, but she accepted a mid-morning coffee invitation. I told her I'd call, then pick her up on Wilson, right off California, as soon as I could get away. I was going to introduce her to Kallie's.

We were getting pretty sloppy about keeping the secret of our configuration-interaction. The top was up in Ta Mia, but I didn't think we were fooling anyone. The Page/Blacker snoop network would know of our sin.

I was wondering how our goth/cosplay/perky-pouty waitress would interpret my substitution of Mia for Clarence. I'd have to keep wondering. Our waitress was an efficient 50-something, professional enough to see my desperate need for coffee.

She stood there while I drank the first cup and refilled it as soon as I slammed the empty cup down on the Formica.

"Solly, we never really talk about our lives, about what we're doing."

Oh no, no. The traditional 'where is this relationship going' chat. I didn't expect it of Mia. I shouldn't have. It wasn't that at all. She wanted to talk about the technical problem she was researching: finding computational models of granular material. A big problem was something called the angle of repose. When you pile gravel or sand or watermelons what's the maximum steepness before stuff slides. Mia thought that a predictive model would mean that they could use observations of the angle of repose to learn about the stuff in the pile. Pretty interesting if you couldn't actually get to the pile. Say it was on Mars for instance.

She was really into this stuff. It was a side of her I hadn't seen. I should have figured there must be that side, but sometimes I don't figure so well. She went on to describe why standard fluid mechanics didn't apply. I might have learned something, but I had drifted off into a semi-dream state. I could hear her words but was more interested in my vision: Mia and Solly, the faculty couple. Oh my god.

She'd be hired at MIT to do astrogeology and we'd have the two-body problem.

We want to hire body A, what do we do about B, her spouse/partner? He's not faculty level. An auxiliary teaching position? I'd be a drag on her career. An embarrassment. I could see the lettering on the door *The Kulpa Group*. She'd be spending most of her time writing grants, sleeping through panel meetings in DC, while her army of grad students take measurements of sliding sand.

I snapped out of it and smiled to show my appreciation of her research and her excitement.

I had one for the road, making it five cups sloshing inside as I slithered into Ta Mia cautious to avoid steering wheel pressure on the bladder. We made it back to California Boulevard without any vehicular or urological accident. I dropped Mia off in a side street, hoped for the best, and drove back to the bathroom in my RA suite carefully but quickly.

With my standard fluid mechanics problem solved, I turned to my bigger problem.

I was worried about Darryl, so I suspended my principle of let them come to me, and went up the stairs and around the two corners.

When I got to his door I could hear him speaking. Since there was no other voice, clever Solly inferred that Darryl was on the phone. I thought about adding privacy to the principles I was suspending, but didn't have to. The hallway was very quiet and without my ear to the door I heard, "I know, Dad, I know."

I thought back to Darryl's description of his family, and especially his admiration for his unappreciated father. The fact that he was on the phone with his father, along with his (door-filtered) tone, were evidence about family relations. In Venice Beach, when Darryl claimed good family communications, maybe he was not lying to me or to himself. But with family relationships it's best to defer judgment.

I went back to the RA suite. I had not been as stealthy as I thought. Darryl had heard me, or used one of his superpowers to sense me at his door, and it wasn't long before I heard his signature knock on my own door and extended a shouted command to enter.

"You wanted to see me, Dr. Sokolsky?"

"Mostly, just to see how you're doing. Hey, how *are* you doing?"

"I'm more rational than I was yesterday. I was upset. I'm sorry if I worried you."

"Worrying is my job. If I remember your schedule, you don't have any classes this morning. I also don't have any classes. Would you like to give a lecture?"

"A lecture? Would you like to hear about quantum entanglement? I'm probably not the best person to try to explain it."

He had regained his desiccated sense of humor. The phone call with his father must have been therapeutic.

"No, I was thinking of Hacking; Part II. You explained how Fang was the queen of person-to-person deception behind most hacking. Where does the king fit in?"

"Hmmm. Yeah, it's interesting. My skills are the opposite of Fang's. You probably see that my strengths are not in personal interactions and fabricating elaborate lies. And Fang – for lack of interest, I think – didn't have the skills with zeroes and ones. This is why we were a good team."

Again, I noticed Darryl's attitude towards Fang. Was it really just respect for her ability? Did he have a derelict crush on her? Or maybe was it some kind of mixture? But I wanted to understand better how the team worked. He was about to tell me.

"I told you that for some people computers are just a tool. (It pains me to say *just* a tool.) Some people are different. They are fascinated by the way the bits move around, how hardware handles source codes, networks, file architecture, packet flow. The guts of the system. They are sort of the theorists of the computer world. Or the mechanics who want to look under the hood. Or the surgeons. There's really no perfect analogy in the non-computer world.

These are the hackers, and they don't consider 'hack' a four-letter word; they consider it an honorable pursuit. These are the Techies who find it a kick to get into commercial and government accounts and scrounge around. It's curiosity and vanity. They like being able to see the bad programming by highly paid IT people. Toobee in Page is this kind of hacker, and he's pretty damn good."

I interrupted.

"Whoa Darryl, you're most interested in the abstract side of physics and math. Doesn't that put you on the 'just a tool' team?"

He smiled. It was at least a smile-like expression.

"There are some people who play on both teams. Nobel physicist Ken Wilson was active in developing parallel processing, but I think that was to speed finding physics answers. I could probably cite better examples if I thought about it for a while.

"I'm a bit unusual, I guess. I'm really interested in the guts of networks because I see it as an intellectual structure, though it's different from math or physics."

"Darryl, you're an expert hacker? Right?"

"I'm an experienced hacker. I've broken into systems just to enjoy reading the code. I've never done any real damage. Sometimes I'd find a vulnerability in an institution's system. A couple of times I reported those, anonymously, to the institution. Often, they paid no attention! It's hard to get good people in IT. Harder in IT administration."

Administrators: the bêtes noires for Darryl's ilk. No surprise. The admins had power, but little expertise.

"You've got to understand that hacking personal computers and systems is no challenge, so it's no fun. What's interesting is institutions. Banks, phone companies, government sites. That kind of thing. Ethical hackers are attracted by challenges and intellectual curiosity. They want to see the code; they don't want to do damage. That's the first principle of ethical hacking. Steve Wozniak did that kind of hacking. You know who Steve Wozniak is, right?"

I nodded. I actually did know. Really.

"For utility companies, government offices: It's a challenge to get in, but most of the time it's just a variation on the theme, the theme that Fang is so good at. The people-hacking details are different, and they have to be adjusted to the situation. It's hard, always different and needs quick thinking; it's fun for Fang."

"At the risk of repeating myself, Darryl where do *you* come in?"

"Yeah. Getting to it. Once we're inside Fang's fun is over and I start having fun.

I need to figure out the file structures, and networking. That's a completely different kind of thing. It's like listening to a foreign language and trying to figure out what the words mean. It takes perseverance. It doesn't require charm. (He looked at me with a self-deprecating shade of a smile. We both knew what he meant.)

"We don't intend to do any harm, but we do screw up from time to time and cause inconvenience. We've gotten people fired, but they were people who needed to be fired.

"It's particularly interesting when the computer system has been set up by a good system engineer, when there are some original tricks in it. It then becomes a kind a game. In cases like that, when I finally figure it out, I usually leave a little joke message. And in those cases, sort of as a sign of respect, we never do any harm. We will usually just leave an explanation of how we got in, so that they will know about their vulnerabilities."

"I'm beginning to get it. Hacking consists of two pretty distinct steps. Step 1 getting in, step 2 rummaging around. You need Fang because there's no electronic, or digital way to get on the system. It takes human deception."

"More or less, but not completely true. Everything is open to signals these days; sometimes no human side is needed. Of course, institutional systems don't use Wi-Fi that can be broken into, but there are some interesting examples of important systems that are open to radio waves, because they have to be."

"Can you give me a for instance?"

"Yeah. Here's a really good one: hacking into a car. For a long time, cars have been on the internet. Cars need that for navigation, and lots of other things. You can get into a car remotely by using the car's cellular connection. It's not that difficult. Really. So with some effort I can find myself inside a car's computer network.

"And *then* it gets really interesting. Just about everything in a car is now run by electric motors. My guess is that a typical US car has 40 of them."

Darryl saw my doubting expression.

"You're skeptical Dr. Sokolsky? Think about it: door locks, vent actuation, blowers, power windows, seat positioner, windshield wipers, AC compressor, fuel pump, water pump, side mirror adjustments..."

"OK. OK. Enough. I get it."

But Darryl wasn't done.

"Everything is changing. Most things in a car were manual 80 years ago, some hydraulic 50 years ago. Great example: steering. It was originally manual, but the steering wheel had to be turned through too many revolutions. But then, in the middle of the last century, along came power steering, an assist from a hydraulic pump. It worked great, except for wasting energy; the hydraulic pump was always running. Energy efficiency became a big thing a few years back and hydraulic steering was replaced by electric steering. Engineers got the glitches out except for the same problem with every other electric motor in a car. It's hackable.

"It's not easy. Everything in a car is connected to everything. It's a challenge. Also, it's different in different cars. I've got to wander around in the file structure to find something called the controller area network, the set of microcontrollers that actually do stuff. All this stuff interacts more or less intelligently, so the source code is – same word, sorry - a challenge. Which is my way of saying it's really fun. I've messed around with a couple of student cars, but of course I let the students in on it. I've thought about controlling a campus police car, but that wouldn't be right. Right?"

There was no visible smile.

"Have I said 'wow'?"

"Pretty sure you have once or twice. I'm assuming then that it's a 'no' to quantum entanglement."

It was a joke. With Darryl it was hard to be sure.

CHAPTER 38

GRIM DISCOVERY; THANKSGIVING, THURSDAY, NOVEMBER 22, 2018

Thursday morning, Thanksgiving, and the 55th anniversary of the JFK assassination, with its turning of a page in American life. A day when my own page was turning.

The day started too early again: 6:30 am again. But started much worse than the previous day, with a sharp knock on my door. "Not Darryl," I mumbled to myself. This was confirmed by the voice of my master, Louis Horvath, his voice dialed up to wake-the-town level.

"Be in my office in 15 minutes."

It didn't sound like a suggestion. Allowing for the one-minute trip to the Housing Office, I had 14 minutes to get dressed and run possibilities through my head. The list didn't include what hit me when I entered Horvath's office.

"The goddamn State Department called me at 6 am! What do you know about this?"

He pointed to the *Pasadena Star-News* he was holding, with the headline: 'Caltech student found murdered in arroyo.' He threw me the paper. I had time only to read the first paragraph. The victim was identified by the Pasadena PD as a female Asian student who dropped out of school the previous spring. Her name was withheld pending notification of the family.

It had to be Fang.

She was murdered late Wednesday; the police were not divulging any details to the public. They'd been made aware of Fang's disappearance, and the FBI had filled them in about the political/international connections. The importance had been put into a bold font with a call from someone in the White House.

Horvath repeated: "What the hell do you know about this?"

The dogs were not used to this tone and whimpered. Ethos looked anxious to help. Mentis studied the situation.

I might also have whimpered. I thought about how to answer. If I said I knew nothing, I could always back out of it, and later make up some excuse for lying. The other choice, telling Horvath about the FBI, was irrevocable; there would be no going back. I could try and tell a partial truth, some of the story but with evasions. I'm not good at that. I'd trip over my evasions and misdirection. It would be a disaster. I was afraid to go that route. The coward's way out was the truth.

I told the whole story, FBI, Darryl, Fang. In an unused corner of my still uncaffeinated brain I wondered how Horvath picked up goddamn as the honorific for State Department. When did he talk to Luk? When he let him into Blacker on Tuesday?

Horvath listened intently, not blinking, not interrupting. It didn't take a great lip reader to see 'holy shit' silently mouthed when I told him about Fang's real estate scheme. The dogs, experts in reading emotions, were stumped by the Horvath's agitation.

Horvath, overwhelmed, or just resigned, knew he had to make a decision about what to do next. He laid out his detailed plan succinctly.

"We do nothing! Go back to Blacker. Don't do anything. Let's wait to see what we get from the Pasadena PD, the FBI, and the goddamn State Department."

As I rushed to obey he stopped me with, "And let me know of any relevant developments."

"Yes, of course."

I almost reflexively saluted. I quashed the instinct, and was back in Blacker in less than the standard one minute, chanting under my breath 'relevant developments,' as a mantra.

Darryl waited for me at the door of the RA suite. His demeanor was worse than the previous day. He was good at controlling his voice. No quavering. But he didn't try to hide anything.

"Dr. Sokolsky, I'm in real danger."

"Oh shit!" I said or maybe thought. It didn't matter.

He assumed I knew about Fang, but asked to be sure. He was told about it by one of the early risers in Blacker, who saw it on his internet news feed and rushed to wake Darryl.

Darryl in danger was a relevant development, but I needed details before reporting to Horvath.

"Why do you think you are in danger?"

Darryl made the day much worse.

"Don't look, but there are two guys hanging around outside. They look dangerous. That's just my impression, maybe because one of them has a scar on his face. And also, there's a black sedan in our parking lot. It has dark windows. Difficult to see inside."

For a change I acted quickly and decisively.

"Darryl, go back to your room. Don't let anyone in except me. Don't answer your phone unless it's a number you recognize. Go."

He went. And I went. I grabbed the electronic bug from my shelf and went around two corners to wake up Smitty, who was bleary eyed but cheerful.

"Solly, is there a fire?"

"Maybe worse. Can you do me a dangerous favor with no questions?"

Her eyes cleared. This seemed to appeal to her, so I spelled it out.

"In the parking lot there's a dark sedan with tinted windows. Could you do whatever to set this thing up and plant it on the sedan. We're going to want to trace it."

"Will do, but I've got a better bug, all set to go."

"Great! Better is better. But wait, Smitty. There's more. There are two thugs hanging around. They're from the sedan. They could be big-time dangerous. Do you think you could approach the car from the Hill Avenue side and keep from being seen?"

"Wow. Even more interesting. I'll use the steam tunnel, and exit on the east of the parking lot. I'll return the same way and send you a text message as soon as I'm back in Blacker. And don't even bother reminding me: Mum's the word. It's my favorite word."

As I turned to go, she added in a serious tone: "So, this isn't about the Page House RA is it?"

It didn't require an answer.

Back to the RA suite, counting the minutes until the next relevant development. It wasn't a long count. There was a soft knock and the voice of Joy, the sophomore math major.

"Dr. Sokolsky, there are two men in dark suits knocking on the entrance door, asking to be let in. Should I let them in?"

Joy jumped at my "NO!" I apologized for my sharp tone.

"Sorry for scaring you, Joy. Thanks for letting me know. I'll handle it."

I grabbed my phone and hurried around the corner to the entrance. I needed to kill a few minutes until Smitty was safely back.

I waited a minute or so, until there was an insistent knocking. I spoke through a peephole in the door.

"I'm Dr. Sokolsky. I'm in charge of Blacker House. Nonmembers are not allowed entrance without clearance from the Housing Office."

This wasn't true. One of them tried to sound friendly. He had a gravelly voice and probably no practice with friendly. He had an accent I couldn't identify. A little like German but very little.

"We only need few minutes. Speak to one student. Very important. If you not let in now we come back later."

The voice scared me. I wasn't used to his crowd, whatever it was. What scared me most was what Luk told me. These guys hadn't been recruited for their brains. They would not be constrained by rationality; they might do something stupid; I wasn't used to stupidity except my own.

There was no point in debating with lethal gunmen. I assumed they wanted Darryl, and there was no way I was going to let them in. I just needed to buy a little time.

After I responded with about a half minute of silence, there was a pounding on the door as if they were using a battering ram. The door shook and the gravelly spokesperson shouted, "You heard me?"

I kept quiet. They didn't. There was an angry exchange between them. It sounded as if one wanted them to force their way in. I hoped the entrance door was bullet proof. I wanted to cross myself, but having been raised mildly Jewish I wasn't quite sure how. If the door was not bulletproof, then what?

I'd worry about that later. My real worry was these thugs hanging around outside maybe trying to get in when a student walked out. Maybe grabbing a student and trying to bargain their way in. It would be stupid, but these guys qualified.

No text yet from Smitty. A sudden realization made me stop breathing for a moment. Why had I assumed there were only two Huns on campus? What if there was another lurking under some rock? I was an idiot. Why hadn't I heard from Smitty? Maybe I was too impatient. I needed to kill a few more minutes before panicking about Smitty.

I shouted through the door. "Coming back later not a good idea. We are on holiday schedule for the Houses." I didn't know what that was supposed to mean, but they bought it, giving me a few minutes. My phone beeped. I got the text from Smitty. She was safe. I resumed shouting.

"Schedule is not known. Maybe check back at noon." (I was winging it.)

There was another loud argument between the thugs. This one longer than the first. At last, Comrade Gravelly said, "Who we see for to get permission?"

Was he trying to seem reasonable? Was he trying to *be* reasonable?

"Housing Office. Louis Horvath."

As soon as I said it I tried to suck the words back. I had momentary terror at what I might have set in motion, but it subsided. They wouldn't know that the Housing office was only a few feet away. They would probably think that they needed to fill out paperwork. These guys were probably as afraid of paper work as I was of them.

Just to be sure: I moved from the door and grabbed the first Mole I saw; it was a frosh who stayed around to study over the holiday. I looked him in the eyes and said in my most "obey-me!" voice: "Super-important: No one goes out; no one comes in. I'll be back in less than five minutes. I'll explain later."

There were very few students who remained in Blacker, a bit of good luck on a bad-luck day. I ran up to the second floor. From an east facing window I could see the parking lot and watched the two thugs get in the black sedan. I could see them still arguing. Maybe they would call home base for instructions from Hun One, Sashi; maybe one of them would shoot the other; maybe anything. No time for guesses. I called Horvath.

"Louis, there's been a relevant development."

I caught him up on the visitors and pointed out that now, or later, they might try to get permission to enter Blacker. As I spoke, I looked out the window and saw the black car pull out. I told this to Louis.

I didn't want to embarrass him by asking him what he would do. The right thing to do would be to call the Pasadena PD. It was passive, but I figured

Louis was too smart to try to handle this with his own spin. And I would hate to see Mentis or Ethos get hurt.

I was sure Louis would keep me updated, so no need to ask. I hurried to take my next step: talk to Darryl. I took the stairs three at a time to Darryl's second floor single. He answered my knock immediately. He was agitated but in control.

"Darryl, it's a good guess the bad guys know about your relationship with Fang. Yesterday you told me Fang swore she would never reveal you were her safety net."

I was in for a surprise that shifted my feelings about Darryl. For the first time, I saw him break down. He fought for control, but lost the fight. His shoulders were shaking and his voice broke, but he got out the words.

"They must have tortured her."

CHAPTER 39

MIA REDUX; THANKSGIVING, THURSDAY, NOVEMBER 22, 2018

I was probably shaking as much as Darryl when I left his room around 8:30 am. I left because I wanted Darryl to see me calm and controlled, and that's not what he would see. I needed a break. The wrong kind of break came a few minutes later. I had ignored two calls from Mia. I didn't like to think of myself as rude.

Mia. Sigh. I had been turning over the Mia question in my mind the way one tosses a salad. No conclusion. In fact, no progress. I needed time away from other concerns to deal with my Mia confusion. That was not Mia's fault; she did not deserve rudeness. I answered the phone.

I was still preparing an excuse for not taking the earlier calls, when she started talking,

"Solly, there's been some brouhaha on campus. Some of my students saw two shady men trying to get into Blacker. A former Caltech student, a Mole, was found dead. What's going on? Do you know?"

Again, I took the easy way out and told the truth,

"Yes. Please accept that I can't talk about it, Mia."

She did another one of those annoying pauses before lying, about five decibels quieter, a half octave lower, and a few degrees chillier.

"Yes, I understand."

I wasn't sure what she understood but this was no time to be faint hearted.

"Mia, *please* really understand, and also that I'm going to be very tied up with this business. We need to talk. Of course, we need to talk. But it won't be today and probably not tomorrow."

"Of course. Well, let's talk as soon as we can. Good bye for now."

I tried not to let that bother me, but failed. Thoughts of Darryl helped push the Mia conundrum away from center stage, so I went up and around two corners to Darryl's room.

I heard his voice before I knocked. I told him not to let anyone in his room, so I was surprised until I realized he was on the phone. I heard Darryl making only brief responses. Was he on the phone with his father again? I would never have considered calling my father in this kind of situation. He wouldn't understand. I wondered: How did I know he wouldn't understand?

Whoever was on the phone with him, it wasn't right to listen. I didn't want to go back to the RA suite and wait for who knows how long, so I knocked. Darryl responded with a request for a few more minutes. So, back down and around to the RA suite, back to inconclusive thoughts about Mia, then after a few more minutes, back to knocking on Darryl's door and announcing myself, as I had before.

When I entered, I was struck by how much calmer he was. Good, but maybe temporary. With the thought of covering my butt if there was an inquiry later,

I modeled professional RA actions: I asked whether Darryl might want me to get him an appointment with a mental health professional. His response was a relief.

"Thank you, Dr. Sokolsky. I needed a good laugh."

I smiled. Reminded him I was there to help if I could. Reminded him he was to let no one in his room except me. I went back to the RA suite and paced back and forth. Waiting. Waiting.

The morning had been like running rapids. There had been a panic, but now, suddenly, everything stopped, and I had to wait. I thought about Pavlov driving dogs crazy with switches like this, and wondered whether I might be part of some malevolent experiment.

Enough of this; I needed to get out and readjust. I called Horvath and asked what was up. Could I leave? He told me I had to be around in the afternoon, but it would be best to stay through the morning also, and be sure Blacker was secure.

I thought about calling Clarence. He was insightful, and experienced with a very varied bunch of humans. But I remembered he was off the grid, and what was I going to tell him if we got together? Did I want to talk about Mia. I didn't think so. Did I want to talk about Darryl and Fang's death? I couldn't.

So I called Mia. I told myself I owed it to her, then told myself that's a rotten attitude for a lover. But I called.

"Might we share a cup of coffee?"

"Do we have to share? I'm willing to pay for my own cup."

The game was on, and I fed her the next line.

"You probably didn't hear me slap my knee in appreciation of your wit. But let me be something like serious: It's going to have to be quick. I can't be away long."

"Yes, I understand, and I understand I'm not allowed to understand why. A quickie will be fine."

I sighed at the implication. And the image. We really needed to meet.

"I need to find someone to guard the door. It shouldn't be hard. I'll call you right back if I can't, otherwise I'll meet you in the Café in five minutes. 'Bye."

To secure Blacker, I went to a corner of the second floor and knocked on the door of a senior, Skate, who had stayed around to work on an undergraduate research problem. His excitement about it stirred memories of my own research, the hundreds of hours of frustration and wrong paths, and the day or two of elation when I made a research micro-breakthrough. There was a thrill for the short time I knew something no one else in the world knew, even if no one else in the world cared. It was worth it. Maybe this was the key to the personality of researchers: They were less frustrated by prolonged failure, and more elated by the rare successes. Normal people (muggles?) had a less extreme punishment/reward payoff schedule. Someone should look into this. Maybe they have.

I once mentioned these musings to a friend who was an amateur pilot. There was a spark of recognition and she made a comparison to flying a small plane: long hours of boredom punctuated by moments of terror. I started rummaging on the internet and found hits about this duality applied to baseball, war and more. Even worse, a few months earlier a bored and terrified graduate student had added the comparison in her blog about PhD research. I thought I had a new insight, but as usual, I had been beaten to it.

At the moment Skate was in the up phase of research manic depression, and it was nice to see. I was loath to do anything to slow him, but was loathsome enough to ask him to stay by the door for half an hour. He agreed, and I was set temporarily free.

At the café, Mia and I were the target of a few stares. We had given up keeping our dating (was that the word?) secret. Everyone knew. The stares were for our boldness to be out in public together. There would have been more stares had there been more students, but it was Thanksgiving. We sat silently in the best isolation the Café could provide. I was used to Mia's pauses and silences, and could sit them out. In a half hour I would leave. She spoke, "Solly, do you remember Tuesday night?"

I had expected a better opening line. Ever the smart-ass, I responded, "Tuesday? Tuesday. Ummm. Oh yes. I remember now."

"Let's be serious. Tuesday meant a lot to me. If you tell me to you it was just casual sex you'll be lying."

I wasn't that good a liar, so I told her the truth.

"It meant a great deal to me also. It left me very uncertain. We are..if our ...whatever... weren't very important, uncertainty wouldn't matter much. I need to think about us, and it's been very difficult. Things I can't talk about have made me put off that thinking."

She wouldn't let it slide by.

"If we are so important, how could we be forced to a join a queue and wait? But I hear myself sounding like the kind of bitch I hate. So, no bitch. Big girl. I can wait if I have to."

"Can we talk about something else Solly?"

Strategic pause.

"Whatever else, you are still my friend, someone I trust. I need to talk to a trusted friend. You are chosen."

"I am honored. What's up?"

"Gilles."

I tried not to groan but could not stop my sarcasm, "How is Ol' Gilles doing?" It turned out Ol' Gilles was not doing well at all.

"I told you... I did, didn't I... about the rumor? The mob rumor. No?"

She *had* told me. It was Monday, three nights ago, but it seemed to be a small detail. There had been a lot of big details Monday night, and in the three days since. Still, I did remember, and nodded my head, wondering whether mobs were suddenly the big thing in 2018.

"Gilles called me last night. It seems the rumors were true."

"Poor Gilles. What does this have to do with you?"

She really didn't like it having anything to do with her. That is what led to the tears welling up on Monday night, and indirectly to what followed. She was emotional about it this time, but went on.

"Gilles says he owes these mobsters, gangsters, –whatever the right word is – and the interest is mounting up. He's heard stories, and seen movies. I think he's really scared. Gilles, being Gilles, he's trying to hide it and pretend he's brave. He's not!"

She stopped, and drifted off, thinking about something. I bumped her back on track with, "So he called you."

She said yes with a small nod of her head and fake smiled then delivered the real issue.

"He says they want some inside information about students at Caltech. They knew about me. Gilles had told them, when they asked him about any connections to Tech. Gilles told me I could keep him from broken knees or a slit throat by helping with some innocent tidbits of information. That's how he put it: innocent tidbits of information."

She understood she would have to give Gilles more than innocent tidbits. Did she understand her choice would be an echo of the business with the young fashion designer, Tommaso Russo? Gilles had some kind of psychological hold on Mia. With Russo she had done the wrong thing. What was she going to do now?

I was hoping I wouldn't have to ask that question, that she would see that it didn't need to bc askcd. No luck. Skate would be getting worried at the Blacker door, so I prodded.

"And?"

She responded with a kind of answer.

"I don't know. Meanwhile I hear there are mobster types hanging around campus. I guess you can't tell me why, so I won't ask. OK. We should be getting back. I'm glad we got together, even for a few minutes. We will need many more minutes."

"Yes, many more minutes."

Chapter 40

LUK AND GALTON VISIT; THURSDAY, NOVEMBER 22, 2018

It was good to have a reason to end the meeting with Mia. I had felt myself melting, and was not happy about it. I needed to be stronger, but need-to and able-to are lightyears apart.

Skate was happy to see my return, so he could get back to rocking science, however gently. He told me he was proud I had trusted him, but he had been nervous about what to do if someone came forcefully banging on the door.

Checklist, item 1: Darryl. Up the stairs and around the corners. He didn't unlock the door until he confirmed I was the knocker. He was a good rule follower. This was a comfort.

I asked whether there was anything to talk about, but no. He understood we were in a waiting phase. He thanked me for my concern and I reversed the corners and stairs back to the RA suite and turned my attention to waiting. Before I could make much progress, there was a knock on my own door. A question mark formed over my head. Darryl? Smitty? Skate? But what followed the knock was the voice of my sort of boss, Louis Horvath.

"Solly, there are people here to see you."

The thought crossed my mind Horvath might have been waylaid by Huns sneaking around campus, but he had told me to be sure to be around in the afternoon. Surely he wouldn't have made an appointment to bring Huns to my RA suite. So I opened the door. Behind Horvath was my old friend Luk, and someone who looked as if he considered himself important and might have been right.

Horvath said, "You know FBI special agent Xi Luk, of course. Let me introduce Bruce Galton, a liaison between the FBI and the State Department."

Horvath hesitated for a millisecond before he said "State Department." It was the moment he would have prefaced State Department with "goddamned." I don't know why the stumbled pause pleased me.

Horvath faded out the door as Galton advanced with a proffered hand. I guessed him to be in his late 50s, and he would be bald when he blew out the candles at his 65th birthday. He was almost my height, but maybe 10 pounds heavier. I wondered about the gym facilities at the FBI, or the goddamned State Department.

Galton's expression and handshake were serious and business-like. He was here to do a job, not to impress anyone. He was wearing a suit, but I forgave him that; Luk was also. It probably wasn't a choice.

Galton was clearly in charge, but he wasn't the sort to push to the front of the line. I supposed being a liaison required a lot of what is called emotional intelligence. With just the right tone he asked Luk whether it would be OK for Galton himself to take the lead. Luk answered, "Certainly Agent Galton." Nice. Luk was showing respect while Galton was showing collegiality.

I would soon see why Luk wanted someone like Galton to lay things out. It was delicate. He began delicately.

"Prof. Sokolsky, Agent Xi tells me you can be completely trusted. In your background I found nothing worrisome. You seem to have been very apolitical."

It made me sound uninterested in what was important, but I kept quiet. As for the Prof business, this wasn't the time for a short talk about academic ranks. But I wondered. The FBI, which knew everything, had to know I was a Senior Lecturer, not a Prof. Was Galton playing to my ego? If so, he was playing on the wrong field. He continued.

"The FBI has been watching the situation Fang Lou got herself into. Agent Xi has told you some of the reasons this was of concern to the State Department."

I could have added my research on the question, but it would have been like a smartass kid showing off that he did more than the assigned reading. Again, I kept quiet. That was twice in a row. Unusual.

Galton had paused for a few seconds to give me a chance to ask a question or be a smartass. Taking his cue from the silence, he continued.

"Prof. Sokolsky, we would like to deal with you in a way we think is warranted by the situation, and will be best for you, and for us. For reasons we hope are obvious, we cannot tell you absolutely everything we know, but we are willing to tell you everything we can, in exchange for your full cooperation."

I didn't think he was out to get me, but why take a chance. I went into lawyer mode.

"What are the details of full cooperation?"

"It means you tell us everything you know."

To avoid seeming sharper than I really am, I want to admit I had been thinking about this meeting and had worried about precisely this demand. Now here it was.

It was presented gently, so I responded gently.

"Like you, I have reasons I may not be able to tell you absolutely everything."

Galton was not put off his stride.

"Could you explain what reasons could be of sufficient importance to interfere with an investigation of a murder and national security?"

A bit much, Galton, I thought. A bit much.

"Agent Galton, I may be told things that require I give promises of confidentiality. If I give such a promise, I will honor it."

Galton was a professional and didn't show any reaction. I would have lost respect for him (which was growing) if he had pretended to praise me for my noble attitude towards promises. He spoke under his breath to Luk, turned to me and asked for permission for them to step out of the room for a moment. I nodded assent.

When they returned, Galton said, "On the basis of Agent Xi's very strong recommendation, we will accept the deal on your terms. You agree to tell us anything that does not violate a promise. We hope you will try to avoid making promises, or agreeing to confidentiality, when you are learning relevant facts."

"You've got a deal. For now, it's not a very good deal for you, because I think you already know everything I know."

Galton did not react, but rather, started in on delivering his side of the deal. A payment against future receipts.

"Here is what you need to know. We have a mole inside the Hun mob. You needn't tell me Mole has a different meaning in Blacker house. Our mole is an undercover member of the gang the FBI calls the Huns. He was one of the locals the Huns brought on board soon after they arrived. If they suspect there is a mole, they'll kill him, and it won't be pretty. Please keep that in mind if you have any weakness about keeping secrets.

"I understand Agent Xi has already hinted to you we have an undercover agent, so let's move on.

"The tragic death of Fang Lou has complicated the international consequences, but ironically, it has simplified an important near-term decision. We know the location of at least some of the hideouts of the Huns. In particular, we know the Culver City address where they were keeping Fang Lou. It's probably their headquarters.

"We had been gathering information about the gang, and their bizarre leader, the one who calls himself Sashi, and we already had enough to put away most of them. We were ready to start the game of getting the lower ones to sell out the higher ones.

"How to do it was the question. In view of the FBI psyche profiles and history of these guys, they weren't the type to surrender peacefully. The alternative was to burst in with tear gas and flashbangs. The FBI is very good with that kind of thing, but the chances Fang would be hurt or killed were unacceptable.

"Please understand I do not mean to be insensitive when I say Fang's death has simplified the situation."

"So why are you hesitating, and what could I learn that might help?"

"Maybe nothing. Maybe some key detail. Since the situation now is no longer urgent, we're adding a cup of 'more careful' to the recipe. We'll move on them within two days, but we want to know everything we can before moving. What do you know that might help us?"

"That's easy, and I won't break promises in answering. Fang was a buddy – that word will have to do – with another Mole, Larry Lagerstrom, who is called Darryl here. On Tuesday evening, two days ago I reported to agent Xi the relationship of Fang and the Huns, and Fang's safety-valve emails."

I gave a brief description of the attempted visit to Blacker by the two Huns and added my opinion.

"The visit may have been connected to Fang's Blacker history, but it was much more likely they were coming for Darryl. Here's the worst part: Fang promised no matter what they did to her, she wouldn't tell them about Darryl. But they knew about Darryl. He is out of his depth here – just as Fang was – and he is terrified. How much of this did you know? Can you tell me that?"

"We knew almost all of it, except for the last point about Darryl. We didn't know about his role in seeking help until you told agent Xi. I will keep you informed of what I learn about that if I can."

"Thank you. Now can I ask you a question or two?"

"Certainly. That's our 'deal.'"

"Did they torture Fang? Did she reveal that Darryl was waiting to summon help?"

"This is delicate, because it involves our mole, but you deserve an answer: No, they did not torture Fang. Things were getting sour in Fang's relationship with the Huns, and she saw an opportunity to make a run for it while a guard was drowsy. He wasn't drowsy enough, and he wasn't smart enough to think through what he should do. So he shot her, and it was a fatal shot to the head."

I would later learn that those details were close, but not quite right.

"The Huns never interrogated her, let alone tortured her. I will ask you *not* to share this with Darryl, since it will endanger our man on the inside."

I nodded that I understood, and I did understand. And I understood Galton, and Luk were asking themselves the same question I was asking myself: "How did the Huns find out about Darryl?" The relationship between Darryl and Fang was well known within Blacker, and around Tech, but how did it get to the Huns?

The Huns had a source at Tech.

CHAPTER 41

ERIK; THANKSGIVING, THURSDAY, NOVEMBER 22, 2018

The evening was quiet; I knew it wouldn't last. My mind was noisy; that would last. Where were my distracting students now when I needed them? Home stuffing themselves, doing laundry, and telling Aunt Cecily and Uncle Ned about Caltech. It would be nice at first. For most of them the tension of being a teenager at home would not be a problem for the short visit. For some of them, even a few days would re-open old issues they thought were closed and sealed. Sociologists theorize the tension in families is nature's way of spreading the seeds, of getting the acorn to move away from the tree. I read that somewhere.

At 6:45 pm I received an email from Mia. I thought about not looking at it. I was worried I missed her and that disturbed me. So, I was proud of my willpower. I waited almost a minute before I read:

> *The empty campus reminds me how much I don't want to lose you.*
> *I don't know what is going on, whether I did something wrong..*
> *but we should at least talk about it. No?*

She was right. She deserved an explanation of what was bothering me, but first I would have to figure out what it was. I had theories, of course. Maybe I was holding her up against the perfection of Shoshana. Maybe. Or maybe I was using her mistakes with Gilles as an excuse to avoid an involvement, a commitment, the future, that kind of thing. I know what you're thinking: Maybe I was a jerk. You may be right.

I didn't want to be a rude jerk. I had been thinking about adding a module to my senior writing course on using the power of language to be evasive. That was the skill I demonstrated in my response.

Mia- We must talk; it is important. And it is important we get it right, which means we need clear minds. I need to clear mine of a great deal. The talk shouldn't be put off, but must be. Things are happening fast, perhaps not fast enough, but perhaps too fast.

I would probably have kept chewing on the Mia situation if Luk hadn't called a little after 7 pm and pushed Mia to the side of the mental desk. He was outside Blacker and wanted in. He got it, and I saw a serious look on his face. Uh oh. We kept silent until we were safely (more or less) in the RA suite. I sat on the bed; I gestured for him to sit in one of the guest chairs. The position of my eyebrows asked him what was up.

"It's time to move on the Huns. Our leadership team has made a decision: They pose a great threat on the loose. There will be some danger in shooting our way in, but not as much as there would be in waiting."

"Luk. Thanks for trusting me, but why are you telling me?"

"This whole business is changing quickly. If you learn anything, *anything* at all, related to the Huns, Darryl, whoever, whatever, let us know immediately. Don't think about it. Don't try to decide if it's important enough. If you're trying to decide, then it's important enough. Here."

He gave me a card, with a phone number, and nothing else, and gave me instructions: "Call the number and just say the words 'wharf rat.' You'll get connected to me immediately."

He smiled weakly and repeated his exit line from his first visit, just two days ago, "Hell of a thing, isn't it?"

I let him find his way out on his own. His appearance was not likely to frighten any of my Moles.

Luk hadn't been specific about when the FBI would do their SWAT thing. I understood it was better for me not to know. Maybe they knew what they were doing. Hell, they promoted Luk. That was a sign they did. A tiny seed of optimism began to sprout.

It was a false sprout. At 7:40 pm I heard Darryl's knock, his unmistakable – not shy, not insistent – knock and shouted my welcome: "Come in Darryl."

When the door opened I saw, standing alongside Darryl, a middle age man in a suit. My first thought was the man was one of the Huns; he had somehow gotten into Blacker and strong-armed Darryl. I was a little off the mark. It was Darryl's father.

It wasn't obvious from his appearance. He looked to be 50-something, moderately fit, and around 6 feet tall. Bigger and bulkier than Darryl. He did share Darryl's fair skin and blond hair, though he was beginning to lose the hair. He also shared with Darryl their unusual affect: neither passive nor aggressive, neither pushy nor needy.

After Darryl had introduced him ("My dad, Erik Lagerstrom"), then Dad spoke up.

"I sensed from Larry's phone call this morning he needed support, so I rushed to the airport and was lucky to get an immediate flight to Burbank. Darryl and I have just returned from a deferred Thanksgiving dinner at a restaurant on Lake Ave. I think it was useful for us to get together."

When Dad/Erik said Larry (a/k/a Darryl) needed support, I didn't take it as a criticism of my RAing. There were more important things to worry about. There was an important addition to that pile when Erik calmly added, "I'm staying at the Nomad motel on Colorado Boulevard."

I not very calmly shouted, "What! The murderers know about Darryl's – Larry's – involvement with the murdered girl. You are in danger. You can't stay in a motel."

He didn't react like someone threatened, nor someone stupidly brave.

"I know the situation, and I'm prepared to deal with it." He opened his jacket to reveal a shoulder holster with a small automatic. Darryl's dad! Flabbergasted wouldn't cover it; I was gobsmacked.

"Dr. Lagerstrom, the criminals are professional killers. I don't know why you have a gun, but with all due respect, you should not" – my voice, already a shout, got louder here – consider confronting these people on your own. The right people are involved and will handle it. Your presence – voice yet louder – will just complicate a dangerous situation."

"I appreciate your worry."

Lagerstrom said in a tone that meant he didn't, but didn't want to be rude. (Yup, Darryl's dad.) "I'll be leaving now so you can get back to your work."

It was crucial he not leave. It was only good luck that let dad and Darryl escape while traipsing around Pasadena. I could not let him push luck any further. I pleaded.

"Dr. Lagerstrom, *please* stay until I contact the FBI." – no point in keeping the FBI a secret. "We'll find a way of keeping you and Larry safe."

"Again, I appreciate your actions and your offer, but I am not as naïve as you may think, and my assessment is bringing in the FBI would just attract attention, and *increase* the danger to us."

I would lose any debate; it would just be a waste time. I thought about blocking the door, then thought how stupid that would be. I let them leave and used trembling fingers to call Luk with the magic number he had given me. I shouted "wharf rat."

He became a Luk I had never known. He exploded.

"How could you let him go?!"

I wanted to explode back but just fizzled.

"He didn't ask my permission, and I decided not to knock him unconscious. Stop wasting time. He's walking from Blacker north towards the Nomad where he's staying. Do whatever has to be done, but do it quickly!"

I slammed the phone down. If Luk had anything more to say he could damn well call me back. I took a deep breath and ran after Lagerstrom to be sure Darryl wasn't going with him. OK. This isn't so bad, right? The Huns don't know Lagerstrom is here. He's just a guy walking north towards Colorado Boulevard. Right?

I guessed it wasn't right when I heard gunshots.

Chapter 42

FATHERS PROLIFERATE; NOVEMBER 22-23, 2018

I was back to the phone in a very loud heartbeat. I didn't know what had happened, but I wasn't rushing outside to take a look. I ran to the door to make sure no Moles were thinking of doing that very thing. I was too well aware of their illusion of invulnerability. Sure enough, there was a small group at the door. They were debating whether they should open the door and have a look around. I ended the debate, and put one of them in charge of guarding the door.

The insistent ringing from my pocket was Luk returning my emergency call. I picked up the phone and shouted, "There were shots fired in front of Blacker. Should I look outside?"

Luk shouted the obvious- "NO! I'll send agents. Keep inside. Keep the door closed. Don't let anyone in unless you're sure of the person and you're sure the person is alone. Please answer immediately when I call."

"Not fair – I always do," I thought, but this was not a time to pout, so I decided against a sarcastic "Sir, yes sir!" and went with an obedient "Will do."

Almost four minutes had passed since the gunshots. Time to share the news with Horvath who would start by asking why I hadn't called him immediately. I was wrong. His response was confusion.

"Louis, we've got a problem with Darryl's father."

"Damn it, Sokolsky. You said Darryl's father. You meant Fang's."

The voice in my head shouted "What!" so loudly it could have been heard by anyone near my head. I lifted my jaw from the floor.

"No. I said, and meant, *Darryl's* father, Erik Lagerstrom. He arrived this afternoon to be a support for Darryl. Darryl brought him to Blacker a half hour ago, and he was abducted and possibly shot when he walked out the door. The FBI is on the way."

It was Horvath's turn to be gob smacked. While he was gathering his scattered wits I added, "Now, what's this about Fang's father?"

In a subdued voice, like someone awaking from surgical anesthesia, Horvath told me Fang's father, Bertrand Lou, had arrived in late afternoon. Horvath had already gone home. Like any big donor, Lou had contacts at Tech, and got quick assistance. A meeting was set up with Horvath, campus police and Pasadena police in the morning. The Caltech administration had contacted the goddamn State Department. They would be joining the party.

I was becoming nostalgic for high tech start-ups. Horvath had not mentioned the FBI, but surely the FBI, and liaison Galton, would know about the other tempest stirring on campus. Still, it was getting too damn complicated, so maybe it would be better to keep separate, at least for a while, the abduction of Erik Lagerstrom, and the vigilantism of Bertrand Lou.

Horvath, demonstrating executive insight, was thinking along similar smudged lines, and decided not to invite me to the meeting (a lack of invitation that was gratefully accepted). That would be necessary if the Darryl story got too entangled in the Lou briefing. Horvath was hoping it wouldn't.

The abduction of Darryl's father would soon be campus common knowledge. I sensed Horvath was happy that the FBI, the PPD, and the goddamn State Department would be making all the decisions. They were welcome to the headlines, the glory, and the blame. I felt the same. And I felt Horvath would be happy to have some division of labor, so I offered.

"Louis, your plate is going to be overfull. Let me deal with the FBI about Darryl's father. I promise to keep you updated on any important changes."

Horvath bought it with the modification "..updated on *any* changes."

I responded with a quick monosyllable "Deal!" and hung up.

It was a few minutes before 9 pm. My blood was drained and replaced by adrenaline. This was needed, I reminded myself, because I had yards to go before I sleep.

There was the matter of Mia, but she was pushed completely off the desk onto the later pile. Darryl was occupying the center. I half ran up and around corners to his room and skipped the knock.

"Darryl, it's Solly. Please let me in."

Darryl was sitting on the bed and – as usual – was impossible to read. I had expected him to be highly agitated, blaming himself for calling his father. I suspected, and later confirmed, that the Pasadena visit was not Darryl's idea. In fact, Erik had not told Darryl he was coming until he arrived at Burbank airport.

Continuing a tradition I had developed in dealing with Darryl, I said the wrong thing.

"Darryl, you mustn't blame yourself for what is happening."

Darryl looked at me quizzically. Vulcans are often surprised at us irrational emotion-drenched normals.

"I don't blame myself, and I'm sure my father doesn't blame me."

I was not deterred. I felt Darryl was faking his lack of emotional involvement. I took another approach.

"Darryl, would it help you to talk about this?"

He thought for a few seconds, much longer than usual. This was something Darryl hadn't already thought through.

"Depending on how things turn out, I might want to talk to someone. I'd prefer you to one of those ridiculous psychologists."

I left with the usual reminder to him to let no one in, and not tell anyone anything. Around the corners and down the stairs, back to the RA suite. I lay down on the bed staring at the acoustical tiles on the ceiling. I was sure I would not be able to sleep. As occasionally happens, I was wrong.

Friday dawned. It was going to be a sort of Fathers' Day. I had gone to bed knowing almost nothing about Erik Lagerstrom, and not nearly enough about why Bertrand Lou was here. Enlightenment would follow before long, but first came Luk, knocking on my door. I didn't know how he got into Blacker, but hey, I reminded myself, he's FBI.

"We've got our confidential informant scrounging around trying to find where they're stashing Darryl's father. We're working up a file on Eric Lagerstrom. I'm not optimistic about the situation."

Silence followed the report on his pessimism. I saw his mood, and kept quiet.

Luk didn't keep quiet. He lost it, with 'it' being professional restraint. He started loud and went louder.

"Goddamn it Solly, we had this wrapped up. It would have all been over in a few days. We would have them in custody with enough evidence to keep them off the streets till the sun burns out. And NOW WHAT?"

With that rhetorical question Luk's crescendo peaked.

I exhibited what there was of my emotional intelligence and kept my expression blank. After an embarrassingly long time, when Luk's breathing slowed, I ventured a statement.

"Yes, now what?"

"Here's what, Solly. Here's the question. How the expletive deleted (he actually said 'expletive deleted') did the mob find out Darryl's father came to Pasadena? There's got to be an informant at Caltech. Shit (expletive undeleted)!"

He went on, though I already had a pretty good idea why expletives were called for. It could be just about anyone at Caltech, so it would be very hard to identify the informant. But until we knew who it was, we would be looking over our shoulder. In fact, both shoulders.

Luk showed himself out, reminding me to inform him immediately if anything developed, anything at all, absolutely anything at all. I cut him some slack for treating me as if I needed to be told this. It was a time for slack cutting.

CHAPTER 43
DARRYL'S PARENTS; FRIDAY, NOVEMBER 23, 2018

I didn't have to be at Horvath's 7:30 am meeting, but I awoke as if I did. And I awoke to the question that plagued me throughout the night: What next? It didn't seem right to be completely passive, just to wait to react to something. But there was no choice. I could call Mia, but I rejected that idea as soon as it passed through my head. I needed a clear head and empty desk to deal with the question of Mia. Even to know what the question was.

It would be nice to meet with Clarence, but I wouldn't be able to tell him anything, and I couldn't figure out whether we were on the outs. So that idea landed in the rejection pile, right on top of 'call Mia.'

I needed something to occupy my preoccupied mind. I had coffee, called it breakfast, then waited for a call from Luk, or Horvath, or for something. I gave up waiting for Darryl's familiar knock. Darryl wasn't coming to me, so at 8:20 am I went to him, up the stairs and around the corners.

He answered my knock with a "Dr. Sokolsky?" I admitted to it, and he let me in.

"I'm fine. Thank you for worrying about me. There's nothing to be done right now."

He was right. But it was unnerving how he was keeping on such an even keel. I forgave him. He was also being polite. Why? Anyway, I'd forgive that also.

By 9 am I overcame my reluctance to put my foot in it and I called Luk. He answered immediately with a rushed "What's up?" I'm not sure he was re-lieved or disappointed that I had the same question for him. Since there was nothing more urgent, I asked whether he had more about Darryl's father. He had indeed, about the father and the mother, and was willing to send me the folder over email. I would, of course, be discreet with it, but that was all he asked. There was nothing so confidential that he was stressed about security.

A few minutes later a pointer to a Google Docs folder arrived. It carried two surprises. The first, an immediate surprise, was how much documentation there was. I wondered whether the FBI had this much on every citizen, and, if so, did they have my past crimes (parking tickets, late library books, talking in kindergarten)? I was not embarrassed about how boring my past had been, but I wasn't happy about the FBI's ability, and motivation, to know so much. It didn't seem needed. What happened to the principle of privacy, once a sacred element of American life? Back when there was a frontier?

The second surprise came when I settled down in the RA easy chair and put my feet up on the bed to begin the dutiful chore of slogging through the prequel of Darryl. The surprise here was that Erik Lagerstrom was not your average high school history teacher, and I read, with increasing fascination, the background on Erik and Kristin, Darryl's parents.

Erik Lagerstrom started out targeting an academic career. (Darryl, the acorn, may not have fallen too far from that oak.) Erik finished his PhD in political science late in 1999 and, as a holding action, took an adjunct teaching job at the University of Chicago. He planned to write a book on his pacifist ideas, become famous and land a plum academic position. Robert Burns had it right; life laughs at our best laid schemes.

The focus of Erik's thesis, and subsequent study, was the dysfunction in the leadership of the Middle East, and how the unrest and violence could be overcome with the appropriate administrative structures and US financial interference. As part of background for his work, he became fluent in Arabic, passable in Farsi, and very knowledgeable about the complex interplay of tribal, governmental, and the Sunni, and Shi'ite sides.

He was an idealist until September 11, 2001. He might have heaved a sigh at the tragedy and adjusted, without abandoning his pacifism, had it not been for Jeffrey. In graduate school, Erik and Jeffrey had that wonderful intellectual relationship of two people with very different points of view, but with a shared love of intelligent debate. Reading about this, I thought about Talmudic debate, and the love of dueling with ideas.

Jeffrey was the realist; Erik the idealist. While Erik headed for ivory towers, Jeffrey took his predictive skills to the commercial side, and rose to the planning team at Lehman brothers. On September 11, 2001, he was at a meeting near the top of World Trade Center One, the North Tower, when it was hit at 8:46 am by a hijacked 767, carrying 20,000 gallons of fuel. During the frantic last hours of the building, many succumbed to death by smoke inhalation. Others chose to jump to their death, making a choice that can't be criticized or understood. Erik learned several days later Jeffrey had been one of those who jumped.

In nightmares, Erik imagined debates with Jeffrey about the choice of death.

Erik requested compassionate leave from teaching for a week, explaining his problem. The University was sympathetic, but his absence meant another faculty member had to cover for him, and there was a limit to how much could be asked.

So, ten days after Jeffrey's death, Erik went back to the semester that had only barely begun. He was not only emotionally shaken. His view of human behavior was shaken. He had been so certain strife could be avoided by better human interaction, and that Jeffrey had been wrong. The FBI analysts did not know whether Erik's complete change of viewpoint was a re-examination of the arguments for his pacifism vs Jeffrey's realism, or whether his change was largely due to his feelings about Jeffrey's terrible end. Either way, the FBI analysts had no doubt the conversion was sincere. Erik was not a threat to national security.

This was relevant to Erik's next step, since it would involve a security clearance. A few days after the terrorist attack, the Department of Homeland Security was formed and started its search for appropriate experts. In interviews with government analysts, Erik told them by joining an effort against terrorism he would bring a rational moderating voice. Again, the analysts saw no reason to doubt his motives.

Having been raised to fulfill obligations, Erik did finish his fall 2001 semester teaching, but was already well along in discussions and preliminary steps of working for Homeland Security, the principle and the department. In those days, before bureaucracy took over, people in the effort were driven by the mission and they saw how valuable Erik would be.

Erik's wife Kristin would not argue with Erik's usefulness in the role he was choosing, but she would, and did, argue strongly against the choice he was making. All this was carefully documented in the FBI's notes, including the conclusion that Kristin's opposition should be noted and watched, but was not an immediate security worry.

Kristin and Erik first met at a pacifist get-together and impressed each other with their seriousness. They married in 1999, when Erik went off to the University of Chicago, leaving Kristin to finish up her graduate work at Purdue. Kristin was a math wunderkind, but was attracted to the applied side of the field. At Purdue she had drifted from the Math Department to the Computer Science Department.

I was gob smacked (a word that was applying too frequently in the last few days). Darryl's math and computer skills came from his mother, not from Erik. I forgave my wrong assumption since Darryl had expressed emotion about how his father had been treated, but had mentioned nothing about his mother. The emotional tie and the early mentorship were different dimensions, so my self-forgiveness wasn't really justified.

Kristin and Erik's marriage was idyllic during the start of Erik's faculty career and the end of Kristin's graduate work. Erik would drive the 45 minutes from Chicago to Purdue every weekend. The FBI notes included a comment on the number of speeding tickets Erik collected during the epoch. It could have been taken as a sign of love, and a sign that Erik's idealism did not extend to vehicular regulations.

Their first and only fight exploded when Erik announced he was going to work for the government. It was a fight that never quite ended. The marriage survived but left emotional and professional scars. Kristin was now a star in the computer science department, and seemed destined to be a star in research. She and Erik envisioned their stellar academic careers just a few years over the horizon.

But the fight with Erik came at a very sensitive time in her career, and Kristin was – at least up to that time – a very sensitive person. At that crucial moment, after the fight began, she lacked the aggressiveness, the taste for self-promotion, necessary to secure a professorship. There was something else. Her disappointment with Erik's decision had soured her view of people in general, and she found the idea of teaching unappealing.

The Computer Science Department at Purdue, like most academic departments, was used to the quirks of people working at the forefront. When it became clear Kristin's passive take on a career was not short-term, they made the best of it and offered her a staff position with no teaching or competition for grants. She took the position immediately though without enthusiasm; she was showing no enthusiasm for anything at the time.

I stopped reading for a moment to think about how the FBI would come up with these conclusions, how they could be psychologists at a distance. I guessed they were creating a personality portrait from bits and pieces extracted from interviews with those who knew Kristin, and especially from the departments at Chicago and Purdue. Academics are typically reluctant to help the FBI, but typically they are anxious to talk.

Erik meanwhile went off to various trainings. He wasn't sure just what branch of Homeland Security he was working for. A minor point of the training, which Erik considered pointless, was craft, skills like avoiding being taken hostage.

I stopped again and thought about the irony.

The skills involved training in firearms. Erik had been taken hunting by his father, so he was not starting from zero, but his new skills involved handguns and firefights. The handgun came with a federal license, good in any state, with no expiration date. Erik returned the gun upon leaving government service, but soon after purchased another gun of the same model. The license was still valid. Probably an oversight.

I wondered whether Erik had reasons for buying the gun, and whether he understood his own reasons. It seemed very likely it was the gun Erik had with him when he was snatched outside the Blacker entrance.

Erik's first year after the training had its surprises, but did give Erik a feeling he was part of a worthwhile cause, and his contributions were appreciated. As happens in all organizations, idealism leaked out and bureaucracy flooded in. (I am inferring this; it was not a major argument in the FBI report.) After a second year, Erik decided he had enough and resigned.

His new view of the world was not compatible with his previous career plan. He needed a new plan, and he wanted it to involve Kristin. Erik was being pushed around by his feelings of guilt, and of responsibility for Kristin's new depressive personality. When he found a notice of an opening for a teaching position at West Lafayette High School, near Purdue, it was a life preserver in the murky waters around him.

Could this explain Darryl's personality? And what about his brother's suicide? More important: What would it mean for Darryl's reaction to what was happening to his father, and to what lay ahead?

CHAPTER 44

JOY AND GIGI; FRIDAY, NOVEMBER 23, 2018

It was now after 9:30 am. I had finished the FBI dossier and had much to chew on. I wanted some time for the chewing, but didn't get it. At around 9:50 am there was a gentle knock on my door. Too gentle to be Darryl. Newly paranoid, I asked "Who is it?" A gentle voice responded, "It's Joy, could I talk to you for a few minutes?"

"Sure, come on in."

Joy was the math major who had sought relationship advice from me (from me!) during my first few days as Mole shepherd. It was the first time I was confronted with the importance of advice-giving. Joy had been struggling with her boyfriend's pressure for physical intimacy. I had done my best, but assumed it wasn't good enough; I was fighting biology. And here she was needing to talk to me. I know what you're thinking. I was thinking the same thing. But we were both wrong, as Joy immediately made clear.

"I want to start by thanking you for your advice. Back in October. I explained to my boyfriend we would just have to wait. You told me to think about the probability we would break up. We did break up. It only took two weeks.

"Again, thank you for your insight and advice, but it's not why I came to talk to you. It's about a friend of mine, my closest friend, also a math major from my region of India. Her name is Jiya, but her Tech tag is Gigi, because she has the cute behavior of an innocent young girl. Anyway, she's a Pagegirl. We decided to avoid being in the same House, so we'd meet more new people."

"Very wise, Joy. Is your friend in some kind of trouble?"

"Yes, big trouble. But this also involves the RA of Page House, Dr. Kulpa. You know her, yes?"

She knew I knew her, and I knew she knew, but the social convention was for us both to pretend and get on with what was important. Joy wasted no time getting to what was important.

"Jiya is pregnant."

Ironic, since I had assumed Joy wanted to talk to me about that issue herself.

Questions streamed through my mind temporarily displacing the hostage taking of Darryl's father. Mia was Jiya's RA, so it was natural she would be involved, but how?

"Jiya told Dr. Kulpa about her problem, and Dr. Kulpa assured her that she, Dr. Kulpa, would handle it. She also told Jiya not to tell anyone about the problem, but – of course – she told me."

She cast her eyes downward, unsure of what she could tell me. After too much silence, I nudged her off the fence. This was something I really needed to know about.

"Joy, if you think it's best not to tell me more, I respect your decision. But if you do tell me more, I promise to keep everything secret, especially to keep secret your role as the source."

She had been waiting for some statement like that. Any statement really. She just wanted a nudge.

"Dr. Kulpa is going to arrange for an abortion. She may have to fake some papers, but Dr. Kulpa assures us there is no chance of real trouble, or of medical complications. Jiya wants to have children someday. Just not at age 18."

I assured Joy that this was a very common background for abortions, and asked,

"Joy, how can I help?"

"Mostly, I guess, to get your opinion on whether this plan really is safe."

I answered that it depended on details, but I assumed the Page House RA knew what she was doing. I was going to add .. and is honorable. I don't know why I stopped myself.

"You did the right thing coming to talk with me. Now try to do the impossible: try not to worry about this. If there turns out to be a way I can help, I'll do what I can, without revealing anything I shouldn't."

As Joy left, I asked myself: "And how are you going to do that Solly? Drop by Page and just mention abortions as part of idle chit chat?" The question would have to wait. But it carried with it a related question. How well did I really know Mia? She had admitted to murky ethics, and had taken the convenient rather than the idealistic road. Now I learn she was possibly going out on a limb, maybe way out, to help a student in trouble. Why can't everything be black or white?

I would have time to waste pondering this, since I could not drop by Page House; this wasn't a time to be away from Blacker. I tried to push the Mia issue off to the side and let the Erik issue take its rightful place, center desk. My mind pushed back, and I lost the push of war.

Waiting. Waiting. I arranged for pizza to be delivered for lunch in Blacker. I covered the cost for the small group in residence over the holiday. I didn't want anyone leaving the House. The Housing Office would probably reimburse me, but that wasn't on my mind.

Right after the pizza lunch, there was a 'relevant development.' Luk and Galton showed up at the RA Suite.

"Solly," Galton began with less formality than earlier, "Unless you have any news for us, we're here to catch you up on developments. Leadership has decided you are likely to be involved."

He then said what didn't need to be said.

"It goes without saying that you must not make decisions or take actions on your own."

I noticed the cadence and internal rhyme of 'make decisions or take actions' and was pretty sure this was a rehearsed speech. I said nothing. He said more.

"Of course, we can imagine situations in which you have no time for consultation. This means it's important we let you know everything possible that might inform the right actions."

I sat quietly admiring the number of words it took Galton to say so little.

"We want to fill you in on the Bertrand Lou situation."

Unnecessary dramatic pause.

"The State Department (my mind filled in the missing word) is going to do whatever is within reason to appease Bertrand Lou. He is a grieving father, of course, but he is also a political figure for whom it is crucial to show strength and good standing with the US.

"He wants to be involved in the pursuit of his daughter's murderers. To that end, he brought with him associates who, he says, have skills valuable in such a pursuit. Of course, for reasons both obvious and not, we cannot let his team be directly involved."

I wondered whether Galton was seeking sympathy. He wouldn't get it from me, but I could appreciate the messy entanglement.

"Got it. Is there anything to do now, or do we just wait to hear from the bad guys?"

He took advantage of the opening I gave him.

"There is something we all need to think about. Bertrand Lou is too well informed about what has been going on. He clearly has a source at Caltech. It's not likely that it's the same source the mob has, but it might be. So, we may have two leaks to worry about. A leak-prone campus, and an internationally delicate mess."

He still didn't get my sympathy, but he did get my "Thanks," as he and Luk unceremoniously left the RA suite.

I lay back on the bed staring at the ceiling. Its lack of activity was pleasing. Before I could get my fill of ceiling, my phone rang. I struggled to free it from its back pocket prison, and saw the caller was Mia.

"Solly, I know you can't say much, but I've missed you and I just wanted to hear your voice."

"This is my voice. It's saying 'I've missed you too Mia.'"

I thought I heard the sounds that go along with crying. The catching of the breath. The unmusical vibrato. I wanted to make it easy for her, so I spoke again.

"Mia, this storm we're in can't last. It will be great when we can talk without constraints. For now, I can't. Is there anything new you want to tell me about?"

An abortion, perhaps? Oh, sigh. She's too damn smart not to realize what I'm fishing for. But, of course, she didn't nibble. We hung up on more relaxed terms than a few minutes earlier. I sighed again. I had obviously softened my feelings about keeping my distance from her.

Solly, you weakling.

CHAPTER 45
ENTER CANFIELD; FRIDAY, NOVEMBER 23, 2018

I wanted to dwell on my weakness, but there wasn't any time; the game was afoot. My phone showed a call from an unfamiliar area code. I wasn't going to ignore any calls. I answered, "Blacker House."

It was Sashi, or someone acting on his behalf. The speaker had a dram of a Brit accent, and perfect formal English, so I figured it was UK-educated Sashi himself.

"We have the father of Darryl. Now listen carefully."

I was listening carefully.

"He is of no use to us except to trade. We do not want him. We want his son. We will give you some time to discuss this. We will call back tomorrow morning. Saturday morning. Meanwhile, pay attention to this. There is a gun trained on Erik Lagerstrom constantly. The safety is off. We hope our associate charged with watching him has no nervous tics. Any attempt to rescue Lagerstrom will provoke nervous tics. And please no more amateurish tricks like the transmitter attached to our car."

That was it. He hung up. Sashi's obsession with ransomware had shifted to Darryl.

Although the phone must have been a burner, his location could have been traced given enough time. The FBI had probably set this up. Sashi rushed because he didn't want to give them enough time.

I also didn't have enough time, so I eliminated thinking and called Luk. I could swear he answered before I had finished making the call. (The FBI had probably hacked into my phone, so they didn't need to wait for me to finish dialing.) Luk's greeting was appropriate.

"What!"

"They've called. They want a trade. They'll hand over Erik in exchange for Darryl."

Of course, Luk already knew that since he had been listening.

"Stay put. I'm going to set up a meeting. I'll call back in a few minutes."

And he did, instructing me to go to the Housing office at 4:30 pm. The office was low security but the Huns wouldn't have any sophisticated listening tools.

Luk told me to bring my phone. He didn't have to. But he was thinking beyond me and said he would be sending three agents over to guard the Blacker doors. I assumed there were already FBI agents watching Blacker from outside. It would be good to have them inside also, to get the Moles to be serious about the danger that had not yet been explained to them.

Luk told me to be sure to let the agents in before leaving for the meeting. I may have thanked him; I may have forgotten to. I did wonder, "Why "three"?"

"One for each entrance; one for the kitchen."

Yow! I thought. The kitchen. Of course. This was a vulnerability I overlooked.

I took comfort in believing the gangsters who called themselves Huns were no smarter than I was, and didn't think of the kitchen. But it was little comfort. I had to up my game. Darryl was still in Blacker. I considered myself responsible for him.

It was 4:02 pm when the FBI agents knocked. I showed them around and told the first Mole I saw – it turned out to be Joy – about their FBI guards. I asked her to spread the word. "It is one of my greatest skills," she joked nervously.

That got me to 4:18 pm. Since it took only seconds to walk to the Housing office, I was confronting 12 minutes of dead time. The devil makes work for idle minds. I thought about Mia and my brain played she loves me/she loves me not. Actually, it was more like I love her/I love her not. The game ended in a draw as I locked the RA suite and sauntered out the front door kidding the FBI guard by making a finger pistol and saying bang. It was probably in bad taste.

The floor-to-ceiling drapes in Horvath's Housing Office were pulled closed, turning the November dusk to a conspiratorial darkness just right for our meeting. "The objective correlative," I said to myself remembering a lesson from my master's classes: a physical condition that evokes the appropriate emotions.

Horvath, Luk, and Galton were there. There was also a new government type, similar to Galton but a little older and a lot sterner. Apologies had been sent to the Chief of the Pasadena Police Force, and to the head of Campus Security. I was told later both were relieved to stay uninvolved. Of course, Mentis and Ethos were there, admirably performing their usual task of lifting the mood, in this instance up to ground level.

Galton spoke first and most. He started by introducing the new person, Trevor Canfield, one of the FBI's top hostage negotiators. He was about an inch shorter than I, twenty pounds heavier, and the color of coffee with just the right amount of cream.

There was no sugar in that coffee. He had a look about him: 'I've seen combat.' He radiated seriousness, I didn't begrudge him the affect. Strangely, Mentis and Ethos favored Canfield; they edged over and allowed him to pet them, which he did – but without smiling. The two dogs sensed something I couldn't. It wasn't the first time.

Galton's said we were in this together, and together we would find the best way of handling the situation. He made it clear what together meant when he told us what we would be doing. He started at the top: We would *not* be making an exchange. He went on to explain the main reason for this was the logistics. How could the Huns possibly arrange the exchange so Erik would be safe? And once they had Darryl, the gangsters would view Erik as someone who knew too much about their locations, identities and procedures. Galton paused, and I took it as an opportunity to seek clarification. (Not to argue, just to seek clarification.)

"If they hurt his dad, Darryl is very likely to be uncooperative. I know Darryl. He would fulfill obligations if his dad is unharmed. But if something happens to his dad, there's no way they could get cooperation from him."

Canfield stepped in. For a hostage negotiator he was surprisingly blunt.

"Dr. Sokolsky, you are arguing based on your alleged understanding of the personality of Larry Lagerstrom (why wouldn't he call him Darryl?). Non-professionals often make the mistake of thinking they understand people. Those mistakes often lead to dead people."

Here his audio rose by a decibel, maybe two.

"Perhaps you're correct about what Larry would or wouldn't do, but the Huns don't know Larry, and their assumptions would be different from yours. They are used to people who can be manipulated with fear. That would be the basis of their decision to keep or shoot Erik Lagerstrom."

Damn. He was right, and he was finished. Galton took over.

"We'll listen to what they propose. Canfield here will do the talking. We won't play any games about who he is. They know the FBI is involved. Canfield will get as much information as possible from them, and try to negotiate the details of an exchange that will give us leverage: the greatest chance to snatch Erik, without putting Darryl in any real danger."

Then there was the matter of handling the next call. My opinion was not sought; it knew when it wasn't wanted, so I kept quiet, listening and thinking about Robert Burns' mouse.

Canfield, Luk, and Galton would come over at 7 am on Saturday morning. My phone would be monitored, and all technical tricks would be used to try to locate the caller. Six FBI cars would be cruising likely areas, anxious to pounce if any location information could be extracted.

Canfield would take the call once we saw an unfamiliar phone number. He would let it ring several times to stretch out the call and the possibility of locating the source. Canfield would then begin negotiations, playing it by ear.

As if everything were clear, Galton asked the group (Mentis and Ethos excepted), "Are there any questions?" There damn well was at least one.

"What about Darryl? What do we let him know?"

It was an easy question for Galton. He answered before Canfield could drain away a bit more of Galton's authority.

"Darryl is to know nothing about any of this."

I knew this was a mistake, but hey, no one asked me.

I went back to Blacker. I thanked the FBI guards and asked them whether there had been any problems or interesting events in my absence. They said that a few of my Moles had taken peeks at them, out of curiosity. The Moles asked permission, and then took photos with their phones of the FBI agents obscuring their faces. They were looking forward to the fun they would have telling stories about this if all went well. They were young. They assumed everything always went well.

I stopped by Darryl's room and played a repetition of my morning's exchange with him. He insisted he was fine. I didn't believe it. I also didn't believe that he was unaware of what was going on. With his hacking superpower he probably knew more than I did.

I went to the RA suite to knit up the raveled sleeve of care. The sleeve was going to get shredded Saturday morning.

And, as was the habit of mornings, it arrived. I was awake to see its entrance, having slept very little Friday night. The FBI trio arrived at 7 am, not taking any chances on just what a Hun might mean by morning. Team FBI was carrying audio equipment, a gallon thermos of coffee, and professional expressions. Luk gave me a quarter smile; Galton and Canfield gave me a ten degree tilt of the head.

There was no small talk except for a brief exchange in which both sides (Solly vs FBI) confirmed nothing had happened since our Friday night session.

Canfield instructed me when the phone rang I would answer. He would take over via the microphone/speaker equipment the FBI had set up. He gave these instructions in his absolutely no nonsense way.

The chat in my head was murmuring "This guy bargains for people's lives; no wonder he's so unsmiling," and then an opposing head voice rebutted, "But a negotiator needs to be empathetic. I wouldn't put that label on Canfield."

They had brought case files to pass the time, and were passing it when my phone rang at 8:40 am. Canfield jumped into action, flipping switches and turning knobs on the equipment attached to my phone. He pointed to me, and I spoke, "Blacker House."

It was the same voice as yesterday. Sashi I assumed.

"Hello, Solly. Do not try to locate the phone; I've taken steps to make that difficult. Games are inappropriate. I'm sure the FBI is there with you. With whom will I be speaking?"

Canfield motioned to me to keep quiet. He started speaking. Each of us had microphones connected to the phone.

"This is FBI Negotiator, Special Agent Trevor Canfield."

I was looking at the same person, but hearing a different Canfield voice, and I was about to witness a very different manner. It occurred to me Canfield had such a strong need for empathy in his job maybe he avoided using it up in ordinary human interactions. Could it be? Do we have a limited amount of empathy so we need to ration it? Maybe a grad student somewhere is writing a thesis on this. Someone should.

Sashi responded with confidence, less terrifying than previously. Maybe he was pleased the FBI had respected him enough to send in a specialist, or maybe Sashi wanted to give the impression he was pleased. Or maybe something else.

"Good morning Agent Canfield, I'm going to tell you how we will exchange Erik Lagerstrom for his son. I don't have to ask whether you have a pen and paper; I'm sure you're recording this."

Canfield responded, "I'm listening."

"We will make the exchange in the Glendale Galleria. It is conveniently close to Pasadena, so it will not be a long trip for your government SUVs. The exchange will take place at 12:30 pm Sunday, that is a half hour after noon, tomorrow. The mall will be crowded with shoppers and with those who are dining after church. Because it is crowded, your team will not take a chance on starting a fire fight."

Canfield then spoke in a business-like voice suited to working out a detail.

"That's a big mall. Could we agree on a specific location to meet?"

Interesting! Canfield was not arguing about the site, he was de-escalating the adversarial tension with a reasonable question. I was getting an education in hostage negotiations.

There was a pause, it was obvious that Sashi was thinking of an answer.

"We will call Dr. Sokolsky's phone at 12:15 pm to tell you precisely where we will make the exchange. This will discourage your little army from setting up some surprise at the site."

"Understood. Will we release the son as the same time you release the father? Will we have them walk across an empty space?"

Canfield continued my hostage negotiation education. He was presenting himself as a hostage exchange technocrat. Creating a persona of someone professional and experienced, and putting Sashi at a slight disadvantage. I was in awe. He was letting Sashi do the talking and was showing he was paying attention, hence paying respect.

Sashi's response suggested perhaps he hadn't quite thought through all these details.

"We'll let you know after we are facing each other in the Galleria. We'll give you instructions over Sokolsky's phone."

Canfield then made his move, gently.

"Could I make a suggestion?"

"Yes, Agent Canfield, what is your suggestion?"

There was irritation creeping into Sashi's voice. A subtle shift was taking place in the balance of power between Sashi and Canfield. It's always a pleasure to observe a real pro at work. Canfield made his suggestion in a relaxed, respectful voice.

"Exchanging Lagerstrom and his son in an open public space may present an opportunity to one of them, or both, to bolt into the crowd. This would lead to a situation neither of us wants."

There was a long pause. Sashi realized Canfield was right but Sashi didn't want to yield the lead in the negotiation. What could he do? He was picturing Erik bolting in one direction, Darryl in the other, the Huns momentarily indecisive and a moment later gunned down.

Canfield may have been having these thoughts about Sashi's thoughts, and – pro that he was – he let Sashi take a long pause, a way of letting Sashi initiate the next step.

"What do you suggest Agent Canfield?"

The irritation had now modified Sashi's voice to a growl. Canfield sensed the need for a pause. It wouldn't look good for him to be too ready with a suggestion.

"I think what might be best is an exchange not in a mall, but in a somewhat remote setting. We probably want a place with an open area for the exchange. There is probably some place with these features that is close enough."

Crafty Canfield had used two 'probablys.' He was not going to pick a specific place. It was going really well and he wanted Sashi to have the last words and the illusion of respect and control.

Those last words were, "The FBI is to be congratulated on the wisdom of its Special Agents. We will call again within a day or so with our choice of the site of the exchange and further details."

Sashi hung up.

Canfield made sure the phone was dead then turned to Luk and me with the question.

"You know the area. What site is he likely to choose?"

Luk and I looked at each other. My mind was blank; Luk's wasn't.

"Chantry Flats picnic area?"

CHAPTER 46

CRUCIAL PIECE MISSING; SATURDAY, NOVEMBER 24, 2018

Canfield returned to his background role, but was paying attention when Galton made it clear we were not finished.

"The leak."

We all knew what he meant, but he wanted to lecture us.

"The Huns are getting information from at least one source on campus. They knew about Darryl and Fang. It wasn't a big secret. Whoever told them could have been naïve and unaware. Not the case with the abduction. Someone informed them Lagerstrom was visiting, and had gone off walking with Darryl. That had to be very intentional. Nothing naïve and innocuous. Leaking any detail about the hostage exchange could now be fatal. We've got to plug that leak. Until we do, we need to be paranoid about secrecy."

There was no arguing with that, but I wanted to argue with his follow up: The source of the leak was most likely in Blacker House. It was possible, but the evidence was weak. Galton added the FBI had its best plumbers doing the investigation and we soon would know. It could be painful, but I would have to accept it.

Sashi hadn't been very specific about when he would be calling back so there was no point in the trio hanging around. We outlined the steps I would take when he made his call. The FBI threesome left around 9:25 am.

Waiting. Waiting. I could now add hostage rescue to the list of 'long periods of boredom punctuated by moments of terror.'

My to-do list had a problem item remaining: Horvath. I had agreed to keep him up to date during our meeting the previous day. There was a promise about relevant developments. At least it would interrupt the monotony, so I started to make the call to him when – in a break with recent tradition – I had some thoughts: There was no reason for Louis to have any suggestions about the leak, so why bother him about it? There was no reason for Louis to know about Canfield and the negotiation with Sashi, so why bother him about it?

Were these details really relevant developments? I decided to do him a favor and not bother him. On the slight (80%?) chance something went wrong, he would be able to claim ignorance and could point a finger at me. In my mind I was running through the scene in which I explained how I had protected him: "But Louis, don't you see that...?" No. Best not to preview it.

It was inevitable that thinking about Horvath raised the specter of Bertrand Lou, a specter that involved Lou's associates opening fire. I would gladly leave that specter to the FBI.

Then there was Mia. The information from Joy had softened my feelings for her, and they were already pretty damn soft, way too soft. And confused. But visiting her was out of the question, light years out. I just had to be patient. Patient. 'They also serve who only stand and wait.' Seventeenth century Brit poet John Milton boasted that his patient acceptance of his blindness was his contribution to God's glory. I didn't draw any inspiration from this since I thought it was bullshit.

I lay back on the bed, waiting, but not serving. I would soon miss the long periods of bored waiting. A moment of terror was on its way.

It had been too long since I had checked on Darryl, so up the stairs and around the corners. I knocked on his door, expecting the usual answer. But there was no answer. I knocked louder, shrugged and wandered off to check around the House.

I returned ten minutes later and again got no response to my knock. You can probably guess the fear that had overtaken me: suicide. The father situation could have hit him harder than he allowed himself to show. I slowly, and nervously, opened the door while repeating "Darryl?" When the door was fully open I could see what wasn't in the room: Darryl. I was worried about how fast my heart was beating, and took a few seconds to let it return to a fast idle.

There was a piece of paper on his bed, placed so it would be noticed. Before stepping into the room I looked around carefully, without knowing what I was looking for. I moved to the bed and read the short statement on the paper:

*I have gone into hiding. Please trust that I know what I'm doing,
and don't try to find me.*

Darryl (Larry Lagerstrom)

Later I would compare this with samples of his handwriting, and confirm
that Darryl wrote it. There was also indirect evidence. The note added Darryl's
pre-Tech name. It was a Darrylian touch for the FBI; their grasp of details
might not include Tech tags. It might also have been Darryl being considerate.
That didn't balance the very inconsiderate touch of turning an extremely difficult situation into an impossible one.

This development would add an element of hilarity to the next negotiation
call with Sashi. He would interpret the claim of Darryl's disappearance in a
way that put Erik in danger. The claim was obviously a lie, a scheme to avoid
the exchange Sashi was angling for.

What now? I needed someone to tell me what now. I punched the Luk
button on my phone, called out wharf rat, and was greeted a few seconds later
with "What!"

"I'll tell you what. Darryl has taken off."

"What do you mean 'taken off?'"

I went on to explain. Luk's voice got louder and he allowed himself the
comfort of strong language before asking, "What the .. what the hell is he
doing?"

"Luk, you're the expert. You tell me. My guess is he is going to try to handle the hostage situation by himself."

Luk offered the observation, "I don't need this crap. I could have worked
in a tech company."

"You would be making the same complaint about different crap."

That was our moment of Kyogen, the comedy break. Now back to the
Noh drama.

"Lock his door. Don't let anyone in. I'm going to send over a forensic
team."

"OK," I said, "I'll let them in."

"No need."

Oh yeah. It's the FBI. Silly me.

"What else, Luk?"

"Nothing else. And I mean nothing. Don't call Horvath. Don't call anyone. Don't talk to anyone. Don't make sounds that suggest anything. Don't make facial expressions."

'Luk's five commandments,' I thought. He then reminded me of something I shouldn't have forgotten.

"Solly, I hope you haven't forgotten there is a leak on campus. This morning we said it was crucial we find it. Now it is beyond crucial. What's an expression for beyond crucial?"

"Critical? Earth-shaking? Super crucial." What did he want? Elegance?

I looked at the heart rate monitor I wore on my wrist. I was in the red zone.

"Never mind the vocabulary quiz Luk. Sashi's going to call back, and it's not as if we have five shopping days left to prepare. What do we do now?"

Luk was more truthful than I expected.

"How the hell do I know?"

It was back to waiting. The punctuating moment of terror had ended, replaced by lower level terror. I longed for a period of boredom.

CHAPTER 47

CANFIELD CALMS SASHI; SATURDAY, NOVEMBER 24, 2018

It was several days, though my clock claimed 12 minutes, until Canfield called. He was the right person to be in charge, and this lowered the terror level to yellowish orange. Canfield said we – the FBI trinity and I- would meet again in the RA suite. If the leak was outside Blacker this would keep the meeting as secret as possible. If it was inside Blacker there was nothing we could do to keep it secret.

Another few days (clocked at 18 minutes) and there were four very grim souls in the RA suite. Canfield started speaking. He sounded calm, and sounded as if he knew what he was doing. I was grateful for both sounds. I was grateful also that he said he would take the call. He saw no need to give us any details. We were not surprised. It was his way, and it would make his performance that much more entertaining.

The FBI trio then went across the corridor to the Blacker library, so they could have conversations beyond my security clearance. They returned less than an hour later, around 10 am, telling us that Sashi was about to call. I reminded myself that they didn't have to wait for the phone to ring; they are the FBI. The next two steps played out according to the script. The phone rang and Canfield took the call.

"Thank you for calling."

Sashi skipped an opening pleasantry and got down to business. His tone told us that he was still irritated at having to follow Canfield's suggestions.

"We have seen the wisdom in your suggestion agent Canfield. We are ready to tell you how we will proceed."

Here we go, I thought. I would have tightened my seatbelt if my RA chair had one.

Canfield's calm voice told the phone, "We'll have to consider changes. Darryl has disappeared."

Interesting. No sneaking up on it. I saw the strategic sense in his full speed ahead approach. He could have dragged out a narrative ("Dr. Sokolsky knocked on Darryl's this morning, and..."). But that would give Sashi many opportunities to become furious. This way Sashi had only one opportunity, and for that opportunity he was back on his heels and off balance. I thought about the FBI negotiator school. Was it extraordinary training, or was Canfield their best student ever? These thoughts flashed quickly through my mind as I wondered what was flashing through Sashi's mind.

Sashi was at a loss for words. After an eternity of 20 seconds he found and delivered the words with a frightening formality.

"Agent Canfield, I am surprised and disappointed. I thought we would have the efficiency of a mutually respectful adversarial interaction. But now you try to fool me. This does not bode well for our negotiation. It is not likely that Erik Lagerstrom will live much longer. I think we are done with our very unsuccessful interaction."

I held my breath. This was getting fatal very quickly. But Canfield responded with no change in his calm tone.

"I completely understand that you would feel that way. In your situation I also would suspect that I was being lied to."

I was taking mental notes on the informal course I was getting in negotiation. Lesson 5: Always show that you understand how the situation looks to your opponent. Canfield continued his master class.

"I have a suggestion, a way for you to confirm that we are not lying to you."

The briefest of pauses before Canfield continued.

"We know, of course, that you have an informant on the Caltech campus."

The 'of course' was a brilliant touch. He continued, "How about we give you a day or so to confer with your informant, and learn that we are telling the truth? After you get the confirmation, we will be anxious to hear how you propose to deal with the very different situation we now face."

Bravo Canfield! Right. We and Sashi are in this together.

Sashi responded. He wanted to sound professional, but he was irked at again having lost the lead in the negotiations. Canfield's suggestion was too good to ignore, and Sashi couldn't ignore it. He was not quick enough on his mental toes to do anything but grudgingly agree without making it sound too grudging.

"Very well, Agent Canfield. I may need more than two days, but I will follow the step you suggest. If we confirm that Darryl has indeed run off, we will present a new proposal."

Canfield hung up without saying good bye. He then turned to me and said "Talk to no one," and left the RA suite, again with no 'goodbye.'

Luk, Galton and I were silent. Canfield had set the tone: Nothing should be said that doesn't need to be said. We couldn't talk, but that didn't keep us from thinking. I wondered whether Luk and Galton were thinking the same thing I was: that this was another example of Canfield's genius. By pushing Sashi to contact his Caltech source the probability would surge for the FBI (no doubt monitoring everything possible) to identify that source.

There were many questions: What deal could be cut with Sashi if we didn't have Darryl? Would Sashi decide this was getting out of control and get rid of Erik? What would Bertrand Lou be told about the hostage situation? And, what the hell was Darryl thinking!

There was no point in the FBI camping out any more in the RA suite, so Luk and Galton took off. The moment of terror had passed, but the hours of boredom weren't on the schedule. My breathing was too rapid. I was proud of my former resting pulse of 47. I hated to think what it was at the moment. I wasn't going to check it; that would just make it rise.

With pressure temporarily and slightly lifted I realized that I could call Horvath, but I remembered Canfield's strict order, which meant I had an excuse not to. So I didn't.

I realized I might be able to call Mia, maybe even meet with her. But I didn't. A month ago I was thinking about doing the Times crossword puzzle in bed with her, amused at the thought that she would put me to shame.

The news about her helping pregnant Gigi reminded me that Mia was – at least in some ways, in some sense, with some things – Mia the sweet. So what was my problem? Or was the right image not Mia the enigma, but rather Solly the lunkhead? Do any of us understand ourselves? I was annoyed that this dysfunction in self-understanding wasn't dealt with in novels. After a little thought, I wondered: maybe it was dealt with in every novel. Enough. Time to do something more useful, or at least different.

I went to the internet to look up FBI hostage negotiation courses. There were other negotiator training programs, but I wanted the FBI, and it seemed that this meant becoming an FBI agent. I shrugged my shoulders; yeah, I could do that. Then I looked at the application process. The cutoff age was 36.

I still thought of myself as young, not quite an adult. Jeez, I blushed entering a motel with a woman. This was the first time I had been too old for something. I would have been depressed about it if there hadn't been so many other things to be depressed about.

CHAPTER 48

VALKYRIES; SATURDAY, NOVEMBER 24, 2018

And there were other things to deal with. Thanksgiving break was ending. Students would return the next day. The Blacker RA suite had been a convenient anti-Hun staging area while Blacker was almost empty. No longer. Now the FBI would move to a trailer parked 1,500 feet to the southwest and 30 feet downward in Tech's underground lot.

The trailer advertised itself as transporting the tools and experts of the Pasadena Asphalt Resurfacing Company. It had a professional looking PARC logo, and a cartoon of a large cheerful figure with a roller, smoothing out a rutted parking lot. Every hour or so, a few people in overalls would emerge with clipboards and would argue about porosity and temperature. The FBI. Unlimited budget; masters of detail.

Along with the inconvenience (and relief) of having the FBI clubroom move, was the inconvenience (and relief) of the resumption of teaching and its interesting subtleties. The return from Thanksgiving marked the beginning of Act V of fall semester 2018, the last two weeks. To be played in four scenes.

Scene 1, the first week back, November 26-30, would open on Monday, with the start of classes. The students would return stuffed with holiday excess, pampered by family, and drained of the self-discipline needed for multivariable calculus, organic chemistry, and thousand-word essays. The academic calendar allowed them to drift during the first week back. The week reminded me of Ahab's *Pequod*, festering in the doldrums, and of the Ancient Mariner becalmed for his sins with water, water everywhere. There were be no strong academic winds blowing. Experienced instructors knew this sticky listlessness, and knew how to deal with it. They mentored the new faculty members who thought they knew better, and eventually learned they didn't. There must be papers about research in this doldrum-week phenomenon. Grad students in educational psychology need topics.

The stagnation did not last. Strong winds and rapid currents brought the 'Oh my God, finals are coming!' week from December 3 to 7. With the calendar ticking students would stop the wasteful practice of getting 8 hours of sleep, would complete some of the incomplete work, and would prepare for battle.

That preparation was Scene 3, study period, the weekend of December 8 and 9, and Monday December 10. The cruelty, of study period had always bothered me. There were no classes on the weekend anyway, so study period was really Monday, study day. It seemed in bad taste to imply it was more. The students had already been studying furiously for days. They didn't need this misrepresentation.

Whether it was study period or study day, it would soon be over. Wednesday, December 12, Scene 4 would begin at 7 am sharp. And therein lies a story.

For reasons no one can explain, and which may not exist, final exams at Tech always start with the playing of *The Ride of the Valkyries* from Richard Wagner's opera *Der Ring des Nibelungen*. It is played very, very loud by many powerful speaker systems everywhere in the undergraduate houses. *The Ride* plays a role in the 1979 movie *Apocalypse Now*. But that can't be the source of the tradition. It dates back far before 1979. It's true the movie is (somewhat) based on Conrad's 1899 novel *Heart of Darkness*, but there are those who claim *The Ride* goes back even before that. The claimers do not specify whether it was played on Edison wax cylinders or whether orchestras were brought to the Throop Institute (which grew up to be Caltech in 1920).

The role of *The Ride* has some aura of the sacred. If it is played, or even hummed, outside of the holy appointed time, the sinner, fully clothed, is cleansed of his (or her, but almost always his) sins in the nearest shower stall. The sin is often an intentional male challenge. Even the biggest, strongest challenger is greatly outnumbered, and ends up wet.

Sociologists say the practices, procedures, and beliefs define what is a 'culture.' *The Ride*, then, is culture, and it is not important whether all the stories about it are true, whether post-graduation Caltech alumni suffered *Ride*-related PTSD symptoms, whether an astronaut was woken by *The Ride* played in the space capsule.

The Ride was the overture to the opening of the last scene, final exams, December 12-14. That they were difficult is obvious. Not obvious is that they exhibited what has become so rare: trust and trustworthiness. It was a rule, and remains a tradition, that all exams are under the honor system. The student picks up the exam, goes to a comfortable setting, and turns it in four hours later. The rules of engagement (what sources can be used and such) are clearly spelled out.

A few years after my beatification as Senior Lecturer, I had a coffee chat with a chemistry colleague about how contrary this was to the *Zeitgeist*. Why, I asked, does anyone think this would work? It was a rhetorical question to introduce my arguments that it couldn't work. "Consider," I pontificated as I laid out my first argument, "there are now commercial software products to check student essays for plagiarism. Cheating is expected. A great deal of effort at most institutions goes into minimizing it. Multiple proctors. Videotaping exams.

"And the students follow the news and are aware of what is going on in international politics. How could they not feel cheating is the way of the world they will be entering, the world they should be preparing for?"

I had saved my best argument for last, "Do you know what's worst? There are students who, despite everything, are honest. Does the honor system not do them a disservice?"

My volume was rising as I made my incontrovertible finis: "And what's worst of the worst is that this may convert them. They will yield; these saints will join the sinners."

The prosecution rested. As is too often the case, I was primarily interested in showing how clever I was, but I really *was* curious about the argument for the honor code. My chemistry colleague began her rebuttal.

"First, the practical side. These kids are painfully clever. If they wanted to cheat, they would find a way. If the administration tried to stop them from cheating, they would take it as a challenge. God knows what schemes they would come up with, but the students would win; the administration would lose and it would be an enormous waste of time for both teams."

Uh oh, I thought as my confidence in winning the debate waned. But there was more.

"Second, there is enormous pride in being part of a very special place with an unusual system. Like most things it's all about ego, isn't it? Getting a high grade boosts that ego, but not if it is from cheating. These students will accept a below average grade at a far above average place. Cheating would be an affront to that special place. Their egos are secure."

I made an ambiguous grunt meant to suggest an ego-saving draw. It wasn't a draw. I had lost. But I had learned something and learning was better than winning.

While walking to class post-coffee I thought back to my senior undergraduate year. Even then, pre-Tech, I had the shallow polymath streak. For reasons I don't remember, I chose to broaden myself with a graduate course in real analysis. The subject title was refreshingly blue collar. Want to impress your friends? Go to the library and find a book titled *Advanced Concepts in Algebraic Topology*. Be sure the title is displayed in a large brightly colored font. If you have to carry around *Real Analysis*, put a cover on it. How could real analysis be difficult?

But it was, and half the grade was the final exam, so I was surprised to learn that the final would be "take home." Not a four-hour take home exam as in Caltech finals, but a *one-week* take home. Any non-human reference source was allowed. No expert consultations. But anything else is allowed. That seemed convenient, but pedagogically curious. Where's the motivation to study the whole subject? I could study during the exam itself. Nothing to worry about; I had a whole week. But the exam took the whole damn week! Aside from an absolute minimum of time for sleeping and eating, every minute went into looking into the depths of the three problems on the exam. I didn't learn the breadth of the material as well as I might have under the standard exam pressure, but it was much better to learn how to focus deeply rather than broadly.

I still remember my solution to one of those exam problems. Maybe.

It was a pleasant change to chuckle to myself about the past, but the present would be crashing in very soon, in the form of a telephone call. The crash came at 7:30 am Sunday morning, but it was not the call we expected from Sashi; it was the call we didn't expect from Darryl.

CHAPTER 49
DARRYL CALLS; SUNDAY, NOVEMBER 25, 2018

Canfield and Luk were on the phone as soon as I answered. (Of course. They knew the call was coming before the phone rang. It's the FBI. Could they trace the source of the call? Probably not. It's Darryl. Where was Galton? Smothering other goddamn State Department fires?)

"I want to apologize for the worry I've caused, and would like to discuss where we go from here."

We assumed Canfield would take over, and he did. Calm voice, the same as he used with Sashi. He had studied files on Darryl, and knew not to try to manipulate him, or to waste words.

"Darryl, I am FBI Special Agent Trevor Canfield. I have been negotiating with the people who have taken your father hostage. What do you propose?"

"I know you were planning on a hostage exchange. Your negotiations had settled on doing it in a place remote from the public."

Had it not been Darryl we would be wondering how he knew this. But it was Darryl. We knew. He continued.

"I want to make a deal with you. A plan. If you agree to it I'll be back in Blacker this afternoon. I will agree to help the criminals if they return my father unharmed."

Agent Canfield again, calm and reasonable, "This will be very dangerous. We cannot assume they will not grab you and keep your father as a way of controlling you."

Darryl, calm and reasonable, "There is no way of eliminating all risk, but it is not likely they will keep my father. They want me to perform services for them. They will want my cooperation. Not releasing my father will threaten that. The good-faith act of releasing my father will be a step towards cooperation."

Agent Canfield in rebuttal: "These people are not practiced in winning cooperation with demonstrations of good faith. Their modus is to threaten and terrify."

Darryl with the counter-argument: "I would agree with your insight, but Sashi seems to be more intelligent than the average of his phylum, and I will leave it to you, Agent Canfield, to point out to Sashi my attitude about co-operation. After dealing with my father for several days, Sashi will have learned of the family pigheadedness.

"In any case, that is my offer. If you accept, I will trust you to carry through with your part."

Darryl then said something that sounded like a few syllables of Russian. When I looked back at his file I saw he had taken a semester of Russian in the spring of his freshman year. I had also taken a semester of Russian. But a semester for Darryl was not a semester for me. After a bit of internet scrounging I concluded Darryl had said 'trust but verify,' a short Russian proverb, "   ,
           ." It rhymed in Russian, "Doveryai, no proveryai," and was popularized (less poetically) in English by Ronald Reagan.

Linguistics aside, what did Darryl have in mind for verifying? It wouldn't be like Darryl not to have a backup plan, but what? I was sure he had something, and that worried me. Darryl's abilities were often astonishing, and he had reason to be confident in whatever he was scheming. But he was not used to playing on this court.

Canfield told Darryl he would have to confer with those higher up in order to sign on to the deal. The car-salesman gambit. It was a rare foolish move by Canfield that didn't fool even me, and certainly not Darryl. Too polite to say what he must have been thinking, Darryl simply said the offer would last only till 2:00 pm.

The car-salesman check-with-my-boss nonsense was only one reason for Darryl's time limit. The other was Darryl's mastery of strategic details. There would be chaos, or at least hubbub, as students returned from Thanksgiving break. This would allow Darryl to slip back with minimal notice from other Moles, and possibly from the informant who reported to the Huns.

Canfield wanted to regain control of the interaction but didn't get his way, "Darryl, this is delicate and important. I may not be able to get permission to do this by 2:00 pm."

Darryl was polite, but may have been losing respect for Canfield. He ended the conversation simply by saying "I will call again at 1:30 pm. Goodbye," followed by hanging up. At least he said goodbye.

I was pretty sure Canfield immediately got in touch with his people to see whether they had located the origin of Darryl's call. Many months later, after a few too many beers, when Luk and I were replaying the whole game, he let slip the information about the FBI trace on the call. They couldn't say where Darryl was starting the call, but the location they reported was the Pasadena Police headquarters. This was a source of some innocent (and admiring) merriment among the FBI telecommunication experts, but Canfield, according to Luk, was not amused.

Two minutes after Darryl hung up, I got a call from Canfield, who told me not to talk to *anyone* about this. This didn't bother me. It reinforced my excuse not to call Horvath. My personal neuroses aside, this was a serious business because the Huns' informant could be anyone, so that is whom I would not talk to: Anyone.

Canfield told me to come to the trailer at 1:00 pm. I inferred (correctly again!) he wanted the call – to my phone, as always – to be handled there. Fine.

It was only 8:00 am. Four hours stretched out ahead, but not hours of boredom. There was my cover identity as Blacker House Resident Associate. I'd need to help the Moles with the return to reality from their jaunts to the past. There were always little fires (lost keys; stuck in an airport, will miss class; broke a leg early-season skiing – on crutches).

On the secret side of Solly the Spy, there were questions about the next steps we'd be taking in the negotiations. Canfield would be talking to Darryl, when – no doubt – some details would be discussed about the interchange of hostages. (Crutches and missed flights were laughable by comparison.)

The devil is said to be in the details. In our case the devil was our psychopath opponent, Sashi, but the details would be important. *If* we got to the details. What was going to happen when Canfield told Sashi that Darryl was back? Our silver-tongued FBI negotiator might reach the limit of his abilities. Darryl and Sashi. Even the Amazing Canfield might be out of his depth.

Or was it all moot? Maybe Sashi had been unsuccessful in confirming Darryl had run off? Might Sashi, a control enthusiast, decide it was all out of control and it's best to bail out, without leaving Erik as a witness. Probably not. But it put in perspective that the life and death issues we were dealing with were really life and death.

What if Sashi *had* received confirmation that Darryl had run off? What would happen when Canfield said to Sashi, "Guess what? New game He's baaaack." Would Sashi reach the end of his patience, maybe think Canfield was jerking him around, and do something we would all regret? Canfield was good, but how the hell was he going to handle this?

How strange it was to have this playing in my mind. I was even a tiny bit embarrassed (or should have been) at how interesting it was to be watching this from a safe seat. I was like a spectator at a bullfight. I would get to see whether Canfield could do the impossible and get Sashi to stay in the evolving game, the game of Erik's life. Maybe Darryl's also. And how strange to have this mist of unreality while the quotidian details of real life sputtered around me.

Oh, and I would have to teach on Monday. Good. I really meant that. Good.

CHAPTER 50

IN THE TRAILER; SUNDAY, NOVEMBER 25, 2018

At 12:45 pm, I left Blacker for my meeting in the parking lot.

The main part of campus is north of California Boulevard. The parking lots, athletic fields, and the new campus astrophysics suburbs were south of the boulevard. I could have walked to the California Boulevard crossing light and immediately been in the north end of the parking lot. But that crossing was a main thoroughfare and the chance of running into an acquaintance was high. Given that it was return to campus day, make the probability 100%. I didn't feel like chatting, and worried that something in my manner or appearance would stir curiosity.

One should not be afraid of being paranoid, so I walked in the direction away from that main crossing. I crossed at the southeast corner of campus and continued on South Hill Avenue. I turned right on Lombardy and then north on Arden Road, and finally took a short path to the parking lot. I had made almost a complete circle – or quadrilateral, I suppose – and hadn't encountered anyone.

The FBI/PARC trailer was in the furthest corner of the underground lot. I wished that I had brought a clipboard as I strolled, nonchalant, through the parking lot, turning to the trailer only in the last few seconds. The trailer door was on the wall side, hidden from the main area of the lot. I walked to that side and found the door had been opened for me. Luk was waiting. Canfield and three telecommunication/asphalt experts were inside. Again, Galton was away. I supposed that this was not politically nuanced stuff requiring his own sensitivity.

Canfield was sitting calmly, probably running scenarios in his mind of what details would need to be negotiated with Darryl. How picky was Darryl going to be about those details? I tried to picture the exchange to get a glimmer of what it might be like. Restrictions on weapons? Time of day? Securing Erik before Darryl was released?

Luk, acting as Canfield's aide-de-camp, took my phone, and gave it to the experts who replaced the sim card with a thermonuclear one, then connected the phone to the speakers, recorders, etc. At exactly 1:30 pm, my phone rang. The phone was connected to a speaker. We heard it ring on the speaker, then heard Darryl's voice.

"Good afternoon. Can we deal with a few matters of my return and the exchange?"

Canfield tried to give the impression 'calm,' but I suspect his toes were crossed. I could guess how much he wanted to be in control, but he would have to cede that to Darryl. He responded to Darryl's question by saying yes, it would be useful to go over these matters. Darryl took it from there. Canfield accepted that a young amateur would be giving directions and acted respectful. But it was an act.

"First, the exchange will be done symmetrically. I will be released at the same time my father is released. We will walk across a neutral space."

"Agreed, Darryl. That was the original plan, and we hope will remain the plan. No problem with that."

"There will be no FBI snipers. It would be too likely that my father would end up dead in the subsequent gun play."

Canfield agreed to this condition, though Darryl knew it would be difficult to enforce. Canfield asked whether this was the end of Darryl's demand list.

"No, I also insist that Dr. Sokolsky be in the vehicle that transports us to the exchange site, and be a witness to the exchange."

Uh oh. I had to leave my safe seat in the stands and climb into the bullring. My suspicions about why were later confirmed by Luk speaking under the influence. Darryl viewed me as neutral, credible, and idealistic. If the FBI cheated on the agreement, if it all got messy –and if I were still alive – I could be relied on to report the blame that could be dumped on the FBI. Darryl knew the FBI would be aware of this. That awareness would be an important constraint.

Canfield resisted Darryl's condition.

"We think we understand your wish to have Dr. Sokolsky for support.."

Bullshit, Canfield, we know as well as you, 'support' is not the reason.

"… but it is against FBI regulations to have civilians take part in a potentially violent event."

We had entered into formal theater, while we all knew the reality. Clarence would have seen a parallel to professional wrestling. Darryl played along, very formal, just short of sarcastic fun. While Darryl could be annoying, he was someone you want on your side in a battle of wits.

"Unless my high regard for the FBI is unwarranted, regulations can be put aside when required for an optimal outcome. I trust you will encounter no barriers in arranging this."

Canfield sighed with a slump of his shoulders. He was losing, but there remained an important issue he needed to mention.

"Darryl, it is important for you to understand the next step will be negotiations with the leader of a violent criminal gang, a man who calls himself Sashi. He may feel the changes in arrangements show that we can't be trusted. It may be difficult to convince him to continue with a hostage exchange."

The unconcerned tone of Darryl's response was interesting: "I have complete confidence you will be successful in taking the next step, Agent Canfield."

Something was going on beneath the surface of that remark. Canfield also sensed it. But what? No time to waste; I'd know soon. Other things were needed now. I pointed to myself, and to the microphone Canfield was holding. He got the idea and said to Darryl, "Dr. Sokolsky would like a few minutes on the phone. Is that acceptable?"

Darryl replied of course it was, and Canfield handed me the mic.

"Hi Darryl," I said, feeling slightly foolish, "How are you going to get back to campus?"

"I have a means of transportation. I will get into Blacker via the steam tunnels. With students returning, I won't be noticed except possibly by someone who was aware that I was gone."

Darryl didn't usually waste words, so his last phrase might have meant the informer. How did he know about that? Oh, right. It's Darryl. I moved on.

"Darryl, classes start tomorrow. It may seem irrelevant, but I need to ask: Will you be attending class?"

He said he would, as part of the effort to keep things looking normal. When he heard this, Canfield sat up at attention as if voltage had been applied to his jockey shorts. He grabbed the mic firmly, just short of rude.

"Darryl, this is Agent Canfield again. We can't let you go to class. The Huns will be watching and could pick you up."

I looked forward to Darryl's explanation of why Canfield wouldn't be getting his way.

"Agent Canfield, I understand why you are worried, but if you stop to think this through..." That was close to an insult. "If you stop to think this through, you'll see they wouldn't try this. I will always be in crowded settings. You will have undercover agents watching me; the gangsters will know that. Any attempt to snatch me will put me in danger. They want me to do things for them. They won't take a chance on hurting me."

There was a pause. Darryl had him on the ropes. I suspected Canfield was wrestling with the decision whether to make another attempt at, 'I've got to talk to my sales manager.' I almost felt sorry for him. He wisely opted for what would be the outcome in any case.

"OK, Darryl. We'll have to accept your insistence on going to class. I hope there are no more conditions you're going to add to the exchange."

"With due respect, Agent Canfield, that is not a condition on the exchange."

Canfield's posture had changed. (He was in a chair, but chair posture can change. Canfield had been sitting upright at the start. He was now slouching.)

"Point taken, Darryl. But please remember: When we make contact with Sashi again, he may be fed up with the changes, and the possibility of an exchange may have evaporated."

Darryl responded, as before, in a strange tone.

"I'm sure your conversation with Sashi will go well."

Again, I wondered what was not being said in what Darryl said.

Chapter 51

IN THE TRAILER; SUNDAY, NOVEMBER 25, 2018

At that point, I figured we were about to enter an hours of boredom phase. We had no idea how long it would be before Sashi would – ironically – get the confirmation from his informant that Darryl truly had disappeared. But it was a day of surprises.

Halfway through retracing my paranoid quadrilateral path back to Blacker, my phone rang. It was Sashi. Of course, the FBI would know this and I thought about the scene back in the trailer. The word tizzy seemed to fit. I told Sashi that Agent Canfield was not close to me and it would take a few minutes to fix that. I assumed Sashi would be worried about having his call traced if it went too long. He was, and he told me he would call back in 15 minutes, from a different phone in a different location. (He was probably driving a route that made it nearly impossible for the FBI to pinpoint his location in time to grab him.)

I started to run back to the trailer, then realized running might attract attention, so I shifted to a quick walk. I wasn't sure I was needed in the trailer. Canfield would do the talking. But I wasn't sure I wouldn't be needed, and Sashi's actions suggested (OK, weakly) he wanted me on the call. My phone rang. It looked like a scam call and I didn't take it.

In the trailer, Canfield, Luk, and the electronics/asphalt team were in position. To varying extents, they all had expressions that asked, 'What the hell is going on? Is it a coincidence that Sashi is calling so soon after Darryl?'

It wasn't. An uncomfortable suspicion was growing in me.

I was in the trailer where Canfield answered when my phone rang again and dived right in.

"Thank you for calling. We are ready to discuss where we go from here. But first I need to let you know an important new development."

This is where we thought Canfield would drop the bomb and Sashi would explode. But it played out in the other direction. Sashi responded quickly to Canfield's statement with, "New development? You mean Darryl's return?"

That certainly changed the scenario for the rest of the call. Acting calmly (I was beginning to understand that it was always an act) Canfield asked the mic: "Would you mind telling me how you knew that?"

"Not at all." Sashi was enjoying this. We could hear it in his voice. He was in control again.

"Darryl called yesterday, and again just a few minutes ago, after his call to you. You may assume that I know everything about the discussion he had with you at that time."

Canfield was the first to recover. It would take a great effort to sound calm; he made a great effort.

"I am happy to hear that. I hope you agree we can now return to the original plan of a hostage exchange in a remote location."

Sashi responded with rude politeness.

"I am happy to be working with a reasonable and efficient opposite. The exchange will take place Monday evening. A few rules: You will arrive in a single vehicle. I assume it will be one of your black government Suburbans, but that is your decision. In the vehicle will be you, Sokolsky, Darryl, and a driver. I hope that you won't be so foolish as to pull a Trojan horse prank and hide FBI gunmen in the vehicle. Any such tricks would prove fatal to many people."

Sashi then added an important wrinkle.

"We will let you know the exact location. You will get this information only far enough in advance for you to safely drive to that location. Not to unsafely set up snipers and a hidden army. Please be prepared to drive when you get a call tomorrow in the late afternoon or early evening." Sashi hung up. He did not say goodbye.

Canfield, talking to me, said he would arrange to have everything needed in place around the trailer at 3:00 pm. I would be there with Darryl at that time. He did not phrase it as a request. Canfield left, walking up out of the underground lot. I supposed someone would pick him up. Maybe he would go home to rest. I couldn't picture him resting. I wasn't sure he had a home.

Luk didn't leave. Instead, he said. "I'm out of gas." He did look wrung out. "Could we meet in the RA suite in a half hour? For a chat?"

Huh? Chat about what? Also, his tone had changed from FBI professional to 'how 'bout it, ol' buddy?'

What was *this* about?

I remember the feeling I had walking into my final exams my first year at Caltech and saying to myself "At least it will all be over soon." I was starting to feel that way now, but what was up with Luk?

My guess was I would waste the next half hour trying to figure out what ol' buddy Luk wanted, and not getting anywhere near the right answer.

My guess was wrong about the next half hour. The call coming in would change that. I didn't recognize the number, or even the area code, so scam appeared in the thought bubble above my head. But karma urged me to answer the phone. I had some minutes to kill during the paranoid quadrilateral walk back to Blacker, so I answered. I think I'm glad I did.

The response to my intentionally rude "Yeah?" was "Hi. It's Clarence."

I deferred my gasp, but still was silent for long enough for him to add "I got a burner phone for this call." I made some asinine reflex statement like "Clarence, so good to hear from you." He gave my statement the lack of attention it deserved and got to the reason for the call.

"You know I hang around with some guys on the edge of society if you'll allow me the euphemism. So I often hear things good citizens don't. OK? I heard something a little while ago, and didn't know how to handle it. I learned it in mid-November just a day or so before we met last time."

I interrupted with, "Clarence is that why…."

He counter-interrupted with, "Shut up and listen. I heard things about Mia, about Ewa Kulpa, and I thought you should know, but I didn't want to be the one to tell you. I got over it and bought this burner phone.

"I don't really know very much, but I think it's important. Can we do coffee at 3 pm today?"

"Hey, Clarence. That would be great, except weird stuff is happening here, and I have a weird meeting at 3 pm. I dread that meeting, and wish I were meeting you for coffee instead, but it's one of those times life isn't giving me a choice."

"OK, Solly. It sounds bad. I'm going to feel like shit if it has something to do with Mia, and I could have helped."

"No. Yes. Well, you're right; all's not well, but Mia is not part of it."

There was a pause as if we weren't sure who was supposed to speak next. Clarence jumped into the ring with, "If the world doesn't end this coming week, let's get together next Sunday. Besides, we need to see how our waitress is doing in her new plumage."

Clarence was using the standard rhetorical light note at the end. But I focused on "If the world doesn't end this coming week." It was ironically appropriate, but I couldn't tell him anything yet.

"Sure, Clarence. I'm happy the cloud over us has lifted. See you on Sunday...if the world doesn't end."

CHAPTER 52

BAD NEWS; SUNDAY, NOVEMBER 25, 2018

Luk was not dressed in his FBI business suit. Suspicious. Something was up. But it might have been a practical choice. Luk did not look anything like his age, so dressed in jeans, a rock-concert hoodie, and November-inappropriate sandals he could pass a casual once-over as a student, even an undergrad.

"Wow, Solly, who woulda thought that we'd be working together on something like this?"

It was a pointless prologue. I wanted to get to the main text.

"I certainly wouldna. What's up?"

"Yeah, what's up? So. It turns out that Canfield was right. He never said it, but we both thought it, right? Canfield had pushed Sashi to contact his informant, remember? Well, he did. I mean, Sashi did. Contact his informant. And we were able to make the identification."

I sat bolt upright.

"Someone in Blacker?"

"Ease up Solly. Let me tell this my way. This isn't going to be easy."

I froze. Not easy meant the source was in Blacker. I let Luk tell it his way.

"Canfield found that the source of information was one Gilles de Patou."

The full name did not immediately trigger the memory circuit, but there was only one Gilles I had ever met. Mia's Gilles. And that particular Gilles had only one likely source of campus information. I was terrified of what was going to come next.

"We didn't want to rock the boat before the exchange tomorrow, but we couldn't leave de Patou at large. We picked him up yesterday late afternoon and have been interrogating him since. We may use him to feed false information to Sashi, but the important thing is to have him in our control."

"Luk, for Christ sake, don't drag it out. Tell me what I need to know! Spill it!"

"Yes. His on-campus source was Ewa Kulpa, your Mia. As I said, we've been interrogating him. We're good at it, but we didn't need to be good. He didn't try to cover up anything."

"Luk! Why the..?"

"Hold on Solly, let me tell the story. What we learned early on is it was blackmail. He had something on her."

"For God's sake…"

"Hold on Solly! As I said, he didn't try to hide anything – Gilles is a guy I would never trust with a secret. Any secret. It seems that Mia was under his spell. Maybe I should say under his thumb, her first year or so in the US. You know about Gilles stealing the ideas of Tommaso Russo?"

"Mia told me the outline."

"Did she tell you that she perjured herself as a witness for Gilles when Russo sued?

"She twisted it a bit."

"I know what you're thinking: It's not enough of a lever to entangle someone in a crime. True enough but yeah, once M. de Patou had perjury to hang over her. She was in his power. At first it was perjury. He made it sound worse for her than it actually was. But Gilles wanted to make it yet worse. He wanted to have something more serious to hold over her. He convinced, cajoled, connived and tricked her into sleeping with an LA mafia boss to help Gilles get a loan he wanted."

"Oh God."

I had pushed Luk to get to it, but now it was coming too fast. I was sitting on the bed, my head in my hands, wanting to stop it, but Luk continued.

"The pillow talk involved a mob hit. She read about it in the news three days later. She tried suicide, but couldn't go through with it. To her credit she managed to pull herself out of it, rebuild her life and end up as a postdoc at Caltech."

I wasn't thinking that. I don't know what I was thinking. Luk continued, with a sheepish look of regret.

He waited for a moment. My head stayed in my hands. I hadn't moved. Luk hesitated. Not sure what else to do, he continued.

"Gilles got in money trouble. His business was not going great and he spent large on his lifestyle. He was optimistic about a new fashion line he was bringing out, so he borrowed from some underworld loan sharks. The sharks sold the contract to Sashi – you probably didn't know about this sort of financing – anyway Sashi started threatening Gilles.

"When Sashi had him in for special treatment, maybe a change in the shape of his head, Gilles looked for a way out. Again, Solly, this is a guy, Gilles, who doesn't keep secrets. He didn't think his physical cowardice was a secret worth keeping. Anyway, somehow the conversation got around to internet hacking. Gilles didn't know a web address from a spider web, but he mentioned Caltech.

"He was planting in fertile soil. It turns out Sashi had an obsession about Caltech, the den of the hacker princes. Sashi figured Gilles could keep his head in its original shape if he could be a useful connection to an insider. Gilles thought of Mia, and the rest is a sad ugly history."

I was looking for a way to avoid accepting the unacceptable. Mia! I had been on the fence, unsure about my feelings for her, about a future with her, but now that a future was slipping away I came off the fence as a passionate defender. The defense attacked.

"Whoa. How did Mia get them the information about Erik?"

"Yeah, good question. We're not sure. We think Gilles, the slime mold he is, wasn't hiding anything, and he wasn't sure how Mia knew about Erik. But something he mentioned might be relevant. Gilles had given Mia some night vision binoculars. Not the several thousand dollar Mil-Spec goggles, the cheap bastard, but good enough.

"Those wouldn't have been of much use to her. There's no line of sight from Page to Blacker, and we don't picture her sneaking around to get a view. We're guessing there was some luck involved. Gilles had put pressure on her that day because Sashi had upped the pressure on him. The bastard laughed in describing it. He said he had developed Hun-induced knee trouble, and was walking with a limp. That became Mia's problem.

"So maybe out of nervousness – who knows – she was spending time just watching Olive Walk and happened to see Darryl and Erik walking west toward Lake Street. If they had walked west on California Blvd, she wouldn't have known a thing, and maybe the grab wouldn't have happened. Fate hangs on details. Who knows?

"But actually we *will* know. After we interrogate her. We haven't picked her up yet. I'll save you the question: We don't want to dance in the canoe until after the exchange tomorrow. We had to pick up Gilles. We don't have to pick up Mia. She's not going anywhere. If we grabbed her, the news would spread, maybe too fast."

"What's going to happen to her? Can you cut her a break?"

"Solly," he sighed, "You know we can't go too easy on her. She's not innocent. She knew what bad stuff was going on and how she was contributing. She's got to do time. The only alternative – if she cooperates and the Bureau Poobahs are charitable - would be to revoke her passport and hand her over to Polish authorities."

"No way out, Luk?"

"No. No way. She could try to make a run for it. You can guess how successful that would be."

"Could you at least minimize the embarrassment to her?"

"Yeah. We would anyway, to preserve relations with Caltech. Horvath will be part of this."

I realized Horvath had to be. He'd have to put a substitute RA in place immediately. Not very important, but still. Secrecy trumped all at the moment, but I made a mental note to let Horvath know as soon as the FBI told me I could. My mental notes were of low reliability, but it made me feel I was doing *something*. It was sort of a trivial detail, but life had to keep going on. I would figure out how to deal with this. Just not right now.

I thanked Luk for letting me know and trusting me not to warn Mia. He started to say something, thought the better of it, just said, "Sorry about all this, Solly." What could he say? He went out the door looking like a student who had just failed an exam.

It was almost time for dinner. I'd have to make an appearance, and fit in with the light spirits of the Moles who had returned to the world of friends from the world of family. 'Compartmentalize,' I said to myself. There are people who can compartmentalize. I'm not one of them. I did my best, and no one asked "Why so down Dr. Sokolsky?" So I guess my best was adequate. More likely my Moles were not paying attention.

The evening stretched out all the way through the evening of the next day, the evening of the exchange. I tried to open the teaching compartment. I would meet with my Lit class at 10 am in the morning. To engage myself in it, I decided to try to create a lecture relevant to what was on my mind in the Mia compartment. Creativity sucked me in.

I would raise the question of the passive protagonist. That's what I was. There was nothing I could do but watch a big story play out. I was an observer. Surely this theme had caught the attention of many pens and keyboards. I searched. There were lots of hits, but they dealt with passivity due to flaws in the protagonist: laziness, indecisiveness, cowardice. My situation was different. I didn't think I had any of those particular flaws (my flaws lay elsewhere). I was passive because I was barred from taking action. I was more a frustrated protagonist than one who was passive by choice. A little bit of thinking got me some answers.

There were lots of science fiction plots with a protagonist who goes back in time with the warning that making any change would lead to a very different future. Maybe the best, or at least the only one I was familiar with, was Bradbury's *A Sound of Thunder*. (This caught my attention because it was built around some real mathematics, chaos theory.) The protagonist was constrained, action was prohibited.

Another justification for this lesson: Unlike me, most of the students were science fiction fans, so this would help reel them in.

I thought about the limitless connections I could make, showing the students the relevance to our moral lives. I remembered Mia's reaction to the cat torturing the sparrow. If we were prohibited from intervening, where did that prohibition come from? Where did moral constraints originate in us? Maybe my students would tell me.

But that would be the next morning. It was still Sunday evening back in reality, and at 9:00 pm there was a familiar not-too-loud, not-too-soft knock at my door. This caused a slamming shut of a compartment, and opening of another. Darryl entered and said in his not too-loud, not-too-soft voice, as if nothing much was going on, "I'm back."

My mind rummaged around looking for a must-do list and I said something like "Thank God," then told him I had to be sure the FBI knew. They probably did. They were the FBI. But Darryl said, "They know. I called them."

CHAPTER 53
NUMBER THEORY; MONDAY, NOVEMBER 26, 2018

The day had come, after a night with more sleep than I thought I would get. Maybe my raveled sleave of care needed more knitting; maybe my aching mind needed an extra dose of balm. Macbeth had even more cares and aches than I did. I felt for him.

Luk called a few minutes after 8:00 am and reminded me we had an event coming up in the evening. We both knew the reminder was a joke in bad taste. Bad was our preference in joke taste. It lightened my mood a little, but it was still down a lot.

As I shaved, I went over the frustrated protagonist arguments for class, then put my body in motion to get to class. I was early; the students were late. In that way, at least, it was a typical day. When we had a quorum, I opened the discussion with "What do we do when we can't do anything?" and warmed to the subject. The students also warmed. They liked the opportunity to compare moral situations in their own lives to frustrated protagonists in literature. I hoped passive misery could learn from company.

It was 10:00 am, more or less, when my class ended. I knew Darryl's schedule: a class from 10:00 am to 11:00 am. I wanted to bump into him quasi-accidentally on his walk back to Blacker. I wanted to see whether I could gauge his mood. Maybe I was the frustrated protagonist trying to do *something*.

This meant I had an hour to kill. The gears turned slowly in my mind and came up with coffee at the Café. The second-thought gears came up with the caveat: Mia. I couldn't take a chance on running into her. Within a day she would be picked up by the FBI, and frustrated protagonist Solly couldn't do a damn thing. One of the many things I couldn't do today was to hide that something was up, way way up. I knew my limitations. So I approached the café with care. My plan was to pretend I was getting a call if I saw her across the room, then turn and walk away. Does this act ever fool anyone?

The coast was clear. A few minutes afterward I realized she might enter after I was seated. She didn't, but I added blindness to possibilities to the list of my limitations.

At 10:50 am, trying to look nonchalant, I ambled in the direction of the building Darryl was in, trying to time my arrival to coincide with him emerging. I was too early. (I should have checked my limitations list for the recent item about poor planning.) After pretending to take a phone call (I have a very limited repertoire of misleading acts), I feigned surprise at seeing Darryl walking down the steps, sauntered over to him and asked whether I might join him. He didn't say no. I tried small talk: "How was the class?"

The class was Math 160, number theory. The subject had always fascinated me as the most inhuman form of mathematics. It was the study of integers, whole numbers. What could be hard, right? In fact, an earlier name for the subject was 'arithmetic.' Mathematicians, in an effort to seem like normal people, or in a subtle form of elitism, like using everyday words for advanced concepts. The word 'almost,' for example, has very precisely defined roles in some math areas. But 'arithmetic' for number theory went too far. I could picture some art history major at a public university looking for a convenient course after 10am and making a disastrous mistake.

Many years ago, I had softly scratched a shallow polymathematical itch concerning number theory. A lot of it had to do with prime numbers, integers like 11 and 89, that weren't the multiplication product of other integers. I could follow a simple proof of the so-called prime number theorem, and then was reminded of my limitations. Perhaps to salve my ego, I concluded that to do number theory you had to be well off the main road of humanity, someone like Paul Erdős, the Johnny Appleseed of mathematics, who would wander from university to university proving theorems.

Interestingly, until recently number theory was considered the purest form of mathematics. Mathematicians took pride in its uselessness. But in the late twentieth century, number theory became critically useful. Prime numbers were used as the key to protecting financial data and transactions, with a technique called public key cryptography. The basis is a huge number that has only two prime factors; there are two unique numbers that multiply to give that huge number. While it is not difficult to find that the number 253 has only the factors 11 and 23, there is no hope of finding the factors of the huge numbers used to safeguard financial transactions. At least, mathematicians can give no basis for hope.

If Sashi had a method of finding the factors of a huge number, he could forget about ransom hacking; that would be micro potatoes. With the factoring method he could transfer all the money in the world into his own account.

I didn't think this was why Darryl was taking the class. But I would let him do the talking. He gave an empty answer to my question about the class.

"It's good."

"This is an advanced grad course. You're competing with grad students who've taken much more math than you have."

Darryl straightened me out.

"Yeah. I have this reputation for being ahead of everyone in everything. It really pisses me off because it means I'm always under pressure. The grad students in this class are *really* smart, but they seem intimidated by me. I'm afraid of asking a question in class. It might turn out to be a stupid question. But it's really interesting stuff, so I listen and keep my hand down."

So much for that box. Darry impressed by the abilities of others. Limitations on Darryl's self-confidence. Go figure. I tiptoed into the area smack dab in the middle of the current compartment.

"How are you feeling about the exchange this evening?"

"I'm feeling OK about it. We've done all we can do. There is a good chance it will go well. If I didn't believe that, I would consider what else we could do."

Darryl was not a passive protagonist. Darryl went to Blacker. I went to seek food elsewhere.

Lunch seemed strangely ordinary. Most everything ordinary was going to seem strange today. A little afterward, maybe 12:40 pm, I looked down at my buzzing phone and saw MIA. My breathing stopped. I was filled with irrational guilt. It was an emotional reaction. In the many rings it took for the phone to give up, I told myself how unlikely it would be for Mia to have any idea of what lay ahead. Still, it took a while for me to return to normal respiration.

I was antsy. I hate waiting. I gave myself the excuse it would be prudent to check on Darryl, so to Blacker, up stairs and around corners. I knocked on his door. He was sitting on the bed apparently, unconcerned about the evening's outing. He put down the book he was reading *An Introduction to Mathematical Cryptography*. I actually knew the book. During my weeks of interest in number theory, I had skimmed a few pages before backing away with regret. It was about public-key cryptography. Was this why Darryl was taking the number theory class? Was he going to break the problem of factoring large numbers and control most of the money in the word? Nah. Probably not. Anyway, I had no room for new worries. I wouldn't even compartmentalize it; I would just ignore it.

"So Darryl, any new things to say about what's going to happen?"

"No. I'm ready."

He pointed to a small pile of electronic equipment on the floor and added, "That's what I'll be taking along."

This was new. I didn't like new. Uh oh.

"How do you know they'll let you bring that stuff?"

"Sashi wants me to hack into networks. The last thing he would do is complain about equipment I'm bringing to do that."

"Umm.. Maybe. But I meant how do you know Canfield will let you bring it?"

Darryl gave his smile-precursor and said, "The FBI doesn't have much bargaining power. Anyway, this stuff will help convince Sashi I am planning on helping with his hacking dreams. Canfield can be persuaded."

He was right, but I didn't want to end the conversation quite yet, so I pointed to a device in his pile, something that looked like a black paperback novel that had sprouted three antennas.

"Hey Darryl, I used to know electronics, but lots of the modern digital stuff is new to me. What's that?"

"That? Nothing very advanced. It's a Wi-Fi pineapple for hacking into Wi-Fi connections. Remember how I told you most people don't bother protecting their Wi-Fi?"

I nodded, and remembered my negligence in not upgrading security in my Duarte Wi-Fi. This wasn't the best time to mention it.

I made a departure-appropriate grunt and left the room.

A few minutes before 2 pm my phone whined. I looked down, asking karma that it not be Mia. I was relieved to see it was Luk, who said we would be meeting in the trailer in a few minutes, and I needed to be there. I quashed the impulse to say 'Yeth, Mathter.' It was time to grow up.

I followed my many-turn route from Blacker to the underground parking lot and casually wandered toward the Pasadena Asphalt Resurfacing Company trailer.

Door open. Solly pulled in by strong arms. Door closed. Many eyes at windows scanning the parking lot. The group accepted that Solly the Spy had not been followed. It was the usual group, Luk and Canfield, with two additions.

One was a very serious looking crag-faced man. Not very tall. He had the physique and complexion of a cement block. His matching grey eyes looked as if they could see through plywood. He was wearing what I inferred (correctly yet again) was a bulletproof vest over military camouflage. His belt made me think of Batman's. A major feature of the belt was a handgun, a big automatic I assumed was a Glock, because Glock is my go-to guess. It wasn't a Glock. With that, my streak of right assumptions came to an end.

The other new face was less stern. It belonged to a woman who appeared to be in her middle 50s, with hair beginning to lose its struggle against grey. I liked her for not trying to hide it. There was a briefcase by her feet, and maps on a small table. It soon became clear she had brought the maps, and her expertise was geography and terrain. Like Luk and Canfield, the woman was wearing boots suitable for outdoor traipsing. Like them, she was wearing a bulletproof vest.

Canfield's briefing began with introductions: Special Agent Mertens (that was the storm trooper) will provide SWAT support and advise us on best practices in the exchange. Special Agent Guzman (the woman) brings her expertise on possible sites for the exchange. If we have an idea of where it will be taking place, we will have a big advantage.

I *had* to interrupt.

"Why will we have an advantage? We have a deal about details. If there is a SWAT team planted it could go badly for Erik or Darryl."

Canfield made a statement he might have considered an explanation: "Trust but verify."

He had heard Darryl say it (though in Russian) in the phone conversation Sunday. Canfield probably looked it up. Or maybe he spoke Russian. Though

Canfield, true to his MO, had not really answered the question, I realized it could be very useful, if things went bad, to have medical help ready to show up quickly.

Canfield turned to Guzman who laid out possible locations.

"I conferred with strategy experts who have local experience. We believe the Hun leader has seen the wisdom of an isolated exchange site. We believe he will seek a place with only one way in, so he can monitor any attempts to bring in firepower. That rules out almost all semi-urban sites, parks, sports fields and such. This means he'll be looking for something like a picnic site or a camping ground, and that means – probably - the San Gabriel mountains. Unfortunately, there are quite a few possibilities.

"We can narrow the list by considering only sites at not too great a distance. Our strategy is also to narrow the list by considering the steps Sashi would take in his own search for a site. Our best guesses are Henniger Flats, Charlton Flats picnic area, and Chantry Flats picnic area. The Hoegee trail camp and Mt. Wilson picnic area are other possibilities, but they may be too far."

Way back on Saturday, after Canfield had manipulated Sashi into favoring a remote exchange, Luk had blurted out Chantry Flats. We would soon see how good Luk's guess was.

But all the names were familiar, and hearing them, I tensed up. This was getting too goddamn real. In a few hours we will be in one of those places witnessing something that could be tragic.

Chapter 54

INFO FROM CLARENCE; MONDAY AFTERNOON, NOVEMBER 26, 2018

I was back in the RA suite. We were back in waiting mode, and we had no idea how long it would be. My attitude was a mixture of terrified and bored. Not equal parts. The back and forth was exacting wear and tear on my nervous system, and again my sympathy was growing for Pavlov's dogs.

A little after 4 pm the phone rang, jangling my already over jangled nerves. My first thought: "Sashi with the location of the exchange site." My second thought was "scam" when I saw an unfamiliar area code. Karma didn't help this time with a hint, and I was so unfocussed I forgot about the earlier call from Clarence's burner phone. I sent it to the scam bin while muttering suggestions to the scammers about self-abuse.

There was an urgent knock on my door a few minutes later, a bit less than the usual time it would take to walk from Page House to the south side of Blacker. I shouted "Come in!" while thinking "What now?" It was Toobee, breathing hard. (This got my attention because panting is uncool and Toobee was, after all, a teenager.)

"Clarence is trying to get in touch with you," he panted. "He says it's important."

"Thank you Toobee. I'll call him right back."

Toobee didn't quite know how to end the interaction, so he just nodded and left.

In a voice I hoped no one outside the suite could hear I told myself what an idiot I was. I spent a few minutes trying to figure out how to rescue a deleted call. I could have called Luk, since the FBI would have a record of all calls coming to my phone, but I conquered the iPhone maze, looked at the number for the last incoming call and dialed it.

"Clarence?"

"Solly. I'm glad you called back. I know you're tied up in something confidential."

He sounded worried. I was now aware he knew Mia had been involved with the LA criminal world, but how would Clarence know about the abduction.

I listened.

"Let me waste 10 seconds. Toobee gave Mia the number of my burner phone. She called me. She said she's worried about you and asked whether I might call to cheer you up or something. That's bullshit of course. No one is saying what's really going on. Solly, don't deny it; I'm not accusing you. You didn't lie, but you evaded it. That's OK. Sometimes it's just gotta be done."

Clarence understood this was awkward for me, but he had the sensitivity to close that compartment as quickly as possible.

"Here's the reason I'm calling. Toobee told me something was brewing around Blacker, something hush-hush, and maybe dangerous. He mentioned a black Crown Vic, vintage 2016, with darkened windows. A couple of Moles mentioned it; they called it the creepmobile. Toobee saw it once himself, toward the end of last week. He said he saw some bad dudes getting out of it and trying to get into Blacker."

I tried to interrupt, although I don't know what I was going to say, but he was having none of it.

"No. Listen. I'm calling for a reason. I was just cruising around Arcadia, north of the 210, maybe thinking about taking a ride up one of the canyons, when I saw a dark Crown Vic with blackened windows. The sunlight was bright and at just the right angle. I could make out there were a couple of guys inside. Could be the bad guys; black Crown Vics aren't that common around here. They were headed up the Chantry Flats Road. That wasn't very long ago. Maybe 15 minutes. I'm at the bottom of the road right now. I can follow them if it will help."

"No! Jeez! That is really useful Clarence. *Really* useful! But please don't follow them."

"Yeah. I get it. It could be dangerous, and you're worried I want to be a hero. No worry. I'm only a hero when it's in the script."

Chantry Flats Road was a paved road that was an extension of Santa Anita Avenue, a major north-south boulevard with two wide lanes separated by a greenery divider.

"OK. Message received. And Solly.. Be careful. You're one of the good guys. Very flawed, God knows, but a good guy. There aren't that many. We can't afford to lose any."

I wondered what Mia would say about that in a day or so.

As soon as Clarence was off the phone I called Luk and asked, "You got that?"

He affirmed, and said it would be helpful to know where to set up a staging area for the SWAT team and the ambulance. (Yin and yang I thought.) Luk didn't go into detail, but did say they would have Special Agent Guzman and her team working on it. The FBI was sure the Huns would have a lookout in position to watch the bottom of the Chantry Flats Road, maybe in the bushes where Santa Anita Avenue splits into Chantry Flats road and a small residential cross street. Luk also let on there would be helicopters on call for whatever, and it would be important for the pilots to familiarize with whatever terrain features and FAA rules are important to helicopters.

The FBI was going to very carefully set up a listening post within a half mile of the likely perch of the lookout. Everything would be in place in plenty of time.

We knew the Huns would be in position very soon. They'd probably want a half hour or so to check out the site. Just in case. They didn't know they harbored an informant, but they didn't know that they didn't. Our informant would be in danger when the Huns learned that we knew about Chantry Flats beforehand. But by the time the Huns knew, the game would be over. For better or worse.

The timing of the evening's events, meant we would be hearing from Sashi very soon and the evening's entertainment would begin.

At around 5:30 pm the phone rang.

CHAPTER 55

SHOW ABOUT TO START; MONDAY EVENING, NOVEMBER 27, 2018

When the phone rang, I was lying in my RA bed, memorizing the ceiling. I awkwardly juggled the phone, which almost escaped. By the time I had it to my ear, Sashi and Canfield were into it. Sashi must already have told Canfield that the site was Chantry Flat. I heard Canfield tell Sashi that he saw it on his map, and it would not be a problem.

"We will need a few minutes to get everything organized. My best estimate is that we'll be there in a little less than an hour."

We had already studied the route and knew that the driving itself would be only a half hour. Canfield was right, though. We would need some cat-herding time.

Sashi accepted the hour estimate and added stage directions.

"We're there now, and are impatient. Please remember the rules. One vehicle. Only Canfield, Sokolsky, and the driver, along with Darryl. No tricks. Any delay, any variation, will be seen as a trick and will be fatal.

"The vehicle will enter the picnic site parking lot where you will see our two vehicles. You will park at a distance of 15 meters from them. You will all exit your vehicle. Erik and Darryl will be released at the same time by you and by us. They will walk on parallel paths, in opposite directions, separated by a few meters. When we have Darryl and you have Erik, we will all get into our vehicles.

"Our two vehicles will exit the parking lot first, and will proceed down the road. We will stop at an overlook and rendezvous with another vehicle. At

285

that point we may move Darryl from one vehicle to another. You will not know which vehicle Darryl is in when we exit the mountain road at the bottom. This will discourage you from certain stupid actions. Each of our vehicles will then proceed in different directions. You will try to keep track of us with helicopters. We know the standard techniques for avoiding being tracked this way; it will be an interesting game, but a dangerous one. We will win it.

"Of course, if you get nervous and start shooting you will not only risk Darryl's life, but also those of the good people of Arcadia, Monrovia, or whatever direction we choose."

Canfield responded to Sashi's many words with only: "Understood. No games."

They both hung up. Neither said goodbye. Canfield then turned to me and ordered: "Get Darryl. Come to the trailer."

I grabbed a jacket, went up the stairs and around the corners. A bit shaky, but trying to hide it, I knocked on Darryl's door, and heard "I'm almost ready. Give me 45 seconds."

In my head I thanked Darryl for that. Who else would have said 45 seconds? A minute yes. A second, yes. But 45 seconds?

The door opened 37 seconds later. (Yes, I was timing him; I needed to distract myself.) He emerged carrying a small backpack. I assumed the backpack held what I had seen on his floor, and shrugged my shoulders envisioning the confrontation with Canfield that Darryl would win.

In the underground parking lot next to the trailer were two black Suburbans with federal plates. (No longer any point in trying to disguise anything. The Huns would know it was us.) The door of one opened. Canfield jumped down, pointed to the backpack and said, "That's not part of the deal." Darryl calmly responded that the deal didn't specify that he couldn't bring along equipment. The tone suggested that Darryl would have preferred a more professional deal, with more details specified, perhaps notarized. Maybe the tone was just Darryl's desert-dry humor; I had given up trying to tell.

Canfield ignored Darryl's implication of lack of professionalism. His irritation showed in the volume he used in calling out, "Agent Xi, please come here and inspect this equipment."

Luk did as he was shouted at and looked through the small pile: a laptop, a thumb drive, the Wi-Fi pineapple, a small soldering iron and some solder, a wire stripper/cutter, a few feet of 18 gauge (I think) wire. (Soldering iron? For what?)

"I don't know what's on the thumb drive or the laptop, but other than that, it all looks OK."

Canfield decided not to make an issue of Darryl's hack-aid kit. He was getting impatient. The show was about to start and he didn't want to delay it. Nor did Darryl, but he delayed it further.

"Agent Canfield, would you please open the backs of both Suburbans."

Were it anyone else making such a request, I think Canfield would have answered with an arrest. But Darryl was not anyone else, and Canfield made do with a laser stare and a sigh. I suspected that Canfield had used more sighs in the last few days than in the last 20 years. He was getting better at it.

"What now, Darryl? Why?"

"I'm sorry to inconvenience you, but I would like to check that you are not hiding someone who will jump out with a gun at the last minute and get us all killed."

Canfield used up another of his improved sighs asking, "You won't take my word for it?"

Darryl looked at him and said Доверяй, но проверяй. (Trust, but verify). I had no idea how Darryl could keep from smiling when he delivered lines like that. Oh. Right. It's Darryl.

Canfield reminded Darryl that they would only be taking one Suburban to Chantry Flats. Since it wasn't a question, Darryl didn't see any reason to respond. I supposed he couldn't trust them to tell him which of the two Suburbans they would be taking. He wanted to check both.

Canfield opened the backs of the Suburbans and said in a resigned voice, "Check to your heart's content."

Darryl quickly went through possible hiding places, and we were ready for the road trip.

We got in. Obeying Sashi's rules meant Luk would be the driver. That was great with me since I trusted him not to panic if things went off the rails. Also, his student memories of Pasadena streets would mean fewer glances at the GPS.

We exited the underground parking lot and turned right at the light on California Boulevard. We stayed on California to Allen Avenue, where we turned left, north, towards the San Gabriel foothills. It was all happening quickly, which was good and was bad. Neither Darryl nor Canfield showed any emotion. At the time, that greatly annoyed me; they should have had the courtesy to show fear. We got on the aptly named Foothill Freeway, the 210, and a quick couple of miles later we turned off on Santa Anita Avenue. About a mile, maybe a mile and a half, later we entered the Chantry Flats Road. The second FBI Suburban had been following us, but turned off here and disappeared into some side streets.

I stared at the bushes in the first big 180 degree turn in the road. It was the perfect place for the lookout, but the light was fading, and it probably wouldn't have been possible to spot anyone, even in bright sunlight.

I told myself that only 4 or 5 miles remained to the picnic site. The trip might be the last few minutes of my life. I told myself to sit back and relax, then scolded myself in four-letter words for the sarcasm. It wasn't even funny.

I was sitting on the left side in the second row, scanning the roadside for anything threatening or interesting. I wasn't sure at that point that there was a difference. I noticed that Canfield, sitting in the front row passenger seat, was doing the same on the right side.

Then we were there. Almost. There was a fork in the road, but it was only a minor hassle. Either side went to connected parking areas. I was pretty familiar with the place and suggested the fork on the right, the one that led to the parking lot on the downhill side. We very slowly edged forward into the parking lot, and saw that we had chosen correctly. Ahead of us, at the furthest point in the lot, were two creepmobiles, black Crown Vics with darkened windows. We stopped at a distance we hoped met Sashi's approval as close enough to 15 meters.

We then followed the script. All four of us got out of the Suburban. The show was starting.

CHAPTER 56

SHOWDOWN AT CHANTRY FLATS; MONDAY EVENING, NOVEMBER 26, 2018

Sashi was standing. Another Hun (Sashi's second in command? The Vice-Creep?) was standing. Sashi was casually holding a handgun. The Vice-Creep had a military rifle aimed in our direction. The doors of one of the two creep-mobiles were open. Sashi and his caddy must have come from that vehicle; the doors left open for a quick retreat. The doors of the second vehicle were closed, and the dark windows hid the interior. I guessed that inside were the Huns with the heavy weapons, the guys who would jump out if a firefight started. Their vehicle was oriented broadside to us, to be used as a shield if fireworks started.

Our Suburban was pointed towards Sashi's vehicles, so Sashi could see both sides as we got out. I got up from my rear second row seat. Pretty much at the same time, Darryl exited the right side of the same row. Canfield waited and watched for a few seconds before leaving from the passenger side of the first row. Luk turned off the engine, made sure the parking brake was on, and stepped out.

It was awkward having us separated on the two sides of the Suburban, so I walked around the back to join Darryl. Walking around the back hid me from Sashi for a few seconds. It was a duffer's unthinking mistake. Sashi and Sashi Jr. knew I was not schooled in their craft and cut me some slack.

Luk went around the front and stood not far from Canfield, so all four of us were on the right side of our Suburban. This business of standing together was a sign of good faith. If a firefight broke out the last thing we wanted to be bunched up, an easy target for automatic weapons. Luk and Canfield knew this. Sashi knew it. Hell, maybe Darryl, the researcher of all detail, knew it. I now know it; I hope it will never again need to know it.

We expected Sashi to balk at Darryl's backpack. We were right. He pointed and said, "That wasn't part of the deal." He was not happy.

I thought I felt my scrotum shrivel. It might have been the cold but I think it was the dread I had been suppressing as we drove up the canyon: These could be the last few minutes of my life.

I waited for Darryl to start lecturing Sashi on properly framed deals. We'd all be dead. But Darryl, raising his voice to span what I hoped was 15 meters, said, "My hacking equipment is in there. May I show you?"

It's a strange feeling to know that your life could end in seconds, or everything might end in smiles. And the difference depended on a tiny detail, a whim, the setting of some synapse in Sashi's nerves. The subtlety of chaos theory joined to the coarse distinction of life and death.

I told myself that Sashi *really* wanted Darryl's help with hacking, so he wouldn't go into batshit shooting mode. But Sashi had a technical problem. He could tell Darryl to bring the backpack to him, but then Darryl could pull a gun out as he approached Sashi. (That wasn't a real possibility, but Sashi didn't know.) He could tell Darryl to leave the backpack behind, but it was plausible Darryl would need some equipment. And Sashi *really* wanted Darryl to do that hacking.

As Sashi stood trying to decide, maybe whether we live or die, Darryl made a suggestion. I've got to hand it to him. He was scared, but he was playing out a script he had written.

"How about I slowly empty the contents on the asphalt?"

It was reasonable, but there was a psychological (i.e., unreasonable) issue. Sashi's ego was getting battered. He wanted to be in control. His ego overcame his judgment and pushed him too far.

"No. How do you Americans say it 'being jerked around.' I've had my fill of it. The deal is off."

We all held our breath. That cold feeling returned inside my jockey shorts. I was an amateur and never asked for this. Lucky us, we had Canfield, the pro who *had* asked for this kind of situation. He saw we were at an impasse because Sashi didn't want to take a suggestion from a boy. Canfield stepped up to the plate as a man. It's hard to believe, but believe me: He sounded perfectly calm.

"Sashi, you and I have dealt openly with each other. We both saw we needed to. It's still true. Agent Xi and I were also taken by surprise when Darryl brought the backpack to the car. We examined it. I can't say we understand the functions of all that's in it, but we're pretty certain nothing could be used as a weapon."

Sashi did not lose his threatening squint. Nothing happened for maybe 10 seconds, then he barked an order to the vice-Creep in what might have been Martian for all I could tell. Holding his rifle at the ready, the assistant sleazed forward and, without ever lowering his eyes, grabbed the backpack and started backing up to the Crown Vics.

Darryl, making a good try to look at ease, started walking forward, toward the Crown Vics, very slowly. Erik picked up Darryl's cue and also started walking toward us, away from the Crown Vics. Sashi was looking back and forth between them. This put Sashi in a confusing situation requiring a quick decision. That might have been Darryl's plan. But then the plot thickened. Darryl reached back under his jacket and pulled out two tools.

One was a hand grenade. A sort of a tool.

Clever Darryl. That little pissant! (Forgive the Omaha Yiddish). The backpack was a ruse. Everyone was so focused on it, they failed to check whether Darryl was carrying anything on his body. It was a risky strategy, but Darryl had something even better than his brain. He did not believe in luck, but damn, he had it! Darryl pulled the pin on the hand grenade. We all gasped. Faces could be seen pressed against the window in the closed Crown Vic.

Sashi just laughed.

"Darryl, you are fooling no one with that toy. Now let's get on with important adult business."

Sashi was striding forward, and taking it in stride, unimpressed by Darryl's hand grenade which was, in fact, only a high quality replica.

Darryl threw the grenade a few feet. Canfield and Luk fell to the pavement. The occupants of the Crown Vic screamed. Only Darryl and Sashi had no reaction. Sashi, the winner of the confrontation, was smiling as he approached Darryl. When there were only about ten feet separating them, Darryl's shaking voice announced, "*This* is not a toy."

He held up a device that looked like a homemade electronics project and, in a sense, was. It was an aluminum box with a small light that was glowing green, five toggle switches, two knobs and a slide switch. Nothing was labeled. He flipped one of the switches. We heard the click of the door locks in the closed Crown Vic, then watched as the Huns in the car tried to open the door, and discovered that the doors were locked, and that Darryl's device was overriding the car's lock controls.

Darryl pushed one of the other switches. The headlights on the Crown Vic flashed, the interior light went on, and the engine started. With the interior lights on, we could see three Huns inside, all holding weapons. They were confused and frightened that their car had come to life on its own. They kept trying to open the doors thinking, for some reason, the doors would yield to repetition. The car, broadside to us, was facing away from the edge of the road and the steep slope only a few feet beyond the edge. One of them broke a car window and began to clear away loose glass for an escape.

The Vice-Creep, Sashi's assistant, had enough of this witchcraft and fired, hitting Erik in the thigh. Erik crumbled to the ground. Darryl turned to Sashi and made a demand in a new voice, "Tell him to drop his weapon."

Darryl then fiddled with the device in his hand and the locked Crown Vic moved backward a few feet. It was now teetering on the edge of the steep slope. It was hard to be sure how much further it could go back before plummeting. Those inside could not be sure, and they sat perfectly still. Plans to escape through a window were shelved.

Sashi shouted to his assistant something that might have meant 'drop it.' The assistant took a moment to make a decision. He was too slow. Sashi raised his handgun and put a bullet through the assistant's head. As if to underscore his annoyance, he fired three more times, once into the head and twice into the inert body lying on the asphalt.

Time stood still as we gazed on the unique spectacle of death. The only motion was the slow seeping of clean red blood forming a pool on the dirty grey asphalt.

The Huns in the remote-controlled Crown Vic were duly impressed with Sashi's management technique, but their attention was focused on the delicate balance of the car on the edge of the road. Sashi moved forward toward Darryl. His expression terrified us. His plans to exploit Darryl's hacking seemed to have been forgotten. His rage had pushed it to the side.

Darryl moved a knob on his control device, and the engine of the Crown Vic raced. Sashi, standing a few feet in front of Darryl, raised his pistol. It was a moment that took an eternity. I could only see one possibility. What happened was something else. A red laser spot danced around for less than a second and disappeared behind Sashi. Then a sharp crack was heard.

Sashi had a strange look on his face. It was meaningless. There was nothing going on behind it. He crumpled. Not forwards or backwards. He just kind of settled to the ground constrained by the connectedness of his limbs.

We saw the barrel of an assault rifle protruding from the broken back window of the Crown Vic. There was a long moment of silence as if everyone had lost their place in the script. Then there was muffled cheering coming from the back of the Crown Vic. It did not last long. The occupants remembered their own unbalanced situation.

The moment of Darryl's certain death was followed by a moment of ours, when the assault rifle turned towards the Suburban. Our only salvation was obvious: Darryl could send the Crown Vic over the edge. Darryl held the control up above his head. The gunman immediately understood the standoff: if the first shot missed the Crown Vic would be their coffin.

The standoff was broken by a deafening thrum. The dusk had turned to night, but we were all bathed in daylight from a small helicopter. Luk had wasted no time. All eyes had been on Darryl and the Crown Vic. Luk took advantage by using a transmitter to contact the helicopters and the troops at the bottom of the road. It was time to move in.

The helicopter landed in the adjacent parking lot. Cement block SWAT agent Mertens jumped from the helicopter slightly before it had fully settled down. He ran in a crouch, out from under the blades then over to the field of action. Others followed. Mertens was quarterback, moving quickly for a cement block and shouting orders. He aimed his weapon at Sashi's body, then spoke to a microphone on his shoulder, giving the SWATTish assurance for under control. Darryl also made that judgment and ran to Erik. Canfield and Sashi dropped to the asphalt. There was terrified shouting from the creepmobile. But there was no explosion.

Darryl, meanwhile, had run to Erik. When the helicopter blades stopped, a medic descended and joined them. Erik was on the asphalt, his back against one of the Suburban tires. Erik was talking to Darryl, both of them seemed emotional. Not normal-person emotional, but very emotional on the Lagerstrom Scale. Darryl seemed to have shiny eyes. Maybe it was the helicopter lighting.

The medic told Erik and Canfield the shot had gone through muscle, and passed through clean. It wouldn't involve much medical intervention, but Erik would be going to the hospital, and it would be better for him to travel down in the Suburban. There was some technical issue about the helicopter landing on the hospital pad, and the drive wasn't a long one.

The helicopter pilot had descended, secured the copter, and came toward the Suburban. Screams were coming from the creepmobile, probably to let them out, but Mertens assumed control, and said to us, with his eyes never leaving the Crown Vic, "Still too many of them and too few of us with arms." Maybe that was his professional judgment, though he seemed to be getting a lot of unprofessional glee from the slight rocking back and forth of the Crown Vic. He wasn't smiling. Those facial muscles had probably atrophied.

We heard something coming. Mertens didn't turn but we did. It was two Suburbans full of serious men and women with serious weapons. One of them was the FBI crisis manager. He approached Mertens and exchanged a few words. He turned to Luk and instructed him to take off, and deliver Erik to the Huntington Memorial Hospital. They pretended not to hear the screams from the creepmobile, but the crisis manager spoke to Darryl.

"As soon as you guys are about to take off, could you release the doors to the Crown Vic? We'll have lots of guns on them but I don't want to take any chances.

I want you out of the parking lot right after the doors are unlocked."

Darryl, always reasonable, said, "Will do. Tell them to have the men in the back exit first." The crisis manager responded, not unkindly, "Will do. I got an A in freshman physics."

Luk was in driving position, with Canfield beside him as he had been on the way up the road. I sat in the third row of the Suburban with Mertens, who kept his attention directed out the back window considering himself some sort of tail gunner.

Darryl was in the middle row with Erik, who had a field dressing on his wound. They were speaking as quietly as possible considering the road noise, and I could more or less hear the conversation. Darryl kept trying to call his mother but there were no bars showing connectivity.

As we exited Chantry Flats Road, we saw two black government Suburbans and a flock of agents. They had a severe looking Hun on the ground, arms out at his sides. He wasn't making snow angels. Mertens showed surprising agility in jumping over the back of the third-row seats, and exiting. He spoke quickly with one of the agents and gave us an update when he was back as tail gunner.

"That was their lookout. I also got word the criminal nest was raided. We got everyone. I can't tell you how I can be sure of that but I am sure."

I knew how he could be sure: the informant. But I saw no point in letting him know that I knew. I remembered Luk's threat to my liver. I preferred to leave his cat hungry.

Darryl looking down at his phone announced, "Bars," and was soon into an emotional (for him) report that all was well, though they were on their way to Huntington Memorial.

At about that time, I also got bars and my own phone rang. I was going to ignore it, but I saw "HRVTH" on my screen.

"Louis. I can't really talk now."

"You goddamn well can talk! This is important. Mia has disappeared. What do you know about it?"

There was a pause as my mind raced looking for an exit.

"Louis, this is a shock to me."

"Do you know *anything* about it?"

"Background, only background. And Louis, listen, I know Mia's disappearance is really important, but *please* believe me I can't talk now. I'm on the road, maybe in danger. Do you have the RA situation covered?"

"Yeah, I asked Gerald Tarsdale to help out."

"Good old Gerry. I'll look in as soon as I can. You have my word. Bye."

I hung up.

Mia was gone.

Did Gilles have a moment of nobility and somehow get a message to her while he was in FBI custody? I didn't know whether the nobility or FBI inattention was less likely. Did Mia not have another source of information? What the hell happened? Did it matter?

Mia was gone.

CHAPTER 57

MIA EXITS; MONDAY–FRIDAY, NOVEMBER 26-30, 2018

I undid the seat belt, leaned forward to put my mouth near Luk's ear. "Mia's disappeared. What can you tell me?"

"Not a thing since this is the first I've heard that she's disappeared. Last I heard she was in Page watched by the government's finest."

I believed him. If he knew anything, he might not tell me. But he wouldn't deny that he knew. I squirmed. I was stuck in that damn moving steel cell, desperate to start the search for information about Mia, maybe even the search for Mia. I was further from rational than usual, but it was a day in which reason wasn't playing much of a role.

"Luk, how do I find out what's going on with Mia?"

"Get a grip Solly. I'll find out what I can, then tell you what I can, but first let's get Erik to the hospital."

Luk was concentrating on driving. We figured we were past the danger, but you never know.

"Luk, I'm not needed at the hospital. Can you drop me off at Caltech?"

"No! I hate to repeat, but for you I'll make an exception: Get a goddamn grip!"

We got Erik to Huntington Memorial. The FBI had smoothed out the way for us as if it were Olympic curling. As soon as we were out of the Suburban, Erik was wheeled away. No questions, no paperwork. There were some new FBI types giving orders, and they gave Darryl an order to get into a car, and me to get in another. It was agony waiting so it was good there wasn't much waiting.

My car took me to Caltech. The chatty driver said, "You'll be debriefed later."

That was it. Four words. Or does the contraction make it five? He didn't need any directions and I wasn't in a mood to make any smartass remarks. I got out in the parking lot near Blacker and closed the door. Saying good bye would have been against some FBI rule. Anyway, I didn't feel like saying anything involving the word good. It wasn't his fault.

I had to change my mood or my affect. My flock knew immediately that the shepherd had returned. Those wonderful kids also knew that something was up, and that I was involved. They just greeted me, asking nothing.

I still had my cell phone. It was exhausted, so I plugged it in and started the quest, first with a call to Louis. With very few words omitted, the phone call was, "Louis, anything?"

"Solly, no."

The few words omitted were short and scatological.

Next: Luk. No luck, no answer.

What the hell, I thought with a shrug of my figurative shoulders, as I dialed the Pasadena Police Department.

"Hello, this is Dr. Saul Sokolsky at Caltech. One of our postdoctoral associates is missing, a woman in her early thirties named…"

"Hold on a minute."

Pause. Muttering in background.

"A body was discovered earlier today. All information is confidential for now."

Time for a white lie.

"I'm her second cousin. Her name is Ewa Kulpa. If she's the one you found I'd like to notify her family ASAP."

"I'm sorry sir. For now no information is being released, even to family."

I tried pulling strings. Louis couldn't get anywhere with the Police. Luk could give me only one bit of information: The matter was not in the hands of the Pasadena PD, but the cop Department of San Marino, the ritzy neighborhood southeast of Pasadena. What the hell? Luk repeated his promise to tell me as soon as he heard anything.

To be sure he remembered, I called him first thing the next morning, Tuesday. Yeah, there was no chance that he would have learned anything after pretty late Monday night, but I wanted to motivate him to avoid more calls.

A half hour later he was just about to receive one, but he took preemptive action. My phone showed his name.

"Solly, promise fulfilled."

"You know what happened to Mia?"

"General outline. It's complicated. Bottom line, she's gone. It *was* Mia that the San Marino PD found."

I knew this was coming, but it still hit me and it took a few seconds and a few deep breaths for me to fake composure. There had been hope. I had been irrational.

"What can you tell me?"

"She was found in Huntington Gardens. An Uber driver had alerted the police. It was suicide. What we know comes from that driver, and much of it is still being kept secret."

Another few breaths.

"When will you be able to give me details?"

"Can't be sure, but I know how you feel, so you know that I'll do what I can."

It's good to have friends in high places.

"Luk, someone has to tell Louis."

"I'll tell him. He's more likely to keep it secret than if you tell him."

"OK. Then be sure to mention that I asked you to tell him."

"I'll swear to him that you threatened me."

I would have, but he was being a friend and I was in need. He made a strong suggestion (gave an order) that it would be best for me not to get the story in incoherent bytes. He somehow managed to get me together with the Uber driver, Ronald McCarthy. Like too many in Southern California, Ron saw his future in acting, or in movies (not sure if they require acting). They bide their time driving cabs and handing out Happy Meals. Ron was a nice kid. He was still shaken by his role in Mia's death when I bought him dinner Thursday night, three days after Mia's death.

What I learned from him had some details that would not have been of interest to the cops. Luk was right about getting the story directly from Ron. This is the story he told me, patched together with Luk's details on the first part of the story and the last.

In a way we can blame the FBI. But just a bit. They assigned two of their youngest agents to hang out at Caltech, keeping an eye on Page House. They dressed in what they thought was student garb. Luk ranted that they had never asked him how a Caltech student dressed. They must have used a J. Crew catalog so they stood out like a drag queen at an Amish barn raising. They were spotted immediately by some Pagefolk who let Mia know. Mia's intuition had told her something bad was waiting just off stage and it was time for her to be leaving. She had been thinking about it for several days, and now it was time.

The young ill-costumed agents were only a minor inconvenience, there were many exits from Page House itself, and many routes for navigating indoors and exiting from another building. She was worried that the helicopter sounds came from police surveillance. It wasn't justified. That would have been too expensive. After all, where could Mia go. The FBI attitude was to hang loose since they'd find her wherever she ran. Yes, since you asked. Yes, they're idiots.

Playing it safe, Mia dressed in a long coat, and man's hat. She walked north and west from Tech until she felt she was in an FBI demilitarized zone, then summoned an Uber. Within minutes Ron McCarthy showed up. Mia asked to be taken to the Colorado Street Bridge.

"I had been doing the Uber thing for more than a year, and had never been asked that. So right off I was kind of worried."

Route 66 runs through Pasadena under the name East Colorado Boulevard. If you're driving west, as Mia instructed Ron to do, you turn south at the Arroyo Parkway to follow Route 66. Mia didn't want Route 66. Ron and Mia continued west. The road had been straight and the terrain level, but a little less than a mile on there was a deep gouge in the land, the Arroyo Seco, the dry gulley. The road showed respect by bending to cross it. Its crossing was the historic West Colorado Street bridge.

The bridge, 'Suicide Bridge,' had been the last platform of dozens who ended their lives there. As Ron told it, Mia had become very talkative as they approached the bridge. It may have been Mia's last burst of human contact, but Ron thought it was something else. She might have been worried that he would stop short of the bridge if he suspected what she had in mind.

She told him she was a civil engineer, and she went on about the engineering details of the famous arches of the bridge. She talked a good game and he was almost convinced.

As they approached, she asked him to turn off to South Arroyo Boulevard so that they could view the famous bridge arches from a better vantage. "She did look up at the arches and said some things about engineering details. She actually seemed interested. But mostly she was looking at the ground, not at the arches. She stopped being so chatty. Her voice became shaky. She wanted me to drive back up to West Colorado Boulevard, to the top of the Bridge. We saw a small blue sign with a phone number for a suicide hotline. She became upset. I wanted to say 'Hey, it can't be that bad.' But I just kept quiet. You know how it is."

I wasn't sure I did, but I kept my mouth shut.

"Then we started across the bridge and she could see that there were high chain link fences on both sides of the bridge. It would have been hard to climb them to get out to the edge of the bridge, you know, where you could jump."

I knew that Mia had no intention of trying the climb. Ron looked at me in a 'this is hard to believe' way as he continued.

"It took her a moment to collect herself, then she was completely calm, and – the hard to believe part – seemed almost happy. She asked me to take her to the entrance to the Huntington Gardens. She started to tell me where it was, but I stopped her. It was popular place for tourists. I knew the way. By now she seemed really relaxed. Even happy. Maybe relieved is a better word. I figured she had changed her mind. But I was worried."

"She got out and handed me two hundred-dollar bills. I objected that it was too much, but she made a joke of it, saying something that worried me, like "I'm not going to need it." Those aren't the right words. It wasn't that obvious, but I was scared for her. I watched her go through the entrance. And I called 911. I worried they would think I was overreacting, so I told them she had said she would kill herself. Hey, who would blame me for that lie?"

The rest came from Luk.

The San Marino cops had a little trouble getting in. The Huntington director had more pull with the city than they did, and he didn't want the cops on the grounds. The forces of law ultimately prevailed, and brought dogs. Her body was not out in the open, and the grounds are huge, so it took a while.

He told me that Mia's body was found in the Japanese garden. As soon as I heard that I thought of seppuku. It had fascinated her, but horrified her. And she would have needed the short sword. It would have taken planning. Seppuku wasn't Mia's way.

She was carrying pills that did the job. I supposed that this was part of some long term planning. She was found lying face up, her coat acting as a blanket. It was a beautiful setting. From her position, her last vision would have been the perfect arc of the Moon footbridge, the focal point of the garden.

It had been three days. For almost all that time I knew that Mia was gone, so my tears were only my reaction to the image. Mia's last moments in peace and beauty.

On Friday I would be taking over teaching my course again, a blessed distraction. The first step on the road back to normal. But there was a roadblock.

A young woman was waiting by the door of the RA suite when I returned from breakfast.

"Hello Prof. Sokolsky. My name is Jiya; people call me Gigi."

A bell rang in my head. I think that there was too much chaff packed in with the bell. I couldn't quite make out what it was ringing. I didn't need the bell to tell me Gigi was very upset. The tears were welling up but not yet giving in to gravity.

Gigi? Of course, she was Joy's friend, a week ago – an eternity ago – Joy had told me about Gigi's trouble and how Mia was arranging an abortion.

"Gigi. You are Joy's friend, right? It's nice to meet you. I understand that Page has a temporary RA for the time being, but I'll be happy to help you if I can."

"No. It's nothing like that. I'm here to give you this." She handed me an envelope that said Solly on it.

"I found this in in my mail this morning. It was in a larger envelope addressed to me. It probably arrived late yesterday. There was no return address on the large envelope, but it was pretty clear that I was supposed to give this to you."

"Thank you Gigi, and I repeat that I will be happy to help if I can."

"She shook her head as tears started."

It was just like Chantry Flats. My heart was racing. I knew that it must have been from Mia. I had to teach in a very short time. I didn't want to rush dealing with it, or arrive for my class incoherent and paralyzed. I put the envelope in the RA suite and left for teaching.

It was probably a mistake since I had trouble concentrating in class. But, clever devil that I am, I threw out a controversial question: "Should a writer write for the reader or for the writer?" It was like throwing corn in the duck pond. They swarmed, loving the clash of thoughts.

I kept myself from running back to Blacker, but my walking was not steady. In the RA suite I kicked off my shoes, opened the envelope and read:

> *My Love,*
>
> *When you get this I will be gone. Since you seek understanding through poetry I'll remind you of some words of an American Poet: "For all sad words of tongue and pen, the saddest are these, "'It might have been.'"*
>
> *I would try to write my own version, but I would fall short. I may be witty, but he was Whittier. Yes, my Love, laugh. Be happy for what we had, not sad for what we missed.*
>
> *Perhaps I can borrow again from Wisława Szymborska. In 'Love at First Sight' she wrote:*
>
> *"But every beginning is only a continuation and the book of fate is always open in the middle."*

I closed the envelope and snuck out. I walked to Colorado Boulevard and walked east, until the police stopped me. Saw that I was not a threat and aimed me back to Caltech.

Mia was gone.

CHAPTER 58

EPILOGUE

By Tuesday, November 27, things around Blacker had returned to Caltech normal. I would just have to wait to hear the details of Mia's suicide. Meanwhile I knew my own life would go on, and things had to be done. That was good. The devil makes pains for idle minds.

Just before I went down to breakfast I heard a particularly annoying ring on my phone, and saw HRVTH on the screen.

"Thank you for having Agent Xi Luk letting me know about Mia. I hope that getting back in the swing of responsibilities will help you get over your loss."

He told me he would arrange a meeting as soon as possible, probably Wednesday, and it was important for me to be there. The meeting was at 9 am Wednesday, not in the Housing Office; too small for all the attendees. It was in the conference room in the Braun Laboratory, way over on the west side of campus. The arrangement of buildings in that area did a good job of shielding who was entering. Long ago, Horvath got (or took) the right to have Mentis and Ethos considered to be Caltech staff, with broad permissions. They were a common sight on campus and would draw no curiosity. They were in attendance, and – as always – very attendant. The Caltech contingent also included the Caltech general counsel and a representative of the president's office.

Luk was there. His look said 'I can only try to imagine your pain.' It was a sincere look. What a shame he worked for the FBI. He could have been a great therapist. He also knew when to keep quiet. After introductions he didn't say a word. The word-saying was left to Galton. The Chief of the Pasadena Police Department was also there, probably as a courtesy, and said nothing. Then there was a guest who was new to me, Bertrand Lou.

Galton did most of the speaking, impressing me with his ability to deliver a partially true narrative without upsetting anyone. The story would be that Bertrand Lou, and his assistants had bravely raided the hideout of the criminals responsible for his daughter's death. Lou had turned them over to the FBI and was going to rely on American justice. The (goddamn) State Department, according to this fable, decided it would be best not to charge Lou for all the laws that had been broken. They praised the Pasadena Police for cooperating in a decision that was best for everyone involved.

And that was that. It wasn't the truth, but it really was best for everyone. Keats had written,

> "Beauty is truth, truth beauty,—that is all
> Ye know on earth, and all ye need to know."

It wasn't that simple in 2018, and I doubt it was for nineteenth century poets. I sensed that Mentis and Ethos agreed, but – socially adept as always – they kept their judgments to themselves.

Time passed and things happened. One of them was a promotion for me. I became a tenured member of the English Department through a special executive action by the President. I had mixed feelings about this since my leaning was play-by-rules, and be politely anti-authority. I salved my troubled conscience by reminding myself that rules in this case were controlled by Department Chair Maurice L'Hommedieu. He was still alive, although the news of my ascendance within his department might affect that. I was sure he wouldn't mess with me. The action by the president would worry him, and he would picture me whining to the President if L'Hommedieu tried stabbing me in the back with his Mont Blanc.

Darryl finished the fall 2018 semester. He did very well, of course, even with the cops-and-Creeps distractions. He then took a leave of absence, a leave that became permanent two years later. He never discussed the reasons with me. What little I know came from what little Luk knew.

Darryl had thought about the meaning of his life. He said he realized he was studying math, computer software and networks and such, because they were fun for him, not from any belief they were important, or were helping anyone. (When Luk reported this, in my head I heard Sweet Caroline's voice.) Darryl had asked Luk whether he would be of any use to the FBI. Luk didn't go into details, but if Luk was able to restrain a laugh and a shout of 'Oh My God Yes!,' he should get credit for it. Maybe a medal.

Darryl-FBI contact was made and the rest is history. Actually, the rest is secret. Luk couldn't tell me just what Darryl was doing. In fact, Luk didn't know. I received two brief email messages from Darryl over the past five years. They simply reported that he was well and felt that he had made the right decision.

I never knew whether any of my own decisions were right, but they worked out more or less well. In the early months of the 2019 spring semester Horvath called me into his office. I entered and greeted Mentis, Ethos, and Horvath in that order. Horvath understood that this was a joke meant to imply the order of importance. I knew that a Biology graduate student, scheduled to defend her thesis in May, had been found to act as RA in Page. We briefly discussed that, before Horvath came to the point.

He told me that he was very happy with the way I handled students and emergencies, and told me that he would like me to remain as RA for the 2019-2020 academic year.

"In fact," he said, "as far as I'm concerned, you can stay on as long as you want."

I have wanted to, and I am still RA. It's a bit like having a family with new teenage children every year. I kept in touch with a few of them after they left Tech. Many went to grad school; some are still there. Many are already successful in different areas, not only science. Some of them had personal problems or accidents. Joy was on a good path, doing very well in grad school, and still planning to take her talents back to India. Dome had been true to his better self and was working for a nonprofit.

Luk had his own personal success. He had been attending weekly folk dancing soirées when he wasn't facing death. In March 2019, Luk attended a small get-together at Blacker to celebrate my 39th birthday. He asked whether he could bring a guest. This sounded interesting, so I simply said "Sure, as long as it's not Canfield." It wasn't. He showed up with a buxom blonde only a few inches taller than Luk. He introduced her as Astrid, and asked me if I would be his best man at his wedding in June. She had a Norwegian accent, a smile the size of a fjord, and I have always wondered about Luk's ability to swing his partner at their folk dancing fests.

It all happened so fast I couldn't make any smartass comments. So the beat went on. Married in June, and wasted no time. They have a toddler and a post-toddler. There is much talk of fusion in cooking and whatever, but fusion of Norwegian and Chinese genes should get some internet space; it makes really cute kids.

I also had real family – the kind that involves sharing of blood or genes. I had Shosh's kids. I visited them a couple of times a year, until the higher education diaspora scattered them. Except for graduations, my visits with them became random but frequent enough for me to keep up.

Niece Delia had taken a year off after college to do volunteer teaching, then entered the Creative Writing Program at the University of Iowa. It seemed that she, I, and Shoshana were connected by literature as well as blood. Conrad had gone STEM and was finishing up his physics major at Cornell. He was interested in the theoretical side of physics, so our career connection was superficial, but our family connection was deep.

On Tuesday, the day after the gunfight at the Chantry Flats parking lot, I went to the hospital to visit Erik. Darryl was there as well as his mother. The interaction among them seemed warmer than what had been painted in the FBI analysis. This proved true in the ensuing months. In the follow up of the big night of November 27, FBI agents visited the Lagerstroms in West Lafayette several times. Luk took part in one of the early visits. He told me that the marriage seemed greatly affected by the trauma of Erik's abduction.

I thought about this as a problem in physics. They had been trapped in a behavior. I pictured it as a physical system trapped in some non-optimal configuration, but needing a kick to get up and out of it. Alpha particles have the same problem in nuclei. The physics of marriage.

It took me a year to think I could handle it, but in the fall of 2020. I thought I could handle a visit to where the curtain fell on the story of Mia. I asked the San Marino PD. They usually deal with well-connected people, and this seems to have made them very helpful. In any case, they were very helpful. They took me to the spot, and pointed to the ground. The officer had photos. I didn't want to see them. I just wanted to feel the atmosphere, see the view of the Moon bridge. I tried to imagine.

Nothing. I don't know what I was expecting, but I was expecting *something*.

Gilles thought that he would be home free after giving detailed answers to all the questions the Feds asked, and some they hadn't. The agents did not strain themselves asking the prosecutors for an easy deal for Gilles. Perhaps they had not developed a deep respect for him. Still, the devil gets his due, and his due was only two years.

Somehow word leaked into the Federal Correctional Institution, Lompoc, that Gilles had made the FBI run out of recording tape when Gilles spilled all about the cast and plot of the Los Angeles mafia. Shortly after the start of his stay, he appears to have cut himself shaving, and bled out. I thought about notifying Tommaso Russo, but Luk shook his head. I said no more. And asked no more about the details of Gilles' tragic accident.

Sunday coffee with Clarence became a fixed point in both of our lives. It filled a need we both had. We could be completely honest with each other. The honesty would sometimes lead to sharply different opinions, but never threatened the friendship.

When November dropped off the calendar and passed into Caltech legend, and it was time to look back and do some 'hey, can you believes?' and some 'what ifs.' I asked Clarence about my relationship with Mia. He had bristled when I first asked him about Mia, but things were very different now.

"Rabbi Decatur, I still think about Mia. Am I stupid?"

"Stupid in general, or just about Mia? I'll assume Mia. It's simple enough that even you can understand it. Physics, start-ups, writing, RA. The history of your life is a set of announcements that you don't want to be locked down too tightly. Jeesus, Solly! You've managed to arrange a just-right life for yourself, but you're always a half-teaspoon dissatisfied. You're always wondering if you've done the right thing."

He was right. I knew he was right. But once a month , sometimes twice, I would have a dream about Mia, always at the RA wine and cheese get-together, or in the Polish restaurant.

ACKNOWLEDGMENTS

The first place in acknowledgments goes to my partner Lin Betancourt, for her time and tolerance as *Mentis & Ethos* grew from two to a hundred thousand words. Her suggestions were an important part of the revisions and development. Most important was her cheerful (perhaps too strong a word) acceptance that not all her suggestions were accepted. What was accepted, and was most important, were the many discussions of the personalities and actions of Solly, Darryl, Mia, and Clarence, Luk, *et al.* They became real people for us.

I thank Lee Lichtenstein who read the first draft and offered insightful criticisms that led to a much more interesting (and believable) second draft.

Thanks go to novelist Gillian McAllister. My interaction with her on her novel *Wrong Place, Wrong Time*, was what started me thinking about writing a novel.